BLOOD OF THE LOTUS

BOOK ONE OF UNDIVIDED

SADE LOUISE

For my mom.
To you, to me, to all we dream.

Contents

AN ETERNAL BLOSSOM

To rise above,
unblemished and pure,
reborn in the daylight,
a never-ending cycle of hope.

To fall below,
blackened and blue,
captive in the night,
a never-ending cycle of despair.

"To what end?" we call.
And she answers.

"Till whatever end."

I

ONCE THERE WAS, AND ONCE THERE WASN'T

My father always told me, "as a hunter, you have a duty to obey"—a verse engraved in my mind before I could even understand what it meant. Yet, standing at the edge of these woods with my mind set on the mission I've recklessly planned, I've realized one thing.

No matter how hard I try, I am not the daughter who obeys.

The wind rattles the leaves and branches of the towering trees, a symphony crying out above me. Its hollow echo seems to warn me back to the confines of my father's estate. I clench my fists, nails digging into my palm.

Stepping out of the protective shadows, I keep my ears open for the footfalls of the guards stationed at the front of the estate, my mind believing they'll catch on to my escape at any moment. In my haste, I had snapped a twig when landing on the other side of the brick wall that kept me confined. A rookie mistake I shouldn't have made. No sound comes, and a sigh of relief leaves my lips in a soft huff. I glance down the dimly lit sidewalk, thankful for the silence except for the wind and tick of a flickering streetlight.

I pull my hoodie over my head and slip onto the sidewalk. Shoving my hands into the pockets, I keep my head low as I walk in the opposite direction. My body is jittery, the summer air biting into me as if winter has come. *My freedom is so close.* When I come back after tonight, everything will change. It has to.

I scan my surroundings, taking in the town I've rarely seen outside of a car. This side of the city is made up of dense woods, which end just ahead and open into a lakeside park. I can glimpse the water, as dark as the night sky, glittering like stars with the reflection of the town just beyond it. My gaze lingers longer than I'd like, the sound of the water beckoning me forward—seventeen years of wishing to escape across the lake too difficult to ignore.

A howl of laughter snaps me out of my daze and draws me to the town made of brick just across the street from the park. The nightlife is roaring, the bustling urban center alive with people who have no idea what the passing hours will bring. I halt in my path. As much as I want to explore there, tonight's not the night.

Eyes on the moon, my hand moves to graze the silver bracelet wrapped around my wrist. Tonight the moon will bleed, and the devil will eat.

I chuckle to myself, letting my hood fall. *I can do this.*

The other side of the street is a long stretch of neighborhood homes. Hunters will prioritize protecting busier areas and areas where people may be carelessly wandering alone. It's not like we can warn the public against a *blood moon...*

My steps are quick as I cross the street, moving into the shadow of a tree. A car passes on the road, and my chest tightens, but it doesn't stop. The loud bass of music thumps in my ears even after the car is gone. I peek around the tree, watching for other hunters.

The silence is deafening. Street lights cast a warm glow on the pavement in front of the brick townhomes. My empty stomach grumbles at the smell of home-cooked food wafting in the air. It mixes with the scent of pine and summer air, intoxicating and repulsive.

Pulling off my hoodie, I toss it into the first trash can I find. The wind feels colder on my bare skin without the layer of warmth, but the excess fabric won't hinder my movements anymore. I rub the goosebumps rising on my arms, adjusting the tactical vest around my torso before I make my way into the neighborhood.

Tonight is my one chance to prove my father wrong. To show him that I'm as capable as any hunter. Someone he should have never kept caged in his estate all these years. I don't care what I have to do. I'll bring him the head of any powerful demon that crosses my path. I'll do anything to see the look on his face when he realizes how wrong he was to say, "You'll never be strong enough."

The street ahead is empty, no patrols nearby. Good. Stepping out into the road, I spin in a slow circle, taking a moment to admire the neighborhood so close to the estate, yet it's like a different world to me.

It's homey here. It has the same Georgian style as the estate: brick construction and tall gridded windows set in an almost mathematical symmetry. But while the estate feels like a cage, this neighborhood feels open and inviting. The houses are so close together as if you could reach your arm from inside one and touch the other, a grand difference from the lonely halls I grew up in. But there's an essence of *care* here. Something my father's estate is lacking, despite its pristine condition.

The homes line one side of the street, another forest of tall trees on the other side. This must be the far edge of the whole neighborhood. The woods are as eerie as the ones I escaped through, the streetlights spaced too far apart to offer much light.

My skin prickles at the sound of laughter floating to my ears. As I follow it, I see a window with a curtain open a crack, just shy of closed. A family gathers in the living room, a young boy in pajamas latching onto his mom as she bends down to kiss him on the forehead.

Nausea fills my stomach, and I turn from the blissful scene. Training my eyes on the silver bracelet, I graze my finger over the reflection mirrored in the black gem and grimace.

"Please be an actual weapon when I summon you this time," I say, ignoring the pit in my stomach.

It hums in response, a shiver running down my spine. *Kioren.* That's what the woman from my vision called it—an unfamiliar name, even after many years of studying angels and angelic artifacts.

I lower my arm, my gaze moving to the moon peeking through the branches of the trees. During a blood moon, demons become ten times stronger, feeding on the essence that seeps from the bleeding eye in the sky. My fists won't be enough, as much as I'd like to believe they would be. Only angelic metals can kill them.

Shaking my head, I scan my surroundings once more for hunters and demons. The wind whispers in my ear as it howls through the trees, shaking the leaves. A door shuts loudly along with a murmur of voices heading in for the night; the lights turned off except for the single one by each front door.

This world is too foreign for someone like me.

Growling rolls across the pavement, stopping me in my tracks. In a swift movement, I swivel around, my hand on my leg holster, to pull the single angelic blade I was able to keep hidden in my room. Black eyes meet mine and my brows furrow. *A hellhound.*

My nostrils flare as the smell of rotting flesh wafts through them. Hellhounds aren't known to travel far from cemeteries. They're creatures that chase lost souls—a nuisance but not usually a menace. I shift back on my feet, sizing up my opponent.

Tall and broad like a wolf, a black inky substance drips from its dark coat of matted fur. A shadow swirls around the creature, moving with each step it takes toward me. Its eyes are glassy as its jaws snap near my leg. I bounce away on light feet, narrowly avoiding the razor-sharp teeth. My brows scrunch together as I raise my dagger. This hellhound isn't normal.

Kioren hums against my wrist as if to remind me of its presence. *It's now or never.* With a deep breath, I recite the incantation gifted to me by the woman from my dream. The memory of her burning light warms my skin. It's as if calling forth the angelic artifact summons her energy along with it.

"Let light and darkness be your essence, your heavenly form in my hands. With the strength to crumble mountains and split the seas, fulfill your purpose as the truth, the protector, and the destroyer. Come forth, Kioren!"

My voice raises as I finish the incantation, lifting my hand into the air. A deafening silence follows. "What?" I lower my wrist, the silver band and black gem the same as before.

The hellhound hurls itself at me, jaws outstretched. I roll to the ground, its sharp teeth skimming my ear. I stand just as large black claws rush toward me. I scramble in the opposite direction. *Shit—*

It jumps in my path, and I skid to a halt. I retrieve the knife secured to my thigh, staring into the hellhound's beady eyes. A growl reverberates behind me, and I look over my shoulder to see two more approach.

The trio circles, taunting me with nips at my heels. I slash back with the blade, my heart rate speeding up as they creep closer. This is definitely not normal. I'm not a lost soul.

"*Kioren*, this was supposed to be your grand reveal," I hiss at the bracelet.

A nip at the heel of my boot quickly refocuses my attention. I spin around, slashing at the snout of the hellhound, and it snarls. The metal of the blade is sticky with black blood.

If only I'd listened to Lance and practiced exorcism incantations. Of course, it's the one skill I always neglected—not that I ever had much of a chance to practice using it.

Large paws land on my back, shoving me to the ground. I flip my body around to face the beast, and, raising my blade, I stab into the jaws of the hellhound and push my other hand into the inky scruff of its neck.

The strange substance burns me, and I gasp, my hand recoiling back. The ink drips to my shoulder, and I bite my tongue to hold in a scream. My mouth tastes like copper, and my stomach threatens to revolt. Forcing my hand to move, I grasp onto the hilt of my blade, arms straining against the weight of the beast.

Adrenaline surges through me as I pull in my leg and kick up, sending the creature squealing off me. I stand, my burning hand dropping at my side as if numb.

"Is that all you got?" I say through gritted teeth. "Come at me."

A hellhound jumps toward my shoulder, and I twist around, slashing it before it can get its jaws around my neck. Teeth dig into my calf as another attacks my blindside, and my legs buckle. I scream, falling to one knee.

"Need help, young miss?" a deep voice asks, raising goosebumps on my arms.

I slice my blade into the neck of the hellhound, its teeth deep in my leg. It doesn't relent.

"You're not safe here," I say to the unfamiliar man. "You have to leave." Blood rushes to my head as I kick the wound I gave the hellhound.

"It's not in my nature to leave a lady in distress," he says, though I can barely hear him over the pounding in my ears. "Well, as long as you have that one—"

"I'm fine! Go!" I kick the hellhound as hard as I can, its teeth separating from my calf. "Kioren, fulfill your purpose as a protector!" A bright light erupts from the bracelet. My mouth gapes at the towering scythe emerging from the bubbling gem.

The scythe curves to my side, moving on its own. It rips into the hellhound, slicing the creature midair. It gives a final cry as it disintegrates into dust.

I stare wide-eyed as the scythe hovers back to my side, the snath straightening. The blade and handle are easily double my height and far less angelic than what I expected. The heel of the blade is adorned with black spikes like the jaws of a beast, a metal railing of sorts seeming to pry it open. A black tendril descends from a gem on the heel and connects with the matching gem on my wrist.

"Are you all right?"

My blood runs cold, and I scramble to my feet. The man is leaning against a nearby tree, examining his hands. He wears a silky black dress shirt opened dangerously low, bronzed chest peeking through. Curly dark hair sways in front of his eyes, the streetlights illuminating the sharp contours of his face. A dangerous smile plays on his lips, and his eyes scan over me until they meet my own.

At his feet, the two hellhounds lie dead.

"Who are you?" I ask, pointing the blade of the scythe at him. It's remarkably light.

He lowers himself into a slight bow, lifting his head to speak. "Rishu, at your service." A curly strand falls in his face, and my stomach twists at the handsome man. I grip the scythe tighter.

"Your name doesn't tell me who you are."

His smirk widens, a warm shade of red glinting across his eyes. Iridescent scales roll across his skin, disappearing as soon as they appear.

My lip twitches in disgust. "A *demon*. Why'd you help me?"

"As I said, it's not in my nature to leave a young lady in distress, especially one such as yourself." His deep voice is laced with amusement, as low and playful as I'd imagine a demon disguised as a human would sound.

My face hardens. Demons don't help humans—especially hunters.

Deadly power radiates from him, chilling me to my core. Even hidden in that human skin, I know a hideous creature lurks beneath. A high-tier like him is not someone even the strongest hunters would want to take on alone.

"You see"—I bring the scythe's blade closer to him—"I don't believe you."

He raises his hands, the smirk never leaving his lips. I lower the blade, but only enough to look into his dark brown eyes—the air around his tall frame trembles with his power. I push the scythe back toward him and take a brave step forward.

"You caught me. It's not my only reason." He pauses. His eyes flash red once more. "Feel like making a deal with the devil?"

I move the blade closer to his throat, and I can somehow feel the scythe enjoying the proximity, expecting the kill. "Not in the least. I'm a hunter. We don't make deals with demons, let alone the devil himself."

His smirk twitches on his face. "Even if it's about your family's secrets? A forgotten weapon you now hold?" He steps forward, placing a finger on the blade to lower it. "A nonexistent mother—one you never knew or heard of, or even the reason your *father* keeps you in that godforsaken estate?" My throat tightens, my knees threatening to buckle under the weight of his words. "Are you curious yet?"

I can't stop the waver in my voice as I speak. "I don't know what you're talking about." But I do know. Not one word he's said has been a lie.

His eyes twinkle as if I've fallen right into his trap, the scythe between us no longer as threatening as I hoped it would be.

"Isn't that the point? *You poor girl.* They hide everything from you." He takes another step closer, and I freeze, my feet unable to move away with the fear coursing through my veins. "Don't you want to know why freedom is so far from your reach?"

I regain control of my body and swing Kioren down at his torso. A laugh spills from his lips as he steps out of reach with unbelievable ease.

"I know who can give you that freedom, all you have to do is listen."

My breathing is heavy as blood drizzles down my calf, my left hand still numb from the strange substance on the hellhound. But still, I grab Kioren and position myself for another fight.

"Don't you want to know it all, *Nova*?"

2

A Beginning

One week earlier

For a moment, I'm light as a feather.

My feet push off the windowsill, my body hovering midair as if I were flying with the clouds above. The breeze holds me up as I stare out past the brick wall lining the estate's property—the glitter of the lake just beyond. The moment passes, my stomach sinking as I fall to the grass below. Sharp pain spreads through my ankle, but I push it aside, rolling up and running for the wall.

Footsteps land behind me, followed by an angry yell. "Nova!"

I push harder, urging my legs to move faster.

He won't catch me today; I'll prove I can outrun him. And once I'm over the wall, I'll keep going until my lungs have no more breath to keep me moving.

"You can't outrun me," Lance yells, his voice growing closer.

I run harder.

It might have been a good idea to have a plan before jumping out of my bedroom window. Not the most subtle way of escaping, but you have to work with what you've got. And there aren't many opportunities with Lance hovering all day, every day. Anyone would become fed up when they can't even remember the last time they left their home—constantly having to train and study, a repeated routine for almost eighteen years.

Leaping over a bush at the edge of the garden, the path clears to an open grassy lawn. My heart hammers in my chest after training all morning, but there's a lightness in my steps as the thought of freedom—even just a little—comes closer with every breath I take.

This is the farthest I've made it before without Lance catching up or catching on to my plan. A smile falls onto my lips at the thought of outdoing my teacher.

I reach the edge of the property, jumping up the six-foot wall to grab onto the wrought-iron spikes at the top. My foot slips on the brick. Regaining my hold, I haul myself up. The lake glitters with the ripples of the afternoon sun reflecting on the water. A soft breeze blows through the loose strands of my hair as if to say, *Go forth and live.*

My shirt tugs at my neck, a hand tightening around the fabric at the back. I desperately hold on to the iron, but my hands can't withstand the strain. Yanked to the ground, the view of the lake shifts to the blue sky above. My back hits hard. Air rushes out of my lungs, black dots swirling across my vision.

In a sudden gasp, my lungs fill. Coughing, I roll over to my side to prop my body up.

'I commend you on getting the best of me today." Lance crouches next to me on the ground, his eyes glittering more than the lake did. "But the student is far from beating the master."

I glare daggers at him. He's the most insufferable person I know.

Lance stands, placing his fedora back over his wavy black hair. A wicked smile appears on his otherwise deceptively soft face—annoying as ever. A dangling earring dances with the movement, the sun sparkling on the autumn-colored gem. He looks toward the wall for a moment before extending a hand to me.

"Don't make me drag you back," he says with a twinkle in his dark eyes.

Slapping his hand away, I huff, standing up alongside him. As much as he would enjoy that, I most definitely would not.

"Pig-headed brute," I mumble under my breath as I turn around and march back toward the estate I had just escaped. Lance lets out a low chuckle, and I scowl. One day I'll be the one laughing.

Heading back up the hill, I'm disappointed the estate seems closer than the wall ever did. Seven acres of land, and yet this place is more of a cage than a home—the wall a barrier between me and the outside world.

It's all the same red brick. Pristine and clean, unlived, and unwelcoming. Only the wall at the end of the property ever seemed inviting, welcoming me toward the lake beyond.

I stare at the eight white pillars holding the canopy above the estate's porch. I can't help but smile devilishly when I see the open window on the second floor of the west wing. The white curtains from my room billow out between the tall black shutters. Lance never anticipated I'd jump from my bedroom window.

Tick that off the list of ways I've tried escaping.

Walking past the garden fountain, I weave through the brightly colored flowers and perfectly groomed box bushes as I head toward the arched glass door beneath the porch canopy. Reaching for the door handle, my fingers graze the angel's wings engraved in the metal. Watching with a thousand eyes, the wings of our angels protect us. Reminding me of the one thing my father keeps me from being—a true demon hunter.

I push the door open. Every hunter knows the mark of angel wings is a sign of protection—a safe haven against demons. As long as they remain, no demon can enter. They are a firm reminder of the foundation of this clan and my family, the Fanderas.

We reside in the North American branch—in Falgens, Michigan. Here we house the largest network of hunters—this town made up of many of us—and the largest hunter university. There are, of course, other headquarters worldwide, but they've only spread in the last few hundred years. The Fanderas originated somewhere between present-day Turkey and Italy, my father's predecessors spreading the hunters to every continent. Nowadays, my father delegates more than his predecessors ever did—having us remain here at this branch.

He also holds all the power in my life. Keeping me here with Lance as my babysitter since I was a child. He has his rules that I obey, at least most of the time, and loves his favorite phrase, "it's not time for you." Whatever that means.

I've trained since birth to be a hunter in his image, to represent the Fandera name as his sole heir. But it's never enough. I'm in the age range of first-year hunters, but my skill level is on par with Lance, who's had years of field experience. Yet, I'm stuck. I can't participate with other hunters. Not in university classes nor hunting patrols. Every action I take is limited to these seven acres. My learning, my training, every single meal I eat. And my father's not even here.

Stepping into the dining room, I let out a sigh. The white walls are alive with delicate engravings, the designs reflecting off the round glass table in the center of the room. Six chairs accompany it as if people eat here—a vase of flowers set in the middle in an act of hominess. I scoff at how pretentious it looks.

My father usually remains at his manor on the university grounds, leaving me here with only Lance and the staff for company. The estate is less than five minutes from the campus. But of course, according to him, it's all part of the job.

We don't talk often, to say the least.

"Go study in the library. Tomorrow we're going over to the campus," Lance says, coming in behind me. "Solomon wants you to spar with the first-years during their evaluation."

"Really?" I ask, spinning around, unable to hide the smile on my face as the reminiscent feelings disappear.

He smirks as if to say yes. It's been seven months since I was at the campus, and last time I wasn't permitted to engage with other hunters. So sparring with anyone, even first-years, will be much-appreciated practice.

"He's going to change his mind." My smile falls from my face. This wasn't the day to misbehave. "I'm so stupid." I lean back against the wall, running a hand through my hair.

Lance leans against the wall beside me. "And why's that? Was it not a training exercise?" He winks at me, causing a smile to creep back to my lips. "See, this pig-headed brute does have your back." He twirls his hat in his hand before placing it back on his head, walking away whistling.

I scratch my head, laughing awkwardly.

Following suit, I head to the library, trying to contain my excitement by focusing on the afternoon study materials I know are already set out for me. I won't thank him, but the least I can do is work on something productive. Because there are security cameras watching my movements, and if my father ever found out Lance lied... My body tenses at the thought.

His punishments are never kind.

The wooden library door creaks open as I step into the room lined with bookshelves. My shoulders relax as the smell of antique books wafts to my nose. These walls contain hundreds of books, manuscripts, and even poems—pure knowledge in this one room. Subjects span from the classics to demonology, hunter history to romance novels. Though those are few and far between, snuck in for me by a friendly staff member before promptly getting fired before they had a chance to do it again.

One subject written in the many manuscripts here is on the Great Demonic Fall. A fascinating topic since it's the origin story of hunters.

It starts a thousand years ago when Lucifer rebelled against the Heavens by breaking into the moon for its power, raising a demon army on the moon's essence. Solomon the First, my father's ancestor, gathered humans together to fight against the uprising. We weren't strong enough against Lucifer's hordes, but seeing Solomon's efforts, God sent the angels to help us. He allowed the angels to link their souls with chosen hunters, and we won the war, defeating Lucifer's army. Though why the angels didn't directly fight the demon army, well, nobody has ever even questioned it in the manuscripts, so there's no clear answer. All I know is hunters have linked their souls to angels since the time of the war.

Honestly, though, while there is undoubtedly some truth to the story, I regard it with skepticism. With so many other mythical stories about a multitude of gods and beings from all around the world, how can the one God we're taught about be the only one involved in all of this? The topic fascinates me, and I wish I could spend more time studying it. I'm sure other hunters would find me crazy for having such beliefs, despite the obvious hypocrisy.

Hunters—though for good reason, I suppose—put too much faith in God when that war was the only time we ever supposedly heard from Him. Of course, we still work with the angels—one of the few things I know to be real. Selected hunters who pass the angelic trials link their souls to them, and become *Undivided,* but they are few and far between. The angelic trials aren't for the weak of heart.

Plopping onto the cool leather sofa chair, I sift through the pile of books left for me while rolling out my aching ankle. A few are on angelology, one is on exorcism incantations, and the last one is something I've read a hundred times—a book on the angelic trials. All are to cultivate my mind, as Lance likes to say in my father's tone, but this book holds a deeper meaning to me.

As hunter-born, before we turn eighteen, it's decided whether or not we will participate in the angelic trials. Crossing through seven moral gates within our minds—our hunter commandments—as dictated by the angels above. All to see if we're worthy to house a part of their soul in our body. The chosen ones are forbidden from sharing their experience, so only the rules and process are known to the rest of us in preparation for our own trials.

It's pretty simple, honestly. The location where the trials take place is a secret and is never to be shared. The seven moral gates are purely within your subconscious, and if you make a single mistake, you'll never be chosen in this lifetime. Do-overs don't exist. And once bonded, the hunter and their angel are inseparable for life.

I clench onto the leatherbound book. There's no way to know what will happen until my trials come. No matter how much I prepare, nothing is guaranteed.

Every year it seems like fewer hunters are chosen for the trials. Those like myself who were born into this life anticipate these trials all our lives. But there aren't as many of us as you'd think, and finding ordinary people with the potential is unusual. I reach up and rub the back of my neck. A set of angel wings tattooed on the skin there... I wonder what it would feel like.

As my father's only child, I'm expected to pass. And because of this, my ceremony is highly anticipated by the clan. Even if I'm not recognized as a capable hunter, not passing would be the greatest dishonor to the Fandera name.

A long sigh leaves my lips. I close my eyes and lean back into the chair, relishing the cool comfort. There's still time before I turn eighteen. What is it? Three weeks? Two? Dread fills me again. Only two weeks and then everything will change. It's not as much time as I had thought.

Setting the books down, I rest my head in my hands. "Get it together," I whisper to myself, brushing thoughts of my future out of my mind.

I sit up as a knock sounds at the door, the color draining from my face as I scramble to grab a book. Lance will kill me if I'm not studying. The door opens, and I pause mid-reach.

"Miss me?" a sly voice says from the doorway.

My mouth parts, eyes widening as I stand. "Adrian?"

He races toward me, enveloping me in a tight embrace. Stunned, my arms splay at his sides. Pulling back, he smiles down at me, his large hand coming up to cup my face. A shy smile forms at the corners of my mouth.

"I had no idea you were coming back already." I lean back to take a good look at him. The same mischievous amber eyes and golden hair I remember, but the boy who left a year ago has returned a man. "And here I've finally gotten used to life without my best sparring partner."

He lets go, grabbing his chest dramatically. "You hurt and flatter me." Stepping forward, he cups my face with both hands this time, his gaze seeming to stare straight into my soul. "But I'm finally home; you'll have to take me back. Promise?"

I nod softly; words lost to me.

"Good," he says, letting go and taking a seat in the opposite chair.

Shaking myself out of my fluster, I sit, wanting to hear about his mission. About how he's been this past year away from home in some foreign part of the world.

Adrian's face is sharper, skin bronzed from the sun, while his hair has become even lighter. The muscles in his body are more defined, a true hunter shining through even with the boyish smile that remains. *I've missed him.*

As this generation's firstborn son of the Bishop family—my family's closest ally and second in command—Adrian's the only person besides Lance allowed to come here. He's been my best friend for as long as I can remember.

"When did you get back? How was the mission?" I ask, unable to stop examining him for injuries. Light flecks of scars line his arms, but nothing recent or deep. "I was worried when I stopped hearing from you."

"I wish I could have had more time to message you, but that's why I came straight here from the airport. The mission was... It was difficult, dangerous, of course, but we accomplished what we went to do." He pauses for a short second, his hands fidgeting. "I can't tell you much more...."

I frown at his answer.

"Classified?" I ask, my nails digging into my palms. He's never been one to keep details from me.

He gives me a small smile. "You know I would tell you if I could."

I don't believe him. If he wanted to tell me, he would. I'm sure my father was the one to give the order not to, and Adrian worships him. Time hasn't changed his loyalty.

Even if I once believed he cared for me more.

"I know," I lie, switching topics. "So when are your angelic trials? I'm sure you're looking forward to them since you had to put it off."

"In five days. Your father doesn't want to put it off any longer." Adrian smiles softly, taking my hand in his. "I really missed you, Nova." He rubs circles with his thumb, and I match his smile, butterflies flurrying in my stomach.

Adrian was only seventeen when he left on his first major assignment. When he turned eighteen, his mission wasn't finished, so he chose to stay, but the trials must be performed with a male Fandera present. As my father is the last one remaining and refuses to travel, our global command centers have no choice but to send their candidates here each year. I once overheard that my father used to spend more time abroad than here in Falgens, but when my grandfather passed and I was born, everything changed. It's a nuisance, I would imagine, but for Adrian, who's finally back, there's no reason to delay.

My father's hopes for Adrian are even higher than his hopes for me. Adrian is the genius son my father never had. Though I suppose they're more alike in both looks and morals than I'll ever be. Mine must have come from my mother, whoever she may be.

My soft, round face seems weak compared to the sharp features they wear. Their blond hair is like a beacon of light compared to my dark brown locks. They're easily well over six feet while I remain five foot four.

As for morals, even though all hunters should have the same goal of protecting humanity, I also have my own selfish wishes, while they always put others before themselves. I've always questioned everything while they preach undying loyalty and faith.

"Are you nervous?" I ask him.

"Not really," he says, letting go of my hand and shifting back in his chair. "I'm confident I'll pass the trials and be chosen. Being nervous won't help or change the outcome." Envy bubbles in my stomach. He's as sure of himself as my father is of him.

Go figure, though. Being assigned to a classified mission at seventeen and being successful. He should be confident.

I jam the nail of my thumb into my pointer finger, smiling at Adrian. "I'm excited for you. I know you'll pass. What angel wouldn't want you?"

He huffs out a laugh, rubbing the back of his head as if embarrassed by my compliment. It's not that I don't believe my own words—everything I said is the truth from my heart—but I hate it all the same.

I'm just as strong of a hunter as he is, but he's the prodigy. My father can show him off at clan gatherings while he tells his daughter to remain at his estate like a caged princess from one of those ridiculous fairytales.

I push a wider smile. It's not his fault.

Leaning over, I grab the angelology book from the side table. "Better study up on your angels. It'd be embarrassing if you didn't recognize the one who chooses you." I toss him the book, which he easily catches in his hand.

Adrian eyes it, smirking. "Isn't this meant for you?"

"I have others." I glance at the pile of books Lance set out for me. "And someone's neglected their studies because of a mission. Unbelievable," I say dramatically, rolling my eyes.

He chuckles but tosses the book back. "Too bad I don't have time to read it." He stands from the couch. "I wish I could stay longer, but I have some matters I need to take care of and parents to see."

Standing, I give him a small hug. "Say hi to your mom and dad for me. I haven't seen them since you left," I say, looking into his amber eyes. He pulls away, heading toward the door. "Adrian, I'm glad you're back."

He pauses, his grin widening. "Me too. I'll come see you again soon."

Without another word, the door shuts behind him. I listen to his footsteps fade as I sit back down in my chair. A low sigh escapes my lips, and I look at my hand, a pink crescent line carved on my finger.

I missed him, but I never missed this.

Swallowing hard, I stare at the door, my foot tapping on the wooden floor. My trials follow just after his, and maybe we'll finally be on equal footing when we both pass.

We'll never be equals. Not even if I pass.

My eyes shut, my head falling into my hands. A gaping hole sits in my heart.

Adrian's back; that's good enough. Isn't it? The evil voice in my head seems to laugh at the thought, echoing the dark feelings I shove away. Even if we both pass, he will always be him, and I will always be me. And that is enough to split the world in two.

I sit up, brushing my hair back. I want my heart to fill with Adrian's return—and a part of it does—the other part... I remember when I first realized we were different, Adrian and I. When my father looked at him with a proud smile after he aced our first exam at only eight years old, and I watched from the sidelines, stunned to know my father could even smile.

Of course, I aced that exam too. I was only seven.

Another sigh escapes my lips as I look at the leatherbound book on angelic trials. Things are changing. Adrian has changed. Whether it's for better or for worse, I don't know.

I have hope for a future that could be and fear for how it might end up.

Grabbing the book, I open to a random page, my finger grazing over an image of an angel as I read the little cursive letters written underneath:

He who acts with true, loyal intentions will always be stronger than he who hides behind his lies. - Archangel Michael

The moral gate of Archangel Michael is all about being true to our role as a hunter to free humanity from the plague of demons. It's said that we must always be loyal to this goal. I close the book and put it aside.

Loyalty. Adrian's loyalty to my father might be the one thing that continues to separate us. The one thing that feeds my fear and eats away my hope.

Because loyalty can be a dangerous thing.

3

MEMORIES

S taring out the car window, I watch the sunlight flicker across the pavement, keeping my eyes off the people wandering about. We pass the grand fountain marking the entrance to the university grounds, trees swaying overhead in the summer breeze.

The campus is vibrant with color—late summer offering a variety of flowers and shades of green. It's more alive than the last time I was here. When winter held each building and plant in its cold, bitter grasp.

Everything is maintained to perfection for the students attending the university, a mixture of both hunters and ordinary people. All to keep up the image of a typical university, carefully hiding the dark work we do from the world around us.

We pass the administration building, stone angel wings resting at the top of the brick entryway—markers of protection. The campus is the largest holy ground in North America. No demons can enter the premises, *ever*.

My great-great-grandfather, who founded the university, utilized the angels' powers to imbue energy into each set of angel wings, connecting them to create a protective barrier around the campus. The estate he built as his home at the same time as the university is protected in the same way.

However, protected or not, it doesn't change the fact that I can't come here often per my father's order. And when I do, Lance escorts me. My eyes trail to the driver's seat, Lance mindfully watching the road. It's not like I'll be eighteen soon or anything...

From the back seat, one of the academic buildings comes into view. Three stories of reddish-brown brick with tall windows standing high among the trees surrounding it. Rich ivy curves around the front of the building, intertwining its way into all the crevices.

We pass the road to the building, and I turn to Lance.

"Solomon wants to meet with you first," he says before I can ask, meeting my eyes in the rearview mirror before looking back at the road.

"Did he say why?" I ask cautiously.

Lance doesn't respond. The whites of his knuckles are prominent as his fingers grip the steering wheel. My heartbeat quickens, my hands fidgeting as I lean back in the seat. A memory of the last conversation we had here comes to mind.

"You ungrateful child," Father says, staring down at me with those cold blue eyes.

I bow my head. "Father, I didn't— I was just—"

"Leave my sight." My chest tightens, and I bite my lip, holding back the tears welling in my eyes. "Reflect on your inferiorities before I see you again. You are a disgrace as a Fandera if you cannot complete even a simple task."

My mouth moves to speak, but I have no words, just regrets. I should have trained harder, then maybe I wouldn't have disappointed him by reading those unnecessary books.

With a wave of his hand, I'm sent out to a waiting Lance to be returned to the estate.

I shiver, running my hands over my arms.

"Lance, you didn't say anything to him, right?"

His shoulders droop, but he doesn't meet my expecting gaze. "No, I didn't."

The car grows quiet, and I bite the inside my cheek. I shouldn't have asked.

"Thank you, Lance," I say to him, hoping it will ease us both. "I wouldn't be here if you had."

Lance nods his head, acknowledging my words. His shoulders relax ever so slightly, but the lump remains in my throat as we turn onto the private road, pulling up around the curved drive to the red brick manor. The wood door is only a few steps from the car, but I hesitate. An uneasy feeling swirls in my stomach as my fingers reach to open the car door.

Two stone lions lay to either side of the entrance, and set above hang a pair of stone angel wings, though slightly faded from the weather. Ivy climbs the brick, creating a solid green side, yet it's as if it was always meant to look this way. Not too sterile and not too unkempt. Just how my father likes it.

My gaze moves up, the two-story manor towering over me. Clouds cover the morning sun, and a chill runs across my skin. Not a bone in my body wants to enter this place.

A breeze comes from behind and nudges me toward the door. Almost as if the manor is taunting me, begging me to enter its cold halls. I don't come here often, which suits me just fine, as I never have pleasant conversations when I do.

"I'll be here," Lance says, and I look over my shoulder to see him leaning on the top of the gray car from the driver's side.

I nod, turning back to the looming doors before me. A gut feeling tells me not to enter, yet in the same breath, it calls me forth. I step toward the door, placing my hand on the intricately carved doorknob, and push my way in.

Entering the breezeway, I make my way into the main foyer, already feeling the chill in these halls. The grand staircase rises to my right, leading to my father's office. A fireplace sits empty to the left side of the room, plush chairs placed in front of it. The hardwood floors creak as I step into the room, and I cringe at the loud sound echoing off the hollow walls. Nobody else seems to be here, though knowing my father, I wouldn't expect anything less.

I head toward the staircase, not daring to keep my father waiting. A door creaks open, and I stop midstep. Beneath the stairwell, faint light creeps its way into the foyer. The entrance to my father's library cracked open, inviting me inward.

Is he in there for a change?

Stepping away from the stairs, I walk closer and peek inside the room. My eyes widen when I enter, not knowing where to look. Bookshelves have been torn apart, papers and books strewn across the floor. Father's desk is buried beneath a heaping pile of documents at the end of the room, a narrow path carved out to walk through without harming the materials.

A single lamp next to the desk lights the room, and I make my way to it like a moth drawn to a flame. I leaf through the old papers, documents, and books piled on each other. I hesitate for a moment, knowing I'm not meant to see them, but I can't help but continue skimming anyway.

Lifting a journal, a few fragile pieces of paper slide out from its pages. Reaching down, I pick them up, recognizing my father's handwriting on the top paper. A checklist of ways to destroy something, lines crossing out a multitude of destructive methods... My brows furrow as I reach the bottom of the page where a note has been scribbled.

This artifact must be destroyed by whatever means necessary.

I move on to the following paper, a crude pencil sketch of a gem set in an intricate bracelet drawn on it—a common style of artifact since most were shaped as wearable items like jewelry. The back of the paper is covered in angelic script, which has been translated with strong cursive letters:

> *I am the key hidden in the shadows of the lost, waiting for the One to call my name. I am the guide to true legitimacy, the answer against falsehood. I am the strength to fight through the blackened waters that hold death and dispute. To hear my name is to know I'm yours.*

My heart stops, and I reread it a few times in disbelief. All known angelic artifacts can be traced back to the Great Demonic Fall. Weapons imbued with divine power, gifted to only the strongest hunters—or at least the ones who fully bonded with their angel, something we haven't seen in years. The artifacts are rare and held in high regard. The clan's artificers have been able to imitate the angelic metal lethal to demons, but their creations do not hold the same power as a genuine artifact.

I mull over the words, a strange feeling welling up inside me. Angelic script isn't usually left behind with an artifact. It only happens when an angel could not convey a message through their hunter. Flipping back to the drawing again, I wonder if this is the artifact my father intends on destroying.

The last piece of paper reads of detailed failed attempts to destroy the artifact—just as I had read on the checklist. A date sits at the top of the page; my eyes widen further. This is from yesterday.

I put the pages down, searching through the desk. There's no way he just left it here...

Silver peeks through from beneath a pile of documents, and I quickly clear them away. The same bracelet from the sketch is in plain sight for anyone to take. It's beautiful in person. Swirls are inlaid in the silver band, a black gem held in a claw-like clasp. The stone is unusual, however. Each angelic artifact contains a different gemstone, so the gem itself isn't a surprise, but the color... It shines in the faint lamp light, compelling me to pick it up and trace my fingers over its smooth black surface. As if, in doing so, I would feel even an ounce of the power contained within.

"Nova."

I jump, startled back by the voice.

"Father," I say, backing away and turning my attention to where he stands at the door.

My face heats as I meet his gaze, quickly turning away. Did he see me reaching for the bracelet? Hands shaking, I hide the bracelet beneath papers as I organize the table mindlessly to avoid the cold stare of my father.

"I thought you were in here, the light was on, and the door was open and—"

"My office, now."

He turns and swiftly leaves the library, not waiting for me to follow. Taking one last look at where I left the angelic artifact under the piles of papers, I leave the room. As I step out of the library, a string pulls on my heart, urging me not to leave the bracelet behind. Shaking my head, I shoo away the thought.

I may be a disobedient, ungrateful child, but I don't need my father to label me a thief.

Hurrying up the grand staircase after my father, I follow him to the end of the hall to his office—the paintings hanging on the wall passing in a blur. I enter behind him, catching the already closing door. He takes a seat behind the large wooden desk, glaring from me to one of the two leather chairs positioned in front of him. I comply with his silent demand without hesitation.

"Father, I really thought you were in there, I—" The room remains silent, and I bite my tongue. My heart pounds in my ears as I avoid his burning glare.

I freeze in my seat when I look up after a long moment. Cold blue stares back at me, unemotional and unrelenting. And I'm glad I don't share those eyes.

His eyes are set deep in his face, brows in a constant furrow. Thin lips are curved in a frown; his thick hair, which is almost as pale as his skin, is slicked back from his face—one weathered but still youthful. Such robust features, fitting for a hunter of his status.

"Adrian's trials are in five days, and as you know, yours will follow the week after," he says, his tone sharp and to the point. I give him a single nod, remaining silent. This isn't a two-way conversation; it never is with him. "My expectations are high for you both."

"I won't disappoint you," I say, forcing my voice to remain steady.

"You will be chosen," he says without hesitation.

There's no way to know such a thing, even for him. The men in my family—specifically the firstborn sons, the ones given the name Solomon—may be something entirely different from a hunter joined with an angel, something only they know the secret of, but that doesn't make them all-knowing. If that were the case, we'd have more angels here on Earth with us.

Is it because I'm his daughter? There's nothing telling in his voice, but honestly, I would have imagined that he didn't want me to pass. Even if it brought disgrace to our family name, he would be able to continue to dictate my life, at least as a hunter. Something to hold over my head once I turn eighteen, and I'm free to do as I please.

"I'm glad you have such *confidence* in my being chosen, but nothing's for sure, as you would know." I pause, waiting for his eyes to give him away. They don't. "So why does it sound like more than that? Father, please, what aren't you telling me?" The bravery of my question startles me.

"You will be chosen," he says, tearing his eyes away from mine to focus on the paperwork in front of him.

I stare at him in disbelief. Since coming here, everything has been so different. The disorganization, the angelic artifact, and now this. Never has he lowered his eyes from mine to avoid a question.

Standing up abruptly from the chair, I use the movement to draw his eyes back to mine, "You expect me to believe you? Because saying it twice makes it more convincing." Anger. The overwhelming feeling rises within me, consuming any sense of logic I have.

"Do you question me?" he asks, his voice becoming harsh. But a flash of uncertainty in his eyes gives him away for the second time.

A smile tugs at my lips. "Question you? Maybe, it's in our nature as hunters; you taught me that, but...."—I drag out the moment, holding his gaze in mine—"trust you? Believe whatever you say? Now that would be a totally different answer." Anger visibly bubbles under the surface of his face. My smile falls, and I replicate the same cold look he always shows me. "If that's all, I'll take my leave." I bow my head in his direction before spinning to the door.

"You'll understand everything after the trials. I promise."

His words stop me before I can leave. Looking over my shoulder, I see his eyes become soft as if they're filled with worry and hope. My chest tightens, and I swallow down my emotions. My eyes must be deceiving me.

"You see, this is exactly what I don't trust." And I leave the room.

I don't wait to be followed, rushing down the stairs to the foyer. My hand reaches the front doorknob, but I hesitate. Turning back, I look to the second floor before my gaze drifts to the library beneath the staircase.

My feet move before my mind can catch up.

Heart hammering in my chest, I head straight to the pile of papers on the desk where the angelic artifact is buried. I rifle through the pile to where the silver bracelet is left untouched. I admire it for a split second before taking it in hand.

The metal is warm, sending a wave of heat through my body as I rub my thumb over the black gem. Remembering the paper with the drawing and angelic script, I quickly find them and shove both into the pocket of my black cargo pants.

Not waiting a moment longer, I race out of the room. This artifact—for whatever reason my father wants it destroyed—is another secret he intends to keep from me. Between this, keeping me locked away, never once mentioning my mother, and acting as if the angelic trials are rigged. I can't take it anymore. Label me a thief.

Bursting out the front door, the wind whips around me as if to fill my lungs with much-needed air. I let my eyes close, calming the adrenaline coursing through my body. All this pent-up anger toward my father still simmers within me, but now that the wind has had its way, it seems to pat me on the back as if to say *good job*.

Opening my eyes, I see Lance waiting in the car, not noticing me yet. Taking the bracelet out, I admire it in the sunlight, a lump stuck in my throat.

I don't let myself regret it, shoving it back into my pocket and hopping into the car.

"Let's go," I say, buckling in. "Please." I meet his eyes in the rearview mirror. He nods softly, confused but thankfully leaving out any questions he may have. I grab my backpack, which is already filled with anything I may need while sparring today, and sneak in the angelic artifact and papers before Lance notices.

Sinking into my seat with a heavy sigh, I try not to think about what will happen when my father realizes the bracelet is missing. At least I'll be able to take out my leftover frustration on the first-years. It'll be a much-needed release after such a useless conversation.

In less than a minute, we arrive at the academic building we had passed earlier. Stepping out of the car, I don't wait for Lance to follow me to the entrance. My eyes trail to the stone arch above the front door, Bishop Academic Center engraved into it. Adrian's heritage and legacy. The only reason he was ever allowed around me.

"We're taking the first-years to the underground sparring arena," Lance says, coming up behind me. "I know you haven't fought others in a while, but remember who you are. Most of these kids may be the same age as you, but you're no first-year."

I nod with a smirk, excitement overriding my anger. "Do you think I look unassuming enough? I'm sure they've only heard rumors about me."

Lance chuckles, holding the door open for me. "They won't know what hit them. Just don't beat them too badly, or we won't have future hunters. Most of them are campus recruits, not hunter-born. Solomon only wants to test their potential ability, using you to taunt them."

"Using me... I suppose there are worse things," I say as he passes me, leading us down the hallway to the first-years. He keeps silent about my remark.

As much as Lance annoys me, he knows I'm capable of so much more. The first-years won't be a challenge for me, yet we both know it's still good practice. Evaluating others' abilities on the spot, responding correctly to their attacks. It'll be easy, but at least my father deems me capable of this one task.

The sparring matches—though I've never been the one to lead them—are the first steps to determining one's potential as not just a hunter but as a participant in the angelic trials. The hunter-born would have been mentally prepared for the trials since they were children, even if the physical aspect has yet to catch up. Recruits, however, will only know the bare minimum of what it means. But even they have a chance to show their potential for it.

My job is to bring out the worst in them. To reveal their true nature. Are they afraid? Easy to anger? Do they run away in the face of danger? All of these are unacceptable.

"No weapons, right?" I say, looking over at Lance. "Have they even picked their classifications?"

"Some have; others are still deciding. The new term started at the beginning of summer, so it hasn't been long with this group."

I nod. There are six different classifications of hunters: healers, who treat demonic wounds; tamers, who can control spirits and low-tier demons; artificers, who create angelic weapons that allow us to kill demons; exorcists, who can recite banishing phrases; dragoons, who use guns as their weapons; and warriors, who fight with various handheld melee weapons. But basic hand-to-hand combat and martial arts are required for all hunters.

Most hunters choose one classification to specialize in—as there are plenty of different skills to focus on within each—but a small number choose a secondary classification. And though each hunter can select their class, part of determining their potential includes seeing what they're best suited for. Some aren't great fighters, so they become healers; others are horrible at metalwork but can easily tame spirits.

As someone who's already been trained in each classification, I'm surprised it's taking so long to choose. Not that I'm good in each area, especially as an exorcist and tamer. Without faith, it's hard to be an exorcist, and being a tamer just never felt right. My main classification is warrior—the same as Adrian. Warriors are usually only skilled in one or two types of weapons, but as hunter-born under the Fandera name, I've been trained to handle as many as time allows me to learn. Adrian's weapon of choice is the greatsword, while I prefer blades that fit my size—though scythes, as impractical as they are, hold a special place in my heart.

Lance comes to a stop in front of a large door, and I follow suit, leaning slightly to peek into the small window and see the trainees. He knocks, and we wait. The door slides open to reveal an older, maybe forty-something, extremely buff man with a shaved head. A deep scar stretches across the left side of his face from the corner of his eye down to his chin, where it crosses his lips. It's an old scar, deep but slowly returning to his deep golden skin color.

The man crosses his arms as he towers over us, his large arms bulging beneath his too-tight shirt. I smile weakly at the intimidating man, recognizing him from around the clan but not knowing his name. Definitely not someone I'd want to mess with. But it does make me wonder why Lance is the one teaching me. I may have behaved better with this guy as my teacher.

"Darius," Lance says, "as Solomon let you know, today we'll start determining the potential of your students."

Darius turns to look back at his students. "Hear that, kids? You're about to get your asses whooped." A collective groan sounds from the students behind him. "Good luck with this group," he scoffs, turning back to face us. On the back of his neck, I glimpse a pair of angel wings tattooed onto his skin.

"You're an Undivided?" I say, and a number of the students snicker. My face flushes. I shouldn't have blurted the thought out loud. Now at least I know why I recognize him.

Darius's dark brown eyes narrow, assessing my ability as he recognizes who I am. "If it isn't Nova Fandera, the spoiled little princess of our renowned leader. What a surprise to see you here."

My eyebrow twitches at the nickname. Spoiled little princess? It seems my reputation has gotten even better within the clan. I mentally roll my eyes. As if my father would ever spoil me.

I train more than any of these first-years ever have. Everyone in the room moves to peek around the large figure of Darius, trying to get a glimpse at me. A few of the boys even mock the stupid nickname.

"I am," I say calmly, extending my hand to him. He takes it, and I squeeze hard, relishing the look of surprise on his face. "But be careful who you underestimate." I let go of his hand. After standing up to my father, he's nothing.

"So the princess has some bite to her. Doesn't make you strong." He sneers. "Even if Solomon sent you, don't pretend to be something you're not."

"Excuse me?" I ask, forcing a friendly smile.

"You're a weak little girl. If you weren't, I would see you on patrols, at clan meetings." He leans down to speak in my ear. "But you're the Fandera princess; you don't have to be like the rest of us hunters. Living in your cushy estate while we fight in the real world."

My jaw clenches, but I force it to relax. "If you'd like, I'll spar with you first. I have no problem proving you wrong."

He lets out a hearty laugh, and I take a step back. Why's he laughing now?

"Maybe another time, princess." He stops laughing, steely eyes looking down on me. "I'll just watch you get crushed by my students for today."

His words tempt me to wipe the sly grin off his face, but Lance steps in before I can do something rash. "I think it'll be the other way around." Lance places a hand on my shoulder. "I did train her myself."

Darius stares at Lance for a long moment before nodding his head ever so slightly. "Then let's see what your little princess is capable of."

4

FIGHT FOR YOUR LIFE

"Listen up, everyone, my ol' pal Lance will be running today's lesson with our sweet little princess," Darius says, his deep voice resounding in the cement sparring arena. "Go easy on her."

I roll my eyes, brushing off his comments. He'll find out who he's messing with soon enough.

Lance steps up next to Darius, taking charge of the room. "Today isn't only about strength, but your conviction as a hunter. This is just the first step toward determining whether you can participate in the angelic trials. And like the angels, we'll also be testing you." Lance motions for me to step forward and stand beside him. "Nova will spar with each of you while I complete your evaluations. Nova, if you could reiterate our seven commandments for the first-years."

Lance gives me the floor to speak. I nod, willing my voice to sound clear to the group before me. "As hunters, we follow seven commandments: To always seek *knowledge*. To commit to the true *intentions* of being a hunter. To understand with *empathy*. To have *courage* in the face of our enemy. To be true to our word of *integrity*. To find *compassion* for those who suffer at the hands of demons. And, most importantly, to have *loyalty* to the clan and our cause. Each of these commandments aligns with one of the seven archangels. If you are lucky to be chosen for the trials, these angels govern them. Fail their test, and you'll never get a second chance." I look around the room. Twenty or so kids of a similar age to me, face me with bewilderment in their eyes. Only a few share the look of having heard this speech countless times—these must be the hunter-born. "So, use this opportunity to show us what you're made of."

"You talk a lot for barely being a hunter," a cocky male voice from the back of the crowd says. "We heard what Mr. Nazeri said. You're weak. Do you think you're better than us?"

I assess the boy moving forward among the majorly male trainees. His features are familiar—shaggy dirty blond hair hanging in front of a sharp nose and amber eyes. The corner of his mouth is raised in an annoying smirk as he eggs on the rest of the trainees to agree with him.

Hushed whispers circle around the room, and I force myself to hold back my own smirk. The kid is tall, but the black athletic wear hangs loosely over his frame, which has yet to fill in with muscle. All while pretending to be the biggest and best of the group. Quite amusing, really.

I step toward the boy. "Do you believe everything you hear? Because your teacher, *Darius*, said I'm weak, makes it true?" The smirk finally makes its way onto my face, finding great joy in calling his teacher by his first name.

His classmates whispers grow louder, curiosity evident on their faces. No one here besides Lance has seen me fight, some rumors say I can't, yet here I am to spar with them for their evaluation. I'd be curious too.

"Prove it then." He takes a step closer to me, invading my personal space. "I volunteer to go first. I'll beat your scrawny ass."

"Theo Bishop, be careful what you ask for," Lance says from behind me.

"So you're Adrian's cousin? I thought you looked familiar," I say to Theo, tilting my head. "You should listen to Lance. I'm not the scrawny one." I stare him down, internally laughing as I watch him try to intimidate me.

"Scared?" he says, puffing out his chest.

I smile. "I'm so scared. What am I going to do with myself? Oh right, maybe you should talk with Adrian. He's my best sparring partner. You could learn something from watching me kick his ass."

His face heats up, tearing his eyes from mine to look at Darius. "I'll fight first, Mr. Nazeri. I know I can beat this shrimp."

"That's the spirit," Darius says, letting out a hearty laugh. He glances at me, obviously curious about my comment. Everyone knows Adrian, but maybe not about us. My fingers curl into fists, nails digging into my palm. I wish I didn't have to throw his name around just to prove a point.

Shrugging my shoulders, I step back nonchalantly. "This okay with you, Lance?" He nods, motioning for everyone to step off the mat and give us space.

Located beneath the academic building, cement walls rise up two stories to create the sizeable rectangular arena. The center space is where we spar, lined with black mats that are harder than they look. Around the outer walls, distinctly different doors lead to other training areas specific to the various classifications and other training exercises. I've been through a few doors during past training sessions. My eyes are drawn to the black-stained door at the far end of the room.

Intricate depictions of demons are carved into the dark wood. I shiver involuntarily. I've entered that one the most. Captured demons are kept in cages for us to practice against in a large pit with a single ladder. Safe to say more than a few hunters have met with unfortunate accidents there.

Weapon racks line the rest of the empty wall spaces. They hold throwing knives, various swords, and other assorted handheld weapons for basic weapon sparring. A skill recommended for all hunters to learn, warrior or otherwise.

I watch Theo prepare, stretching my arms, tension rippling through his body. If I remember correctly, Adrian once said Theo had been sent abroad to another Bishop academic branch, but considering he's in the first-year group, I don't think it went well. Not that he could ever compare to his cousin anyway. No one can.

I move into position, loosely raising my fists to give the illusion of an unskilled fighter. Theo flexes his small muscles, posturing himself to tower over me. As he assesses my poor stance, a cocky grin rests permanently on his face.

cocky grin rests permanently on his face as he assesses my poor stance.

Oh, Theo, you have no idea what's about to hit you.

"Ready, Little Bishop?" I say to Theo.

His eyes flare with anger at the nickname, but he nods. Turning back, I throw a wink at Lance before he starts the match. Theo stalks closer, waiting to strike as he watches my movements. Lowering my arms, I fake a yawn to taunt him forward. It hits a nerve, and he rushes at me, throwing a soft punch at my jaw.

"Too slow." I sidestep out of the way, his punch missing with room to spare.

With his ribcage exposed, I throw a quick jab at it before moving behind him to playfully kick his back. He stumbles forward but regains his footing after a moment. He glares as he circles back, his face red with frustration.

"Is that all you got, Little Bishop?" I say, spinning to look around the room at his classmates. "I thought I was weak."

Theo's eyes fill with anger. Rushing toward me without thinking, he throws a cross punch toward my jaw *again*, smirking as he expects it to hit. Dodging his fist, I almost let out a laugh. I grab his forearm and use his momentum to knee him hard in the stomach.

A pained gasp leaves his lips.

Spinning back, I kick over his head, letting my shoe graze over his dirty blond hair. The room is quiet, Theo's classmates watching intently. I make eye contact with one of the few girls, throwing a wink her way as I dodge his jabs from behind me. Dancing back around to face Theo, I smile at the red color rising to his cheeks.

"So, how's it going beating the shrimp?" I ask tauntingly.

I hit him with a jab. He attempts a sloppy roundhouse kick in response, but I grab onto his leg, flipping him to the ground. A grunt echoes in the cement room as he thuds onto the hard mat.

"Fighting like this... You won't ever be considered strong. Anger will get you killed when facing a demon," I say, standing over him.

His breaths are heavy, sweat glistening on his brow. Steam seems to burst out of his ears, his anger fueling what little energy he has left. Pushing himself up, he tackles me onto the ground. He digs his knee into my stomach, pinning me to the mat.

"Good move."

Mimicking the smirk of victory plastered on his face, I grab hold of his ankle with one hand and use my other to push his knee. Unbalanced, he topples over, and we switch positions. I land on top, pinning him down with a stronger hold.

"But not good enough." I lean close to whisper into his ear. "Weakness isn't tolerated in this world, and cockiness will get you killed."

Resisting the urge to punch him and end this, I release my hold and stand. I wipe my hands on the fabric of my leggings, looking at Lance as he scribbles on his clipboard. The room fills with whispers; the silence was broken the moment I won.

I chuckle to myself. Theo wasn't the first Bishop I thought I'd spar against since Adrian got back. I tighten my ponytail, eyes trained on Lance as I wait for his queue. Theo should be sixteen or seventeen, yet his skill as a fighter seems to be lacking. He's a Bishop; he should have the basics down by now. It would still be unlikely that he'd win, but the Bishops are known for having some of the most highly trained members of the clan. Just look at Adrian's father—right hand to my father and bonded with one of the seven archangels.

"Good job Nova. Theo, you could do better," Lance says, still scribbling notes.

The chatter in the room grows louder. I sigh, letting my gaze travel over each trainee. Most seem to be between fifteen and seventeen—their faces filled with innocence and excitement. A group of students laugh together; a few others roughhouse while they wait. I look back to Lance. With Theo's first reaction being anger—even as a Bishop—I have to wonder if he'll be allowed to partake in the angelic trials.

My eyes trail to my bag sitting harmlessly beside a cement pillar of the arena. A buzz rings in my ear, every other sound fading into muffled noise. Blood thunders in my ears, my heartbeat racing as my eyesight goes blurry. I reach a hand to my head to shake the feeling when a cool blade presses against my throat.

"Thought you beat me?" Theo says, pressing the blade in, drawing a small trickle of blood. "I'm a Bishop; I don't go down that easy."

Whispers ring throughout the arena as my senses come back to me. Did nobody notice this idiot grabbing a knife from the wall? Lance's eyes meet mine, and I smirk at him, a loud laugh bursting from my lips, breaking the tense air.

"Shut up!" Theo yells in my ear, but I continue laughing.

Grabbing his wrist, I pull the blade from my neck, dislocating his shoulder as I spin around to face him. He screams, the blade dropping from his hand. I catch it, applying more pressure to his wrist. Aiming the knife at his throat, I don't hide the anger in my voice.

"Don't you *dare* put a knife to my throat."

Letting go, I step back and land a roundhouse kick to his face. He slams to the ground, knocked out cold. Silence follows, no whispers or chatter this time.

I stare at Theo, a scowl set on my face. There are rules to sparring, to being a hunter, that you never break. Shaking my head, I walk from his limp body to Lance waiting on the sidelines.

Reaching a hand to my throat, I wipe the warm blood dripping down my neck. It stings, but I pay it no mind.

"I don't know about you, but I'm thinking no angel for him," I say to Lance.

He lets out a sigh, "Someone take him to a medic." A few hesitant trainees step forward to drag him off the arena mat. As they move him away his head lolls to the side, a dead weight in their hands.

Father keeps me in the estate, not letting me become a true hunter when *these* are the hunters he's training? Even if Theo is a Bishop, there's no excuse for breaking the rules of loyalty and respect for your fellow hunters. My hands tighten into fists while I master my face into perfect calmness.

"Your feet need to move faster. He was catching up to you," Lance says, and I roll my eyes.

"I doubt that," Darius says, coming to stand beside us. "She has a good stance and a strong kick. You've surprised me, Nova."

Lance nods, distracted by whatever he's writing on his clipboard.

"What can I say? The rumors have me all wrong." I smile at Darius, and he lets out an amused huff.

"Get back to your job," Lance says, turning away from us. We ignore him.

"I hope you'll be joining us on Monday's full moon patrol. I'd like to see you against a real demon." Darius crosses his arms, a somewhat approving smile on his stern face. "Theo is one thing. A mid or high-tier demon is another."

"Well, you're in luck. My father already promised I could go since it's almost my eighteenth."

"Then we'll see if you're worth it."

I tilt my head at the odd phrasing but nod softly. It'll take more than a fight with Theo to prove my capability to someone like Darius.

Turning my attention back to the group of trainees, I can't help but smile at the terrified yet impressed expressions they wear. I meet their eyes, skimming over the group, trying to see whatever it is that Lance is looking for. Searching for some clue as to what this so-called potential is.

Long silver hair flits across my vision, and I suddenly notice a woman weaving between the trainees. I take a step back, ears ringing. A sweet floral scent tickles my nose, masking the smell of sweat and disinfectant. The woman stops in front of me, and my heart pounds in my chest. Though her face appears blurry, her bright golden eyes are clear. I stumble back, goosebumps raising the hairs on my arms.

She disappears, and I realize everyone's waiting on me expectantly, their eyes pointed in my direction. I gulp, squaring my shoulders and turning to face Lance. *Weakness is not tolerated.*

"So, who's next?"

5

A BROKEN PROMISE

Pinning my last match to the mat, I look to Lance for confirmation to stop. He nods, and I loosen my grip, lending a hand to the girl I sparred against. She takes it, and I pull her up.

"Thanks," she says.

"No problem." The girl smiles as I fidget with my hands. "You fought well. Better than some of the guys even," I say awkwardly. I watch as she heads back to the rest of the trainees—not even getting her name. They laugh as she approaches, teasing her for losing even though they all lost to me.

I smile weakly, turning away from them. The rest of the matches went far better than the one with Theo, considering no one else pulled a stunt like he did. A few first-years have talent, their abilities just waiting to be honed, but it'll take time. The majority of them are campus recruits, not hunter-born. They have a lot to learn before they can catch up to someone like me, who's trained for as long as I can remember.

Stepping off the mat, I grab my towel from my bag, wiping my sweaty forehead before downing an entire water bottle. My

46

athletic wear sticks uncomfortably to my body, and I think of how nice it'll be to take a shower once I get back.

I plop to the ground, exhausted and sore from sparring with so many people in one day. They might not be as strong as me, but there's strength in numbers. I smile again, wishing things could stay like this.

Looking over my shoulder at the room of trainees, I watch them pack up and start doing the same. Silver peeks out from behind all the stuff in my bag, and hesitantly, I reach in and graze a finger over it. The metal is warm to the touch, even in the cool air-conditioned arena. I swallow hard, the image of the woman stuck in my head.

Letting go, I zip my bag and pull it over my shoulder as I rise and head to where Lance is finishing up his notes.

"Is there anything else we need to do?" I ask at the exact time his phone rings. He raises a finger and steps away.

I wait patiently, lost in thought, as I look around the arena. The full moon patrol is coming up, a night where demon activity rises, and we send out larger patrols to protect the town. Falgens is known for being a hotspot for demons. Some say we live on a portal to Hell—or Gehenna. A dimension they rule yet never seem to want to stay in. Maybe it's because here they can feed on humans' fear, anger, desire, and even blood. Thankfully, they're primarily creatures of the night. Still, we work with local police to monitor CCTVs around town to sight demons before they can do any harm. It's the high-tiers and up that are the real problem. Immersed in society due to their unique ability to wear a human face. You never know when or where they'll hit, but when they do, they hit hard.

Father doesn't normally let me go, but he promised I could since I'll be eighteen soon. I grip the strap of my bag. As long as he doesn't realize I took the angelic bracelet...

At the other end of the arena, Darius raises a hand in goodbye, exiting up the stairs with the last few trainees. I turn back to Lance, who's still on the phone. His voice is hushed, speaking in short responses and glancing over at me every so often. My body tenses, recognizing the behavior. It must be my father.

Lance hangs up, grabbing his bag. "We have to go, now."

I nod, following after him. We move quickly up the stairs, exiting from the hidden doorway into the academic halls. I jog to keep pace as we head to the front doors, my sore body protesting against the movement.

A warm glow hangs in the sky as we burst through the front doors. The setting sun casts golden light across the campus, and I stop for a moment to admire it.

Lance circles back around, grabbing my wrist and dragging me to the car. "What the hell, Lance!" I stumble, but he doesn't stop until I'm in the car.

"We need to get back to the estate, now," Lance says, voice laced with urgency as he clambers into the driver's seat.

He peels out of the parking lot faster than he should, and I bounce in my seat. Quickly, I attach my seat buckle, holding on to the seat in front of me to keep steady. Father couldn't have found out already... Right?

"Lance, slow down," I protest but am ignored.

We peel out onto the main road back to the estate. He swerves as we almost hit another car, and a loud honk blares behind us as we zip through traffic with complete disregard of all traffic laws. In less than five minutes, the estate's gate opens, and we're pulling into the curved driveway.

"Lance, what's going on? You drove like a mad man." He doesn't respond, ushering me out of the car into the house even as I protest.

"Inside, now," he commands, and I freeze, nodding stiffly in compliance.

We enter the main foyer, and before I can question him again, Lance pushes me farther into the room. I turn at the sound of another set of footsteps. Father stands at the bottom of the staircase, his cold blue gaze set on me. My thundering heart sinks. He has to know.

"Father," I say, forcing my voice to remain steady.

"I heard you didn't lose a single match," he says, walking toward us with his hands behind his back.

"She did well today," Lance says with a curt nod.

Father gives him a look that says—I wasn't talking to you—and Lance bows his head, stepping back from us. Father moves closer, towering over me with an aura of cold, steely authority. My hands tremble, but I tighten my grip on my bag, which suddenly feels much heavier.

"I'm ashamed of the Bishop boy, so unlike Adrian." His words are slow and controlled. As if biding his time before delivering bad news. A pit forms in my stomach.

"I handled the situation," I say, struggling to keep my voice steady.

"That you did," he says and swiftly turns away from me to walk toward the grand staircase.

I let out a breath I didn't know I was holding in. He hasn't realized I took the angelic artifact yet. Adjusting the bag on my shoulder, I loosen my grip on the strap.

Watching him go up the stairs, I wonder if this is another step toward change. I still hate his secrecy and the answers he dangles like carrots to ensure his control over me, but I can't help but hope this means he's starting to see me as a valued hunter.

Halfway up the staircase, Father stops.

"We didn't finish earlier." His head turns slightly back to us without fully meeting my waiting gaze. "You won't be participating in the patrol Monday. I expect nothing but training before your trials."

My heart stops. Emotions I've shoved down since I was little fight against the chains I locked them in, clawing at my insides to be unleashed.

"You promised me," I say, my voice strained.

I take a step forward, and Lance grabs my arm to hold me back. Father continues up the stairs, not saying another word on the matter.

"Father!" I yell out, struggling to break from Lance's grip. He ignores me, disappearing down the hall.

The grip on my arm loosens, and I yank myself free, whipping around to face Lance. "You knew." He doesn't respond. "So? Was the sparring supposed to appease me? Compensation for yet another broken promise?"

"Nova, I—" Lance reaches for me, but I step away, raising my hand to stop him. I don't need his excuses.

Leaving him behind, I head to my room. Tears prick at the corners of my eyes, but I blink them away. No amount of tears will change my father's mind. Unbidden, a memory resurfaces from when I was a young girl.

I was only seven years old but had just returned from training. I was exhausted, hurt, and lonely... always lonely. I had approached my father with tears in my eyes, hoping for just an ounce of comfort. But Father's eyes were cold, hard.

"What have I told you about crying, Nova?"

"Only the weak cry," I sniffled.

"And are you weak, Nova? Fanderas cannot be weak. Weakness is not tolerated in this world."

"No, Father. I'm a Fandera. I'm strong."

"Then I better not see you crying again. Do not disappoint me."
And with that, he turned and walked away.

Slamming my bedroom door shut, I shake off the memory and throw my bag into an empty chair. I stare at my room, unmoving. The rage is still there, simmering quietly, but an empty feeling reigns.

All I want is to prove I can be the hunter I know I am. To show my father and the clan that they have me all wrong. I'm not the weak princess they all assume I am; I'm stronger than all of them.

My nails dig into my palms. Another day, another broken promise. How many more until I'm set free?

I sink down next to my bed. Closing my eyes, my head falls to my knees, and I wrap my arms around my legs. No matter how many times I've thought about it, I can't figure out why he does this. No rhyme or reason to keep me locked away, to shroud my life in mystery.

A soft breeze wraps around my trembling body, and I lift my head. The room is dark, with no window open. I blink, searching the room—I must be going crazy. A sigh leaves my lips as I lean back against the soft mattress. Trailing my eyes over the outlines of the furniture, I notice the crumpled bag on the chair. Standing, I take the bag into my hands and reach inside for the angelic bracelet.

It's still warm to the touch. Unease settles into my stomach as I suddenly recall the silver-haired woman from the arena. I turn the bracelet over, the black gem shining with the faint moonlight coming from the window. What if... I shake my head. An angelic artifact is an extension of an angel's power, but it can't summon an actual angel.

But if I could use it... I rub my forehead. What am I even thinking?

Either way, I should see if the library has anything on this artifact. I go to set it down when an idea sparks in my mind. The full moon is in five days. If I can convince Lance and my father that I agree I should just train before my angelic trials, when the day actually comes, they won't suspect me of escaping and taking things into my own hands.

The thought is tempting. An opportunity to recklessly prove myself as a hunter. I sigh, tucking the bracelet into my pocket. Heading to my closet, I pull out a single inconspicuous blade. It's not much, but it's made of angelic metal. And knowing my father, he'll have Lance make sure all my personal weapons are taken—and I can't fight demons without one.

I scan the various weapons still lining my shelf. Lance shouldn't notice if one is missing... Tucking the blade into a hidden crevice I made as a kid, I leave the closet. This might actually work.

Walking to the closed window, I stare at the partially full moon in the sky. This time, I won't let Father dictate my life. The wind sweeps past me again, brushing its subtle touch through my hair—reassuring me in my next move. Strange, no window is open... But somehow, I've found my answer.

I'm a hunter; it's time I show up as one.

6

KIOREN

The TV plays in the background, the news—the only channel I have access to—filling the empty silence in the library. I've been flipping through books all night, hoping to find anything about this angelic bracelet. We have records of all known angelic artifacts, yet I can't find anything matching the description of the one my father wants to destroy—the one I carry.

I know it's not one of the angelic artifacts of the seven archangels. None have a black aura to match the unusual gemstone, and none of their artifacts take the form of a bracelet. But I've been researching hundreds of angels this morning, and not a single one has any connection to this bracelet. Is it even angelic?

I finish skimming another book and toss it aside. Leaning back into my leather chair with a long sigh, I rub my tired eyes. There are only two days left until the full moon. My father left almost as soon as he came, and Lance is wary but convinced I've moved on from the broken promise, nonetheless.

The mumble of the TV pulls my attention. *"Nearly fifteen hundred refugee children in the Chicago area have gone missing in the past month. Officials are still searching for the undocumented children, but so far there is no new information on the case..."*

The library door swings open, and I sit up, startled. Lance strides toward me, the news returning to background noise.

"You missed practice"—he grabs the remote from the side table next to me, turning off the TV—"and now you're watching TV."

My eyes go wide. It's Saturday; we always spar with weapons early in the morning. Looking from the sliver of light through closed curtains to the ticking clock on the wall, I see it's well past noon. How did I lose track of so much time?

"I—" I try to think of an excuse but come up short. I'm not even wearing my training gear; still in my shorts and an oversized T-shirt.

"Is this about Adrian's trials tomorrow?" Lance's face relaxes, a sort of sadness passing over his dark brown eyes.

"I mean, well, I don't... I guess so?" He came up with an excuse for me. Lucky.

Lance takes a seat in the chair across from me, leaning toward me with his elbows on his knees, fingers intertwined. He lets out a sigh, taking a moment before speaking.

"Nova, you don't need to compare yourself to Adrian." He locks his eyes with mine. "You can be a great hunter with or without an angel. You already are. You might not realize it, but you have a strength inside you that nobody else has. Hold on to it."

My lips part as he speaks. I would expect him to reinforce what my father told me—that I'll pass the angelic trials. Or at least urge me to show everyone the hunter he's turned me into. It's comforting but confusing. Maybe it's because he understands, having not passed his own trials, as proven by the bare skin on the back of his neck.

"Inner strength or not, you know I can't think that way," I say to him. "My father will always expect more than that."

He nods, but his phone rings before he can say anything more.

"What is it?" he says upon answering, his eyes widening as he listens.

He puts his finger up for me to wait, standing from the chair and walking toward the door. His voice is hushed as he leaves the room, but before he's gone, I hear two words. *Blood moon.*

The door closes, and I jump to my feet, racing to the bookshelves. Skimming through the titles, I search for books on demonology, specifically relating to the moon phases. Finding a few promising ones, I take them back to my seat, flipping through the pages with renewed enthusiasm. If I'm not mistaken, a blood moon means... I find the words confirming my thinking. A rare night where the full moon turns red, demons eating off its essence, their powers growing tenfold.

Closing the books, I smile. *This is fantastic.*

Because full moons bring out the worst in demons, headquarters track the ebb and flow of the demonic power in the air. If they've sensed a blood moon, then Monday's patrol will be much crazier than any of us anticipated.

Lance once told me the legend of the blood moon or the *Night of Helel*, a hunter tale to scare children and remind us of our history.

Legend has it that a thousand years ago, when Lucifer fell from the Heavens, he declared war against God and His angels, intent on stealing the throne in the glass castle of the Heavens. Using his gift as the Lightbringer, Lucifer cracked open the moon and stole its power to raise a demonic army from Hell. But stripping the moon of its power caused an imbalance in the world, and the moon cried tears of blood—its essence dripping to Earth, feeding the demons and granting them even greater strength. We humans were caught in the crossfire, and our cities burned as Lucifer's demon army rampaged. Lucifer almost succeeded in winning the war, but God used His power to seal the moon and restore balance. He then sent us the angels to aid us in our fight for survival. And so the first Undivided were created; the only part of this legend I know is a fact. Led by Solomon Fandera the First, my ancestor, we won the war, now known as the Great Demonic Fall, because of this incredible gift.

Nowadays, hunters say that whenever Lucifer's anger rises from the depths of Hell, the moon will turn red once again—that the damage the fallen angel caused was too significant for God to fix completely. No one truly understands why this is, or if the legend holds any truth at all, but the fact is that when the full moon rises and turns red, demons become stronger.

My mind travels to the single blade hidden in my closet—my other weapons already confiscated until the full moon passes—and my heart sinks. It won't be enough.

Grazing my fingers over the title of the book, I return it to the shelf. My father and the long line of Solomons before him are the only hunters who have ever been able to use angelic artifacts without an angelic bond—the source of their power something else entirely, a secret only they are privy to.

I pull the bracelet from my pocket. Its warmth is intoxicating; I can feel the power emanating from it. Whatever this artifact is, it could be strong enough to fight with, and if my father and his father before him can use them without an angel, who's to say I can't?

It's a dangerous thought.

I wrap my fingers around the bracelet, and pull it close to my chest. But if I can use this... The bracelet pulses in response, a heartbeat within the silver metal. Holding it out in front of me, I stare into the black gem, my reflection distorted in its faceted, gleaming surface.

Please, give me a miracle.

Lance never returns, forgetting about our sparring for the first time ever. This blood moon must be keeping him more preoccupied than I would have thought possible. I keep reading all day, searching for more answers. The bracelet has been quiet but is still warm to the touch as it rests in my pocket.

Yawning, I look to the sun casting its final glow. It highlights the scattered books and papers throughout the library, and I dread having to clean this up later. With a long sigh, I put the latest useless book aside and stand from my chair. I only have tomorrow and the day of the blood moon to see if this will work, or I won't be able to go through with my plan.

I am the key hidden in the shadows of the lost, waiting for the One to call my name. I am the guide to true legitimacy, the answer against falsehood. I am the strength to fight through the blackened waters that hold death and dispute. To hear my name is to know I'm yours.

The angelic script is ingrained in my head—I had hoped it'd help me in my research—but I don't know what it's supposed to mean.

Leaving the library, I head for my room, yawning again as the tiredness sets in. Golden light shines through the windows, and I stop to watch the last red rays shimmering on the lake. Can I make the impossible possible?

I look above for the first evening stars in the sky, thinking I might find an answer. Instead, my mind drifts to thoughts of tomorrow—Adrian's trials. I haven't seen him again since he's come back. Though I suppose he's busy preparing for his trials. Another sigh leaves my lips.

A tiny flutter outside the window catches my eye. Black wings of a butterfly rising into the darkening sky. My head grows dizzy and begins to ache as I watch it, and I place a hand on my brow as I turn away and continue to my room.

Plopping onto my bed, I stare at the ceiling as I sink into the mattress. The room feels empty. White walls, white sheets, white furniture, beautiful and opulent. But all the wealth in the world can't buy away loneliness.

Rolling to my side, I curl into a ball, hugging my knees. Lance lives on the property as well, but he has a separate house. It's only a few housekeepers who keep to the shadows in the estate itself and me. Pulling the bracelet from my pocket, I stare at it as my room darkens. Whatever happens tomorrow, I'll get through it. If Adrian is chosen, I'll support him as I always have. If this bracelet can't be used as a weapon, I'll find another way.

My eyes grow heavy, but through my lashes, I notice a dark figure standing in the corner of my room. I quickly push my body upright, but the figure is gone. I rub my eyes. I must be overtired. Lying back down, I begin to relax, but the shadowy shape appears again.

I swing my legs over the edge of my bed and stand. I watch the entity sway softly, unmoving. There's no face, no solid form, just a dense black mist in the night. I take a step forward, a cold shiver running over my skin as it seems to beckon me closer.

I reach a hand out as I take another step toward it, curiosity stronger than fear. Another step, and I'm almost touching it. I cross the final distance, my fingertips grazing the black mist.

Time freezes for a moment, the warmth of the shadow somehow familiar. My pulse quickens, and my head begins to throb. I try to step away, but the shadow reaches out and wraps its tendrils around my arm, holding me in place.

In a gust of movement, it pushes me back and pins me to the bed. My eyes widen as I stare into nothing, frozen in its hold.

Slowly, the shadowy figure leans down and whispers in my ear. The voice is ancient, guttural. Something powerful finally awoken from a long slumber.

"Sleep."

It's dark. The room around me has disappeared into solid blackness. I'm alone, the shadowy figure nowhere to be seen. There's no light in this space, not even a trace of sound besides my own soft breaths. It's too quiet, too empty.

Standing on uneasy legs, I spin in a slow circle, my mind twirling as up and down blend together. I take a step, feeling for solid ground beneath my feet.

A faint glow from above draws my attention, and I look up as a large pink petal floats down in front of me. A heady floral scent fills the space, intoxicating me with its rich and vibrant smell. The petal lands in my hand, and I rub it delicately between my fingers. More petals follow, illuminating the darkness. They fall like snowflakes, and all I can do is stare in wonder.

"It's time to remember," a woman's voice speaks faintly.

"Remember?" I whisper back, mesmerized by the petals pooling at my feet.

"It's time to return." Her voice is soft, familiar.

"Return?" I ask, regaining my senses enough to search for the source of the voice.

"They're waiting."

"Who's waiting?"

Pressure rises in my chest, and I fall to my knees. The petals swirl up around me, and I grab onto my head as pounding erupts within my mind. My fingers tighten around my hair as I curl over, gasping.

"Nova," she says my name, the pain fading for a moment. "There isn't time."

"Time for what?"

She doesn't respond, but I feel her presence materializing behind me. I turn to see her face, but hands come up and cover my eyes.

"I'm sorry," she says.

Light erupts from her palms, searing into my eyes. I scream, my voice obscuring the foreign words she speaks as her light burns through my entire being. I claw at her hands, desperate to pull them away, but they don't budge. Tears stream down my face as my arms fall to my sides, my body spent.

Her hands move away, the light fading. A scene remains in my mind's eye, flickering incomprehensibly of a silver blade. I reach to my eyes, which are tender to the touch. A deep pounding beats through me like a drum.

"*Kioren* will protect you, as only you can speak its name, hear it called." I turn around, looking for her, but she's not there. "You must remember. The lotus longs for your return."

"I don't understand," I say, my voice sounding muffled to my ringing ears.

"You must go. He's waiting for you."

"Who's waiting?"

"Our most beloved."

Blood splatters the petals on the ground. I scramble back, scooting to escape the river of red forming around me. Standing, I start running with no clear direction. The floor is slick; my bare feet slip on the blood and petals. The petals fall faster, the darkness turning to a pink flurry. Blood drenches my hands and clothes as it pools on the ground, rising over my ankles.

For a moment, golden eyes stare back at me. The woman's face is a blur, but I know she's the one I saw. She turns away, long silver hair disappearing in the frenzy of petals. I reach out a hand to follow after her, desperate for answers. Slipping, I fall to my hands and knees as my world returns to darkness.

Yet as I lose myself, the sound of a piano echoes in my mind. The song is painfully beautiful and achingly familiar, but I can't remember where or when I've heard it before. A sweet song of remembrance, hope, and agonizing loss. Tears fill my eyes with each fading note.

7

LOST HOPE

Jolting up in bed, I squint at the morning sun. The room is bright and empty, no remnants of the shadowed figure or the woman and her bloody petals. Her words remain in my mind, and the pain lingers in my body. Something wet drips down my nose to my lip, and I wipe at it, pulling my hand away to see blood. Nausea rises in my stomach.

Warm metal grazes my skin, and I look to see the angelic bracelet wrapped around my wrist. I suck in a breath, hesitantly touching the black gemstone.

"She showed me," I say to myself, eyes darting back and forth as clarity forms in my mind. The blinding light... Whatever she did, I know how to use this bracelet now. To summon *Kioren.*

I jump at the sound of a knock. "Come in," I say, racing to my bathroom to wash away the traces of blood on my face.

I hear the door open and turn to find Lance standing at my bathroom door. His brows are furrowed, but there's a lighthearted look in his eyes. "First TV, and now you're sleeping in past nine, unbelievable." His mouth cracks into a smile as he jokes, "I'll let it go for today." His face becomes serious, and I can only stare, my heart thudding in my chest. "I came to tell you Adrian's trials are starting now."

I wrap my head around that, my movements stiff as I dry my hands on a towel. "Do you think he'll make it?" I ask, hoping for an honest answer.

He doesn't respond right away, eyeing me carefully. For many years, Lance has helped determine those who have the potential to pass the trials. He has to know more about it than he lets on.

"I do."

I should have known; anyone would think so.

Realizing I'm holding the towel in a death grip, I let go and walk past Lance, and head to my closet to grab my training gear. "Let's spar. I don't want to think about the trials today."

He nods and turns to leave my room. "Meet me outside in ten."

Warm metal slides on my wrist, and my eyes widen as I remember the bracelet. Turning to the door, my heart drops. *Please tell me Lance didn't see it.* Shaking my head, I slide the bracelet off, placing it in the crevice of my closet for safekeeping. He would have said something if he had...

The thought doesn't ease my mind.

I quickly change into black moisture-wicking workout clothes and slip on a pair of sneakers. Tying my hair into a ponytail, I look myself over in my mirror, deeming myself ready.

Rushing downstairs, I head out through the dining room to the sparring field beyond the gardens. The air is warm, with harsh sun beating down as noon approaches. I pause as I pass my daily sparring partner—a wooden post, as wide and round as a mature tree, stuck in the ground. Deep indents are carved into its sides, dug out from the years of use—hours upon hours of practicing my punches. My hands curl into fists as I pass by, knuckles tingling with phantom pain.

Lance waits by the grassy edge of the sandy sparring pit under the single tree we have for shade on this end of the property. He takes a swig of water, setting it aside when he sees me.

"Ready?" he says as I jog over. His curly hair is pushed back with a red headband, adding to his already youthful look.

"You look like a kid," I say, tightening my ponytail.

Lance walks past me into the sparring pit. "Antagonizing your sparring partners again, are you?"

"Apparently, it's my specialty," I say with a mock bow, wondering what happened to Theo after he was taken out of the arena.

My foot slides back on the sand, palms raised. A smirk makes its way onto Lance's face as he mimics my position. I breathe out, and Lance charges forward with an onslaught of jabs and kicks. I dodge and block, unable to switch to offense as he quickly pushes me back to the edge of the pit with each move he throws.

Our arms cross as I grab his wrist to stop his attack, my muscles straining to push him back. A kick lands on my shin, and I'm sent rolling to the ground. Lance jumps back, a wide smirk plastered on his face as I spit sand from my mouth.

"You should be mindful of who you antagonize," Lance says, his forehead beading with sweat from the sun.

"So I shouldn't call you a pig-headed brute again?"

I sweep his legs out from under him, using the ground to push up and roundhouse kick with my other leg as he falls. He catches my leg, dragging me back to the ground as I attempt to stand.

Rolling away from each other, we both jump to our feet, standing at opposite ends of the pit. We circle the clearing, watching each other's movements with a close eye. Sweat trickles down my face, and my clothes stick to my skin. The buzz of cicadas fills the air, mixing with the sound of our heavy breaths.

Lance rushes forward, his jabs and kicks quicker than before. A few land, a painful thud resounding off my limbs with each one, but I return them with equal force.

I block his following few jabs by cornering his arms close to his body. Open to attack, I throw a cross punch toward his jaw. He sidesteps at the last moment, grabbing my arm and flipping me over onto the ground. My back hits the sand hard, but I roll over to retaliate at his open backside. A reverse kick hits my side, sending me flying over to the grassy edge. Out of breath, I prop myself up on sore arms—already feeling the bruises forming on my body.

"I know you can fight better than this," Lance comes over and kneels in front of me.

"You think you won?" I knock him over, pinning him to the ground.

He laughs from underneath me but easily rolls me over, switching our positions. "You're still confident even when you're not fighting like your normal self?"

Shoving him off, I stand and head over to the shade of the nearby tree. Not only is he a pig-headed brute, but he has an annoying mouth too. Grabbing the water he brought me, I take a long drink, avoiding his gaze.

"Nova, you can't let doubt cloud your judgment. Today it's just me, but others won't go easy on you."

"This was you going easy?" I turn to him, an eyebrow raised.

He smiles, but it doesn't reach his eyes. "I know you're strong, but doubt cannot come in the way of—" He stops abruptly and walks over to join me in the shade. "Listen, strength only matters if your head is clear and you trust in yourself. Otherwise, you get hurt, or someone else does in your place."

I close my eyes, listening to the soft sway of leaves brushing together. "I know. It's just—" I don't know how to explain it. How do you even begin to comprehend all the things in my head? My father and his secrets. Adrian's trials. My own trials. The shadowy figure in my room. And now this woman who has given me the key to using this mysterious angelic artifact... It's too much.

"Let me tell you something." He reaches into his bag and takes out two apples, tossing one to me. "You know I wasn't born into a hunter family. Everyone doubted my abilities, including myself. But had I let that get to me, I wouldn't be here, training you. Through my trust in myself, I gained Solomon's and the clan's respect."

"But still—"

"Let me continue." He takes a bite of his apple. "My point is, people will always question your strength. And for you, you will have an even harder time proving your worth to the clan. So things like doubt, you have to rid them from your mind and trust in yourself. Everyone else can doubt you as long as you don't doubt yourself. And today, you did, and you lost."

He's not wrong.

"You're right," I finally say, nodding in agreement. "I'll always be Solomon's daughter—the *princess*—so I'll always be doubted." Looking off in the direction of the wall that blocks our view of the lake, I let out a long sigh. "But I can only pretend to be so confident." The last words come out before I can process them. My cheeks heat and I focus on wiping the sweat from my forehead to avoid Lance's eyes.

When I finally look at him, he's staring down at his apple, black curls falling so low over his face that I almost miss the sadness in his eyes. I narrow my eyes and tilt my head at him. He looks up and gives me a soft smile before continuing to eat his apple. Joining him, I bite into the fruit, relishing the sweet flavor.

We're silent as we eat, sitting in the shadow of the tree. I watch the summer clouds in the sky, creating images from the shapes. Lance doesn't normally open up to me like this. Somehow I'm always on the outside with him, even when we've known each other for so many years.

I glance over at his soft face, one which makes him look younger than he is—not that thirty-two is old. I've known him since I was four, and he was eighteen, yet it's unfamiliar to me when he acts differently than the normal pig-headed brute I'm used to. Part of me is thankful, wanting to share the rest of my worries with him to get his advice. But I know I can't. It isn't fair to make him choose between me and his loyalty to my father.

Lance sees me looking and smiles, but his eyes quickly move past me, his face hardening. I follow his gaze.

"Adrian," I say as I see him approach, a radiant glow around him. He still wears the white pants, and tunic male hunters wear during their angelic trials.

A wide smile is plastered on his face, the answer so obvious it hurts. My heart beats wildly as I stand to meet him. He races over, wrapping me in a hug and spinning me around. I'm too stunned to react as he puts me down, stepping back to meet my eyes.

"I did it, Nova." He wraps his arms around me again, the heat of his embrace suffocating under the hot sun. "I have an angel. I'm an Undivided."

Remembering Lance's words, I hug him back. "Congrats, Adrian." Stepping back, I put on a smile for him. "I knew you would pass."

Turning back toward a now standing Lance, I watch as he gives a slight nod to Adrian. His face is hard, solemn even, as his eyes dart to the large gold ring on Adrian's index finger.

"To finally have Archangel Michael back in our presence, the clan must be grateful."

Adrian's thumb rubs over the large blue gem set into the ring. The smile I put on falters. Michael, the one we call *Quis ut Deus*—who is like God. One of the most renowned angels viewed as a great savior during the Great Demonic Fall. I stare at the ring on Adrian's hand. Archangel Michael's angelic artifact... Father must have gifted it to him.

My voice catches in my throat. It can't be.

"It's an honor to be joined with him. One I plan to live up to," Adrian says, his eyes squinting as if to consider how Lance figured it out so quickly.

Adrian turns back to me, unconcerned. My stomach twists as I try to return his smile. I'll never surpass him now. My hands curl in, nails biting into my palms.

"My father must be proud to have a hunter like you." I hold his gaze, forcing my smile wider. "I'm proud of you." A long pause sits between us, one I'm not sure will ever end.

"Nova, you have things you need to do inside," Lance intervenes.

Turning to Lance, I nod. "Then I should go. I'll see you later, Adrian."

I don't wait for either to say anything more, their eyes burning into my back as I leave the sparring field. Reaching the dining room door, I enter the estate and fall to the floor. Despair overwhelms me the moment I stop moving.

The prodigy hunter—my *best friend*—is beyond my reach now. I'll never compare, never stand as an equal to him even if I pass my angelic trials. Archangel Michael doesn't share his soul with any hunter; his standards are far beyond what an average hunter can achieve. It's been hundreds of years since he last decided to do so, yet here he is with Adrian.

A sob forms in my throat, but I swallow it down. Pulling myself from the floor, I head to my bedroom—to the one thing that chose *me*.

I breathe easier as soon as the silver bracelet is back in my hands, its warmth enveloping my trembling fingers. The bracelet pulses gently as if trying to comfort me. I pull it close to my chest, wondering how something inanimate could offer me anything close to solace.

"The woman showed me how to use you, but I hope you don't mind helping me during the blood moon—" This is my one chance to prove myself before my angelic trials.

I trace a finger over the silver swirls etched into the band. Maybe whichever angel this belongs to is listening to me. Pulling the bracelet closer to my lips, I whisper words that almost draw another tear from my eyes.

"I don't think I can set myself free without you."

8

SHATTERED

A sigh leaves my lips as I enter the library, running a hand through my hair to help it dry. Plopping into my favorite leather chair, I sink my sore body into its cool cushions. My eyelids are heavy after tossing and turning all night. A knock at the door startles me, and I look up to see Adrian's head popping in.

"Can I come in?"

I hesitate to answer, shifting in my seat. "Of course."

He smiles, strutting in with the confidence he should have after being chosen by Michael. Adrian takes a seat in the chair opposite me, already in all his hunter gear for tonight's blood moon.

"You didn't dry your hair?" he asks.

I touch the damp strands, a blush rushing to my cheeks. "I just finished my morning training."

He hums sympathetically, but then his smile falls from his face.

"Solomon told me—"

I jerk back as if slapped. "Don't," I snap, holding a hand to stop him. His eyes are soft, a look of empathy crossing his face, but he doesn't understand—he can't. "I don't care what my father said. If it's important, he can come to tell me himself."

Adrian sighs, hanging his head before looking up through his blond strands. "Come on, Nova, I know you know what tonight is. Please give him and me a break for today." My eyes narrow, but I stay silent. Adrian runs a hand through his hair, looking everywhere but my eyes. "Just... just don't do anything rash tonight."

I scoff, looking away from him. As if that wouldn't make me suspicious.

"I have no weapons, no gear, and no team. What can I do but stay here and let my abilities go to waste," I say with a sarcastic smile. "If that's all you came to say, please leave. I have better things to do." Grabbing a nearby book, I wave it in his face.

Adrian reaches over, placing a hand on my knee. "You know I would change things if I could."

I open the book and pretend to study its pages, pointedly ignoring him.

"Just think how it'll be after your trials; the clan won't know what hit them. You just have to stay positive until then."

The book tumbles off my lap as I burst to my feet, all of my pent-up anger breaking loose inside me. "Stay positive?" I laugh, staring at the confusion crossing Adrian's face. "That's your solution? Honestly, I'm beginning to think you wouldn't change anything, Adrian. You pretend to be my friend, yet you come to *my* house and order me around like you hold superiority over me just because my father favors you."

"He doesn't favor me," Adrian says, a scowl on his face. "You're just projecting. Calm down and think rationally for once."

My heart tears at his words. "Projecting... Right, that's what I'm doing." I shake my head, sadness and anger warring inside me. "Adrian, you have so much sway in this clan, you're the prodigy everyone loves, and now you're bonded with Archangel Michael. If you said something to the clan, my father would have no choice but to listen, and I would be out of this godforsaken cage. So don't come to me preaching positivity and rational thinking like that's some magic solution to my problems. I've been positive and rational my whole life, and where has that gotten me? At this point, the only thing that could probably help me is you. But you don't. You've never even tried."

"Nova, I—"

"Leave, please," I say, pointing to the partially open door.

He stands, his eyes pleading, but I stay firm. I watch him walk to the doorway, but he stops with his hand on the doorknob. "Please, just don't do anything stupid tonight."

The door shuts, and I plop into my chair, staring at where he had been. I barely recognize this Adrian. Wrapping my arms around my body, I push the thought of him and Archangel Michael from my mind.

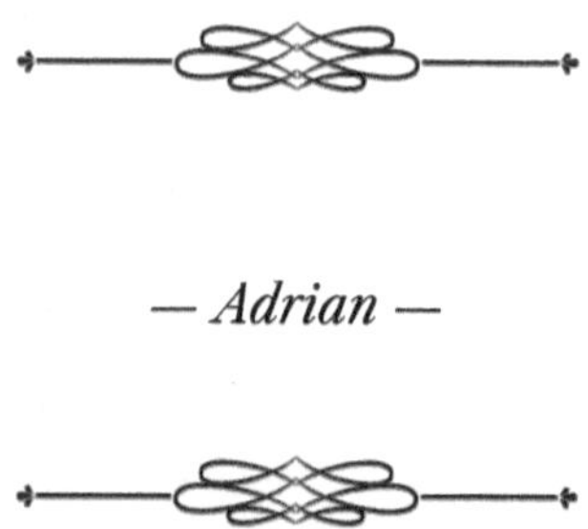

— *Adrian* —

Nova's words sting as I storm out of the Fandera Estate. I don't hold as much power as she claims. I gaze down at the gold and sapphire ring that feels heavy on my finger. No one in this clan can go against Solomon; even now, with Archangel Michael, I stand no chance.

Waiting for me in the large circle driveway is my new cadre—a group of hunters entrusted to me to lead after my angelic trials. Most are older than I am, ranging in age from twenty to twenty-four, and all are highly skilled. People I trained with yet have since far surpassed.

One woman is among them—Eva—a slim tamer and healer like my mother with a preference for hellhounds despite the catalog of creatures she can summon. Her straight brown hair is tied up in a bun as she watches me approach the group. Two dragoon users linger at her sides as if vying for her affection. Roman and Aril are like two sides of the same coin, one of sunshine and one of darkness. Both men are capable of handling a variety of guns but always carry dual pistols in their holsters.

Aril, however, easily took the spot as my second. Despite not being chosen for the angelic trials, he's made a name for himself in our clan as a dragoon while also honing his skills in several other hunter classes, particularly warrior and artificer. He's six years older than I am—the eldest among us eight—but he's been a friend since I was fourteen. A newbie at the time and now his leader almost five years later.

The last four I command are all warriors like myself. Ewan, a tall redhead, carries a greatsword much like my own. Beside him, Anders, who is by far the largest of us, swings his mace over his shoulder as if it hardly weighs an ounce. Many assume he must be slow because of his size, but I've seen how fast he can move and know underestimating him is a deadly mistake. The last of my team, half-Japanese identical twins, Cain and Callan, stand at the back of the group. Cain stands still as a ghost, hand resting on his angelic katana, while Callan scans the estate as if a demon might jump out in the middle of the day. His fingers twitch, ready to swing his bow over his shoulder or throw one of the many knives he keeps hidden beneath the black layers of his gear at a moment's notice.

A deadly group to support their Undivided—support me—in battle. The demons won't know what hit them tonight. Even a blood moon can't prevent the wrath we'll bring down on them. A loose grin tugs at my lips despite the simmering hurt from Nova's words.

"Handle the princess?" Callan says, a smirk on his cocky face.

I shoot him a glare, but his dark eyes twinkle as if enjoying the reaction. "It's taken care of," I say through gritted teeth.

Ewan nudges Callan, shaking his head. Good. At least one of them knows to not press their new leader. "Meet me at the compound in an hour. I have other business to attend to before tonight."

They nod silently and then disperse, loading back into the large black SUV we came in. Eva's blue eyes meet my own, and her lips part as if to say something, but the door slams before she has the chance. When the armored vehicle is gone down the road, I head in the opposite direction.

It's been so long since I've spent time with Nova. I was hoping after my trials Lance would grant us time together. Yesterday proved otherwise. But it wasn't Lance who didn't want me around.

I saw the look in her eyes, her hands fisted, and how she *tried* so hard not to let her emotions show. At least, not anything besides happiness for me. It hurt to watch. But I didn't want to say anything with Lance around, and then I didn't get the chance to say much before she kicked me out of the library. I run a hand through my hair. I'm proud to have Archangel Michael bonded to me, happy to play my role as a hunter, but the devastation on her face... I would give it all up if I could to prevent ever seeing that look on her face again.

The walk is short, and soon I'm in front of the Bishop Estate. Walking up the pristine drive, smaller but nearly identical to the Fandera Estate's, I look up the front steps to find my mother already opening the door. Her golden hair, the exact same color as my own, is pulled back into a tight knot, and a frown settles across her still youthful face.

"I was wondering if I'd see you before tonight," she says, eyes softening.

My steps slow as I say, "I just forgot something."

I go to pass her when her hand falls on my shoulder. "Your father's not here, but Theo's waiting for you."

I grimace. After the stunt he pulled with Nova, I hardly have any desire to meet with him. Still, I nod to her, her hand slipping off my shoulder as I head around her and up the curved staircase to my room. The door is already open as I approach to find Theo sitting in one of the leather lounge chairs. He stands as I enter, shutting the door behind me. Anger seethes inside me, egged on by the angel urging me to put him in his place. *Inferior*, Michael seems to whisper distantly.

"What do you want, Theo?" I say, my voice hard as I turn from the lanky boy.

Only a few years younger than I am, but far from the image my uncle had in mind for his son, Theo has brought nothing but disgrace to the Bishop name. Disrespect and dishonor I've had to make up for all these years. To prove the next generation of our family is still fit to hold the position of second in command.

"Take me with you tonight."

I whip around. "After what you did? Why would I even consider letting you near my team when you're still on probation? It's only because of my father that your punishment wasn't worse." Desperation and a hint of fear shine in his eyes, but he holds his stance, and I have to give him credit for it. To face my rage head-on after hurting the one person I want to protect.

"*Please*, Adrian," Theo says, the desperation reaching his voice.

I sneer, but before I can respond, the door creaks open. "Take the boy with you." I turn to the man leaning against the doorframe. "Ensure he makes up for tarnishing *our* family name."

The anger burns brighter, but I shove it down. "Yes, Father."

"Good. Then I suppose you should get moving. Your team is to take the neighborhoods while mine scouts the town."

I barely nod, but he leaves, the door lingering open behind him. Glancing over my shoulder, I scan Theo up and down. He stands stunned, unsure what to make of my father's command.

"Be ready in five if you're coming," I say, motioning for him to leave.

He doesn't say anything as he rushes out of my room to gear up. Closing the door behind him, I let out a long sigh.

It was better being away...

I shake my head. No, there's still someone here for me. I refuse to believe otherwise.

Reaching into my pocket, I pull out the small black box carrying the earrings I had planned to give Nova before her eighteenth birthday. I open the box and stare at the small gold hoops. Rectangular emeralds matching her sparkling green eyes hang from the delicate loops.

Another sigh leaves my lips as I tuck the present into my sock drawer. Maybe she's right. Maybe I could've done something. *Princess.* That's what the clan calls her without knowing she could have their asses on the ground in a matter of seconds. My jaw tenses as my gaze lifts to the hot sun outside my window.

And knowing the *princess*, there's no way she'll sit pretty at the estate.

I almost chuckle at the thought, wondering what kind of damage she might leave in her wake, but my stomach sinks instead. Tonight, of all nights, she can't be reckless. Archangel Michael warned me so. Whatever secrets he keeps from me, one thing is for sure—

Nova cannot leave that estate.

9

FREEDOM

O ut the window, the sun still shines brightly in the sky. It won't be long before it sets and the blood moon rises. Anticipation gnaws at my stomach. Reaching into my pocket, I pull out the angelic bracelet, *Kioren.* I can... I can still prove myself with this. Running my fingers over the shining black gem, I recall the mysterious woman, the searing light, and the vision that burned behind my eyes. Could it really be possible? An unknown angel and an unbonded hunter trying to call it forth. Definitely not a recipe for disaster...

"Shall we try you out?"

Sitting up straight, I close my eyes and replay the scene the woman showed me. *Blinding white light. Silver metal powerful enough to destroy anything in its path, to protect what is worthy. Mumbled words spoken as if a secret, a chant meant only for the wielder of Kioren—a name only I can hear and call forth.* The memory flows through my mind, and goosebumps rise along my arms. My head screams to stop, yet my heart urges me to speak the ancient words.

I recall what Adrian said. *Think rationally.* But I'm tired of being rational; it's time for me to follow my heart. Confident in my decision, I slide the bracelet onto my wrist and say the words the woman gave me.

"Let light and darkness be your essence, your heavenly form in my hands. With the strength to crumble mountains and split the sea, fulfill your purpose as the truth, the protector, and the destroyer. Come forth, Kioren!"

I peek an eye open and see the black gem beginning to bubble like boiling water. I stretch my arm far from my face, unsure of what it might do. A silver tip glistens under the black, the weapon piercing its way out of the gemstone. I pull it closer, and it shoots out past my head, almost grazing my cheek. A black tendril is attached to the end of the blade, connecting it to the gem it came from. It zooms around the library, scattering books and papers in a wild frenzy.

I duck, barely avoiding it as it comes near my head again. "*Kioren*," I say, trying to get its attention. It perks up at the sound of its name but doesn't stop its crazed flight.

Watching it carefully, I wait until it passes, grabbing its tail and rendering it immobile. My face falls as I look more closely, all my hopes vanishing in an instant. I press my thumb against the blade. Short, dull. Great, this is just *fantastic*. The amazing angelic artifact my father wants to destroy, the one I had an epic vision about, is no better than a butter knife.

A knock sounds at the door, and I scrabble to gather the rest of the long black tendril, shoving it and the knife behind my back. The door opens, and Lance enters the library.

"Busy?" he says, peering to one side to see what's behind me.

"A little, you know, with studying and all," I say with a forced smile as I feel the knife creep up behind my shoulder, trying to peek around me. Tugging it, I shift it back down, so Lance doesn't notice. What the hell is wrong with this thing?

"Okay, well, never mind then." The corner of Lance's mouth curls up, but he continues eyeing me.

Not good. Think of something, anything... "It's just"—I pause as I rack my brain—"Adrian came, and I think he's trying to take your job."

"What?" Lance looks at me incredulously.

"Well, I mean, he's running errands for my father now, telling me he said I can't do anything rash tonight. Like seriously, what does everyone think I'm going to do?" He looks at me like I'm going crazy. "So I'm going to study all night to prove a point to them both. Which is that I'm not that rash, and I only need one babysitter in my life."

Lance's eyebrows raise. "*Right*... Then I'll leave you to it." He pauses at the doorway. "The hunters stationed here are leaving soon to get a head start on the moon, and I'll be going with them since I haven't been out in the field for a while. We'll train together tomorrow, okay?"

I nod with a small smile, watching as he closes the door behind him and listening as his steps fade away. Spinning around, I face the butter knife floating in midair. The black strand sways in front of me as if waiting for me to say something.

"That could have gone really, *really*, badly," I say to it.

The blade seems to shrug, moving around me as if to now carefully examine the room.

So this thing is Kioren... The angelic weapon meant to crumble mountains and split seas. Seems unlikely. I continue to examine the blade, but there's nothing remarkable about it. And even though the woman gave it a name, I never expected it to be so... *alive*.

"You need to go back for now," I say to Kioren, and it tilts itself as if confused.

Sighing, I walk toward the door. Lance said the hunters will be leaving soon—my father's letting some of the Undivided and their teams take weapons from the estate. And with Lance gone tonight, the only guards here will be stationed out front and by the far edge of the property line. While everyone's preoccupied, I should prepare the rest of my things.

I reach for the doorknob and twist, but it doesn't budge. I pull harder, trying to open the door, but it's no use. Did Lance seriously lock me in here?

I slam my hand on the door. Of course. He noticed something was up and took the proper precautions. He has known me for fourteen years.

A tap on my shoulder distracts me from the locked door. Turning, I see the silver of Kioren liquefy, the butter knife melting and changing shape. My eyes widen as I watch. When it finishes, a key—a replica of the one for this door—hangs before me.

"I've changed my mind, Kioren. You're not so useless after all."

I watch as Kioren slips under the crack at the bottom of the door and listen as the lock clicks and unbolts. I open the door to the foyer, scanning the open space. Sneaking out of the library, I shut the door quietly and smile as Kioren relocks the door behind me. *Smart.* Better if they think I'm still in there. Grabbing Kioren, I hold the silver key and black tendril close. It tugs against my hold, curious to look around, but I tighten my grip.

Voices of hunters can be heard out front as I race up the staircase, careful not to make a sound. Reaching my room, I slip inside, quietly closing the door behind me.

A little longer, and I'll be able to get out of this place. I wish I could see the look on Lance's face when he realizes I got the best of everyone. The thought curls my lips into a smirk.

Changing into black training gear—the best I could do without the proper tactical wear—I equip myself with the few things I have at my disposal: Kioren's bracelet on my wrist, fingerless leather gloves, and a small tactical vest. I head into my closet and retrieve the single angelic blade I was able to hide, attaching it to my thigh. I grab a medical wrap from the adjoined bathroom in case of injuries and tuck it into the vest pouch.

Pulling a black hoodie over my head, I look in the mirror to tie my hair up. I nod approvingly when I finish. *I can do this.*

Kioren slides back into the black gem, disappearing as the sun falls past the horizon. I breathe a long breath, cracking a window open an inch to listen for the hunters outside. The last birds bid farewell to the day as bats replace them in the sky. The wind carries the scent of flowers, the cool breeze curling around me and gently nudging me out into the night. A black butterfly flutters within my grasp, its wings shimmering with a faint silver gleam. I reach toward it as it flys higher, disappearing from my line of sight. Strange... I've been seeing those black butterfly's more often as of late. The last rays of light fade from the sky, and I know it's time.

"Please be more than a butter knife when I summon you next time," I say to the bracelet peeking out from beneath my hoodie sleeve.

Closing my eyes, I listen for any remaining sounds of hunters and engines. Hearing only silence, I smile.

Opening the window wider, I scan the yard before lowering myself as far as possible before dropping to the grass below. Pain shoots up my ankles, but rolling out would have me caught on the security cameras I know are being watched with an eagle's eye.

The ache fades as I scoot along the estate's brick wall. Passing the entrance to the dining room, I reach the other wing of the estate. A dark forest rises beyond the brick wall—only a few steps away from the estate's corner. Above, a security camera moves back and forth, watching for any suspicious activity—demon or otherwise.

Pinning myself to the wall, I scoot along to the edge of the estate to see the other camera at the opposite end. Thankfully there are only two along this side of the estate. Hugging the wall, I slip into the blind spots of the cameras, pausing to time my run and jump perfectly. This is the last obstacle, and I'll be free.

I freeze, listening carefully to the sounds coming from the nearby gate. Four male voices. Weapons shifting against tactical gear. I tense, pushing myself closer to the wall. I'm close to the gate; if they round the side and see me... I don't let myself continue the thought as the cameras come into position.

I run forward, jumping high to grab the iron spikes at the top of the brick wall. Lifting myself over, I land in the dark shadows of the trees with a crunch. I wince at the sound, not moving for a moment. Looking up, a guard rushes to the sidewalk to investigate the outer wall. Slinking behind a wide tree, I pray the shadows protect me.

"What was that?" I hear the first hunter say—a voice I don't recognize.

It's silent for a moment before another speaks. "Probably a squirrel. Leave it be."

My shoulders relax as I listen to their steps fade as they return to their positions. Breathing a sigh of relief, I move through the woods, watching my steps to not make any more noise. Once the estate is no longer in sight, I pause and listen for the footfalls of pursuers—thinking they'll discover my escape at any moment. When no sound comes, I pull my hood over my head and slip onto the sidewalk.

I did it. *I did it.* I'm free.

A smile rises on my lips as I walk in the opposite direction of the estate. The shadows pull me in—allies just for the night. Excitement jitters through my bones, my steps quickening down the long sidewalk as I shove my hands into my pockets.

I will show everyone exactly the kind of hunter my father has kept hidden away. No one will call me *princess* ever again. Not when I place the head of a demon on their table.

10

AND THE MOON CRIED

Present moment

My breaths are heavy, my left hand numb, tingly. Whatever that strange inky substance was on that hellhound, it isn't natural and hurts like hell. Blood pools at my foot from the teeth marks that punctured my skin, reminding me of the other grave injury I've already sustained tonight. I don't let it show as I scan the demon standing across from me. The summer night air feels cool against the sweat beading on my skin. My fingers tighten around the scythe's—Kioren's—handle. A forgotten weapon, a nonexistent mother, the reason I'm kept in the Fandera Estate... How does a demon know all this?

"Don't you want to know it all, *Nova*?"

My heart falters, thudding in fear no matter how I try to rein it in. How does he know my name?

I eye him carefully, from the sleek human skin he wears to the subtle inhuman way his eyes glisten. Handsome, dangerous, powerful. But it isn't *just* him.

"Who sent you?"

Red flashes across the demon's eyes, his words floating over on the breeze.

"Amon."

A cold chill races down my spine. Amon—a Marquis of Hell and a highly sought-after kill. The clan has been tracking his movements for years, but he's as elusive as most high-tier demons are.

"Now, I've piqued your interest."

My jaw tightens as I hold back the questions. "I wouldn't have taken you for a foot soldier. You seem more powerful than that... Then again, I guess you're actually more like a messenger. One I have no intention of dealing with."

Hunters don't converse with demons; I chide myself. But a small voice whispers to listen, to learn what this demon has to say. I shove it down. Only my father has the answers to my questions. No demon would know such things. Not even Amon.

The demon's face seems to tighten; I've hit a nerve. It's quickly masked as he says, "Amon wants to strike a deal. Your help in exchange for information, answers." He pulls a golden necklace with a ruby pendant from his pants pocket, hanging it on one of Kioren's black spikes. "Think about it. And when you decide to come to us, break the gem. Then Amon will discuss his terms." He turns around to walk away, stopping midstep to look back at me. "And you might learn something about that scythe of yours." He waves his hand, a sly smile crossing his face. "You have two weeks. Don't die tonight."

My mouth gapes, "Wait, you can't just—"

He vanishes in a cloud of black smoke.

The street grows quiet once more with only the wind to accompany me. I glance at the angelic artifact on my wrist, at the scythe that emerged from it. Looking back at the spot where the demon disappeared, I scowl.

A lost opportunity.

I fall to one knee, my injured calf giving out. My shoulder is no better. I reach up and touch the skin with my good hand, hissing at the contact and wishing I had taken salve for demon wounds before I escaped. Not that I had any on hand... The demon, Rishu, distracted me from my injuries, but the hellhounds did a number on me, and the blood moon has yet to rise.

I grip the scythe's handle and pull myself upright. Allowing Kioren to support my weight, I limp over to the curb and sit down. I let go once situated, and Kioren hovers above me as I peel up my pant leg to examine the bite wound first. I hiss through my teeth as the fabric pulls at the torn skin. Reaching into my tactical vest, I pull out the single bandage wrap I brought. I wrap it tightly around my calf to stop the bleeding and provide support for the rest of the night. Hopefully, the infection holds off until I get my hands on a demon.

I touch my shoulder again, where the inky substance burned through my clothes, wishing I had more medical wrap. I should have been more careful with the hellhounds. I haven't prepared to fight demons my whole life to make such a stupid mistake.

"They weren't normal, though, right?" I look up at Kioren, waiting for an answer. The scythe doesn't move, holding its position above me.

I let out a long sigh, my head dropping into my hands. What a night it's been. Hellhounds abnormally attacking, Kioren coming out as a huge scythe—one I'm surprised I can even lift—and a proposal from a high-tier demon, a Marquis of Hell.

"How would they know anything...."

Kioren curves down, bending at an odd angle until the ruby necklace dangles in front of my face. My brows pull together as I watch the movement; no physical weapon should be able to move like that.

In every book I've read on angelic artifacts, I've found no evidence of a weapon, a *being*, quite like this. I reach to touch the black tendril that connects the scythe to the gemstone of the bracelet; it's tacky, almost like rubber, solid but flexible. Kioren doesn't flinch away. I can practically feel its trust—as if a bond is settling between us. The silver blade curves closer so the heel rests in front of me. I admire the design, which resembles an ornate metal gate holding open the jaws of a vicious beast—one with black spikes for teeth.

Letting go of the tendril, Father's promise rings in my mind. *You'll understand everything after your angelic trials. Everything will be clear then.*

Taking the ruby pendant from Kioren, I turn it over in my hands. They couldn't possibly know anything; this must be a trick. Shaking my head, I stand to leave, shoving the necklace into a pouch on my tactical vest. I only have tonight to prove myself as a hunter; I don't have time for games.

My calf throbs as I limp along the shadows of the neighborhood. The pain is a reminder to do better. To be *better*.

Forcing myself forward, I trudge to the end of the street. A remote part of town comes into view, and I scan the area, listening for other hunters. It's a place I'm not too familiar with—no streets I would have driven past with Lance and a place I've never visited on the few patrols I've been on. I scowl at the thought. My father did a good job preventing me from knowing much about this town.

To my right, a large gray metal warehouse stands abandoned, overgrown with weeds. The moon reflects off broken window glass in the street, shining on the graffiti written across the side. I look in the other direction, eyeing an empty four-story parking ramp with a few flickering lights. Dark graffiti can be made out around the small building, though the designs are lost with each flicker of lights.

The scythe doesn't return to the bracelet, the black tendril that connects the two circling protectively around my body. Humans shouldn't be able to see it if it is an angelic weapon, though I'm still holding judgment on that one.

Turning back to the two locations in front of me, I close my eyes and listen. Low-tier demons I've hunted in past patrols won't be here since there aren't humans to prey on. Most low-tiers attach themselves to people, eating off their fear, anger, sadness, and greed. But that's why it's much more dangerous here. In empty spaces on the edge of the bustling streets, mid-tier demons can converge. Especially if they already feel the coming blood moon. They'll rise from the depths of Hell, not for the human prey but for the bleeding moon they can feast upon.

Glancing up, I look at the moon where it sits bright white, unbroken.

"I wonder if the legend is true," I say to no one in particular. Lucifer hasn't been seen since the Great Demonic Fall; some say he's dead. Others say he's building an army again or hiding in shame from his defeat. Maybe he never truly existed at all.

A long sigh leaves my lips. It's early, but I anxiously wait to see the moon turn red. It's only then that I'll finally be able to prove myself.

Taking a step toward the open lot between the warehouse and parking ramp, the scythe breaks from my grasp and curves in front of me to block my path.

"What's your deal?" I grab the handle and pull. It doesn't budge.

I huff, moving to step around it, but it blocks me again.

"I thought you're supposed to listen to me"—I stare at the scythe, feeling a little ridiculous arguing with it—"but it seems you have a mind of your own."

Kioren doesn't make a move, standing firm. I let out a small, frustrated sound, finding a new curb to sit on. Dead hellhounds won't buy me freedom. Father might even laugh if he knew what happened with them. I look at the monstrous scythe above me. And now this thing won't listen to me.

My head falls into my hands. What am I doing out here? I'm not helping anyone, especially not myself. Red seeps through the wrap around my calf, which throbs painfully.

A blood-curdling scream pierces the summer night, ringing through my ears. My heart beats wildly in my chest as I jump to my feet and spin in a circle, searching. Someone's in danger, and I—

Closing my eyes, I calm my beating heart and focus on the drawn-out sound. It stops for a moment, and I'm unable to pinpoint the location. Goosebumps rise on my arms as a cool breeze shuffles the leaves of the nearby trees. The scream sounds again—like a child crying for help. My eyes open wide as I turn to the parking ramp, ready to run. Human or demon, I have to go.

The scythe races in front of me again, blocking my path.

"Listen, I think someone's in danger." Grabbing the handle, I stare at the blade towering above. "So we're going whether you like it or not." Kioren hesitates but curves away in defeat, letting me lift the giant scythe. "Thank you."

I run toward the parking ramp as fast as I can, the scythe light in my hands. *Wait for me, whoever you are, I will help you.*
Or kill you.

A stairway entrance is open to the left as I near the small parking ramp, a single sputtering light above it. I race toward it, the smell of damp cement reaching my nose. From what I heard, it sounded like the scream came from above. Entering the stairway, I climb two steps at a time—gritting my teeth as my leg throbs more with each step, blood trickling through the bandage. The sound of my footfalls reverberate in the small space as the scythe bends and curves behind me to fit in the restricted space.

The metal door to the top level comes into sight, and I burst out into the open space. It clangs as it hits the wall before slamming shut behind me. I scan the barren parking lot, spinning in a slow circle. Bright lights from the main street can be seen just beyond the cluster of trees surrounding the ramp, but it's silent.

Turning on my heel, I head back to the stairway to check another floor. A howl of wind swoops around me, whipping my ponytail into my face. It pushes me back from the door—compelling me to stay, to wait.

The wind cools my skin, wrapping around me like silky fingers. Caressing my exposed skin and kissing the wounds on my body. I shiver. My gaze moves to the moon in the sky...

And I see it.

A red filter creeps across the white of the moon. The light pierces down, racing across the parking ramp and encasing everything in its red glow. I gasp, sucking in a deep breath at the rush of power tingling in the air.

Fluttering wings cross my vision, a black butterfly against the red light of the moon. *Didn't I just see you?* It flies higher, dancing in the wind that calls to me. Something tingles at the back of my brain as I watch its flight, beckoning me closer.

The butterfly disperses into a cloud of black ash, and I take a step back. Where it once flew, a figure now stands on the spire of a church just beyond the parking ramp. Fabric floats around him in the wind, a shadow outlined by the red tears of the moon. A prince of the night without his wings.

A tear slips down my cheek.

How do I know you?

My heart freezes, the question racing through me as if struck by lightning. I stop breathing, a strange power holding me in place, an ache in my heart to reach out to him... I take a step back.

A scream pierces the night, and I spin, looking for the source. There's nothing in sight but the empty ramp. I turn back to the shadow in the sky, but he's gone. I reach a hand over my heart, pressing my palm into my chest in hopes of easing its rapid beat. He was a demon. There's no way I knew him; it's impossible. *Our beloved.* The words the woman spoke pop into my head.

"One, two, three, I sing a song for thee!" A laugh echoes around the ramp, a sickly sweet sound. "Oh, what a nice night indeed, won't you play with me?"

A little girl steps out of the shadows into the red moonlight. Her skin is enveloped in inky shadows, swirling around her just as it had with the hellhound. She skips around as she sings her song. Speaking to me while keeping her distance.

"Let's be friends until your end!"

"What the hell...." I tense as I watch the young girl. Is it possession? I examine the inky black seeping off her, all too similar to that of the hellhound.

A demented laugh erupts from her mouth, her head drooping down and hanging low as she stops her dance. "Play a game with me, sing a song with me, Nova, Nova, won't you die for me?"

My hair stands on end as she calls my name. Her head flings back with her laughter, and I cringe at the inhuman movement. Slowly, she cranks her head back up, black eyes staring into mine—no white left to be seen.

I blink, and she's above me. Grabbing the scythe, I block her with the top of the blade. Swinging herself off, she jumps back to the other end of the ramp. Her dance begins again.

Dark energy coils around her small form. Black shadows ebbing in and out as if consuming her. A part of my soul yells at me that this is *wrong*, but I have no time to ponder the situation.

"An interesting game indeed; master desires this scythe I see." She stops and turns to look back at me. "I'll take what doesn't belong to thee."

She charges toward me again, moving even faster than before. Her feet land on the tip of my blade, and I swing to shake her off again. She flips backward, racing back at me in a single breath. A ball of black energy forms in her hand as she nears. She shoots it in my direction, and I slice it in half, the energy exploding around me. The scythe's tendril spreads out to protect me from the blast. I cough as I inhale the smoke. It's cold and putrid, toxic in my lungs.

When the smoke clears, the child is gone.

A low laugh sounds behind me. I turn to find her standing directly behind me, a sadistic grin on her face and an energy ball aimed at my chest. The energy hits me square on, and I fly backward. Kioren's black tendrils enclose around my body—but not fast enough. My back hits the cement wall. Air bursts from my lungs; blurry dots float across my vision.

Time stops, and I can't hear a sound over the ringing in my ears. Air rushes back into my lungs, and I gasp, coughing up blood. I wince as I try to move, a whimper leaving my lips. Braving a look down at my burning chest, I gag and force myself to look away from the bloody mess.

A warm liquid slides down my face, and I drag my hand up to wipe it away, pulling back to see my fingertips dipped in blood.

I shut my eyes as the world spins, calming my breathing as best as possible.

"Nova, Nova, you bleed so freely. Now your scythe is mine, really!"

The child's maniacal laughter reverberates in the parking ramp, and my blood boils. The black tendril unravels from my body, the scythe waiting at my side. I reach for the handle and somehow pull my battered body from the ground. A smile forms on my face as my head hangs low.

Laughter escapes my lips, growing louder as I limp toward the girl. She watches me curiously, silent for the moment.

"To think I've been this injured," I say through a chuckle, "by you? My father will love to hear about this."

"Nova, Nova, the game is over! The game is over!"

She charges forward, and I catch her on my blade, stopping her in her tracks. Fire burns within me as a wave of adrenaline passes through my body. I swing the blade out, unleashing a violent wave of energy.

She rolls to the ground, the single attack strong enough to halt her movements. Dread is written across her childlike face as she pulls herself up. With each step, the pain in my body fades. No longer limping as strength enters my limbs.

Her small form scoots back as I near, desperately trying to escape. I swing Kioren's blade into the cement by her head.

"This can't be," she screams, scrambling away from the blade. "I must go to master."

Lifting the blade from the pavement, I pound the handle into the ground. Energy waves shake the floor beneath her feet. She stumbles, peering over her shoulder as she tries to flee. My smile widens as I watch the demon, fear in the eyes of my enemy.

To think they'd stoop so low as to look like a child. As I approach, the whites of her eyes appear through all the darkness. *Pain.* It fills my chest, almost bringing me to my knees.

Someone *did* this to her.

The shadows lick at her skin, fighting for control. Anger replaces the pain, a spark flaring inside me. I reach for it, and a dam breaks loose inside me. Light bursts from my chest, flooding the vicinity.

It envelopes everything, red moonlight vanishing as it holds the child in its warm embrace. The shadow separates from her body, screeching as it tries to escape. I reach out and take its inky form in my hand, strangling it in my grasp. It squirms and struggles to break free. The light intensifies, burning the shadow into dust. It slips through my fingers, turning to nothing. The child falls limp to the ground, and I kneel next to her.

Her chest rises and falls softly, free of the shadow possessing her. She's okay; I've saved her. My eyes blur, a calm breath leaving my lips. My worries disappear as the light takes me into its arms. I saved her.

Blinking away the tears that had formed in my eyes, a blurry woman seems to stand before me. A vague similarity to the one from my vision. I see her mouth move, but no voice reaches my ears. She smiles, turns away, and fades with the waning light.

When the last embers of light fade, my body crumbles. My eyes close as I fall, waiting to hit the hard cement.

Strong arms catch me instead, cradling me gently. An earthy scent fills my nose, calming me as I peek through my heavy lashes. A blurry face stares down at me, but his eyes are as clear as day. Eyes as silver as the moon above.

Then it all turns black.

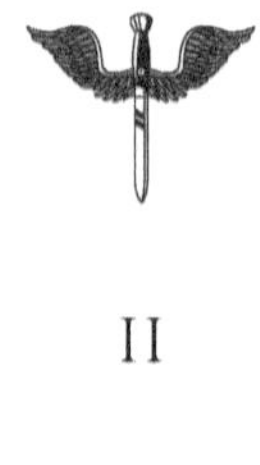

II

ALONE

— Adrian —

A boom shatters across the sky as I finish slicing the head from a ghoul—its thin gray body shriveling to dust at my feet. My heart hammers in my chest, Michael whispering *go* in my ear.

My feet move faster than I can shout a command, but my cadre and Theo follow behind without question. Whatever made that sound is no ordinary demon. Rounding a street end, an abandoned warehouse and parking ramp comes into sight. Another boom sounds and a black wave of energy emanates out from the top of the ramp. My stomach twists as I turn to my team.

"Aril," I say to the dark-haired dragoon, "Take Eva, Cain, Ewan, and Theo to the far-right staircase while we take the left. Meet at the top, prepare for a high-tier."

They nod, setting off as I lead the others toward the left stairwell. White light explodes across the red-stained world, momentarily blinding me and forcing me to a halt. My mouth gapes as the red of the moon fades within the light.

"Keep moving," I say, my steps quicker than ever as I race past my team, not waiting for them to keep up as I enter the stairwell.

Archangel Michael urges me on, doing nothing to quell the anxiety clawing its way up my throat. I burst through the door to the top of the ramp, but the empty parking lot is dark—the light now faded. My eyes land on a child curled up asleep on the pavement, then on the figure crouched in the center of the ramp. I pull my greatsword, Severance—the beginning starting with the end, the splitting of bonds—into my hands. Archangel Michael's power vibrates through the sword, blessing me with strength and swiftness.

The cloaked figure shifts, exposing the body held in his arms. My face pales as I see Nova, a gaping wound on her torso, blood dripping from her head. I surge forward without a sound, my blade aimed at the one who did this, who *hurt* her. The figure glances over his shoulder, silver eyes piercing into mine. Michael yells within my head, commanding me to slice down the man. An urgency unlike anything I've ever felt from the angel's soul inside of me.

Before my blade can hit, the figure vanishes as if swallowed by the shadows themselves, leaving Nova behind. I spin in a circle, searching, scanning, but he's gone. Not even the speed of my Undivided powers were swift enough to land a blow. The thought doesn't ease my overwhelming panic as I turn back to Nova.

The doors on either end of the ramp burst open. My team takes over as I fall to my knees beside Nova. I brush her blood-stained hair from her face, taking in the bruises and cuts littering her body. Blood seeps through a cloth wrapped around her calf, and a gruesome burn scars her shoulder. But those aren't the worst. No, the blast was. The call that brought us here had slammed into her chest, ripping through the thin fabric of her vest. Only a shoddy piece of black cloth has been pressed into the wound to stop the bleeding.

My throat tightens. She didn't even wear the proper gear... She couldn't *get* any. Anger flares deep inside of me. At the demon who touched her, at the moon that did indeed bleed, and at Solomon for not doing enough to prevent this from happening. He let her escape. Let her fight without a team, without a weapon, without anything.

"I can heal her," Eva says, brushing a fallen strand of hair aside as she kneels down on Nova's other side. She pulls out a tin of demonic salve from her pocket, passing it to me. I take it, unwrapping Nova's calf. Bite marks. My frown deepens as I spread the salve into the wound, then the one on her shoulder.

Eva's blue eyes glow as she holds her hands over the worst of the wounds, murmuring words under her breath. The skin stitches itself together slowly, so painfully slow. A whimper escapes Nova's lips, but her eyes don't open.

"I called for backup," Aril says, the worry in his eyes mirroring my own as his gaze falls to Eva's hands, still at work on the wounds. He shifts to look around. "Where's Theo?"

I follow his gaze; my cousin is nowhere in sight. My frown deepens. He'll have hell to pay for not following simple orders.

"Solomon won't like this," Callan mumbles, earning him a jab from his brother. Between Nova and my missing cousin, he's not wrong. My frown deepens as my eyes trail to the silver bracelet wrapped around her wrist. *Isn't that...*

"I've done what I can, but she needs more than one healer." Eva sits back on her legs, blue eyes lifting to mine.

Roman crouches over Nova, scanning her body up and down. "That light saved her, along with that cloth." His gaze falls to me as I snarl at his words. "Whatever caused it, she might have bled out without it."

I glance down at the wounds, at the trickle of light knitting the wounds together. Not from Eva but from something entirely different. Was it that cloaked figure? The thought makes me queasy.

"Did you see where it came from?" Ewan asks, running a hand through his red hair as he looks around the ramp for any evidence.

I shake my head. "The light was gone by the time I got here. Only—" My mind races as those demonic silver eyes linger in my memory. "Only a cloaked figure was hovering over her. He vanished before I caught him." I don't mention how that had never been part of the plan. His blood was meant to be on my hands. "There's a child over there. She needs our attention too."

Cain is the fastest to move to where I pointed, lifting the child and carrying her over to Eva. Sweat beads at Eva's forehead, but she just brushes it away as her eyes shimmer once more, checking the little girl for injuries.

My gaze falls back to Nova, her chest rising and falling with soft, labored breaths. She whimpers again, and my hand moves to her cheek, stroking away the tears and blood staining her skin.

"It's okay. I'm here."

— *Nova* —

My head pounds as light flickers between my heavy lashes. Where am I? Rolling to my side, I force myself up on sore arms. I'm in my room, lying on the white sheets of my bed. The air in the room is stale. I gaze at the window, wishing to open it but not having the energy to do so.

I reach for my head, the pounding slowly easing as I rub small circles on my scalp. Cool metal slides down my arm, and I look to my wrists, my breath catching. Glowing chains of translucent yet tangible metal accompany the angelic bracelet. I frown as I inspect the chains, wrapped so tightly around my wrists that I can see red lines digging into my skin through the luminous metal.

A knock sounds at my door, and Lance enters without waiting for a response, my father at his heels.

Lance's stance is stiff. His curly hair falls in his eyes, free of the fedora he usually wears. My breaths are shallow, my heart hammering in my chest.

"You disobeyed direct orders, stole an angelic artifact, and put yourself in danger by leaving the estate last night," Lance says, his dark eyes meeting mine. "All privileges you had will be stripped, all weapons will be taken out of your possession, and training halted until further notice."

I look between the two of them. "You can't be serious."

They ignore me, Lance not even blinking his eyes in acknowledgment.

"However, your trials will happen tomorrow as planned. Until then, you are confined to the estate, bound with the angelic chains of Ansiel," Lance says, bowing his head and turning to leave. He whispers something quietly in my father's ear before closing the door behind him.

My father and I stare silently at each other from across the room. Though my mind is hazy, the memories of last night are clear in my mind. I killed hellhounds, saved a child from possession. Did I get injured? Sure. But it doesn't warrant this. I did my duty as a hunter.

"Take off the bracelet."

I look down, admiring the glistening black gem and silver spirals. "No."

Returning his gaze, I wince at the familiar anger burning in his eyes. "That wasn't a suggestion."

"And I'm choosing to disobey."

He strides over to me, yanking my arm toward him and pulling me off the bed. "Stop," I say as I fight against his firm grip.

Father reaches for the bracelet as I struggle, powerless against him, limbs weak from my injuries. No, he can't take Kioren. I won't let him!

"No!"

His fingers graze the silver band, and long spikes burst from the black gem. They race toward my father, stopping right before his throat. I suck in a breath, meeting the cold blue gaze glaring down at me.

The grip around my arm loosens, and I fall to his feet.

"It would seem it doesn't want you to take it from me," I say with a hollow chuckle, rising from the ground.

"You summoned it," he says, eyes filled with an emotion I've never seen him show before. *Fear.* "You have no idea what you've done. The consequences you'll bring... And I don't know if I can stop it."

I step back, brows furrowing. Stop what? He turns to leave, but the black spikes surge after him. "Enough," I whisper, and they recede into the gem.

"Father," I say, and he stops at the door. "Why can't you just tell me?"

He turns around, his face hardening into the stony facade I'm used to. "A disgrace such as yourself doesn't deserve to know." My heart clenches, and I bite my cheek to stop the tears brimming in my eyes. "A hunter's duty is to obey, yet it's the one thing you can never seem to do. My only child; it'd be easier if you didn't exist."

"Father, I—"

"You've always been a disappointment, but I never expected this from you."

The door slams shut, and my body trembles, frozen where I stand, as I listen to his footsteps fade away.

I fall back onto my bed, defeated. I look down at my hands curled in my lap, following the trail of glowing chains to where they pool on the floor. They clink together as I raise my arms, grabbing and pulling as if I could shatter the chains and break free. I cry out, my hands digging into my hair. They're the angelic chains of Ansiel; they won't just break.

The sun sets outside my window, a red glow hanging low in the sky. A hellhound's teeth sinking into my calf, a demon offering me a deal, a child's cry, a demented laugh... Pain shoots through my head as I recall the events of the previous night. Healers have been here to treat my wounds—the faint scars left behind where there should be gaping wounds are proof of that—but it'll be a while until the pain fades.

Shaking my head, I think harder. A child was possessed by a shadowy entity; she attacked me with a ball of dark energy, and then... Light? Memories of a blinding light flood my mind. It separated the demon from the child. How did I do that? My cheeks warm as I remember silver eyes and strong arms catching me as I fell.

None of this makes sense.

My tattered tactical vest catches my attention from across the room. Laid carefully over a chair as if it's not barely hanging together by threads. Lifting myself from the bed, I stumble my way to the vest. Reaching into the last surviving pouch, I pull out the ruby necklace to find it undamaged.

He's lucky this was the pouch I put it in. I step back, throwing the pendant to the ground. What am I thinking? Lucky? A *demon* gave this to me to make a deal with the Marquis of Hell. This isn't lucky; it's cursed.

I sink to the ground, closing my eyes and curling my arms around my body. The demon shouldn't be trusted. He *can't* be trusted, but... I look up, staring at the necklace on the ground.

But how can I continue to live like this?

Reaching forward, I take the ruby back into my hands, holding it close to my chest. Secrets and uncertainties keep piling up. What is my father trying so desperately to hide?

The door bursts open, and I'm embraced in a hug before I can even stand.

"Why don't you ever listen?" Adrian squeezes me tighter.

"Adrian," I say as he suffocates me in his embrace. My wounds ache in protest, but I try to keep it from showing on my face.

He pulls away, helping me stand from the awkward position. His hands fall to my shoulders, locking onto them. "We were so worried when we found you"—he pauses, amber eyes searching mine—"I was so worried."

Slowly, I remove his arms. The chains drag behind me as I walk to the window, the rattling sound filling the room. Opening the window, I take a deep breath of the fresh summer air and exhale slowly.

The breeze whispers in my ear as it glides into my room, caressing my cheek. Licking my lips, I try to find the words to say to Adrian.

"It wasn't my intention to worry everyone"—I turn ever so slightly toward him—"to worry you."

"But why, Nova? What did you think you could accomplish?" He comes to my side, spinning me to face him. He places his hand on my cheek, searching my eyes. "How could you fight demons on your own during a blood moon? How could you risk yourself like that? You could have died. I would have lost—"

I grind my teeth as a whirlwind of emotions rips through me. "You don't get it at all." I step back from his touch. "You've always had freedom, so you can't even imagine what it's like for me—unable to prove my strength as a hunter, unable to even step outside my home without a chaperone! I'm not even allowed to have a phone or a computer!" My hand's fist at my sides. "And now, you're linked with Archangel Michael!" I shake my head, incredulous. "How could I risk myself? If it meant I might get an *ounce* of freedom in return, I would do it all over again." Adrian steps back, eyes growing wider with every word. "Fourteen years of training, of blood, sweat, and tears, and I'm stuck in this place day and night, unable to leave, to fight, to do anything! Does that make any sense to you?" I stop yelling, eyes turning to the ground as the energy drains from my body and my shoulders slump. I've had enough of this. "Please, just leave me alone."

"So what? You blame me for everything?"

I meet his gaze, which flickers to Kioren, but he says nothing about the angelic artifact. I don't know what to say anymore. Even with these chains tied around my wrists, he thinks I only blame him. That our failing friendship is the worst part of all of this.

He scoffs, turning around and leaving my room without another word. The door slams shut, and I sink to the floor, a tear rolling down my cheek. I choke on a sob as my world falls apart around me. *How did everything go so wrong?*

I don't want this to be our relationship. Adrian's my best friend—my only friend. But living in his shadow with my wings clipped like a caged bird... I can't take it anymore. How can he call himself my friend when he repeatedly chooses my father over me, oblivious to the pain it causes?

Sighing, I rub my eyes and drag my hands over my face. Tomorrow is so uncertain. Will I pass the trials and be chosen by an angel? Will my father unlock these chains and set me free? I don't know. I don't know anything anymore.

A tear slips from the corner of my eye, and I curse myself for being so weak. Crawling my way back onto my bed, I curl myself into the soft sheets, which rub like sandpaper against my skin. My hatred for this place—this prison—radiates into everything I touch. Closing my eyes, I know tomorrow my fate will unravel.

12

THE ANGELS AWAKEN

"It's time, Nova," Lance says upon entering my room.

I don't face him, staring instead at my reflection in the mirror. "Okay," I mumble, tugging at the ivory dress. It seems to hang limply over my toned body despite the corseted waist and fitted bodice. A breeze brushes against my arms, and goosebumps rise beneath the long sheer sleeves. I rub them mindlessly as I study the delicate embroidered flowers and tiny pearlescent beads that line the square neckline. The skirt drapes loosely around my hips, the hem nearly reaching the floor to hide the bandages around my still healing calf. The traditional dress for the women who perform their angelic trials—the men are allowed to wear pants and a shirt as long as they're white. I frown.

My hair has been combed to silky perfection, falling in long waves around my round face and stopping just short of my waist. I would say I look pretty if not for the dark circles beneath my eyes. My olive skin looks paler, gaunter.

Eighteen.

I sigh; it doesn't feel like my birthday today. Not that anything special usually happens when it is. A gift from Lance, more rigorous training, maybe a new blade from my father if I'm lucky—normal things for hunters, I suppose. The excitement I used to feel for this day has long since faded. Instead, all I feel is emptiness.

I run my fingers over Kioren, finding comfort in the warm bracelet, but my eyes trail to the angelic chains wrapped around my wrists, and cold settles over me.

"It'll be all right." I look at Lance waiting at the door. "We've trained all this time... Just because Adrian bonded with Archangel Michael doesn't mean you won't succeed."

Tugging at my dress one last time, I pass him at the door. "It's more than that, and you know it."

He doesn't say anything else as we head downstairs to the front door where my father awaits us. He wears all black, from his dress pants and vest to the long dress coat overtop. His blond hair is slicked back, cold blue eyes staring down at me as I approach.

I watch his eyes trace over Kioren as I stick my wrists out, waiting for him to release me from the angelic chains. Reaching into his pocket, he pulls out a gold rosary with a clear gem set in the cross—the angelic artifact of Ansiel.

He waves it over my wrists, and the silver bands dissipate into thin air as they fall away. The gem on the cross turns blue, Ansiel's aura color returned along with the power. I linger on the gem, mastering my face as I consider Kioren. The black never faded like Ansiel's gem, like all angelic artifacts are supposed to. Only when the power is returned should it hold the aura of the angel it's connected to.

Turning from my father, I walk out the door first, skipping any pleasantries as my fingers reach for Kioren's gem. Father's dark gray BMW is parked at the front of the estate, steps away from the door. Behind it, the gate has been left open. For a moment,

I consider running and getting as far away from my father as I can.

I head toward the car.

Getting into the backseat, I wait for my father and Lance. Silence weighs heavy in the air as they enter. Father said I will be chosen, but those words make me question the trials even more. I study his profile from the backseat, searching each line in his face for the answers he hides.

The angelic artifact of Ansiel hangs slightly out of his pocket, and I wonder what other artifacts he has access to—and what power he possesses that allows him, *us*, to use them without being bonded to an angel. Father is respected in the clan as our leader, but the knowledge of his strength and power aren't known to anyone but himself and the Solomons before him. He's made it blatantly clear that his only daughter, his sole heir, is a disgrace and a disappointment. Undeserving of the truth. *Of any truth...*

I shift in my seat, closing my eyes and trying to control the beating of my heart, the butterflies in my stomach. I've always anticipated this day; I just never thought it'd be like this. A small part of me always hoped my father would be encouraging, wishing for my success. Instead, he fills my head with promises and regret.

The scenery throughout the campus is darker today as we enter the grounds. Gray clouds hover in the sky, the flowers and trees still and lifeless as we drive by. The air feels heavy, suffocating, seeping into the car and filling my lungs with more unease. I choke it down as my father's manor passes by. The clan's chapel at the far end of the campus grounds comes into sight—the place where all angelic trials are held nowadays. Built with the same red brick as the rest of the campus, its pointed roof seems to reach to the glass Heavens. Ivy grows up the entirety of the front as if to keep it hidden from sight. Fitting, since it's the only building on campus non-hunters aren't allowed to enter.

My breaths start to come faster as we pull up to the sidewalk at the front. Most hunters aren't particularly religious, but we all have a certain respect for the truth we've been told. A reality I face today. Hunters put their trust in the God who saved us and the angels He sent, though we may never know how any of it really works. All we can do is put faith in the choice they make when it comes time for these trials. I glance at my father. Maybe he knows the entire truth but chooses not to share, as he does with everything else.

Stepping out of the car, I'm greeted by the silence of the headquarters small group of Undivided. They were asked to be despite going against tradition. Normally, only my father is required to be present for the trials, but today it's me—our leader's only daughter—and the weight of it sits heavy on my shoulders.

A disgrace... A disappointment... You will be chosen... It's a wonder my father assumes I'll be immediately chosen when he seems to wish I never existed in the first place.

I force myself to stand straighter, looking ahead without meeting the eyes of the other hunters. Lance comes to my side as I lift my gaze to the large stone angel wings hanging above the wooden chapel doors. A sign of protection, yet all it makes me want to do is run and hide.

"Nova." Darius steps forward to greet the three of us. He turns to my father, and I wonder if I'm the only one intimidated. "Solomon, you've been holding out on us. Who would have thought your daughter is such a strong fighter, being stuck in your estate all the time." He arches a dark eyebrow. "Makes one wonder why she wasn't on patrol for the blood moon. She is your heir, after all."

Father stares him down without response. He steps past Darius, the other hunters parting for him as he enters the chapel.

"Still a stick up his ass," Darius says, bringing a small smile to my face.

"Let's go," Lance says, placing a hand gently on my shoulder and leading me forward.

We pass Adrian, and our eyes meet for a split second before I turn away. *Not now, not today.*

Entering the chapel, I let out a small gasp, one quiet enough to not be heard. A rainbow of light shines down on the large room, illuminating the aisle lined with bouquets of white flowers attached to the wooden pews. At the far end of the chapel, my father stands before a statue of an angel, its wings spread wide beneath the enormous stained-glass window depicting our history and giving light to the room. I study the details of the glass as I move toward it. A continuous story unfolding with each pane. The colors, the lines... they tell a tale of death and despair, of hope and salvation.

I approach my father's side, trying not to gawk as the statue's enormity blocks most of my view of the stained glass window behind it. A hood and veil lay over the angel's head, a human face delicately outlined beneath. So lifelike—as if an angel turned itself into stone just to be set here. Its arms are extended forward, a sword in its grasp pointing to the ground. I step closer, examining the markings engraved on the length of the blade. *Angelic script.*

Stepping back, I take in the entirety of the chapel.

I've never been here before, even though it's open to all hunters. I suppose my father never saw the need, and for once, I'm not mad. While beautiful, this place reeks of something I don't like, something I can't pinpoint. My throat tightens; nausea forms in my stomach, but I swallow it down.

Father reaches toward the angel's hands, placing his palm on top. The ground trembles as a faint blue light emanates from the engravings on the blade. A scraping sound follows, and I take a step back, bumping into Lance. He rests his hands on my shoulders, steadying me as I watch the statue turn and reveal a secret underground stairwell. I creep forward to peer in but see nothing but the shadowed steps.

"This is where I leave you," Lance says, and I turn to face him, my heart sinking, "*Remember* who you are."

I nod, a cold numbness settling over me. My father's footsteps already tap softly as he descends the stairwell. Taking a deep breath, I turn and follow after him.

The other hunters trail behind, their bodies blocking any light from the surface. Our steps echo through the stone stairwell; no one speaks. I shiver as darkness wraps me in its arms the farther we descend.

I make out the end of the stairwell as my eyes adjust to the darkness. Stepping down carefully from the last step, I hesitate at the entrance of a long room.

Seven arches are chiseled into the walls—seven gateways. The air is cold and stale and smells of damp stone. The Undivided walk past me, spreading out into the room as if it were routine. Father walks to the far end of the room, his golden hair shining despite the darkness. He kneels before what I make out as another angel statue—almost identical to the one upstairs.

Turning from my father, my gaze follows the hunters. Some I've seen in passing, but most are unfamiliar. They know nothing of me and probably assume I'm here because of who my father is. A feeling of unworthiness surfaces, but I shove it down as best as I can.

Most of the hunters remain near the back of the room, but three step out toward the arches. Adrian's eyes lock with mine as he passes by, his hand tapping me lightly on my elbow as if to reassure me. My body recoils from the touch, but I force myself not to back away. He continues to the end of the long room to stand in front of the arch nearest to the statue.

Biting my lip, I turn from him and approach the closest arch—empty of any hunter. I squint my eyes to see a set of intricately sculpted angel wings, an angelic symbol carved into the stone between them. I shuffle back, taking a second glance at the room. Seven arches for seven archangels. The three hunters here must be the only ones currently at the Falgens branch to hold one of the seven archangels within them. I look to the empty arches in the room with hope, trying to remember which of the archangels have yet to bond with a hunter.

I walk down the room, quietly reading each angelic symbol. "In Selaphiel, our *intentions*." I pass the older woman linked to Selaphiel, her face hardened by years of hunting. I don't recognize her. "In Azrael, our *empathy*; in Raguel, our *integrity*." Raguel is the next to have a hunter, and I recognize him as Adrian's dad, my father's second. He smiles fondly at me—strange, considering I've only met him a handful of times over the last eighteen years since he was always away on confidential missions. I nod to him and move to the next tunnel. "In Gabriel, our *courage*; in Uriel, our *compassion*; in Raphael, our *knowledge*; and"—face-to-face with Adrian, I whisper out the last words—"in Michael; our *loyalty*."

We stare at each other through the darkness. Adrian's lips part as if to speak, but I turn away as butterflies flutter in my stomach. I can't do this with him, not before my trials. I move to stand next to my father, still kneeling before the angelic statue.

After another minute of tense silence, he finally stands, facing the audience of the hunters.

"The time has come for Nova to embark on her angelic trials, to determine if she has the ability to possess the soul of an angel within her body, to become an *Undivided*," Father says, his voice crisp as it echoes throughout the room. He turns his attention to me. "Do you accept the responsibility if you succeed and are chosen." His words aren't a question but a statement. *You will be chosen.*

"I do."

"Every hunter must overcome different challenges in order to pass through each of the seven moral gates. If even one is failed, the trials end." His eyes lock with mine. "Are you ready?"

I nod and take a deep breath, steeling myself for what's to come. This is what I've trained for.

"Then we begin."

He reaches into his long suit jacket, pulling out a small dagger. Grabbing my wrist, he pulls me toward the stone angel. "Will you take the bracelet off, or will it remain?" he says for only me to hear.

"It stays," I say, expecting him to demand I take it off, but he only nods. My brows knit together, and my heart aches. He's promised that I'll understand everything once my trials are over, but after yesterday... Nails dig into the palm of my free hand.

Flipping my palm up, he punctures the tips of each of my fingers, tiny droplets of blood welling at the surface. I gulp, remembering reading about these nuanced details of the trials. Traditions passed down from generation to generation of hunters—since the first Undivided. Guiding me closer to the statue, he places my hand over the angels.

"Remember what I said."

I turn to face him, but his cold expression is fixed on the angel before us. Blood drips from my fingertips, trailing down the angel's hands to the sword it holds.

"You will be chosen," Father repeats, and my head swivels to him. "Trust me. If only this once."

A breath catches in my throat, and I lick my lips, feeling parched even in the damp underground. Trust... How can I when it's always like this with him?

Blue light emanates from the statue and seven arches, and the Undivided behind me begin to chant softly. Ancient words of encouragement to send me off into my trials. I swallow hard, their hymn for the last child of the Fandera name like an ungodly weight. I focus on the angel—its veiled face unsettling—and I don't look away. The light becomes brighter, bathing the space in a cold blue glow. The chanting grows louder, though the words seem far off, the sound steadily becoming distant. Brighter and brighter, the light surrounds me until the statue and the room disappear.

My hands raise over my eyes, blue light fading into warm sunlight. Soft, damp moss tickles my skin, and I slowly sit up as my eyes adjust to the sudden brightness. Lush greens and vibrant flowers surround me, filling the humid air with their heady scent. I stand, my bare feet digging into the moist dirt.

Dark green leaves twice my size sway in the hot breeze, carrying the scent of soil and fresh vegetation. Vines climb the tropical trees, visibly inching along in a way I didn't think was possible. I watch them for a moment, goosebumps rising across my skin.

I blink, and the scenery changes. I fall to the grass, slick and wet beneath my bare feet. A large pond of lotuses spreads out before me. The lotus leaves rise high out of the water, reaching for the sky, yet the flowers themselves have yet to bloom. I stand and walk closer.

The water is clear, the roots and stems of the lotuses visible all the way to the bottom. Sunlight reflects off the still water, and I look up. Dense trees bend toward the center of the pond, leaving only a small circle of blue sky above. I spin around to find no exit, only an impenetrable jungle—no way in or out.

Approaching the pond, I dip a foot into the water. It wraps around my skin in a cool embrace. Small ripples spread out along the surface. Stepping in fully, a contented sigh leaves my lips. My white dress floats with me as I gently push the emerging lotus leaves gently aside, my steps creating clouds from the rich soil beneath my feet.

I wonder what trial this is supposed to be...

My eyes widen at the thought. This *is* my trial; what am I doing swimming? Turning back to the edge, I wade my way through the pond, the water becoming heavier the more I try to push through. The color quickly changes from clear to a murky brown, then continues darkening until it's completely black and thick like tar. It stains the white dress I wear and coats my skin and hair. I reach out to grab the grassy edge, watching in horror as it moves back every time it's almost in my grasp.

The pond floor disappears beneath my feet, and my head sinks underwater. I kick my way to the surface, gasping as I burst through. Black liquid slides down my skin, stinging my eyes. Treading water, I spin, searching for a way out. My heart pounds in my chest as the water desperately tugs at me, attempting to drag me down into its depths.

"There's no time." A man's voice, both silky and guttural, booms throughout the clearing, thrumming in my ears. I look up at the circle of sky visible above and recoil as the pale blue turns to a sickly green. The trees begin shaking as a vicious wind whips down through the opening.

Waves form on the water, and I tread harder to stay afloat. The light darkens, and I spin around to find myself face-to-face with a towering black wave. I suck in a breath, squeezing my eyes shut as it crashes down. I'm dragged under, blackened water gripping my skin, pulling me deeper and deeper. Air bubbles rise above me; my lungs burn as I twist and turn in the darkness.

All sense of direction disappears as the water suddenly lets go. A light appears above me, and I swim toward it. I exhale, letting out precious air from my lungs—but the light is not leading me to the surface. A memory that isn't mine plays out before me as if I had been there, a bystander watching, hiding.

Father stands with my grandfather, whose face is even harder and colder than his. Though I never met him while he was alive, I recognize him immediately. Father's younger here, maybe in his late twenties. They stand together in what is now my father's office at the estate. My grandfather hands him a leatherbound book. I glimpse the cover as Father turns it over—*The Eternal Keeper* inscribed in gold in the dark, worn leather.

The pages flip open, but I'm unable to get close enough to read the words within. Father's face falls, shock registering across his eyes. He looks to his father, shoving the book back at him with angry shouts, which sound muffled to my ears. Tears stream down his face—a father I don't recognize. The two of them angle toward me, and I turn to see a door opening, a blurred face, and blond hair appearing. Grandfather yells, pointing for the man to leave, his face becoming red as he clasps a hand on my father's shoulder and shoves the book back into his hands.

The water swirls and the scene disappears.

I hear muted voices and turn to find a new memory playing before me. A young girl around my age climbs a hill to a stone cottage—something not from this century. Smoke rises from the chimney as she turns and looks straight through me, a smile on her face. I pause, staring into all too familiar eyes. *My eyes.* Though her face isn't mine, there's recognition of being one and the same. I turn to find what holds her attention, but the water drags me away again, pulling me to a row of scenes playing out in frames almost like a film strip.

Images pass by and disappear into the darkness—none of them as clear as the first two scenes. But one thing is as clear as day, and a sinking feeling settles in my chest. Each face I see, in different centuries, different lifetimes, *it's mine.* Across ages, ethnicities, genders, the face is never quite the same as the one I have now, but all the same, I am looking at myself. Looking into those familiar green eyes.

My head spins, the memories vanishing. Frantically, I try to recall them, but they're gone. An empty pocket within my mind. The same woman who granted me how to use Kioren speaks again, unmuffled by the water.

Remember, remember, remember, she says into my ears on repeat, the sound filling the space around me. Shutting my eyes, I swim for the surface, unable to bear the burning in my lungs any longer. The black liquid grabs hold of my ankle, dragging me back down.

Look and remember. My eyes are forced open.

Kioren and I are in the next image, the night of the blood moon. I wince as I watch my grip loosen from the scythe's handle. Falling back toward the hard cement of the parking ramp. A flash of black fabric flutters across my vision. I blink, and in the next moment my body is being cradled by a cloaked figure. His head is turned away as if to hide his identity, but I recognize him. He was the one I saw in the night sky. Kioren stands at my side protectively but doesn't attack. Almost as if welcoming him to my side. My heart squeezes, and my hand inches forward, aching to reach out and uncover the hidden face of the man holding me in his arms.

Water swirls, and the scene changes again. My body floats in a lotus pond similar to the one I'm immersed in now. The pond is blackened by the same tar-like liquid, but the surface is still as my body rests upon it. Seven small lotus flowers—each a different color—rest on my chest. A golden glow hums around my body.

A wave washes the image away, and I become light-headed, lungs desperate for air. Black liquid sweeps me away to a line of angels cloaked in white, faces veiled. They speak, and for once, I hear them, yet I can't understand their language. The only words comprehensible to me: *remember, remember, remember.*

An angel steps forward; its cloak undulates as it moves behind me. They place their hands over my eyes, bringing me into greater darkness. Light erupts, and I scream, bubbles escaping my mouth. I feel the angel pry their way into my body, splitting me apart from the inside out, and I'm powerless to do anything.

My lungs collapse, and my vision begins to gray—eyes on the brink of closing forever. The angels disappear, and I sink into the black water.

Remember.

The water pushes me up, and I burst through the surface into a black room, coming out from one of the walls. Air rushes into my burning lungs, and I gasp, coughing fiercely as I collapse on the ground. I look at where I came from, the wall of water shimmering. I reach out to touch it, but it becomes solid—I'm locked within this room.

Hair sticks to my face, and I push it back as I stand on wobbly legs. Water drips to the floor, the sound echoing in the silence. A single full-length mirror appears, and I step forward and gaze at the young woman reflected in the glass. Wet hair strewed messily over her head and a dirty white dress plastered to her skin. Remnants of the black liquid linger and drip down my body, and I shiver, rubbing my arms in the cool space.

A clunk resounds in the room, and another mirror appears. I turn to it, stepping back as more mirrors appear, clicking into place until all I can see, no matter where I look, is my own reflection. I race forward and pound on the glass, panicking.

My hands bounce off with no effect. I spin around, but my reflection twirls with me in a kaleidoscope of chaos. Something pricks the space over my heart, and I run a hand over it.

"How do I—" The pain is more intense this time, stopping me mid-sentence. The excruciating sensation of being branded follows, and I cry out, falling to a knee. Looking up into the mirror in front of me through watery eyes, I notice a red glow emanating from the area over my heart. I drag myself closer, limbs weakening with each movement. Leaning forward, I pull down the collar of my dress, the fabric peeling off my skin like it had been sticking to an open wound. I grit my teeth, holding in the whimper desperate to burst from my lips.

My breaths are labored, and sweat beads on my forehead as I reveal the skin beneath my dress. A red line emanating from my heart glows like a laser burning me from the inside out. It moves, and I scream, unable to withstand the pain any longer. Slowly, it begins to etch a design into my skin. Tattooing me in a way that feels much deeper than just a surface mark.

The red glow ebbs away, the design complete. My head drops forward to rest against the mirror. On weak arms, I push myself up and trace a shaky finger over the tattoo, the skin around it raw to the touch. A red lotus, seven petals—the lines thin and delicate but unyielding.

"What are you?" I breathe out, my brows pulling together.

Black lines shoot out around the tattoo. My ears fill with the sound of my screams before I can even process the agonizing pain spreading across my body. Knives seem to cut into my skin as the black lines cascade over me, spreading like vines until I'm covered in the black ink.

I collapse onto the ground, tears falling from my eyes, vision dotting black.

"Haven't you ever heard, curiosity killed the cat?" A man's voice—calm and smooth—echoes around the room. Through heavy lashes, I see a figure approach. The toes of his shiny black shoes fill my sight as he towers over my crumpled form. Waves of fear wash across my skin with each word he speaks. "We wouldn't want all of Solomon's begging to go to waste. Right, *Nova?*" He laughs at my pain, continuing to walk around me.

"Who are you?" I mumble, my voice barely a trickle of sound.

The man halts, darkness spreading out from around him to black out the mirrors around us.

"I am the King. The Savior. The Holy. Fail to heed my warning, and it will not just be you in pain, my dear." He turns and walks away, each step cracking the glass beneath us.

"Why? Who are you?" I whimper as I push my body upright. The man's face is blurred in darkness, and fear grips my heart.

He chuckles, and I begin to tremble. "It's been a long time since you yielded so much power. I might have a use for you yet."

The man turns away, and the mirrors shatter into a million pieces. I fall from the room into endless darkness. I flail as I try to grab hold of something, empty space slipping through my fingers. Blue light crowds the edges of my vision, and I slam into a body of water.

Knives dig into my back, twisting and turning in my skin as I exit my mind—my screams carrying over into reality. My eyes open wider, taking in the blue light illuminating the cavernous underground room. I glimpse my hand still over the angel's, unable to pull away. I move my feet only to feel them dangling in midair, no ground beneath me.

My heart races, thumping wildly in my chest. The pain pierces me harder, and a wail rips from my lips before I can bite it back. It grows, reaching a crescendo of agony. Tears unwillingly stream down my cheeks. *Is this what my failure feels like?*

A pop sounds, something soft tracing my skin as it unfurls from my back. Relief floods through me, and I glance up to find the face of my father. His eyes are wide as he takes a slow step back, the knife he used to pierce my fingertips clattering to the stone floor. I blink, vision still hazy, but from the corner of my teary eyes...

Wings. They spread out wide behind me, glorious. But a heartbeat later, the blue light fades, and I drop to the ground in a heap.

My head spins. Two voices speaking to me within my mind. *Remember.*

13

CHAINED CHOICES

Bright light wakes me from dreams filled with darkness—shadowy creatures clawing at me, black vines consuming me until death grasped me in its cold embrace. I slowly sit, my room spinning as I look around. Reaching up to rub my aching head, I feel the cold slide of metal against my wrists. I freeze, bringing my hands before me. The angelic chains of Ansiel curled around my skin once again. A wave of déjà vu washes over me.

My head clears, memories filling the empty throb in my mind. Goosebumps rise along my body as I recall everything from my trials—not that I can really call it that... I shake my head, not understanding the scenes shown to me. Memories that aren't mine yet felt entirely too familiar.

I brush the thought aside as I reach a hand to my chest, and I tense, looking down at the collar of the white dress I still wear. Is it there like I saw? *The lotus tattoo?* My hand slides to the back of my neck as if I can feel for the lines of angel wings to mark me as an Undivided. Was my father right?

Standing from the bed, I walk to the bathroom. My heart thrums in my chest, every sensation heightened with each slow

122

step I take. When I finally look at my reflection, I wonder who it is I'm staring at. I saw them, the faces that used to be mine. I close my eyes, shifting my hair over my shoulder.

Slowly, I reach my fingers up and peel down the collar of my dress to reveal the space over my heart. My body recoils at the sensation, remembering what it was like to peel the fabric off raw skin. I take a deep breath, opening my eyes to face the truth.

The seven-petaled lotus is tattooed in red ink right over my heart.

I let go of my collar, stepping back from the mirror as I try to wrap my head around the marking. A million questions race through my mind, but answers elude me, no matter how hard I think.

I meet the gaze of my reflection, searching my eyes. "What does this mean?"

Taking a deep breath, I calm myself, knowing I need to look at the back of my neck. Lifting my hair, I crane my head to see the back and freeze—too stunned to move. Two sets of angel wings are tattooed on my skin, the black ink both delicate and bold on my olive skin.

My hair falls from my hands, a smile creeping up onto my face. "I'm an Undivided." My voice is breathy to my ears; excitement wells inside my chest. I did it, I passed. Father wasn't wrong, he knew, he—

I look down at the familiar chains wrapped around my wrists. Kioren sits comfortably next to them, the bracelet quiet. If I'm an Undivided, why am I in chains again? I lift my hair again, brows drawing together as I examine the two distinct sets of wings. My gaze trails down; the back of my dress is ripped to shreds. *This isn't possible.*

Backing out of the bathroom, I leave my room, searching for Father. I trip on rushed feet, falling to the carpeted floor.

Pushing myself back up, I wince at the weakness in my arms. I scramble down the hall and go to fling his door open but hesitate. Thinking better of it, I knock, waiting for a response. When no voice comes through, I open the door, searching the empty room for his face.

Dizziness overcomes me, and I lean against the door frame, composing myself when it passes. I need answers... He *promised*. After everything I witnessed within my trials, I must speak with him.

I hear the front door creak open, and I race down the hall to the staircase. Lance stands at the bottom, and I take two steps at a time, fighting my dizziness until I'm standing before him.

"Lance." I stumble forward, and he catches me in his arms. "Where's my father?" I say, searching his eyes.

He sets me straight, but I don't let go of his sleeve—waiting. He removes my hand and walks away without a word.

"Lance." I turn to face his receding back, heart racing in my chest. "I need to see my father."

He stops but doesn't face me, a sense of pain laced into each word. "He doesn't wish to see you."

My stomach sinks, a piece of me shattering inside. Lance starts walking away again, and I collapse onto the floor, numbness spreading across my body.

I must have done something wrong during my trials... My eyes dart back and forth as I rake my mind, groping for any sliver of reason.

Father's face flits into my mind. The fear in his eyes as he stepped away from me as wings burst from my back—something that only happens to hunters whose angels give them full control of their power. A complete bond.

My head pounds. "*Curiosity killed the cat,*" the man's voice echoes through my mind, and a tremor runs through my body.

He with no name but Darkness. For I would never call such a *thing* a king, a savior, or holy.

And answers are the only thing that will set me free.

Pulling myself from the ground, I stare ahead aimlessly. An Undivided, yet still a prisoner in this estate. Glancing at the silver chains wrapped so tightly around my wrists that they're on the verge of bleeding, my body shakes with rage. Kioren pulses angrily against my wrist, the black gem bubbling as if reflecting my emotions.

"Let light and darkness be your essence." The words sound hollow to my ears—emotionless, dead. "Your heavenly form in my hands, with the strength to crumble mountains and split the sea." Lance turns back around, eyes filling with realization. The world moves in slow motion as he races toward me, reaching out. "Fulfill your purpose as the truth, the protector, and the destroyer. Come forth, Kioren."

Black tendrils shoot out from the bracelet, unfurling to reveal the monstrous scythe I remember. I take hold of Kioren's handle as the black tendril unfurls and circles protectively around me.

If this estate is the cage I won't be freed from, I will tear it down until there's nothing left. I may not have answers, but I will at least free myself from this place.

"Destroy it all."

Letting go of the scythe, I watch, unfeeling, as it whips around my body, shredding the staircase railing with its blade. Lance ducks as splinters of wood shoot toward him. Kioren slices the couches and chairs in the main foyer in half, its black tendrils shooting out and tearing into the walls and ceiling. Pieces of the estate crumble around me as I stand frozen, too numb to move. Kioren blocks chunks from hitting me, protecting me as much as it destroys.

The windows shatter as black tendrils pierce through them, and glass rains down around us. Lance raises his arms over his head to block the falling debris.

"Nova!"

Someone calls to me, but their voice is distant. Kioren moves faster, and I wrap my arms around my body. The shouts grow louder, but I block out the sound, retreating into myself.

A breeze brushes against my skin, gentle as if arms are wrapping around me. I ease into it as a soft, silvery voice whispers in my mind. *"Calm your mind, my sweet child. This destruction is not what you seek."*

"I can't...." I say in my mind, shutting my eyes tighter.

"There is another way, my child." The red ruby pendant sways in my mind's eye. *"There is another way..."* the voice repeats.

I look up as sensation returns to my body, the wind slipping off my skin. I gasp. Around me, everything is in pieces, scattered across the foyer as if a tornado had hit.

"There is another way." I shut my eyes again as I gather my strength.

Reaching my hand out, I call Kioren back to my side. It obeys with silent ease, the bracelet on my wrist humming as if to comfort me. I nod to it, and the scythe shrinks into the bracelet, black tendrils coiling back into the gem. My arms drop to my sides, a numbness settling over my body once again. There is another way... But can I really make that choice?

My legs give out, and I fall backward, eyes fluttering shut. Arms catch me before I hit the ground, holding onto me tightly. I peek through hooded lids to see the face hovering above mine.

"Nova," Adrian says. His brows are furrowed as he places a hand on my forehead. "She's running a fever."

My body lifts from the ground, Adrian taking me into his arms. I hear him speaking to Lance again, but I can't make out the words. He carries me up the surviving sections of the staircase, careful to keep us steady. Resting my head against his chest, a chill runs up my arms.

He places me on my bed when we reach my room, pulling the sheets over me. Resting a hand on my forehead again, he brushes damp strands of hair away from my face. "Wait here."

I mumble incoherently in response. He leaves the room, and I'm left alone once more. Opening my eyes, I stare at the white ceiling above, vision blurring in and out of focus. Slowly I sit up, reaching over to my side drawer to pull out the ruby necklace. Laying back down, I hold it above me, the red gem sparkling in the incoming sunlight. Lance enters the room, and I lower the necklace, hiding it in my palm.

"Nova, let me see your neck."

Lance walks over to my bed, and I sit up.

"Now you'll talk to me?" He frowns, and I roll my eyes. "Will it change anything?"

He reaches into his pocket for a cloth, wiping my sweaty forehead. "Show me."

I hesitate for a moment but turn my back to him. He lifts my hair over my shoulder, lightly tracing his fingers over the tattoos. It tickles softly, and goosebumps pebble on my arms.

"Why are there two?" I ask, glancing over my shoulder at him.

He moves away, letting my hair fall back over the tattoos.

"I don't know," he speaks low—rushed—glancing around the room. "None of the Undivided have spoken a word about your trials. It seems Solomon is keeping it—"

"Secret." I finish his sentence. "He doesn't want anyone outside the Undivided present to know I have two angels. It doesn't make any sense, my trials—" I stop myself, the words threatening to burst out, to explain what I experienced. To ask about the lotus on my chest.

"Do you remember them? What did you see? Who are your angels?"

I close my eyes as I recall the fragmented images, the seven-petaled lotus tattoo, the black vines encasing my body, Darkness, and his cold laughter. My eyes open, and I examine Lance's expression, one I'm not entirely sure how to interpret. He knows better than to ask things I cannot share with him.

"That's the problem. I remember too much."

Lance searches my face.

"And there's more, so much more," I say, letting the full extent of my fear shine through my eyes.

Lance's face pulls to a grimace, grasping the enormity of what I might've seen while inside my mind. His hand reaches toward mine, but the door bursts open, and Adrian enters with a small medical box and a bowl of water. He rushes to my bedside, and Lance steps out of his way.

"You should be resting," he says as he gently lays me back down and feels my forehead. "You're burning up."

"I'm fine," I say with a feeble attempt to brush his hand away.

Adrian grabs my hand, looking at the ground. For a moment, I think about the ruby necklace curled in my palm, and I force my fingers to remain shut tight. I glance at Lance, but he only turns away. Sighing, I place my free hand on Adrian's cheek. I try to get him to bring his eyes to mine, but he doesn't budge.

"Lance, can you give us a moment?"

He nods, giving me a final glance before leaving the room. I turn my attention from the door and back to Adrian, who lifts his face, amber eyes searching mine.

"I wasn't going to ask because of your fever, but what was that in the foyer? I've never seen you like that before. I've never seen that kind of weapon...." His voice trails off as his eyes move to the angelic bracelet accompanying the chains on my wrist.

I take a deep breath. How can I explain it to finally make him understand? To choose me over his stupid loyalty to my father. To realize how trapped I am in this estate, secrets waved in front of my face, and now Darkness lingering at my doorstep, threats and promises made that I know he intends to fulfill. Is Adrian capable of choosing *me*?

"Can you open the window?" I ask him, finding something to say.

He nods, standing to open the window. The summer breeze wafts into the room, my white curtains billowing out in a dance of wind and fabric. Light and shadows flicker across my bedroom floor as the sun lowers in the sky. Wind brushes tenderly against my cheek, fading away when Adrian returns to my side at the edge of my bed.

"I like the summer sun and the colors of the leaves in the fall. I like seeing the winter snow and watching new growth bloom from the decay in spring. I want to go to the beach in the summer and go skiing in the winter—just like I've seen on TV. I want to pick flowers in the spring and apples in the fall. But most of all, no matter the season, I want to protect people. I want to hunt the demons who torment our society. I want to show the clan I'm not some spoiled princess. I want to show everyone how capable I am," I say to him, a tear sliding down my cheek without my consent. "This estate is my cage, and I can't free myself from it." My eyes remain trained on the angelic chains circling my wrists, red welts beneath the luminescent metal. "I could give up everything else if only to be a hunter."

He stares wide-eyed, a sigh leaving his lips as he reaches to wipe away my stray tear. "Nova, you don't have to explain yourself to me, I get it. I just... I just want you safe. I never meant for you to feel like you didn't have me, because you do." He lets go, reaching to hold on to my hands instead.

"I hated not being able to do anything during your trials. It was so different from mine, and when you screamed"—his voice catches in his throat, and he shuts his eyes—"I was so scared. I didn't know what was wrong... I didn't know how to help you. Then two sets of wings burst from your back, and... It was beautiful... terrifying."

My body begins to tremble, and my voice quivers as I say, "How is it possible? I've never heard or read of anything like this. It's—" It's too much for one person, one hunter, to bear. No human, no mortal, soul can contain this much divinity. At least, not for long.

He shakes his head. "I don't know. Solomon threatened everyone into keeping their mouths shut. No one else in the clan knows."

I look at the chains around my wrists. Despite everything that's happened, nothing has changed.

"How can I trust my father?" I say, a look of shock appearing on Adrian's face. "He told me before my trials I would pass and be chosen. That I would understand everything once it was all over. Now he won't speak to me." I shove the chains in his face, the links glimmering in the light. "Does this make sense to you?"

"Nova..." His face falls as he finally takes in the chains wrapped around my wrists. He reaches to touch them, but his fingers pass through the nearly invisible metal, only tangible to the wearer and the wielder.

"I don't want to be hidden away in the estate anymore. I want the freedom to be a hunter. To be me."

More tears fall as I speak to him. How could I have forgotten how easy it is to talk with Adrian? He pulls me into his embrace as I sob into his shirt, soaking the fabric. Pent-up feelings I haven't released in years flowing freely. Letting my weakness show for just this one moment with him. The only one I trust enough to display my vulnerability.

"It'll be okay, I promise. We'll figure it out together. Just have a little more faith in your father. He'll come around. You'll see."

Rubbing small circles on my back, he remains quiet for a while, letting me cry. I dig my head into his shoulder, one hand fisting the fabric of his shirt while the other rests in my lap, still hiding the necklace. I missed this... *Please let Adrian be right. Please let my father just tell me the truth and finally free me.* My fingertips tighten around the large ruby pendant, warm in my palm. *Please don't make me choose this, a path I can never walk back from.*

A knock sounds from the door, and I pull away, Adrian still rubbing circles on my back. Lance enters the room, a solemn look cast over his face, posture rigid.

"Your father would like to speak with you now. He just arrived and is in his office."

My heart stutters, and I look to Adrian, who nods in support. Lance leaves the room, and I stand to follow after him. As I enter the hallway, Lance pulls me aside, wrapping his hand around my arm as he leans in close. His dark eyes hold mine, his voice but a whisper.

"Don't falter before him. Do what you must." He lets go, nodding in the direction of my father's office.

I stare at him, searching his face, but his lips remain pressed tightly together. Turning away, I head toward my father's office, unease growing in my stomach. *Do what you must.* He couldn't mean... The pendant heats in my hand.

Reaching the door, I shake my head to clear my thoughts and knock softly. Father's voice bids me to enter, and I make my way in, not bothering to take a seat in front of him.

Cold blue eyes study me: red, puffy eyes; tear-stained cheeks. He must be disgusted by my weakness. I scoff in my head at the irony. *How could someone weak be chosen by two angels...* The lotus tattoo throbs on my chest as if to remind me of its presence and what I endured during my trials. I resist the urge to reach for it.

"Sit," he commands.

"I'll stand."

Lifting my chin, I keep my head held high before him. This is his last chance to explain. All of it. If not... *Please, just answer my questions.*

"You made a mess of the foyer."

"The estate needed some remodeling." My joke doesn't lighten the tense atmosphere. "I have two angels," I say, reopening the conversation.

"Do you now?" he says casually.

I stare in shocked silence. Really? *This* is how he wants to play? Promising me answers and then pretending not to know anything. Until now, I've never thought of my father as a coward. As much as I hate his rules, I've always respected his strength. But the man before me isn't strong—no, this man is as weak as the tears drying on my cheeks.

"You promised I would understand everything after my trials, that you would finally answer my questions. I think I deserve to know the truth after everything that's happened," I say, a slight waver finding its way into my voice.

"Is that how you interpreted it?"

My heart cracks open in my chest, but I keep trying. *Please, Father, I beg you.*

"Why do I have two angels? You said I'd be chosen. Did you also know this would happen?" He remains quiet, unmoving. "Or what about the lotus tattooed on my chest? Or the mother I've never known? Or even better, why do you keep me locked up here? You know I'm a good hunter... I don't know how else I can prove myself to you."

"It's not time yet...." He tears his eyes from mine and begins leafing through some papers on his desk.

My world crumbles around me. There's nothing left for me here. Nothing I can do to change his mind.

"The man from my trials... *Darkness*... What about him?"

His eyes shoot up to mine, widening with fear for a fraction of a second before settling back into the cool, stoic glare I know so well. "I don't know what you're talking about." A lie, and he knows I caught his reaction but says nothing more, returning to the papers on his desk.

My jaw clenches, and tears well in my hot, fevered eyes once again. *Why are you making me make this choice?* I look down at the chains digging painfully into my wrists. *You intend to keep me locked in this cage forever, don't you?*

I take a deep breath and close my eyes, trying to gather my thoughts. I try to think rationally—I'm a hunter, an Undivided, with not one but two angels. I think of Adrian's embrace, the comfort of his shoulder. *Do what you must.* Lance's words replay in my mind, and one answer is clear—as much as I wish it wasn't.

"Then I see no reason why I need to be here."

I turn from his desk and walk slowly to the door. *Please, Father. Stop me from leaving. Say something, anything.* His lips remain shut as the door closes behind me. A single tear falls down my cheek, a silent goodbye.

Walking down the hall, I stand straighter, holding my head high. The fever makes me dizzy, but I push through it. My decision has been made; there's no looking back now. *But it's not only my father I'll be leaving behind...*

I shove thoughts of Adrian out of my mind. Not even my best friend can stop me. Not when he still has faith in my father.

Lance waits outside my door as I approach. He looks up when he hears my footsteps, a single dark curl falling in front of his brow. His eyes sparkle with understanding as he smiles sadly at me. I almost laugh. Of course, he would know when I plan to do something rash. Hasn't he always known my every move?

I guess you could say we've become close, at least in some ways.

"Adrian's gone," he says, and I look toward the open bedroom door.

"You always knew I'd choose the rash route," I say, meeting his gaze. "Don't try and stop me."

"I won't."

I freeze. Turning to look at him, I ask, "Why?"

He smirks, his autumn-colored earring twinkling in the light. "Let's call it intuition."

And with that, he walks away, leaving me standing alone in front of my door. I watch in confusion as he runs a hand through his curly hair and places his fedora back on his head, whistling as he disappears from my sight.

I scoff. What a suspicious guy.

I've known him for fourteen years, yet I have no idea what's going through his mind. But his unspoken approval somehow makes me believe I'm doing the right thing.

With that thought in mind, I enter my room and lean against the closed door. My thoughts circle back to Adrian. I'm glad he left, but I can't disappear without another word. Even if I'm betraying what it means to be a hunter.

I swallow the lump in my throat. Is this what it feels like to give up on your dreams?

"You must leave now. There will not be a second chance," a different voice rumbles within my mind. Deep and gravelly.

"You're my angels, right? Can I only talk with you sometimes?" I say out loud as I retrieve a pen and a pad of paper.

"Child, we are always here. We are one now," the soft, silvery voice speaks, comforting to the ear like a lullaby.

"I know nothing about you two. Everyone's keeping secrets from me, and I don't even know what angels are with me."

"I am Uriel, the one who is God's light." I pause as I write my note. One of the seven archangels. Her voice is beautiful—warm, and kind—unsurprising for the angel we associate with compassion.

"You're an archangel... Then why are there two of you? I don't understand how this is possible. A human—a hunter—shouldn't even be alive after what happened in those trials," I mumble, my mind going blank as I try to think of what to write to Adrian—how to say goodbye.

"There is much to learn, but you must leave now," the deeper voice speaks. Though his voice is raspy and strained as if unused for a long time, it somehow feels familiar.

"Who are you?"

He's quiet for a moment before he speaks. *"I am called Zerachiel, God's command that has long been forgotten."* I pause again, the hair on the back of my neck bristles. I've never heard of such an angel...

"Am I really doing the right thing?" I ask, distracting myself from the thought.

"No path is right or wrong, but you must act quickly. Hesitation can change the course of your future, whichever path you may choose," Uriel says.

I stare at the piece of paper—my message to Adrian. Holding the ruby necklace out in front of me, I wonder how certain my future is. All I have to do is break this gem, and I'll be gone, taken to the demon Rishu and then brought to Amon. *I so hope he has some real answers...* But even if he doesn't, at least I'll be free.

The setting sun shines through the window, illuminating the glittering ruby. Adrian's face flashes through my mind. *I'm sorry.*

I glance down at the paper to review my note one last time, and my heart sinks as I place it on my bed without a second glance.

I tie my hair up, slide on my leather boots, and quickly pack a bag of essentials to take with me. With the angelic chains it'll be difficult to change but I'll need clothes once I get out of here. Closing my eyes, I gather my courage. My heart races with excitement and fear, adrenaline rushing through me as I drop the gem to the floor.

The lotus tattoo on my chest throbs along with Kioren on my wrist, and I clutch the fabric over my chest, opening my eyes to catch one last look at the setting sun. I lift my boot over the sparkling pendant and take a deep breath; I know there's no turning back.

The ruby crunches beneath my foot.

I'm sorry, Adrian.

14

AMON

R ed mist seeps from the broken shards beneath my foot, hissing as it coils around my legs like a snake climbing my limbs. It winds to my torso, silky threads tightening around me. My heart thuds in my chest, and I don't dare move as it glides over my skin. The mist wraps around my throat before rising over my face and covering my mouth—sucking the air from my lungs. I shut my eyes as I'm completely taken into its hold.

The door creaks open.

I drag open my heavy eyes to see Adrian's shocked face. His amber eyes are wide as he stares at my entrapped figure. I hold his gaze, my heart shattering as he runs toward me, shouting my name in desperation.

His panicked eyes are the last thing I see as I plummet into darkness.

I should have locked my door.

My eyes fly open, and I gasp as I slam down onto hard cement. For a moment, everything seems to stop as dull pain washes through me. Air rushes back into my lungs in one agonizing swoop, and I'm suddenly racked with violent coughs. I roll over

137

and prop myself up on my elbows as the red mist slithers off my limbs and vanishes.

I look around and slowly take in my surroundings. Concrete. Dim flickering lights. *An underground parking garage?* It smells of dampness and car fumes. My nose crinkles. The world sways around me as I try to lift myself from the cool cement, and I fall back down.

A car door slams shut, and my instincts kick in as I jump into a fighting stance. The world spins, but I steady myself, turning to the figure standing beside a black Porsche—the demon from the night of the blood moon. Rishu. His black hair is pushed neatly to one side to match the black suit he wears, top buttons undone. In the dim light, shadows flicker across his sharp, pointed features. A face so unnaturally beautiful that it can only belong to a high-tier demon.

"It really took me to you," I say, lowering my fists. "I must say, I'm a bit surprised."

Metal scrapes against the ground, and I look at my wrists, the angelic chains still attached. Following the trail of glowing links into a square cement pillar, I curse. They didn't break when I came through. The light around the chain pulses as it recovers, soft tugging gradually increasing with each second.

I turn back to the demon standing motionless beside his car. "Listen, we need to get these chains off *now*."

As if finally realizing my predicament, he steps forward. "Well, I suppose I'm obligated to help you." He reaches his hand toward the metal, and it singes his fingertips before he even makes contact. "Angelic metal." He stares at the burned skin—already healing.

My body lurches forward, and I'm pulled to the ground as the chains regain more of their power. I skid along the floor, swinging my legs around to plant my feet. I grab ahold of the chains, my arms straining to keep myself from being sucked into the swirl of darkness waiting to take me back to the estate.

Think, Nova... I look around the garage for anything that could help me. My feet slide on the smooth cement, veins bulging in my arms as I try to hold on. Kioren hums on my wrist, waiting for an order.

"Kioren, break the chains," I yell.

The giant scythe bursts from my wrist, slicing down on the angelic metal. The chains break, swinging wildly into the cement pillar and disappearing along with the dark void they were trying to suck me into. I collapse to the ground, exhausted. Calling Kioren back into the bracelet, I watch as the scythe slithers into the black gem, and the room goes quiet. The pieces of chain still attached to my wrists dissipate into thin air, and I let out a sigh, collapsing onto my back. Breathing heavily, my head spins as my cheeks heat—the fever taking hold again. Why didn't I use Kioren sooner?

Clapping sounds from above, and I look up at the demon standing over me. "I have to say, I'm impressed." He reaches a hand down, and I hesitantly take it. "But let's not waste any more time. Follow me."

Rishu turns around, his Porsche beeping as he locks it. Elevator doors open with a *ding,* and bright lights flood the dim parking lot. I enter after him, wrists throbbing, and gaze bitterly at the angry red marks left by the chains. The doors shut as the demon pushes the button for 107—the top floor.

— Adrian —

She's gone. It was as if death itself had wrapped its claws around her small frame, dragging her into oblivion. I fall to my knees at the spot where Nova had stood. *She's gone.*

Out of the corner of my eye, I notice a glimmer of gold. Reaching over, I scoop up the gold chain and empty pendant lying on the floor, studying it for a moment before sticking it in my pocket to examine it more thoroughly later.

I feel like I'm going to throw up, but I pull myself together. There has to be something, *anything*, I can do. A breeze rolls through the open window, and I hear a piece of paper crinkling on the bed. I stand, snatching the letter.

Adrian,

I'm sorry. I really wanted to believe that I could still have faith in my father. That these chains would vanish, and there would be no more secrets caging me to the estate. Just know, this decision had nothing to do with you. You're still my best friend, that won't ever change, but I can't stay. Not with Darkness looming.

I know it doesn't make any more sense to you than it does to me, but don't trust my father. I said it once, but I'll say it again because there is more than I ever thought possible that he's been hiding from me—from all of us. When I figure out what all of this means, I'll return to you, but please don't come after me.

I'm sorry.
— Nova

The door bursts open, and I crumble the letter into a ball, shoving it in my pocket with the gold necklace.

"Where is she?" Deathly cold eyes lock onto my own. "Where is my daughter?"

My jaw ticks as my teeth grind together. "Something took her. She's gone," I say, choosing my words carefully. What kind of trouble has she gotten herself into now?

For a moment, darkness flares across his harsh features as Lance races into the bedroom.

"Where's Nova?" the hunter says, black curls bouncing as he scans the room.

I shake my head. Where could she have gone? She has to be okay... Michael seems to chuckle in my mind, but the sound is distant with the newly formed bond. Does it have to do with the strange angelic artifact I brought back from my mission? The one I saw Nova wearing on her wrist? It even summoned that monstrous-looking scythe...

Solomon's jaw flexes, blue fire burning in his eyes. "Find her. Whatever you must do, bring her back."

— Nova —

It's silent as the elevator ascends. Although it was my choice to come here, it doesn't mean I trust these demons or this deal. I'm a hunter, an Undivided; I have no intention of switching my loyalties. This arrangement is just a means to an end.

"Nice dress," Rishu says, breaking the heavy silence.

I scowl at the remark. At least he can't see the shredded back, my bag covering the flimsy pieces. Remnants from the all too literal wings that appeared.

He clears his throat. "So tell me," Rishu says, the elevator dinging as we pass the sixty-sixth floor, "what were those chains?"

I stare at my reflection in the shiny metal panel in front of me, belatedly noticing the blood smeared across my forehead. I must have hit my head when I fell. No wonder I'm so dizzy.

He glances over at me, but I stay silent. *Like I'd tell a demon anything.*

He chuckles. "Fine, don't answer. But please, enlighten me as to why you made this decision. I was the only one who didn't think you'd come... But here you are."

I continue to stare ahead silently. A black handkerchief with golden letters *R.N.* embroidered in the corner suddenly appears in front of my face, and I jerk back. "At least wipe the blood off your face before meeting Amon."

Rolling my eyes, I take it from his hand. *How considerate.* Bringing it gently to my head, I carefully wipe away the blood, wincing when I hit the wound. The demon watches curiously as I make slow work of cleaning the cut, but he says nothing more.

Amon, the Grand Marquis of Hell. The one who governs forty infernal legions in Gehenna—the shadowy Hell world demons rule—and is sometimes referred to as a prince. In our records, he's referenced as appearing with features of a wolf and a serpent's tail. I recall that he can also breathe fire. *Wonderful.*

Not a creature I ever thought I'd encounter. Nor one I really want to meet on my own—even if that form is most likely not what he'll show me, considering his status as an S-class. His human form isn't listed in our database, however, so I'm not sure what to expect.

S-class—our categorization for demons beyond high-tier. A title only a few demons outside of the Seven Princes of Hell hold. This tier is given to only the most powerful and notorious demons and fallen angels—the ones who like Earth a little too much. The only being ranked higher is Lucifer himself. An SS-class enemy of the clan—if he even still exists.

I gulp, reining in my growing fear. I don't have enough strength right now to face a fire-breathing wolf-serpent hybrid. My hands tremble, and I hope the demon beside me didn't notice.

The floors tick by slowly, doubt kicking in as we near the ninetieth floor.

I'm not completely insane for coming here, right? I mean, who would stay in a place that chains you up? Then again, I have no idea how this night will end...

I rub my raw wrists.

"Ease your mind, child," Uriel says, and surprisingly, my breathing eases.

The elevator dings as we reach the top floor, and the doors open to a dark hallway. Rishu exits first, and I follow closely behind. My steps are hesitant as we make our way through the darkness, but I'm careful to keep pace, not wanting to lose sight of the demon.

He could have at least turned on a light.

We weave back and forth through the hallways in a labyrinth of twists and turns. Left then right, then right again. It would be easy to get lost here if you didn't know where you were going, especially with the absence of light. The demon doesn't look to see if I'm following him as I struggle to keep up with his long strides.

Passing an open lounge space with floor-to-ceiling windows, I stop without thinking. An entire city is displayed. Towering skyscrapers, lights twinkling in the dark like stars, spanning as far as my eyes can see. I walk toward the glass, mesmerized; my fingertips graze the cool window.

"It's beautiful," I say, my breath fogging up the glass.

The city seems to be filled with life, excitement. I recognize a few landmarks I've seen pictures of in books or on the news. We must be in Chicago, a city bigger than I could ever imagine. Falgens is only a short drive away, but I've never left the town before.

A smile rises to my cheeks. It's safe to say I like the view of being up high.

"We shouldn't keep him waiting," Rishu says, waiting by the entrance of the lounge.

I reluctantly pull myself away from the glass, following behind the demon once more. He winds us through a few more hallways until we reach an imposing wooden door. Hanging at the center is a gold nameplate that reads:

CEO
Marq Otsoa

The demon knocks, opening the door to a large office with a window spanning the entire far wall behind an elegant wooden desk—another stunning city view shining before us. Two plush chairs sit in front of the desk; behind it, a tall black leather chair faces the glass. The room is dark, the sparkling city outside providing the only light.

"My lord, the girl has come."

Fingers snap, and the door behind me shuts as warm light fills the room. The chair swivels around to face us, and I look upon the fearsome Grand Marquis of Hell, *Amon*.

"Silly Rishu, I told you she would come."

My mouth gapes. A little boy sits in the chair, wearing a mini suit. Short pale blond hair and unnaturally pale chubby cheeks. His eyes shine light blue as they look me over, curiosity twinkling in his pearly smile.

I know I'm feverish and probably concussed, but... *Am I going crazy?* This can't be Amon... Maybe his child? The kid, who can't be older than six, jumps off the chair and walks over to stand before me.

He peers up at me with a devilish smile, extending a small chubby hand. "Nice to meet you, Nova. You can call me Amon."

I freeze, every thought I had about Amon vanishing into thin air. How can this kid be the great, mysterious demon lord Amon? Let alone a CEO? Shaking myself out of my confused trance, I reach down to grasp his chubby little fingers.

"Come, take a seat." He smiles widely, heading back to his chair. "We have much to discuss."

I follow him to the desk, hesitantly taking a seat in one of the leather chairs before him. I don't have much experience with kids, but hearing a child talk the way he does is... unsettling.

Amon props his little elbows on the desk, resting his head on his hands as he smiles widely. Rishu stands off to the side in the shadows of the room. I sit still, Amon's staring unnerving. In all my life, I would have never guessed demons to be so... Well, whatever this is.

"Ah, Nova, you're quite a beauty. I see why he—" Amon stops mid-sentence, tilting his head to one side as if considering something. "Anyway, you're here, as I knew you would be. Though it makes me more curious than ever. A hunter joining the demons will surely make history." He throws his arms in the air, falling back into the chair in a fit of giggles.

"I'm not joining the demons. You're just the only one who has offered me what I want," I say, keeping my face cold, serious. The one useful thing I learned from my father.

"Yes, yes, I know. But isn't it exciting?" His eyes glitter as he speaks. "For the first time in hundreds of years, a hunter, an *Undivided*, asking a demon for help. I just *love* it."

"How did you—"

"Know you're an Undivided? Easy, even without seeing those horrible tattoos on your neck, I can *smell* it." Amon giggles. "But I do wonder why you decided to come. Being an Undivided is a stupid honor for you hunters. You don't disrespect it easily. So do tell, my sweet Nova."

I cringe at the pet name, considering if I should say anything at all. "I wasn't going to come... But sometimes you're put into situations that leave you with no other choice." I pause, looking into Amon's eyes. A sense of knowing passes over his face—hidden wisdom beneath those chubby cheeks.

"Does this have to do with the angelic chains?" Rishu asks, and I nod.

"Secrets, lies, betrayal. Humans are so fickle," Amon says, his childish face holding no joy. "But you wouldn't have come unless you believed I have the answers you seek."

"Listen, I don't know what information you have or if it'll be useful to me... I just... I just wanted freedom." My nails dig into my palms. Freedom always comes with a price. "So tell me what you know and your terms. I wasn't born yesterday, and I know this isn't free, but maybe you'll convince me it's worth my time."

Amon claps his hands together, "Free it is not, but some good faith goes a long way. How about some information about the bracelet you wear?"

I look at Kioren, the silver warm against my skin. It hums in response to Amon, a quiet vibration as if saying *listen*.

"The Heavens are looking for it. Why? Well, even I can't speak for the idiots up there. But I do know it chose you. Something both angelic and something that is not—an energy I don't think anyone on Earth can quite explain."

My brows furrow as I recall the research in my father's library—information on having the bracelet destroyed. But if the Heavens are searching for it, why wouldn't my father give it to them? *The consequences you'll bring... And I don't know if I can stop it.* I thought those were pointless words, reminders of my disobedience, but he obviously knows something more.

"My father wanted it destroyed. Do you know why?"

Amon smiles. "The Heavens aren't as kind as you think. Maybe your father is starting to recognize that fact."

I let that thought run through my mind. The Heavens have served us as much as we them. I know my father well enough to know he wouldn't go against them.

"I may not know what the Heavens want, but I can tell you the things you desire to know. Secrets your father hides, the truth about who you are and where you come from. That is, of course, if you agree to my terms."

I hold back from letting my face show anything but strength as nerves buzz through me. His wording is strange... Bait to trap me in his ploy. Amon stares at me with wide blue eyes. He may look like a child, but a dark power radiates beneath that innocent face. This is not someone to mess with.

"Tell me your terms."

He grins. "In the world of demons, there exists such things called cambions, half-demon half-human offspring. Creatures who are lost, alone, abandoned, hurt, afraid, and maybe even guilty. Most of us couldn't care less about them; they're usually never strong enough to survive. But"—he leans his elbows back on the desk, mischievousness returning to his face—"some have unmeasured capability. Though, as they grow, they find themselves at a crossroad. Not human enough to live in society, and not demon enough to survive among us."

I arch a brow. "What do they have to do with me?"

Amon leans back in his chair, looking me up and down, "I want you to train a few of them, six to be exact. To hone their powers and give them the control they lack."

I scoff. "You've got to be kidding me." I'm not training demons, even if they're only half. "Why do you even need them? You're powerful enough on your own, and like you said, demons don't care about them. So why do you?"

An unnerving smile rises to the child's lips, and in that moment, I'm unsure if I want the answer. "Because someone has to."

Amon jumps from his chair, walking over to the window. "Come, stand here with me."

I cautiously rise, glancing at Rishu, who nods silently. Walking over to the window, I stand next to Amon. The vast city glows below us, the view still taking my breath away.

"In this city live both humans and demons, but these cambions cannot live in either world. As they are now, they will be killed. If not by the hunters, then by the lords of Hell themselves."

I take a step back and turn to Amon, surprised by the cruel words. "The demons would kill their own?"

"We will never risk our own lives for the sake of half breeds." He looks at me, his face emotionless.

I search his eyes, trying to wrap my head around what he's asking.

"Then why are you doing this?" I ask.

He smiles, turning back to the view. "Call it a precautionary measure for the future."

His explanation does little to ease my curiosity or explain why he needs these six. "Even so... I'm a hunter. What makes you think I can train demons?"

"Cambions," he corrects. "I'm sure you can figure out a way to help them harness their powers, especially with the right motivation. That is, of course, if you still want answers."

I don't say anything for a long moment, turning instead to gaze out at the city lights. There are pieces I'm still missing—lots of them. A whole story coming together but falling short before I can understand it.

Images from my trials flit through my mind, my head stinging as they pass. Such a simple contract, and maybe I'll figure out what it all means. I wait for the hum from Kioren or a whisper from my angels, or even the wind that seems to come and push me in the right direction whenever I need it—but nothing comes.

"Let me ask just two things."

"You're asking a lot, my sweet Nova, but I will at least listen."

I tear my eyes from the city and meet Amon's gaze. "Darkness and the lotus, what do they mean to you?"

He freezes as my question registers but then hums with amusement. "The darkness is many things... We demons are born from it, but everyone has it living inside them—whether it consumes them or not is dependent on the individual."

I cross my arms and lean back against the window. Not much of an answer, but maybe he doesn't know about the man I call Darkness. After all, he only appeared in my mind.

"As for the lotus, it's a flower that blooms from adversity to share its beauty with the surface. One who perseveres, much like yourself." Amon stares for a moment, eyes narrowing slightly. "Though I suppose only time will tell if you'll have the strength to emerge from the blackened waters holding you captive."

My mouth goes dry. *Blackened waters.* His words are so carefully chosen. Another trap, another piece of bait.

If I choose to do this, I'm turning my back on the hunter's code, on the life I've always desired. Adrian's face pops into my mind, his amber eyes filled with fear as he watched me vanish from my room...

I shake the image. *Do what you must* is what Lance said. Closing my eyes, I brush away the pain, the regret, the dream of becoming a recognized hunter within the clan and fighting as Adrian's equal. When it's all gone, I meet Amon's all-too-knowing gaze once more—resolution setting in.

"I'll do it. But I have my own conditions to add." The words feel foreign on my lips. A devilish grin makes its way back onto Amon's face, and I wonder if this is the right move after all.

"Then we have an agreement."

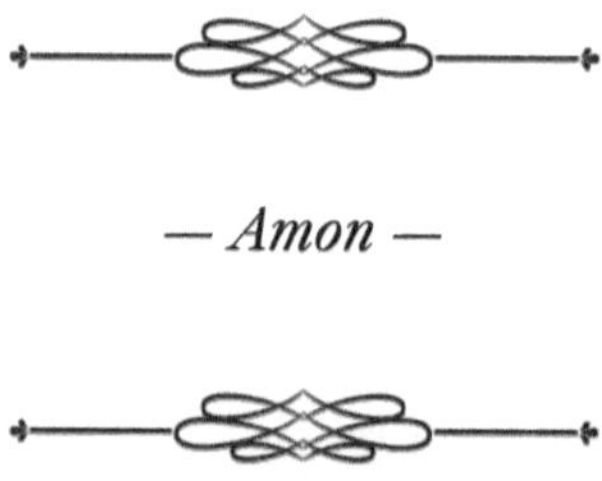

— Amon —

A contract is signed, a means to an end for both myself and Nova. And time waits like dominoes lined up in a long row—the catalyst already falling toward the next piece. It's a butterfly effect of events long since determined yet still uncertain.

I tsk at the annoyance of being unable to see Nova's future clearly. Her unpredictability is alarming in a way I'm unaccustomed to, challenging my well-honed abilities as I maneuver the pieces around the board.

"Nova's in a room resting," Rishu says as he returns to the office.

I nod, rhythmically tapping my fingers on the desk. The fatigue and strain on her body was as clear as day despite how strong she tried to seem. It would be laughable had I not known what she had already endured and what is to come. The ticking sound of her fate echoes at a distance, mocking me for the destiny I cannot fully see.

Standing, I peer down at the glittering city. It's time to forgo this charade.

Bones crack, and my skin tears as I morph out of the childlike body and into my preferred form. I rise in height, white-blond hair growing long down my sculpted naked back. The nails on my fingers turn black and sharp, a hint of the lupine claws hidden within. My ears elongate into slightly pointed tips as I sigh out a breath of fire—the transition complete.

Eyes the color of fresh blood stare back at me from my reflection in the window. I stretch my muscles and smile, relishing this gorgeous form. Pulling my waist-long hair over my shoulder, I turn to Rishu. The demon places a black silk robe over my shoulders, gathering the discarded children's clothes at my feet.

"My lord, if I may ask, why show her that appearance?" Rishu says from behind in a slight bow, not raising his head to speak.

"Don't you think it's amusing? They're so easy to manipulate."

A black shadow steps out from the darkness, moving forward into the faint glow from the city lights. I tilt my head to the figure, a grin rising on my lips. Two birds with one stone, I achieved everyone's desire in a single blow.

"My king," Rishu says, turning and deepening his bow to the shadowed figure.

"As agreed upon, she will be by your side, and you will fight for me," I say as I turn back to look at my city. "There's a war coming. Things of the past and what is yet to come—the lines are blurring. It will be different from all the wars before... even if Solomon is once again involved." I pause as a vision of both the past and the future spreads across my mind. A war I need to prevent, the ones we've already faced that led us here. "My king, just how precious is Nova to you? For I sense death close to her soul, a darkness peering in. Her fate is shrouded unlike any I've seen before...." I smirk as shadows dance across the floor; the king is displeased. "Tell me, is the girl more than what you've let on?"

"Do not concern yourself with idle questions. Keep your bargain with her, and I will handle everything else." The low, commanding voice rings out through the room. Surprisingly soft yet still radiating with immense power.

"Yes, my king." I grin as the king disappears back into the shadows of the room.

The game my king is playing is a dangerous one. With Nova by his side, the gears of fate will move faster. With all players stepping onto the board, it's only a matter of time until the past comes crashing down on them both. The red string of fate connecting them, ready to go taut and snap. So obvious, so painful to watch.

"Rishu, make the necessary preparations to satisfy Nova's conditions. We cannot waste any more time."

Rishu bows once more, vanishing from the room in a cloud of smoke. I'm left alone in the dark office with only my thoughts and visions to accompany me. They dance behind my eyes, taunting me with fragments I can't quite understand. The shadows of something beyond human or demon. Golden hair. Black eyes. Darkness.

I consider the word—the question the girl asked me. The way she said it, like the name of Death itself... Unease curls in my stomach despite the hope of everything finally aligning. I have the king, the five, and now Nova. Everything should feel right... But what am I missing?

A sigh escapes my lips, and I frown, crossing my arms. There is no room for failure in this game against destiny. No matter what, my king *cannot* hold back.

"What does the lotus mean to me..." my voice trails off, recalling the other odd question asked by the girl. "I suppose I have yet to find the whole truth of it myself."

15

IN THE FACE OF THE ENEMY

"Take this." Rishu pulls a necklace out of his pocket as we stand beside his car in the parking garage. "The properties of this gem will hide those horrid tattoos." I scowl, but he doesn't give me a chance to retort. "As long as you wear this, no one will see them."

He hands me the necklace, and I clasp it around my neck, lifting the gem to admire the inlaid lines of red and orange on the brown stone—like an autumn forest floor. "What about the smell Amon talked about? If they can sense it, isn't this pointless?"

"My lord is far stronger than these cambions. They most likely won't notice."

"Most likely?"

He smirks, opening the passenger door for me. My scowl deepens as I climb in. Rishu closes my door and walks around the car, entering the driver's side. "Now, young miss, we've kept them waiting long enough by letting you rest. How inconvenient that humans need sleep." He clicks his tongue, turning the car on with a push of a button.

"Geez, sorry to disappoint with my human tendencies." I sink into my seat. "So do I get some sort of cover? They're going to question this random human showing up to train them with zero background."

Rishu looks deep in thought as we pull out of the underground. Bright light blinds me for a moment. A sly grin slides across his face. "What about a human injected with demonic power?" My eyebrows raise, unamused. "Fine, maybe not that."

I sigh, looking out at the magnificent city around us. "Have they ever heard of the Undivided? If not, then maybe I can just be a human that is, well, *other*..." The lotus tattoo on my chest warms; my hand itches to touch it. It's far enough from the truth without being a complete lie. Something about me *is* other, even if I don't understand why or what that means.

"Other... It doesn't have a bad ring to it."

I look over at him, his eyes trained on the road ahead. He's handsome, his face deceptively young but sharp—ancient power radiating off his bronzed skin. Sly like a fox. I wonder what type of demon he is to be so powerful yet still subservient to Amon.

"The place we're going, I hope it isn't easy to find. My father will already be looking for me." I'm struck again with the image of Adrian's panicked eyes, his hand outstretched to me. I consider the letter I left behind. "They already know I'm gone."

Rishu snorts. "The hunters won't find us."

The car grows quiet. People and places pass in a blur, lives I wanted to protect from the very being I just signed a contract with. My heart squeezes, and I look at my hands, at the healing red abrasions around my wrists.

"Have you met them? The cambions." I fill the silence with the question, avoiding the window.

"I was the one to bring them all together."

I look at him, more questions brimming. "Then you know their powers?" He doesn't say anything. "Do you think they'll be able to harness them?"

He sighs. "Young miss, it is not my place to speculate."

I frown but drop the questions.

"You know, you can stop calling me young miss already. Call me Nova."

A devilish smirk, befitting for the demon, rises to his lips. "Then, Nova, I need you to take a little rest." His hand fills with black smoke, and before I can open my mouth to ask what he's doing, the smoke shoots across the car and over my eyes. All I see is darkness as I begin to fade from consciousness...

Damn demons.

Blinking my eyes open, I awake in an unknown room, laying on top of ivory bedsheets. Flowing white drapes hang from the four-post bed frame above me, billowing softly as a breeze blows through the open balcony doors of sparkling colored glass. The wind circles me as if urging me to get up and move.

The high walls are painted a light sage green; wide planks of polished dark wood line the floors. Three of the walls feature closed wooden doors of the same color. Curious, I stand from the bed and tiptoe to peek inside each door.

The first leads to a long carpeted hallway, but I decide to leave further exploration for later.

Opening the next door, my jaw drops. The walk-in closet before me is massive, filled with clothing, gear, and an impressive arsenal of weapons. I rush to the wall of blades prepared for my delight. I pick up a long dagger, marveling at the exquisite craftsmanship. It's not angelic metal, but I suppose they wouldn't want me to have something like that here. Setting the dagger back on the shelf, I glance at the racks of clothes.

My hands go to my hips as I take it all in, wondering when I'll need half the things here. As much as I love pretty clothes, I'm here to train the cambions, not walk a fashion show. Still, I should be grateful Amon has done this much. I was expecting to have to remind him that I have nothing but the single bag I brought.

Leaving the treasure trove of a closet after a quick change, I open the last door and step into a large bathroom. Gleaming black-and-white checkered marble tiles cover the floor. A large vanity with pale cabinetry and a walk-in shower with glass walls and elegant black tiles take up most of one side of the room, and an obsidian clawfoot tub big enough for two sits at the other. I close the door and leave, even though I'm tempted to draw a bath and wash away the grime from the last couple days, not to mention the sweat from the fever that finally broke last night.

A fresh, flowery scent wafts to my nose as another breeze slithers through the room. I follow it to the open balcony doors. As I step out into the warm sunlight, I take in the vast forest stretching out from the edge of the property, seemingly extending for miles. *Where are we?*

I lean against the tan stone railing, admiring the garden below. It blooms in a vibrant array of colorful flowers, soft petals, and leaves swishing gently together. A large fountain sits in the center, and I smile as I watch the birds playing in the spouting water. I breathe in deeply, basking in the feeling of fresh air filling my lungs.

"Jump down," Uriel's voice rings in my mind. *"The demon will come for you soon."*

Nodding, I hop over the railing, landing easily on the stone pathway. "Is this your doing?" I ask out loud, careful to keep my voice low so I'm not overheard. She hums in response. I feel her power brimming beneath my skin, a tingling sensation I haven't quite gotten used to. We were always told the Undivided become stronger—it only makes sense when a literal angel bonds with your soul—but I wonder what else they couldn't tell us before, what secrets are left to be discovered now that I've become one of them. I shake away the thought. Uriel and Zerachiel can fill me in on the details later.

I walk toward the first flower beds, brushing my fingers over the colorful flowers. I'm here for the cambions, yet I'll also need to train if I ever want to become a strong Undivided. My skin tingles with awareness; someone is watching from a distance. Circling the fountain, I revel in the feeling of the warm sun on my skin, the sweet smell of the flowers, the cool spray of the water, and the delicate touch of the breeze. Everything seems brighter, more beautiful now that I'm finally free.

As I complete my leisurely stroll around the fountain, my eyes go wide. A giant castle-like manor, far grander than the Fandera Estate, rises high above me as if lifted straight out of a European fairy tale. The manor is shaped like a U, with the middle section rising up four stories, while the wings, which wrap around the garden, rise to only two. The imposing walls are built in a pale tan stone, and a pointed gray roof rests over the top. Tall glass windows—some artfully speckled with colored glass like my balcony door—line each floor, beautiful stone carvings etched around each pane. Shadows move inside, but I choose to ignore them for now.

Soft steps sound behind me, approaching slowly as if to not startle me. "I see you're making use of your *other* abilities." I turn to Rishu. "But was it necessary to jump from your balcony?"

I chuckle. "It's a habit." The memory of my almost escape that sunny day snags my heart. Had I stayed, Lance probably wouldn't have known what to do with me anymore.

Rishu raises a brow, changing the topic. "So, what do you think? Is this place suitable enough for the young miss?"

I roll my eyes. "Don't be so pretentious. I told you to call me Nova." A shadow on the third floor moves to another window, and I watch from my peripheral vision. "But yeah, wow. It's... it's more than I expected. I guess Amon really cares about these cambions." My shoulders tense. As long as this place doesn't turn into another prison, I don't care how nice it is or how much Amon provides for us. I look at Rishu, plastering on a smile. "But was it really necessary to knock me out?"

Rishu shrugs. "Would you believe me if I said it was for your safety? If it makes you feel any better, I did the same to the others. This was a part of the contract you asked for." A twinkle flashes in his eyes.

I cross my arms. "A heads up would have been nice. I get that this is to make sure no one can find us but doesn't this place stand out too much?"

"Amon's power protects the Moonlit Château. A barrier separates us from the outside world, so no one can even see that this place exists."

I hold his gaze, searching for a trick. If a barrier has been placed, it means we're also trapped inside. "So he's done what I asked, now he just has to stay true to my last condition. I won't wait forever for answers." Shifting my gaze to the window, I smile. "Now, I suppose I should meet my admirers."

"You noticed," Rishu says, following my gaze. "They've been watching since you landed in the garden."

I smirk at the demon. "If I was so oblivious, do you think Amon would want me to train them? I may have other ideas about *demons*, but I'm not an idiot. I've trained far too much not to notice."

He shifts uncomfortably but says nothing. His arms cross, the partially undone button-up he wears creasing around solid arms.

I meet his gaze, letting out a sigh. "The night of the blood moon, I escaped and was reckless. I had nothing but this"—I gesture to Kioren—"which I didn't even know would work, and a single dagger. Plus, as you know, I'm much stronger now." He remains silent, so I continue. "Training and fighting is the only thing I've ever known. And even though I wish these cambions weren't standing in the way of my answers, I won't fail to follow through on our agreement." I walk past him, looking to the third floor. Who knew Amon had a flair for French aesthetics? *Maybe we really are in Europe...*

"I know better than to doubt Amon. You are indeed something that is *other*." He draws out his last word, and a shiver runs down my spine.

I give him a final side-eye before examining the stone siding of the château. I measure the distance between the crevices as I say to my angels, *"Should we have some reckless fun?"* Uriel hums in response, her power tingling stronger. A wide grin spreads across my face.

I sprint to one of the inner corners of the building, where the center and east wings meet. Jumping up, I grab ahold of a stone carving jutting from the wall and use my momentum to quickly pull myself up. The corner the perfect place for climbing, and I use the stone ledges and carvings to propel myself up the wall. I feel the power of Uriel rush through me, like a buzz of energy sizzling beneath my skin—making me faster, stronger. I mentally thank her for the help while wondering what

Zerachiel's power feels like—his silence is strange when I can still feel his presence.

I reach the third level with one last jump, landing on a wide windowsill. A small shadow watches from inside, shifting back from the window as I approach. Adrenaline pumps through my body, and my heartbeat rings in my ears. Pushing the glass pane aside, I smile at the young, wide-eyed girl.

"See something interesting?" I ask her. She looks so human with her dark skin and flopping black pigtails. Only a hunter would recognize the power lurking in those stormy gray eyes. A gentle reminder of what I've gotten myself into.

Let's just hope it pays off.

"How did you...." Her voice sounds small as she steps farther back into the large living space. "Aren't you human?"

I step down from the windowsill. "Yes and no," I say, examining each cambion.

Lounging on a red velvet couch in the center of the room, a pale boy with thick brown hair and strong, arrogant features doesn't bother looking my way. He's dressed in a simple cotton shirt and jeans, and he tosses a ball into the air repeatedly, disinterest written across his face. In the chair beside him, a girl with elfin features glares at me with fire blazing in her eyes. Her short brown hair swishes as she looks me over, and I notice the ends of her hair have been tinted black as if singed with soot. On the wooden armrest of her chair, a tall boy with skin like night and a delicate nonchalance about him winds a leafy green vine around his body. Curly black hair is cut close to his head, dark brown eyes calculating my every move.

At the other end of the room, a girl with long straight black hair stands with her arms crossed, face pursed in annoyance. She flicks her head away from me, tension radiating from each movement. I move my eyes past her to the last cambion, who seems to also be of Asian descent, possibly Korean. He leans against a dark corner of the room, his posture rigid as dark strands fall in front of his eyes. The shadows seem to embrace him, wrapping around his body and falling gently across his face, sharpening his angular features. He stares back at me with an intensity that makes me shiver. Something about him feels dangerous, yet there's a softness in how he looks at me. I hold his gaze for a little too long, drawn to him like a moth to a flame.

Rishu poofs into the room in a cloud of black smoke, and I quickly look away from the last cambion, reining in my features. "It seems everyone's met each other," Rishu says calmly as he walks to the center of the room.

He stops in front of the cute girl with pigtails, who must be the youngest here. A faint trace of a smile appears on his face before flickering away. I make a mental note of the interaction.

"I wouldn't go that far," the pale boy reclining on the couch says with a light accent I can't quite place. Italian maybe?

"Then I'll start," I say to the group—ignoring the pounding of my heart. The fear I won't let myself feel. "My name's Nova. I'm sure you've been told why I'm here, so I'll cut to the chase. Amon has assigned me to help train you, to hone your powers." And this is simply a means to an end for me, though they'll never have to know that.

Something touches my ankle, and I jerk my foot back, looking down to find leafy tendrils grazing my exposed skin. *"Human."* I follow the path of the vine as it recedes from around my ankle and wraps back around its owner. His dark eyes rise to meet mine, narrowing his brows as he sneers.

"A human is supposed to train us?" asks the fae-like girl sitting in the chair he rests on. She crosses her arms in front of her, leaning back in her seat. "Amon has to be joking."

I go to speak, but Rishu beats me to it. "Nova is more capable than you think." He throws a wink my way. I cringe but try not to let it show on my face.

Nobody responds to his comment. Kioren vibrates on my wrist—a reassuring presence amid the hostility saturating the room. They're not unlike the first-years I trained with—doubtful of my abilities and eager to pick a fight.

Rishu sighs as he rubs his temple. "No matter. You're all just going to have to deal with her, so—"

A ball of fire blazes toward me, and I dodge without thinking a split second before it slams into the wall behind me. My eyes slide from Rishu to the flames climbing the heavy curtains. Fire crackles and I spin to face the source.

This time I'm not fast enough, and a ball of fire slams into my body. Crossing my arms, I crash backward through the open window. The flames shatter the glass, raining sharp pieces around me as I fall the three stories to the garden below. My stomach sinks, but Uriel's power surges through me, and I flip midair, the fire dispersing as I land with a slight wobble but otherwise steady footing. *"Thanks, Uriel,"* I say quickly in my mind. No human could survive a fall like that.

Looking up at the broken window, I watch as my attacker jumps down, and I raise my arm as more pieces of glass scatter around me. *Maybe Theo's surprise knife attack wasn't so bad after all...*

"What gives you the right to think you can train us?" I meet her gaze and realize the fire I saw burning behind her eyes was a very literal representation of her powers. Pyrokinesis, *great.*

Above, the other cambions peer out the windows—watching not only the fight but what I might say and do. To them, I'm just a simple human tasked with training them. If I were in their position, I wouldn't trust me either.

"Only that I'm me?" I smirk, and flames burst from her palms.

She yells, running straight at me. Raising my fists, I wait until she nears before faking to her left. Her right side opens, and I grin—she's untrained in hand-to-hand combat. I land a swift kick to her ribcage, and she flies to the other end of the garden. Skidding to a halt, her eyes raise to mine as she bares her teeth, seething with anger. My eyes widen as I look from my foot to how far it sent her. *"Was that you, Uriel?"* A chuckle echoes in my mind.

Fire crackles at the girl's fists as she stomps toward me. Rubble falls, and I look back to the broken window where the young girl with pigtails peers down with a mischievous grin. Refocusing on my opponent, my hands clench tighter as I slide my foot back to brace myself for more balls of fire.

The girl punches flames at me as if she's realized she can't beat me with her fists. I make note of her quick thinking. Dancing careful steps around her, I maneuver to avoid the licking flames. The heat coming off her is intense, but I move in closer with each step. Kioren vibrates on my wrist, begging to be let out to play.

"I've said this before to someone," I say, ducking under another fireball, "anger is not the way to win a fight."

Her eyes widen when I suddenly appear right next to her. Dropping low to the ground, I sweep her feet out from under her before she can react. The flames puff and disappear as she lands with a thud.

"I will give you credit for moving me to defense like that."

She bangs her fist on the ground with a frustrated scream. Flaming eyes rise to mine, and I take a step back. Her tan skin burns red as fire threatens to bubble out from beneath the surface. She stands from the ground, her moves quicker than before as she throws stronger but uncoordinated punches. I dodge and block, feeling my shirt sleeves singe as her fists graze past me.

If things keep going like this—

Something small hits my head, and I look to where it landed on the ground. *Is that a grape?* I whip my head back to the window again to see the girl with the pigtails shoving a small grape into her mouth.

"You're only human!" A fireball speeds past me in my distraction.

Focusing on the flaming cambion again, I land a kick to her gut—the contact almost enough to burn me. "Be careful judging a book by its cover. I may be human, but I'm also something *other.*"

Her flames sputter, but when her eyes meet mine once more—it isn't the girl with the flames I'm staring at but the powerful, rageful demon encased inside her human form. The flames around her burst high into the sky, and I jump back to avoid the heat. But even from a greater distance, they threaten to burn my skin.

Kioren vibrates with urgency. I clasp my hand around the silver bracelet, hoping to calm it. *"It isn't time for you."*

The girl's flames recede to encase her body—the human part of her seemingly lost. My stomach turns.

She races forward faster than I have time to react. A flaming hand wraps around my arm, and a knee slams into my stomach. I gasp for breath. I can't be weak, not here, *not ever.* The flames lick at my skin, and I feel a deep ache throughout my body as she takes my strength and turns it into hers.

"Focus our energy," I hear the gravelly voice of Zerachiel say within my head. The first time I've heard him since I left my old life behind. *"Douse her flames."*

Tingling energy sparks at my fingertips. Zerachiel's energy is different from Uriel's. But while I expected it to feel heavy, his energy is actually like a breath of fresh air—like the wind rushing by.

I focus on the feeling, time seeming to slow as the power grows around my fist.

She surges forward with another punch, but I swerve, sending all the strength in my fist into her stomach. I watch the air leave her lips, the flames in her eyes sputtering along with the rest around her body. She drops to the ground, coughing. Her hand remains fisted at her side, but the fire is dispersed, unwilling to come to her aid again.

Despite the hits I've taken, the pain is nowhere near what it should be—a perk of being an Undivided—and I hobble over to her. "Are we done?"

"What are you?" Her voice is but a whisper—the fire and rage from before gone with the flames.

"Like I said, I may be human, but I'm also something more," I say with a shrug, internally debating whether or not I should help her up. "If anyone should understand what it is to be *other*, it's you all." I turn from her, looking at the others jumping down to join us. "So you'll just have to deal with a mostly human training you."

I clasp a hand over my arm—the fabric burned, my skin sore to the touch. But the wound is healing rapidly.

"You're strong for a human." The girl stands, wiping the dirt from her black cargo pants. She's about my height—maybe a little taller—and her body is lean and wiry. There's a subtle twang in the way she says *human*, a bit of that spark still shining through.

"What's your name?" I ask her.

She looks me over uneasily. "Azura."

"Okay, Azura. Now that I've seen what you're capable of, we have some things to work on. Starting with your form. It sucks." The thought turns my stomach, but I keep my voice light. Making them stronger, teaching them control... The things they can do even without my help is enough to make me sick. *So much for my hunter past.*

She nods, keeping her distance as I turn to the others. "Anyone else want to introduce themselves?" Their faces flash with mixed emotions—impressed, wary, and maybe even a little fearful. I let go of my arm, revealing the visibly healing skin beneath. A few release small gasps, their attention on something that should be impossible for humans.

Their features are clearer in the daylight. All six are so different, but they're all so intangibly beautiful; it's almost surreal.

"Human," the boy with the vine says. Long dark fingers play with the green strand as he shifts back, recoiling as he assesses me. "You may call me Tevari." The vine coils around his body. A protective feeling radiates from it, reminding me of Kioren's black tendrils.

I nod to him, cautious to start any more fights.

My gaze shifts to the girl with long black hair, just shorter than I am, standing beside Tevari. Her expression is tight, lips pursed in disgust like Tevari's. But her eyes... The tapered shape widens in careful observation, revealing the swirling violet irises within. She crosses her arms, and I notice she's wearing long sleeves even on this hot summer day. "Lei Jing," she says as if I forced it out of her.

"Ignore her," the pale, lanky boy with Roman features says, shoving an exasperated Lei Jing out of the way with a dramatic shift in his demeanor. "I'm Oliver, and I must say I am *thoroughly* impressed with your fighting skills." He smirks as he takes my free hand in his, towering over me. I quickly pull back—an uncomfortable smile on my face.

"And I'm Meena," the girl with pigtails says, popping out from behind Oliver.

I regard her carefully, recalling the mischievous grin she sent my way after throwing a grape at me. The girl waves a small hand, smiling with all her teeth. She must be the youngest of the group, maybe thirteen or fourteen. A gentle smile comes to my lips as I watch her, giving her a small wave back. Her joyful demeanor is infectious even with the hostile atmosphere—and foul play.

Like before, the last cambion stands apart from the rest of the group, somehow having found another shadow to hide in despite the hot afternoon sun. I wait for him to approach, an unusual shyness coming over me, making me uneasy yet curious. He steps into the sunlight, and I can see doubt reflecting in his sharp eyes. It's a cold stare. Mesmerizing.

He reaches his hand out to meet mine, and I'm momentarily distracted by the many rings on his fingers, bejeweled as if to serve some meaning. Two rings stand out, my eyes lingering on them. They're a matching set of gold bands with green gems—the only gold among the other silver jewelry. One sits on his ring finger and the other on his pinky.

I hesitate for a moment before grasping his hand. A spark shoots up my arm when we touch, and my eyes dart to meet his. His face is calm—a single silver earring twinkling in the breeze. His skin glows in the soft sunlight; a few strands of his black hair falls in front of his eyes. Bright silver irises seem to study my face, and I squirm. A dark power—more dangerous than any of the other cambions'—prowls beneath the quiet calm he wears.

"Luka," he says, his voice deep but quiet, sweet like honey, with a slight accent I'm unable to place. "My name is Luka."

I nod softly, forcing my hand to let go. He's dangerous, yet somehow... I look at my hand, the shock still tingling my skin. Maybe it was my imagination.

"It's nice to meet all of you." I dare one last glance at Luka, the lotus tattoo on my chest throbbing. "I hope we all get along."

They remain quiet, and an awkward silence grows between us.

Rishu steps forward, clapping his hands together. "How about lunch?"

16

DISTRUST

My skin tingles as I trace over the red burns on my arms. It's only been an hour, yet the wounds are fading faster than I expected. They prick like bee stings, the sensation more uncomfortable than painful.

With a long sigh, I stand from the bed—ivory bed sheets wrinkled where I sat. No one stuck around after Azura's battle, especially not for lunch. I head to the bathroom in search of a medical wrap, hoping Amon would have prepared the basics for a human, considering everything else he's done. Finding what I'm looking for in one of the cabinets, I turn to leave the bathroom but catch my reflection in the mirror.

I don't look nearly as tired as before—the fever from my trials long gone as the two angels settle within my body. Staring at the spot over my chest, I can't help but pull my collar down to see the fine red lines of the lotus tattoo.

Seven petals, the lines overlapping delicately as if it is more of a decoration than a brand on my skin. The black vines I saw during my trials are nowhere to be seen, and I breathe a sigh of relief. How can I train the cambions when all I can think about is this? I draw a finger over the design before letting my collar go.

"Do you guys know anything?" I ask my angels out loud as I leave the bathroom.

It's quiet for a moment before I hear Uriel's clear voice. *"If words could be spoken, fate would be much easier than the reality of what it is."*

I frown. "So what you're saying is, you can't tell me anything?"

She doesn't respond. I let out a huff, taking a seat back on the bed to carefully tend to the burns. They're healing quickly, but there's no reason not to help the process.

A knock sounds at my door, and I hesitantly call out to invite whoever it is in.

"I was getting worried Azura would win," Rishu says as he enters the room, "but you didn't disappoint."

I focus on wrapping my wounds, only glancing up as he comes closer. "She's strong," I say, my words clipped. He stays quiet for once, the silence forcing my eyes to fully meet his. I grimace at the smirk resting on his lips. "What is it?"

"I came to check on your wounds," he says in his annoyingly seductive voice, stalking forward as if I were prey. He leans in, black curls falling in his face. "Azura may only be half-demon, but you're still *mostly* human." His fingers reach toward the bandages, but I stand and step away.

"I'm fine," I say, watching as he retracts his hand.

His face purses in annoyance. "I'll be killed if your employer finds out I didn't treat your wounds. Let me look."

There's a desperation in his voice that I can only gawk at, wondering where it came from. *Employer.* Said as if Amon weren't his lord, the one he obeys. My stomach turns, the lunch I ate alone spoiled.

I roll my eyes, moving my arm closer to him, the bandages unraveling. "See? I told you I'm fine."

His cool fingers graze over my exposed skin, and I almost flinch. "Incredible, it must be your—" He cuts himself short. His eyes remain on the healing wound before rising again to meet mine. "Still, there is a salve for demonic wounds in your closet. Put that on before wrapping it."

"How did you get your hands on demonic salve?" Only healers of the clan know how to make it.

The mischievous grin he seems to always wear returns. "We have our ways," he says, "which makes my job much easier. I can leave knowing you have things handled. Amon's servants will be around to manage the household, but I doubt even you will notice them."

I step toward the receding demon. "Wait, what do you mean leave?"

"This château is now yours to run. Good luck, Nova," he says before vanishing in a cloud of black smoke.

My jaw drops to the ground as I stare at the empty spot on the antique rug where he stood only a moment ago.

"He can't be serious," I say, but I know it's not a petty demon trick. He's really gone.

Taking a deep breath, I try to cool my anger. It hasn't even been a day, and I'm left to take care of everything? *Damn demons.* Always a forgotten clause, a trick you don't notice.

Uriel's laughter fills my mind, and I frown. She's not the one who has to deal with this on her own. With a long sigh, I settle on a cool shower and head into the luxurious bathroom. I should clean up after that brawl with Azura, change these torn clothes... Sifting through the multitude of scented soaps, I pick my favorite—lavender, to calm my nerves. My shower is quick as

I finally wash away all the filth I've accumulated since my angelic trials.

It's only been a day. One day since everything changed.

I stare down at my body, taking in the scars that litter my skin—the night of the blood moon just adding to my vast collection. My father, Lance, they were never gentle with my training. I fought so hard to prove myself, but none of the scars I earned were ever enough.

I frown as I look at my wrists. And now, these—the ones left behind where the angelic chains cut into my skin. Uriel and Zerachiel can't seem to speed along the healing; the skin is still red. Maybe because it was caused by an angelic artifact. Maybe it's to remind me why I left in the first place.

I don't loiter longer in the bathroom, drying quickly and dressing in loose jeans and a white t-shirt, slipping on a pair of sneakers. Soft humming floats to my ears through the open doors of my balcony, and I walk toward the sound. Peering over the railing, I see the source in the center of the garden.

Tevari. His elegant features are well suited to the flowers swaying around him in the breeze. He hums softly as he flips through the pages of a book, unbothered, as the cicadas buzz around him.

I watch from the balcony. He didn't seem fond of me earlier. The way he said *human* all too telling of his experiences with us.

My eyes scrunch as I peer closer at the flowers down below. They seem to dance to the tune of his song. He shifts in his seat on a bench, the garden swaying with him—desperate to draw nearer.

It's a beautiful scene. Unfamiliar to me in many ways.

The garden at the estate was never like this. Nobody ever enjoyed it as he seems to. So peaceful and at home with the plants and flowers at his side. He must have chlorokinetic abilities if they react as such around him.

Jumping over the railing, I land on the stone walkway. He doesn't lower his book, casually flipping to the next page as I approach. The flowers beside him seem to watch me carefully, questioning if I'm friend or foe.

"Is that necessary?" The vine around Tevari moves ever so slowly around his tall frame.

"Rishu asked me the same thing." I chuckle, hoping to break the awkward tension between us. "Maybe not, but it is faster. This place is huge."

He looks up, and my mouth parts as I stare into his eyes, which shine like pure liquid gold in the sunlight. Weren't they so dark they were nearly black earlier? His golden gaze reminds me of the woman from my vision—the one who showed me how to use Kioren.

I hold back from spreading my hand over the lotus tattoo on my chest.

"I'm curious," he says, putting his book aside, "why choose you? You beat Azura, but she's not as strong as she thinks. Your life force, though... It's different from a human."

I feel something brush against the back of my hand and look down at his vine lightly touching my exposed skin. "And I'm curious about this vine of yours."

"Avoiding the question." The vine shoots to my throat, curling tightly around my neck. Tears form in my eyes, but I don't reach to pull it away. "Whatever you are, remember who you're dealing with."

"So you can control it?" I smirk at him, speaking through tight breaths. "I'm getting to know you more and more by the minute." Its grip tightens, squeezing around my throat.

"I can't tell if you're arrogant or just unafraid of death." The vine releases its hold, returning to his side. I sag a little, air rushing back in. "I'd suggest you keep your distance. You're not the first one to try and *tame* us."

I can't hold back the choked laughter that comes out. "Tame you?" I stand straight, a smile cracking on my lips. "I honestly couldn't care less about you. I was given a job, and I plan on going through with it. What happens after... Well, like I said, I don't care." I rub my throat, a trace of the pain lingering.

"So you say now, but humans are all the same."

"And I could say the same about demons, but here I am."

Silence thickens as we enter into a staring contest. Anger and sadness seem to churn in his golden eyes. His distrust is so evident in his posture. Confident, but only to a certain point. A subtle shift back to create distance. Stoic and stern—forcing himself to remain solid and whole in front of the enemy. It's all too familiar.

"Look, we're both something other. You're not completely demon, and I'm not entirely human." He doesn't look convinced. "Give me one day to prove I can train you. And if you still don't like me, I won't bother you again."

He stares at me, amusement replacing his previously grim demeanor. "You truly are arrogant. But I can agree to those terms."

"Good." I extend my hand, which he hesitantly takes. "Meet me here tomorrow at dawn."

— Adrian —

The clan's been in an uproar all day and night. The first seventy-two hours are the most crucial if we stand a chance at finding Nova. Any clue of who took her, how they got within the estate's angelic barrier, or where she might be will decide our direction and her own fate.

I run my hands through my hair, coming up short on answers.

The broken necklace was the only thing left behind. Made from a simple gold chain, the pendant was empty with no residue of what rested inside. It's the only thing we've been able to guess at. That whatever gem had been within was the thing that took her from the estate. Whether it was by force or her own volition—they don't know.

The letter she left weighs heavy in my pocket. I have to trust Nova on at least one thing she wrote—not trusting Solomon. Especially after seeing that angelic artifact on her wrist. Solomon wouldn't have spent years searching for it for nothing. Not going after her, however... Well, she will just have to deal with me ignoring that part after I bring her home.

"Adrian." I hear Cain's voice as he approaches from behind, his steps noticeable only because he wants them to be. He's a shadow in the room—dark hair and eyes contributing to the effect. I turn to him, the others of my cadre on their own separate hunts tonight.

"Did you find anything?" I ask him.

Cain extends his gloved hand, placing something wrapped in cloth on the table in front of me. He moves back, letting me unravel the fabric. My nose crinkles at the overwhelming stench.

"Flesh of a hellhound," Cain says as I examine the piece he brought back. "No team reported being in that area—probably why she chose it."

I poke at the ash-like substance beside the flesh. "And this?"

Cain barely moves as he says, "I've never seen anything like it."

Another dead end.

"But,"—the hunter starts, and I turn to him. Shadows pass over Cain's face, his dark eyes flaring with fatal precision—"its residue is hellhound." Meaning at least two hellhounds were killed, and in two different ways. Whether it was all Nova or someone else alongside her... "Demonic residue was found on the hellhound's flesh. Serpentine poison. Possibly from a lamia or a naga."

Lamia... Naga... It's not impossible, but this territory is far from their usual hunting grounds. Lamias go after children, which fits with the child we found, but this attack was on a hellhound. As for a naga... Semi-divine, semi-demonic, some even worship them in Southeast Asia. I almost scoff at the thought. They're merely another breed of demon, nothing more.

Still, it's hard to say why either might assist Nova. Her killing the hellhounds herself seems more plausible, but then where did the necklace come from? Who—or *what*—offered her a deal? I inhale a sharp breath at the conclusion I come to.

What were you thinking, Nova?

The sun sets outside the two windows at the far end of the Bishop library. I commandeered the space for my team, but sitting here sifting through ideas and papers isn't helping me. All these speculations won't lead me to Nova.

"There've been rumors," Cain says, "of a high-tier on the move."

"Who?" I ask, almost breathless.

Cain smirks, his dark hair falling in front of his eyes. "Amon."

A grin forms on my lips. "Find Aril and gather the others. We're going hunting."

17

BENEATH BLUE SKIES

The morning light shines a pale yellow into my room as the sun rises from the horizon. A cool breeze blows through my open balcony doors, brushing gently over my skin not covered by the silk sheets.

Rising from the bed, I ready myself for the day ahead. I grab a dagger from my new collection on the way out, twirling it aimlessly in my hands.

I venture out into the dimly lit hallways of the château. It's quiet as I walk along the dark wooden floors draped in long red runners. Shadows change shape as I pass, a ghostly whisper of the servants maintaining the château, as Rishu had mentioned. A faint smell of breakfast wafts down from the kitchen, and I head to the open door to find the room empty—pots still steaming on the stove.

"Anyone here?" I ask, peeking around for signs of life. No one appears, so I grab an apple and head back into the hall.

There's a stark contrast between the style of my room and that of the hallways. While mine is filled with light greens and white, the rest of the interior follows a much different theme. Dark wood furnishings, deep red curtains with the occasional

179

red plush chair. The pale stone walls are carved artfully and embellished with hints of gold. Antique paintings hang in every corridor. It's ornate and beautiful... A place of my choosing but not permanent.

I sigh, heading down the main staircase to the lower level. No place has ever truly been a home to me, and I don't plan to make one among demons—or cambions.

Finding the doors leading to the garden, I exit the château and step outside. I walk to the grand fountain in the center and take a seat on the ledge, running my fingers through the cool water and watching as it glitters playfully in the sunlight. The morning light grows stronger, and I close my eyes as I listen to the birds singing their daily song, relishing the sense of peace the garden offers.

"You came," I say, opening my eyes as I sense Tevari's presence.

"I made an agreement with you."

I smile. "That you did."

Turning around to face him, I flick the water from my fingers toward his face. His eyes widen as he raises his hand, stopping the droplets midair before they reach his skin. Flicking his hand to the side, he sends the droplets flying away. He towers over me—somewhere around six feet tall—a frown on his face and arms crossing, unamused. His eyes have returned to the almost-black color I knew I had seen before.

"Now I can't decide if you're arrogant or just juvenile."

"Call it getting to know you better." I keep my demeanor light enough, but rather than relaxing, his posture stiffens, and his ever-present vine tightens around him protectively. "So tell me, what are your powers? Chlorokinesis and hydrokinesis seem the most likely... Or better yet, who's your demonic parent?"

His eyes narrow. "Not holding back, I see. Ever consider it might be a sensitive subject?"

I shrug. "For me to have any chance of helping you, there are things I need to know."

Tevari lifts his chin and glares down at me, eyes flashing gold for a moment. "My family is from Zimbabwe, though I only lived there for the first five years of my life."

"That's not exactly—"

He cuts me off. "And for the last thirteen years, I've survived without anyone. Because I may not have total control, but I'm no fool."

Flowers shoot forward in my direction, and I roll to the side off the ledge of the fountain to avoid them. I spring to my feet and continue dodging his attacks, using my dagger to slice through the flowers which follow my every move. His vine wraps around my ankle, yanking my foot out from under me. I land hard on the stone ground, now carpeted with flower petals. Tevari hisses in pain as I slash at the vine, freeing my ankle. I make a mental note of his reaction as I roll out of the way—more flowers crashing onto the stone path behind me. My nostrils flare as an overpowering floral scent begins to rise.

Tevari steps through the array of flowers, his eyes burning bright like molten gold. A single golden line runs down his forehead to the bridge of his nose, glowing through his dark skin. I gasp, pressing a hand over my chest as his pain radiates from his body. Overwhelming emotions of hurt and anger flow into me, and I fall to my knees.

"I've studied demons," I say through clenched teeth as I rack my brain, quickly flipping through a mental catalog of all the demons I've researched, "so let me guess who your parent is." He doesn't say anything as he watches me, but he refrains from attacking. "Does the name Buer ring a bell?"

The flowers suddenly shrink back, returning to their positions in the flowerbeds. Only his vine remains around him. His emotions leave my body as well, allowing me to breathe again as I stand from the ground.

"Huh. You actually figured it out. I'm impressed," he says, the vivid gold color in his eyes fading back to black—the line of gold down his forehead disappearing along with it.

I brush the flower petals from my clothing and hair. "It was an easy conclusion to come to. Amon wouldn't have selected cambions who didn't have...." I catch myself before using hunter terminology. "A powerful demonic parent, and not many of them have control over plants like you do."

"You're smarter than you look," he says, "and easier to beat than I expected. Or was it that energy inside you getting in the way?"

My body goes rigid. What does he mean? The image of Darkness prowling his way toward me, the words he spoke—his threats—race in my mind. Can this cambion sense him?

"I was going easy on you, okay? Leave it at that."

"Fine. For now." He turns to head back toward the château.

"Hey!" I sprint forward and cut him off. "Where do you think you're going? I still have a whole day with you."

Tevari glances over his shoulder to the forest beyond. "You have to deal with that," he says, nodding his head in the direction of the dense woods. I turn to follow his gaze but see nothing; the birds silent in the trees.

A loud yell echoes from a distance, and I flinch. Rising into the sky, a tree flies up before crashing back to the ground somewhere in the forest. Another shoots up, and I internally wince.

"Good luck," Tevari says, disappearing back into the château.

I stare at the door for a moment, considering my options.

Well, it could have gone worse with him, considering I didn't have a plan. Looking back toward the forest, I breathe out a long sigh. Do I even want to know which cambion it is?

Shaking my head, I jog toward the woods, heading in the direction where I saw the tree fly into the sky. Whoever's out there is either practicing to kill me or super pissed off. Neither of which I want to deal with.

Branches crunch underfoot as I race through the trees, not bothering to hide my presence. It wouldn't be a good idea to sneak up on an angry demon—even if they're only half. I approach a clearing, trees uprooted and thrown aside. Bits and pieces of trees scatter the ground; other trees are still standing but with gaping holes through their centers. Standing in the middle is the cambion in question. *Oliver.*

The last uninjured tree left within the clearing stands before him. He yells out, and black scales replace the skin on his arms as his fingers shift into talons. They race far past his body, latching onto a tree before tearing it from its base. It flies overhead as he tosses it, and I dodge to the side. The tree crashes down next to me, and I raise my arms to block the debris and rising dust. Oliver pants heavily, falling to his knees. His arms slowly shift back to his usual pale skin, and I consider him for a moment. A shapeshifter.

"Having fun?" I call out from the cover of the bushes.

Oliver glances over his shoulder and smirks when he sees me. He stands from the ground, turning in my direction. "I'd say you could join, but we wouldn't want to tear up the entire forest, now would we?"

I snort. "I think you did a pretty good job of that on your own."

"Well," he says, walking closer, "I have to prepare to fight you one day. A human who holds her own against one of us...

It makes me... *curious*." His lilting accent slips through, and I wonder about his story, how he ended up here.

"I wouldn't get too curious if I were you," I say, scoffing at the flirtatious look in his eyes, which swirl between grayish blue and yellow—hypnotizing as they change color as if he controls every inch of his being. Interesting.

"Why? Do you have something to hide?" he says, a slow smile crossing his face as he steps closer.

Oliver's not as tall as the other guys in our little group, but he still stands well above my own height. The earthy scent of the forest clings to him, his clothes covered in dirt, pale arms lined with long red scratches.

"Don't we all?" I say, my face mastered to calm perfection.

He shrugs. "You got me there. Maybe this can be our own little secret."

His hand reaches toward a loose strand of my hair. I grab his wrist and spin his arm around to his back, pinning him against a tree. "Seems like you'll need more training before you take me on if you couldn't see that coming."

Beneath my hands, I feel his muscles tense, his breath catching in his lungs. An uneasy chuckle leaves his lips as I shove him away.

"Yes, perhaps." He hesitates before turning to face me. When he does, it's as if nothing happened—shoulders loose, a sly grin playing at his lips. He's just as bad as Rishu.

"I can train you," I say, the words vile on my lips. I don't think I'll ever get used to this—offering to train the very beings I was raised to hunt.

"Another day, love." Walking past me, he heads away from the messy clearing he made.

I yell to him before he gets too far, "Why? What are you afraid of?" I need to know more about his powers—this opportunity too good to pass on.

Oliver freezes, looking over his shoulder. "Nothing, I just don't feel like it." His eyes twinkle as he leaves me standing alone amid the destruction.

A sigh leaves my lips. It's only my second day here, and I'm already utterly confused about what to do. It's not like I can ask Amon or Rishu for help when they're technically my employers—so to speak. Not to mention they didn't leave a way to contact them. I rub my temples, my stress levels increasing.

The way Lance trained me, I can't imagine it working for these half-demon, half-human hybrids. Drills would be ineffective when they'd be focused on how to strangle me instead. Tevari proved that one. Sparring would be too aggressive at this point since, again, they want to kill me—thank you, Azura. Add in the fact nobody here trusts me, and I can hardly say I trust them, and it's a recipe for disaster.

"You have to start somewhere, like how you began," Uriel says softly.

"But how I started was—" Faded memories of my father putting me in front of the sparring pole at four years old flash in my mind's eye. *Get strong, or the world will kill you.* He'd have me practice my punches and kicks until my knuckles bled and my body ached. Until the wood splintered beneath my fists, new scars and bruises forming with each blow. And when morning came, I'd do it all over again. Almost fourteen years of training. Each year progressively more intense.

"I somehow doubt that would work with them either," I mumble under my breath, kicking a stray stone.

The sound of a branch snapping off to my right causes me to freeze in place, and my head swerves in its direction. Body tense, I scan the area for what made the sound. Someone's watching...

I take a step forward.

Movement catches my eye—just a blur, a subtle distortion in the air—something or someone invisible disappearing back into the woods. I can't help but sigh again. Amon gave me this job to do, but I have no idea how to uphold my end of the contract. Distrust weighs too heavily in all our hearts. I look at them and see my enemy; they see me and feel the same—even if they're part human too.

"You must remember who you are."

I perk up as I hear the golden-eyed woman from my visions. Her voice is not within my mind but as if she were beside me, whispering in my ear. *"He's waiting... our most beloved..."* she says. The lotus tattoo on my chest begins to ache. I groan. Too many voices in my head recently.

"God, I'm going crazy."

Leaving Oliver's clearing, I head back to the château. Forget the things I need to remember, I first need to figure out how to train these cambions, or I'll never find out what information Amon has—per the clause I ensured was added.

> *Clause 3: Answers and information regarding Party B's questions will be given at each increment of the cambions improved power and control, determined by biweekly observations. Party A swears to judge fairly and honestly and will provide Party B with an answer to a single question per improved cambion.*

With deals, especially the demonic kind, every word counts. Amon might never give me any information without a time frame, a way to gauge the cambions progression.

Moving through the woods, images from my trials cross my vision: being pulled beneath the black water, suffocating in strange memories that I want to understand—that I *need* to understand, the lotus tattoo, the black vines of death, Darkness...

A frown settles on my face as the château comes into sight, the blue sky bright above it. Training these cambions is the only option I have if I want answers.

Guess I better get to work.

18

THE VINE THAT SPEAKS
THE TRUTH

"**Y**ou still owe me."

Standing in front of Tevari—a book in his hands once again—I stare at him, blocking his exit. If he thinks he's getting away this time, then he's very, *very* wrong.

He lowers the book, crossing his denim-covered legs as he leans farther back in the red plush chair of yet another living space in the château—this one just as opulent as the others. The same overwhelming yet gentle floral scent rises from where he sits as if he's a walking bouquet of flowers.

"Owe you?" His face remains impassive.

I nod. "You promised a whole day; we made a deal. Now it's been two weeks, and I doubt I've convinced you of anything." I try to hide the depth of my annoyance from my voice.

Two weeks of searching high and low with no luck. And not just for him but for all the cambions. Their eyes always seem to trail me as I wander the château, yet they keep their distance, even to the point of locking themselves in their rooms. Not even waking up early to catch them at breakfast has worked. Rishu hasn't returned to check the progress of Amon's beloved

188

cambions based on our agreed-upon terms, a saving grace since it means he won't report on my utter incompetence. Even if it's frustrating that I can't get in contact with them.

Tevari crosses his arms. "No, you haven't"—he sets his book aside and stands to meet me—"but I'll work with you. For now."

I examine him, waiting for a catch. Why the sudden change of heart? "Good. Then let's go." Spinning around, I head toward the door, not waiting for him to follow.

It was luck, I suppose, that Tevari let himself be found in this room. The others... Well, Oliver, despite saying he wants to spar, has locked himself away somewhere or disappears before I can get close enough. And Luka has all but vanished. I've searched everywhere, but he just isn't here. Out of everyone, he intrigues me the most. Something about him has nagged at me from the moment we made eye contact, and that spark when our skin touched...

As a hunter, I'm not stupid enough to fall for such things. But it's... intriguing.

The girls haven't been any better. Azura, our resident fire user, threatens me with flames before racing away every time I try to get near her. Childish, if you ask me. Lei Jing, on the other hand, is around—I've caught glimpses of her—but then she just... disappears. It's entirely possible she has some invisibility powers, though I can't be certain it was her that I heard in the woods. And Meena, the cute girl who seems like a younger sister to Rishu—I often hear her pacing after me, curious, but not quite enough to approach.

At least their absence has given me plenty of time to familiarize myself with the château, the forest, and the unusual beings maintaining it all. Which has led to a discovery Tevari is sure to appreciate.

Heading down various hallways and winding staircases, I take us to the main level of the château. Tevari follows closely enough, silent despite the curiosity I can feel ebbing off him. So much for the reserved, impassive attitude he tries to hide behind.

We arrive at a grand set of wooden doors, ones that took a whole day to find the key to. I push them open and step aside, watching Tevari's mouth part in awe. Two stories of books—shelves lining every wall. Light cascades in from the beautiful stained-glass windows across the room, red curtains hanging from the second level to the wooden floor. The arched ceiling above is painted with a scene of the Great Demonic Fall, so detailed and realistically rendered, it feels as if the tableau might come alive at any moment.

I step in first, heading toward the nearest shelf. Reaching for the first heavy tome my sight lands on, I breathe in the familiar scent of antique books. So similar to the Fandera Estate's library, yet here I feel like I can actually enjoy reading without worrying about getting in trouble.

Flipping through the pages, I turn my gaze to him. "I'm surprised I'm the one who found the key to this place. You're never without a book."

Tevari takes a tentative step inside, eyeing the book I'm holding. He doesn't say anything as he walks farther into the library, but his eyes are wide with wonder and reverence. I watch his vine reach out to grab a book for him, retracting to place it gently in his hands. His dark eyes turn to me as he regains his composure.

"Why are we here?"

"Don't you like it? I found it and thought of you," I say, placing the book I grabbed back on the shelf. "Plus, I think we need to do some research." I look at him, waiting to see if he wants me to continue. He nods ever so softly. "How I was trained... Well, we focused on cultivating the mind as much as the body. And based on how you controlled the flowers in the garden, I think before we start training you to fight, you need to understand what exactly you're doing—which I don't think you really know." His nostrils flare, but I continue. "And unfortunately, this is my first time training a cambion, so"—I motion to the library behind me—"what better place to learn together."

A single brow raises on his face. "Who have you trained, *human?* If not cambions, then why would Amon consider you qualified?"

I roll my eyes. "That's the one thing you got from everything I said?" Tevari remains impassive, waiting for an answer. "I trained novices like you." Which isn't a complete lie—if you count the few times I worked with the first-year trainees... "Speaking of, did you even realize you summoned other plants that day you attacked me?"

His jaw tightens. "And?"

"And maybe there's a reason you summon different plants. And once you can understand the why, we can figure out the how." He doesn't look convinced. A long sigh falls from my lips. "What I'm saying is, I think if we look into it, you'll be able to do more than summoning and controlling." In many ways, his powers seem to act similarly to how tamers summon low-tier demons and spirits to aid in combat. It's a skill I never liked much, but my knowledge from training in the tamer classification might help us.

"And why do you think that?"

I smile. "Intuition."

There's a long pause between us. His gaze shifts back to his vine, which seems to be waiting for his command. Turning back to the shelf, I skim through the titles. My gaze falls to the bracelet on my wrist, the black gem reflecting the incoming light. Kioren hums, and I feel bad I haven't let it out recently.

"What books do you need?" Tevari asks.

"I was thinking basic scientific books about plants and any that mention Buer would be a good place to start. I have some knowledge about him, but a refresher is never bad, and I'm sure there's lots more we can learn." Hopefully, it's not too strange for a human to have knowledge on demonology.

He nods, taking the end of his vine into his hand, and whispers in a language I recognize as his native tongue. When his gaze moves upward, the golden line down his forehead shines bright through his dark skin. The vine shoots out from around his body, growing into separate tendrils. It reaches out and takes books from the shelves, sending them flying to the wooden tables in the center of the room.

I duck as it plucks a book next to my head. This vine of his... It's more than what he's letting on. The main body of the vine ends its pursuit of books, returning to his side as the smaller tendrils make sure the books are all in order on the tables.

"I'm impressed," I say as I head over to the table. Around fifty books are stacked for us to read through.

Picking up the first book I see—a beautiful, timeworn leatherbound tome—I flip it open and skim the first paragraph. *Growing in blackened waters, the lotus blooms from the muddy depths, overcoming its difficulties to rise above as an object of beauty.*

My brows furrow as I keep reading. *The flower closes and sinks underwater at night, only to rise and open again at dawn. Untouched by impurity, the lotus symbolizes the pure of heart and mind across many cultures and religions.* Without thinking, my hand reaches up to rub the lotus emblazoned on my chest.

"Find something interesting?"

I jump as Tevari peers over my shoulder at the book in my hand. Slamming it closed with a *snap*, I turn to him with a smile. Even if he read it, it means as much to him as it does to me. I glance at his vine suspiciously. It tilts itself as if saying, *"I got this one just for you."* I gulp, not sure if I like the sentience of this vine—it seems to know too much.

"Not really... We should get started. There are a lot of books to get through and theories to test out. And you'll have information to memorize."

I meet his gaze, a haughty smirk playing on his lips. "I have a photographic memory," he says, taking a pile of books and plopping himself onto a plush velvet chair.

"Of course you do."

I grab my own stack of books and settle into the chair opposite him, tucking away the leatherbound book I don't dare try to continue reading—saving it for when I'm alone. I suppose it would be good to read up on the lotus. There has to be something that can help explain my visions and this tattoo.

The sun shines brightly into the library, casting a rainbow of colors across the room. Lance would send me running laps until I passed out if he found me spending my whole day reading. The memory causes me to chuckle before I can suppress it.

I startle as the leatherbound book suddenly flies out from the bottom of the pile next to me, Tevari's vine sending it flying into his hands. I stand as he opens it and quickly skims the first page.

"So this is what you were hiding? A lotus flower?" He arches a brow, dark eyes fixed intently on mine, and I tense.

"I wasn't hiding it." I walk to him, snatching the book from his hand. "I said it wasn't interesting. So, just forget you saw it."

"Photographic memory, I can't." He stands, and I turn away, not willing to face him. "And I don't want to either. Your secrets are becoming much more intriguing than the training you offer."

Heat rises in my chest, and I whip around. "I said to forget it, and you'll do just that. Remember your place."

He flinches slightly, and the lightness in his eyes disappears.

Guilt washes over me, but the anger still burns in my chest—unfamiliar, dark.

"Calm yourself, my child. The boy means no harm." Uriel's voice echoes quietly in my mind, soothing the horrible feeling from my body. Darkness. That's what it felt like. My stomach turns rotten.

"Sorry," I mumble to him, returning to my chair and holding up the book to cover my red cheeks.

Closing my eyes, I smack myself in the forehead with the book. The same controlling, cold, and unfeeling voice my father always used on me. *Darkness.* I've probably taken ten giant steps backward in this new—well, not quite—friendship.

Tevari laughs, and I peek up over the book.

"Did you think that scared me away?" he says, but I don't say anything as I search his face. "There's something about you... some part of you"—he tilts his head as he looks me up and down—"that isn't you."

My breath hitches as my gaze falls to his vine. Can it sense my angels? Does he know I'm a hunter? An Undivided? Just how much has his vine found out about me? I guess I've been underestimating the cambions abilities if Tevari's vine can read energy, see truth, just by grazing my skin. I gulp, my throat tightening.

They can never find out about me. Not if I want to survive.

19

WEB OF SECRETS

— Adrian —

Two weeks.

Two weeks and nothing. Cain's tidbit on Amon led to one dead end after another. As one of the few S-class demon's out there, the outcome was almost too predictable. If none of the Undivided before me could find information regarding the demon, how could I?

I pound my fist into the wooden desk. Another failed day... My seven sit silently in various chairs in the Bishop's library.

Solomon commanded us to find Nova. A test of sorts, I presume. Why he wouldn't send more teams after her, though, is beyond me. Isn't she important to him?

The chains around her wrists the last time I saw her slither into mind. Maybe he doesn't care about his daughter—his heir. That, too, is beyond me.

"What next, Adrian?" Aril says, and I turn to my second.

His brown hair hangs shaggy in front of tired blue eyes. We've been moving nonstop these past two weeks. Though not unusual for hunters, without making any progress, it wears us down.

"Honestly, I don't know...."

The room falls silent.

"Maybe..." Eva begins, avoiding eye contact. "Maybe she doesn't want to be found."

My nostrils flare, and my lips curl into a snarl, but my third speaks first. "Are you suggesting she's betrayed the clan?" Cain says, moving off the wall he was leaning against. Eva turns her gaze to the floor. "Don't dare say that again, Eva."

My anger cools with Cain's response, but Nova's letter is a heavy weight in my pocket. She asked to not be found, to not trust Solomon. But she's *always* wanted to be a hunter. Even if she did something stupid, it wasn't out of betrayal. It has to be something more.

I'm about to speak when the door bursts open. Theo stands there, tall, unbothered. My cousin's gaze falls on me, and I sit up straight. What the hell is he doing here?

"Theo now is not the time," I say through gritted teeth.

He only smirks, pushing me to my limit. I stand, ready to show him his place, when he finally speaks. The sound is cold, unnatural. Unlike anything I've heard from my cousin.

"Don't you want to know what I found about Nova?"

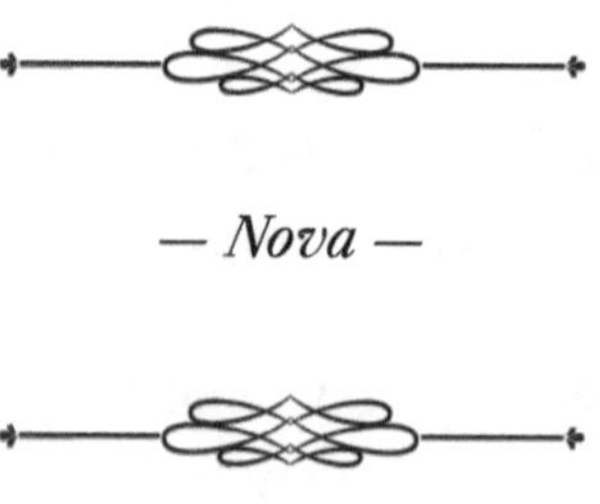

— Nova —

Walking through the château halls, I stare aimlessly at my feet. Night fell quicker than I expected. The hazy sunset already below the horizon, the day gone as quick as it came.

Tevari never brought up our conversation again, but it eats away at my mind. The anger and darkness inside me... A chaos that calls to me to be something I'm not. It scares me, and I'm not sure what to do about it. I rub the space over the lotus tattoo as it throbs softly. *A warning*, a cold voice whispers in my ear, but I ignore it.

Before I left the library, Tevari said he'd meet me tomorrow to continue our research and training. Something his vine picked up on is changing his opinion about me, intriguing him enough to want to stick around. I'm not sure that's a good thing. In fact, it *terrifies* me.

Looking up, I find myself in front of the back doors leading to the garden. Pushing them open, I breathe in deeply as a rush of cool air blows over my skin, curling around me and gently nudging me forward.

I step outside and turn my gaze toward the blue-black sky, counting the growing number of stars. I pick out the constellations I recognize, tracing the shapes with my finger. The lotus on my chest burns, and I glance down as I press my palm into it, trying to ease the growing pain.

When I lift my eyes, I notice a figure sitting on the edge of the fountain at the center of the garden. *Luka*... He trails his fingers in the water, looking ahead at something I can't see, unaware I watch from a distance.

Moonlight casts an ethereal glow over his skin, illuminating his profile even in the dark. Wind billows the fabric of his dark button-up, and his black hair sways messily in front of his eyes. His hand lifts to his face, delicately holding a single flower beneath his nose.

I'm utterly hypnotized, unable to look away from the scene he's created beneath the moon. I lift my foot to step forward but hesitate, wanting nothing more than to join him but knowing better than to disturb his quiet thoughts. The lotus on my chest cuts into me like a knife tracing over the design, and I wince.

Luka's head shifts, eyes connecting with mine. The flower drops from his hand, and he tenses as if preparing to bolt. *Why do you want to run from me?* Yet my instincts scream for me to do the same while my heart begs to go closer.

A step toward him, and then another. As if in a spell, I can't turn back—stopping a breath away from him. I stare into his eyes like moonlight, watching as a soft smile graces his lips. Hesitancy filled with delight because I approached first. Is this his power? I shiver at the thought. Dangerous indeed.

"Hi." My voice is breathy, the sound taking me by surprise.

"Hi."

His voice is but a whisper in my ear, but it wraps around my heart, squeezing it in a way I've never felt before. The burning edge of the lotus tattoo fades amid the pure contentment of the moment.

I open my mouth to say something, *anything*. Words fall short as the soft, gentle scent of him reaches my nose. It stands apart from the flowery scents lifting from the garden around us. A subtle citrus blended with delicate florals, yet it's deeper and more seductive with an undertone of the earthy woods. He breaks from our gaze, reaching to retrieve the fallen flower.

"For you," he says, handing me the white rose.

Tentatively, I take it, lifting it to my nose. My eyes close as I smell the sweet flower. The scent is strong, but my nose is still filled with his scent. I open my eyes and find him staring thoughtfully at my face. I swallow hard, a pang in my chest waking me to reality.

"Thank you," I say, swiftly turning around and almost running from him and the fountain.

His eyes burn into my back as I slip inside. Closing the door, I collapse to the ground, my heart thrumming in my chest. I only stay a moment, not risking having him enter while I sit here on the floor. Slowly, I stand, shaking my head and trying to clear my clouded mind. If this is his power... I'll have to be more careful. Taking one last look out the window behind me, I'm surprised to see that the garden is now empty. I sigh and start heading back to my room.

Rounding a corner, my heart drops to the floor. Amber eyes and mischievous grin. *Adrian?* Tears well in my eyes as I pull out a dagger I keep on hand, throwing it in his direction. The image shatters like glass, and the dagger falls to the ground with a *thump*. A wide-eyed girl peeps her head around the corner before disappearing again. Sighing, I cross my arms. So she finally confronts me...

"Meena?" I say to her. "Please come out. I'm not mad."

She peeks her head back around the corner but doesn't step out into the hallway.

"Who was he?" she asks softly, her stormy gray eyes bright with the scattered moonlight falling into the hallway.

I examine her round face, considering the powers she may possess. "How did you summon that? Are illusions your skill?" I say, copying her soft tone.

She creeps out into the hallway. "He's there, constantly on your mind." Tiptoeing closer, I notice her bare feet on the plush carpet, wiggling as if unable to hide her discomfort. "So much *human* emotion tied to him... You make it too easy to use it against you."

My jaw clenches. I don't like the sounds of that at all.

"So you can create illusions from these emotions?" I ask, doing my best to keep my voice steady.

She nods, a sweet smile forming on her lips. "The others may hide their true abilities from you, but I don't fear you."

She raises a hand, a silver thread tinted with a faint pink glow glimmers between her fingers. I blink, and the whole hall is covered in these webs.

"I'm a mind-weaver. I can create any image and turn it into something physical." The sweet smile turns to something wicked. Illusions of Adrian form all around me from the strands, disappearing and reappearing before I can even make a move. Meena lowers her hand, and the illusions shatter as the silver threads disappear. "And sometimes I use it to see into the mind of someone. Rishu told me it'd be useful one day."

Meena's gray eyes meet mine, and my heart breaks—a very hurt child is staring back at me.

"You seem to have good control... But you wouldn't be here unless Amon thought you needed more." Innocence returns to her face as she pads closer, big, round eyes staring at me. "Do you want to train with me?"

Her smile widens tenfold, and she nods rapidly, pigtails swinging back and forth. She takes my hand, pulling me down the hall. "Let's start now!" I can't help but smile. Her attitude is like a breath of fresh air compared to the others.

She's almost jumping as she rambles on and on, asking question after question about how I'll train her. It makes me want to help this sweet girl that much more. Because not once have I felt any malice in her small frame—despite the time she threw a grape at my head.

"You see, it was Rishu who found me in India when I was a kid," she says, her words catching my attention. "I did bad things when I was little to survive. Happens when your mother abandons you on the side of a road." She laughs, but there's deep pain hidden behind her words.

"How long were you on your own?" I say as we enter a room off the main hallway.

She puts a hand on her chin as if deep in thought. "I was four when I was abandoned, and then brother Rishu found me when I was almost seven, so only three years." Her voice is calm as she recounts her past, but my heart breaks even more. And here I thought my situation was bad... How ignorant of me.

"I'm sorry," I say, not knowing what else to respond with, "but you're here now, and I want to help you in any way I can."

Meena examines me carefully. "You know... I didn't trust you at first, mostly because I couldn't get into your mind—I was actually only able to see that boy because you're projecting thoughts about him all the time...." She rolls her eyes, and my heart skips a beat as I struggle not to give myself away by showing how extraordinarily relieved I am to hear that. "But you remind me of Rishu in a way. He's always kind to me like you are now." She smiles softly, a small blush rising to her tanned cheeks.

"I've never been compared to a demon before, but I'll take it as a compliment," I say with a wink. She giggles, and I echo it, the joyful sound warming the small, dimly lit room we enter.

We find a comfortable-looking set of chairs and take a seat together. It's less opulent than the rest of the château, possibly a drawing room of sorts, with simple wood furnishings and a small lounge couch taking up the rest of the space. Moonlight trickles in from the opened windows, and a breeze floats through, causing the candle on the table to flicker.

"How old are you, Meena?" I ask the girl.

"Thirteen. I'll be fourteen soon, though."

I chuckle to distract myself from the pang in my chest. "You've been using your powers for so long. What's left to harness?"

Her long pigtails fall over her shoulders, a sheepish look crossing her face. "Well…" She hesitates, biting her lip and tucking her legs under herself.

"It's okay, whatever it is, you can tell me," I say, encouraging her without trying to put too much pressure on her.

"Well… I have some control, but the illusion stuff is easy." She glances back and forth, her hands fidgeting together. "But I… Well, I… It happens kinda unintentionally… And I, um—"

"Meena, just tell me," I say, cutting off her babbling.

She turns her gaze to mine, mustering up a small smile. Her eyes glitter as she stares at me. "I sometimes kill people unintentionally."

20

DARK REMINDERS

"What do you mean? How do you kill people unintentionally?"

"Well, you see...." She scratches her head with an awkward laugh. "Most of the time, my powers are at a normal level, but sometimes if I'm like, really upset or emotional... Well, they... They can cause temptations or fears to rise... And then, you know, people die. Like this one time, a man was harassing me, so I reached into his mind and found his darkest fear—spiders, ironically—so I gave them to him. Let them crawl down his throat by the dozens. He thought he was suffocating, so he just... did." I stare at her in shock. "I didn't mean to kill him... but on the bright side, at least he won't be harassing little girls anymore."

A lot of demons cause desires or fears that lead to, well, nothing good. "Do you know who your demonic parent is? I've studied many demons, so knowing your parent will help me help you."

"Really? Why? Was it to help us? How many demons do you know of? Do you know—"

"Meena, who's your parent?"

She frowns. "Rishu said Mara, but it doesn't mean anything to me since it's not like I ever met them."

I freeze at the name. Raking my mind, I skim over all the texts on demons I've studied. The name is ancient, nothing too specific comes to mind, but the one thing I can say is I'd pick a fight with Buer over Mara any day. A demon of deception, confusion, possession, and all sorts of horrible phenomena that incite fear in the hearts of mortals. A demon I don't think many hunters would ever want to encounter—another S-class.

"And you're sure?"

"Yeah, why?" She cocks her head, curiosity twinkling in her stormy eyes.

"It's not a demon I'm very familiar with, but... I do have an idea of why you have your problem with control and impulse."

She jumps up, a huge grin on her face. "Really! Then you can help me? I don't really like killing people. I mean, unless they're bad people, but—" Her rambling begins again, and I can't help but chuckle. "What?"

"I never expected you to get so excited." I smile softly. "I'll read up on Mara later, but from what I know, he's ancient and binds someone with desire or fear—much like your own abilities." Meena nods in perceived understanding, and I fight not to laugh. "How about we just see what you can do?"

"Focus, Meena," I say, watching her brows furrow as she moves her fingers to lift a doll's hand. It crumbles to the table, and I look at the sweat beading on her forehead. "Let's give it a rest for now." The clock on the wall ticks by, showing 2:17 a.m.

"But I haven't mastered it," Meena whines.

I smile at her sleepily as I stand from the chair I've been sitting in for the past four hours. "You just discovered this skill an hour ago. You'll exhaust yourself if you continue at this rate."

"But—"

"No buts. If you really want to keep practicing, focus on meditating. You control your thoughts and actions; they don't control you. Meditation will help you master that."

She frowns but nods, jumping up from her chair with more energy than should be possible. "Fine," she skips to the door, opening it to leave, then pauses and turns back. "Goodnight, Nova." With a small wave, she disappears into the hallway, leaving me behind.

I sigh. It's hard not to like Meena. In fact, it's hard to really dislike any of the cambions too much, and that's... confusing. Something I never thought possible as a hunter. Meena, while she's had a difficult and strange life, is quite normal. Not the evil demon I might've expected her to be...

My thoughts trail to the illusion of Adrian she had created. Of how she delved into my thoughts and picked out every detail perfectly. Another sigh escapes my lips. Adrian would think I'm insane for thinking Meena is anything but a demon. He'd chastise me for helping the cambions, for making this choice to begin with.

I didn't give him a chance to help me, not that he could have. My father was never going to tell me anything, no matter how much faith Adrian or I had in him. Something I should have recognized from the moment my father promised to explain everything. Honestly, I should've known long ago, since the time he refused to tell me about my mother...

Picking up the white rose Luka gave me from the table, I lift it to my nose. Two weeks... Time has passed faster than I thought it would; it's a slow process getting these cambions to trust me enough to train them. I would say two out of six is pretty good, considering my odds.

I leave the drawing room, stopping to look out the window at the moon high in the sky. Thoughts race through my mind, ones I'm not sure I want to consider. Of the clan that never knew me, a father who didn't love me. Besides Adrian, how can I miss my past? Being a hunter was always my dream, but everything's changed with all the secrets that keep piling up.

It goes beyond the lotus tattoo and the two angels I'm bonded with. There's everything I saw in my angelic trials—things even my angels won't, or can't, clarify. Those memories that felt too real... Then there's the woman who showed me how to summon Kioren. She's as much a mystery to me as the faceless Darkness who continues to threaten me. I shudder. It'd be too soon if I never heard his voice again.

Then there's the light I summoned on the night of the blood moon and the man who caught me before I fell. I've hardly had a moment to think about any of this with everything else that's happened.

Questions keep adding up with no answers. All Amon gave me was the free tidbit about Kioren being both angelic but also *not*—whatever that means—and that the Heavens are looking for the scythe. It's refreshing to have some clarity but also terrifying since even Amon doesn't know why they're looking for it.

Pain sparks in my chest, and I rub the spot over the lotus tattoo. A vision of black vines cascading over my body flashes in my mind. I catch myself on the wall as the world tilts. Darkness threatened my life with those vines. Even if I don't understand why I can sense it was his doing.

I breathe deeply through the throbbing ache. Meena and the others aren't the only ones with powers threatening their lives.

I snort at the thought. This shared struggle for us to continue to live against all odds. *It'd probably be easier to just give up.*

Entering my room, I head to the bathroom, knowing I must face my fear of the lotus. "Uriel, Zerachiel, why does it hurts so much?" I ask out loud, the pain more intense than when the black vines encased me during my angelic trials. They don't respond, not even a soft hum.

Pulling off the T-shirt I wear over my athletic tank top, the tattoo comes into full view. The seven petals glow softly—amplifying with each second. My breathing becomes shallow as my heart begins to beat faster and faster in my chest. Needles seem to prick me as the tattoo is set aflame, a burning sensation slithering across my skin. I grip the counter to hold myself up, my arms weakening as I bite my lip to stop any sound from escaping. I force my eyes to remain open, watching in horror as the deathly black vines begin to emerge from my chest and encircle the tattoo. My hand goes to my mouth, quieting my whimpers as I stumble back from the mirror and slide to the cool floor.

"A reminder, my dear…" a dark, sinister voice, so unlike that of my angels or the golden-eyed woman, speaks. I begin to shake uncontrollably. *Darkness.* I spoke too soon.

Tears fall from my eyes as I try to calm my gasping breaths. The burning light of the lotus fades slowly. My breathing eases, but the pain lingers, draining my body of all energy. Never came too soon—Darkness's voice more terrifying than I remember. And still, I cannot help but succumb to it as my head lolls back, my world going dark.

A knock sounds and I jolt awake. Raising my hand, I block the incoming sunlight streaming through the open bathroom door. I achingly stand from the cold tile, a groan leaving my lips. The knock sounds again, harsher this time. I face myself in the mirror, dark bags under my eyes, an unhealthy paleness to my normally glowing skin. My stomach sinks as I risk a glance down at the lotus tattoo. The curving tips of black vines spread out around the tattoo. *A reminder...* I lurch forward and vomit into the sink, shaking with weakness and fear.

Splashing my face with water, I pull my T-shirt back on as I make my way to the door. Opening it, I find Meena standing beside Tevari, a worried expression on their faces.

"Nova, you have to come quick," Meena says, grabbing my hand and pulling me out the door before I can say anything.

"What's going on?" I ask, looking between her and Tevari. It's strange; I haven't seen two or more cambions together since the first day I was here.

"You'll see," Tevari says, his jaw tight.

A body crashes through the window before us, slamming into the wall. Wood and glass shatter in every direction, paintings crashing to the carpeted floor. Tevari's vine blocks the shards as I hold back Kioren from emerging. Azura stands from the destruction, wiping her mouth as she looks out into the garden. She pays us no attention as she races back out, anger flaring in her eyes.

"That little bitch," Azura cries out, jumping back out in a burst of flames.

I run to the broken window, my eyes widening at the destruction in the garden. Azura's body of flames lands on a creature I've never seen before. At least twice her size and covered with scaly flesh, the creature opens its mouth, revealing rows of dagger-like teeth. Her fire burns its skin, and it lets out a nasty snarl. Scaly arms extend far past their original reach, long claws grasping onto her and slamming her against the stone exterior of the château. She screams as the creature grabs onto her body once more, pulling her in close as its face slowly shifts into the Roman-like features of Oliver.

Definitely *not* good.

Swinging my body out the window, I land in the garden, the two-story fall cushioned by my angels' power. Glancing at my wrist, I consider if this is a good time to show them the power of Kioren. After Darkness reappeared... I'm not sure I have the strength to stop two angry cambions on my own.

"Come forth, *Kioren*," I say, and the black gem begins bubbling as the silver scythe emerges. I grin as the monstrous weapon appears, thankful I no longer need to recite the long incantation to call it forth.

From above, I hear a small gasp from Meena, and I look over my shoulder at the two surprised faces peering through the broken window. Turning back to the destruction, I head toward the brawling cambions. Azura and Oliver don't notice my approach. They tear into each other without remorse, neither willing to give in. Fireballs flare across the garden as Azura attacks; debris flies in every direction as Oliver deflects them. From a distance, I can tell that neither are in the best shape. Claw marks are engraved in Azura's skin, blood soaking her clothes. Oliver himself is scorched with fire. His attacks are strong, but he doesn't move nearly fast enough to avoid her flames.

Another roar sounds from the two cambions, and I make my move. Racing forward, I jump up between the two, swinging Kioren's blade in a wide arch and slamming it into the ground between them. A blast of energy ripples out from the impact, and the ground trembles. Azura and Oliver freeze, flames dissipating, scaly skin shrinking away.

"You…" Azura says, her voice fading as she stares at the giant form of Kioren.

Oliver's wide-eyed gaze is also fixed on Kioren, but he recovers quickly, lifting his hands in surrender. "Nova, you see—" I cut him off with a cold glare.

I pull Kioren from the ground, holding the staff in my hands. Motioning for Meena and Tevari to join us, I wait for them before saying anything. If they think they're getting away with this, then they are very, *very* wrong.

The garden is a disaster. The fountain's spewing water everywhere. Flower beds are torn from the ground, petals crushed into the smashed stone pathway. The château nearby isn't much better—windows are shattered, and chunks of the stone siding are crumbling off around body-shaped imprints.

Meena and Tevari approach slowly, and I smile at the group of four. This is one way to get a move on with my side of the deal…

"Great, now that you're all here," I say, addressing the two destroyers and the two bystanders, "it's the perfect opportunity to start a different kind of training."

Azura scoffs, her black-tipped brown hair swaying above her shoulders. "Who said I'm gonna train with you?"

"I only said I wanted to fight you, not train," Oliver says with a cocky grin.

I raise my hand, and Kioren's black tendrils race toward both of their throats, stopping at the last second. "You don't have a choice anymore." They gulp, not mouthing off any more complaints. Calling Kioren away, I smile at the four of them. "Since you all seem to be so inclined to fight, instead of destroying our place of residence, you'll be sparring against each other in *friendly* combat. And there you'll learn to work together."

"Work together? You're joking, right?" Oliver says, the grin falling from his face.

I smile at him. "I think you and Azura will make great partners." His jaw drops, and I turn away, heading back toward the manor.

"There's no way I'm working with him, he—"

"Honestly, Azura"—I turn back to face the girl—"I couldn't care less right now why you were fighting. Get to know each other while cleaning this mess up. We start tomorrow at dawn." They grumble, kicking pebbles around, but a flash of Kioren turning toward them quickly shuts them up. "Oh, and if this happens again, I won't let you off so lightly."

Meena grabs my shirt sleeve before I can leave. "But, Nova, what about us?"

"We had nothing to do with this," Tevari adds, his dark eyes glancing over in annoyance at the other two. "These fools did it themselves."

I gently remove Meena's hand and turn back to the group. "You're a team now. When one of you messes up, you'll all suffer the consequences. Besides, it'll be good character building." With a devilish smile, I turn away, leaving them in the wreckage of the garden.

Maybe I should have introduced Kioren on day one... They might have been more agreeable in letting me do my job. Calling the giant scythe back into the bracelet, I enter the château. The inside, thankfully, remains mostly untouched by the destruction. Only the outside tells a different story.

Sighing, I lean against the nearest wall. Even that much exertion has taken me to my limit. Whatever happened last night... Why Darkness came back... I shake my head as I rest my hand over the lotus tattoo. With those vines appearing now—

"Interesting tactic," a sweet, lightly accented voice says from behind, startling me from my thoughts.

I turn to find Lei Jing standing before me. She wears long sleeves despite the blossoming heat, and her long black hair is drawn over her shoulders. But it's her eyes that captivate. Swirling violet unlike any color I've seen before. A trait not naturally possible for humans.

"Finally decided to show yourself?" I say to her.

Her face purses, sharp eyes narrowing. "They'll be busy for the rest of the day, so you won't have to worry about anyone finding out your secret. Though if I'm being honest, I don't think it'll last long."

"You're welcome to help them," I say to her, crossing my arms as I approach her, "and as for my secret, it depends on what you're talking about. Unless, of course, you're bluffing." My voice remains steady despite the thundering in my chest.

She flips her silky black hair over her shoulder. "I might not know what it is, but I saw the lotus tattoo." I bite my tongue to stifle the growl building in my throat. "Seemed to hurt, if you ask me."

She begins to walk past me, but I grab onto her wrist, stopping her in her tracks. "Thank you," I say with a smirk, "you've confirmed what I thought your powers are."

She yanks her arm from my hand. "You may have their attention now, but you're still human, *weak*," she says with a huff. "But nice scythe. I wouldn't mind taking it for a spin someday."

Leaving me alone in the hallway, her graceful steps fade into the distance. Spinning around, I yell out as I punch a hole in the wall beside me. Anger boils inside. I made a mistake. If she starts asking questions about the tattoo that even I don't understand... I shake off the thought. It's time I talk with Amon.

21

Two Truths and a Lie

"You can't just barge in there," Rishu says as he reaches out to stop me before I make my way to Amon's office unannounced. The upper floor is like a maze of hallways, but they underestimated me if they thought I couldn't find my way after my first visit with Amon. It only takes once to remember when your life is at stake.

"If you hadn't been so hard to reach, I wouldn't have to," I yell over my shoulder, skipping ahead of him before he can block me.

"It's not my fault you don't know how to use the phone," Rishu yells from behind.

As soon as Rishu popped in as per our third clause, I demanded he take me here to speak with Amon. He insisted I could've used the landline on the main floor if it was an emergency but left out the part of one existing, let alone how to actually use it.

"And why didn't we teleport the first time? You just had to knock me out instead," I say as I pick up my pace.

With his initial annoyance, I was half expecting him to ignore me, keep me in the château, but a moment later, he teleported

213

us here with a snap of his fingers. A painful vortex of black smoke that sent me to the ground with my stomach in shambles but here nonetheless. So much for using his fancy Porsche...

A scoff of disbelief sounds from Rishu. "Because it's dangerous and taxing. You try teleporting other people and then tell me how you like it."

I scowl as I approach Amon's door, the big CEO letters shining bright in the daytime. Banging the door open, sunlight blinds me from the large glass window. Amon sits facing the city view.

"We need to talk," I say, calling out to him as I ignore the impending demon at my heels. They could've at least told me there was a landline; I'm sure I could've figured it out—

The chair swivels around to reveal a drop-dead gorgeous man with long, silvery-blond hair. I scoff, rolling my eyes. Of course, the child was just a facade. This man wearing an elegant black suit is as beautiful as I'd expect of an S-class demon wearing human skin. Unnatural, captivating. His face is angular and sharp; piercing blue eyes lift to meet mine.

"I have to say, I think I preferred you as a kid," I say, walking over to take a seat in front of him. I rein in my emotions, not wanting him to see my surprise. "Then again, I'll have less of a guilty conscience making you bleed for how difficult it was to contact you."

He smiles, a cold glint in his pale blue eyes. "It's good to see you too, Nova." His voice is hypnotizing compared to the childish giggle he first used on me. Smooth and charismatic as it draws you into its depth. Makes me sick.

"It's been over two weeks, and you haven't checked my progress. Am I to believe you're not following through with your end of the deal?" I say, my voice cold. Amon smiles with a slight shake of his head. "Good. Then since I now have four cambions training under me, you can answer some questions."

Amon leans back in his chair as he says, "Go ahead."

I inhale slowly, remembering Darkness's promise—his warning. *Curiosity killed the cat.* I brush it aside, my thoughts lingering on the pointed black lines spreading around the lotus tattoo on my chest. Ones that I know will try to kill me.

"Tell me what the lotus tattoo means." I cut to the chase, skipping over any sort of pleasantries. "What are the black vines, and will they—"

"Kill you?" he finishes for me, standing from his seat and walking around the desk. He leans against it, his gaze piercing down at me. "One day, they might."

My heart thunders in my chest. "You're lying." I don't believe my own words.

"Sadly, I'm not." He doesn't sound sad in the least. A strand of his pale hair falls into his face as he continues. "The past and what's to come are always with me. I see pieces of your future. Your death is part of your long journey. As unclear as that journey may be."

I stand, my hands pulling at my hair as I approach the large window. "It's like I saw... I never thought—" I pace in front of the city view, my mind racing with the images from my angelic trials. "What does this mean? How will it kill me?" I ask. Who is Darkness, and why is he doing this to me? I shudder at the memory of his voice as he released just the tips of the black vines.

"My cambions aren't trained. I don't think you've warranted more answers—"

I raise my hand, cutting him off. "Uriel, Zerachiel, what are you hiding?"

My eyes blaze as I reach into my mind, searching frantically for any hint of their presence. This all started with my angelic trials, yet they've never spoken a word about what happened.

Hell, it was barely even a trial, considering the memories that were shoved into my mind or how Darkness appeared with his threats.

"My death, just how long have you known?" My voice raises an octave. "Why won't you answer me?"

Amon and Rishu share a look, but I ignore their curious faces. I should have gone to my angels first. This is a matter I believe even Amon can't see. My angels were the ones who showed me the lotus in my trials; they *gave me the lotus tattoo*. Because of them that I saw how the black vines would consume my body. They brought Darkness to me. If anyone knows anything, it's them.

"Tell me now!" I scream, but their voices remain silent in my mind.

"Nova," Rishu's voice comes from behind me, and I feel his hand on my shoulder.

Grabbing his wrist, I flip him over onto the ground. He lands with a thud, eyes wide. My breaths are heavy, and my palms sweat as I remember the pain, the fear, Darkness instills in me. Rishu's brows furrow together as he looks at me, but the anger continues to boil, eating away at my sense of self, just waiting for me to break so it can tear loose.

"Calm yourself, child," Zerachiel says, his gravelly voice a whisper in my mind.

I tear my gaze from Rishu. "I'll calm down when you explain why this tattoo is going to kill me! You're the one who gave it to me in the first place!"

"It's not as simple as that," Uriel says, her voice finally rising in my mind.

"Do the demons know?" I look at Amon and Rishu. "I'm sick of you lying to me. So either you tell me, or I'll make them."

"The time will come for you to know. Do not rush what is meant to be," Zerachiel says, his voice booming with anger rivaling my own.

Uriel's silvery voice follows as she says, *"We do not know how much they know, but, Nova... We are not the only ones listening. For now, the less you know, the safer you are."*

I breathe in deeply, closing my eyes. *"If I wanted to be safe, I would have stayed with my father,"* my voice rings in my mind, speaking directly to them and whoever else is supposedly listening. These truths no one is willing to share—these lies of omission—they'll kill me before anything else does.

"To hell with this." I shut their voices out, building a wall between them and me. Turning back to Amon, I take a moment to calm my anger before speaking. "I don't care what you have to do, but until I know the whole truth, I'm not letting this tattoo kill me. Consider this an extension of our deal."

Rishu rises from the ground. "I don't think I'm catching on. What tattoo?"

Stripping down to my tank top, I expose the seven-petaled lotus inked in red on my chest—tips of black vines twined in a circle around it. The beginning of my death.

A smirk comes to Amon's lips. "You are far more interesting than I could have expected. No wonder he—" He cuts himself off but not before I hear his last word. *He?*

"Just do what I say. If I die, I can't help your precious cambions." I put aside his mistaken comment, ignoring the matter for now.

"True. If only I could replace you," Amon says, and I tense at his words. "Sadly, I cannot."

"I think we're done here." I turn, heading toward the door. "Let's go, Rishu. If we leave the cambions alone for too long, they'll destroy the place again."

He shares a final glance with Amon before following me out of the office. I storm down the hallway, my mind still racing. Uriel and Zerachiel fight against the mental block I placed in my mind, their voices threatening to break through. They're hiding things from me, things I should have asked about from the moment I first spoke with them. Maybe it was stupid to come here, to sign a deal with Amon, when they obviously know more than they're letting on.

Rishu's hand lands on my shoulder again, stopping me in my tracks. "We teleported here, remember?" he says softly, a somber look on his face.

"Oh. Right," I say, my gaze falling to the floor. "Let's go then."

I reach my hand out, grasping onto his, and we fall into darkness, spinning painfully as he takes us back to the château. Landing hard on my back in the garden, a rough cough escapes my lips as the air returns to my lungs.

"I'll stay at the château for a while," Rishu says. Looking up at him, I nod, barely comprehending his words. "Are you sure you're okay? I can manage the cambions for now if you need me to."

"I'm *fine*," I snarl as I push myself to my feet.

I leave him standing in the garden as I walk toward the château, getting away before he can call me out on the blatant lie. In truth, I don't know if I'll ever be fine. Not without answers. Not with the promise of a painful death looming over me.

22

REMEMBRANCE

Laying in the soft comfort of my bed, I stare at the princess canopy above. Numbness overwhelms me as I build a brick wall in my mind. A skill I didn't know I had until I tried. Stacking one layer up after another to quell their voices. Even under the unrelenting pursuit of my angels trying to tear it down, it remains whole. Closing my eyes, I add another layer, and the pounding grows quieter.

The sun is already setting, trickles of golden light shining into my room from the balcony. My hand moves to touch the lotus tattoo, where the tips of the black vines surround it. The pain is long gone, but I know I'll remember it for the rest of my life. *My short-lived life.* I roll to my side, curling into the ivory sheets.

I can still hear my angels shouting at my mental walls, and I sigh, finally deciding to hear them out. I open the barrier a fraction. "If you're going to lie and hide the truth again, I'm not interested," I say, exhaustion setting in.

"There is much you do not know, much we cannot tell you," Uriel says, her soft tone turning sad. *"And for you to continue to live, we must be careful. Trust that there is a plan."*

A plan... "Because Darkness is listening?" I curl my body tighter. "That voice I heard... I didn't imagine it, did I?"

Their silence is all the confirmation I need. Darkness is very much real. But who is he, and why do this to me? I'm just a girl who wanted to be a hunter. A girl who wants to know why she never could be.

"There are those who wish for you to fail when you must succeed. Therefore, when we cannot speak the truth, other doors may open for the answers you seek. But it takes time and careful moves. We cannot risk you, Nova," Uriel says.

"Is that why you didn't stop me from making a deal with Amon? Because he can provide the answers you can't?" A sense of understanding begins to form in my mind.

"Sometimes there is more than one door," Zerachiel says.

The sound of a piano floats into my room from the hallway. Rising from my bed, I open the door, closing my eyes as I listen to the sweet, sad song. My bare feet pad along the hall, following the music like the Pied Piper is calling me forth. It's an ocean-drowned tune in the beginning, deep and sensual. But soon, the melody changes, becoming delicate and sweet; high notes trilling gently. As I draw closer, the song reaches a climax—I can hear the soft sound of the fingers striking the keys as the notes grow louder. Tears well in my eyes. Pain, sadness, joy, love, and loss. It pulls at my heartstrings, drawing out long-buried emotions I wasn't even aware of until this moment.

Turning the corner, I approach a door that's slightly ajar and peek inside. I listen to the tapping of a foot on the piano pedals and watch as if in a trance as long fingers move with ease over the key. My chest burns as the lotus ignites, the black vines inching across my chest. I dig my nails into the wooden door frame, unable to turn away even as the pain cascades over my skin. An indescribable sensation washes over me as I listen, like a wave crashing down on my unprepared heart. *I know this song.* But the words are lost in my memories.

Pushing the door open, I step inside, unable to stop myself. *He's waiting. Our most beloved. Remember...* The last note sounds, echoing in the quiet room as I meet the player's gaze.

"Luka?" His name is painful on my tongue, my mind aching as if I truly need to remember something but can't.

He stands from the piano bench, his silver eyes wide. "Nova..."

The black vines around the lotus suddenly burst forward, growing rapidly across my skin. I scream as the pain intensifies. They race down my arm and ribcage. Stretching over my body as I saw in the vision.

Luka catches me as I collapse to the floor, unable to hold myself upright any longer. My eyes squeeze shut as tears fall. The pain is excruciating, incomparable to how it felt during my angelic trials. The reality of it is a hundred times worse. Luka's hand gently caresses my cheek as he softly murmurs in my ear. I peek through watery lashes to see Rishu appear beside him, but my eyes are unable to focus on either of their faces.

"This is going to hurt," Rishu says.

Rishu's hand slams onto my chest; Luka holds onto me as all the breath leaves my lungs. A different kind of pain spreads through my chest as the vines are drawn back. Every bit of energy is zapped away in a single moment. I feel my body rise as Luka takes me into his arms, but my eyes are too heavy to keep open.

"It's okay," he whispers into my ear, "I'm here."

— Adrian —

Another week gone, and I'm going insane.

Theo, however he discovered it, found that Nova might not be as far as we initially thought. A concealed compound where she's been hidden away... But it's taken another week to narrow down where it might be.

I pull the letter she wrote from my pocket, my eyes tracing the words like a poem. The only thing I have left of her. A month and still nothing... Can I really believe she doesn't want to be found after so long? Is she safe? Does she think of me?

Crumbling the paper, I shove it back into my pocket as the door to my bedroom opens. I look up to see my father. His light brown hair is pushed back, and his amber eyes are harsh as he scans me over, disapproving.

"It seems to me your cousin has been more of a help than you have in finding Nova." I wince at the disappointment in his voice. "Don't fail Solomon."

He leaves before I can say anything back, shutting the door behind him. My hands ball into fists, knuckles cracking. What does he know? Not even Solomon is looking for his daughter. I release my fists, running my fingers through my hair. I need to find her.

A chuckle rumbles through my mind, Archangel Michael's voice pushing forward. *"Do you want me to lead you to her?"* My eyes widen at his words.

"You know where she is?" I stand from my bed as if Michael was standing before me with all the answers. "Tell me."

And so he does.

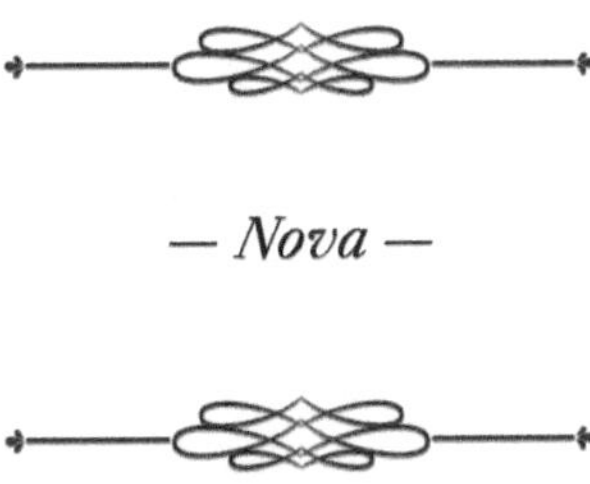

— Nova —

The château is louder than usual when I awaken—hungrier than I've ever been. Laughter echoes up to my room, distinguishable voices of the cambions piercing through the walls. Did they destroy the place again?

My body aches, but there's also a new lightness to it. Standing from my bed, I head into the bathroom. I pull down my shirt to check my tattoo—the vines have been drawn back, forming a twisted circle around the lotus. White symbols are carved into my skin as if to tie it in place. I gulp as I examine it. I hope this lasts.

After quickly showering, I dress in comfortable athletic wear, placing Kioren back on my wrist before I leave the room to find where the commotion is coming from. The sound of voices conversing grows louder as I approach the dining hall, stomach growling. I crack open the door and peek inside. My eyes go wide at the sight; most of the cambions are together in one room. Well, this should be interesting...

They sit at the long wooden dining table, eating their breakfast as they joyfully speak with each other. Azura and Meena are in a rapid conversation as they shovel food into their mouths. Beside them, Tevari reads his book but cracks a smile every time he hears something amusing. Lei Jing sits the furthest away from the others as she picks at her food, meeting my eyes briefly as I enter.

"See something interesting?" a voice says from behind, and I jump.

"Seriously, Oliver?" He shrugs innocently, pushing past me into the room. I follow him in, greeting everyone present. Only Luka is nowhere to be seen... Taking a seat at the table, I begin packing a plate full of fruits and sliced meats. "Is... is Luka not coming?" I ask Tevari, not wanting to disturb the two girls, now bantering with Oliver, or ask Lei Jing.

He shrugs his shoulders, not looking up from his book. I nod back with a small sigh. Popping a grape into my mouth, I lose myself in my thoughts. A song I recognize but don't remember. A cambion who spoke my name and caused the vines to go rampant. Does it have to do with the golden-eyed woman? Her words resonated in my mind when I heard the song Luka played... *Remembrance*, that's what I'll call her. Just another entity to differentiate inside my mind.

I stare off in the distance, eyes unfocused, recalling the heartbreakingly beautiful song. I can't imagine where I heard it before... I've never heard someone play the piano in person before. Father never kept musical instruments in the estate either. In his eyes, they're a waste of time for a hunter. As for music in general, I can't say I've ever listened to classical piano. So how the hell did I recognize that song? None of it connects together... My hand itches to reach for the lotus tattoo. Why does it threaten Darkness?

"So, are we going to finally do the team training?" Meena asks, shaking me out of my thoughts.

All five of them turn to me. "Well yeah," I say, looking around at them, confused. "I said we'd be doing it today...."

"You made us wait almost a week," Azura says, arching an eyebrow.

"Rishu wouldn't tell us why either," Meena adds.

"A week?" I say, my mouth parting slightly. Have I really been out for so long? "Luka didn't say anything?"

"So he got private training?" Oliver says teasingly as he takes a seat across from me.

I roll my eyes. Since when were we all so comfortable around each other? "Then what have you all been up to?"

"We did what you said. We got to know each other better," Oliver says before shoving a piece of bread into his mouth. "They're not as bad as they seem."

My eyes widen. "And that's all it took?"

Oliver shrugs, returning to his eating. The two girls barely glance up as they continue their conversation. Tevari remains aloof, having never stopped reading.

Who would have thought giving a random order and disappearing for a week was all it would take.

Peeking through my lashes at Lei Jing, I notice she still separates herself from the others. Her violet eyes meet mine before swiftly turning away. I wonder what made her join in when my order had only been to the other four in the room.

The door opens, and the room goes quiet. Luka enters, ignoring the stares from the others. I glance at him quickly but look away before he notices. He takes a seat at the table, mumbling a soft "morning." His gaze lifts to mine, and my cheeks heat. Mortified, I immediately turn my head to hide the pink tint.

"Uri, Zera..." I whisper in my mind as if someone in the room might hear.

"I must say, the nickname is sweet," Uriel says with a glittery laugh.

I smile to myself as I take a bite of my breakfast. *"I know you said to wait...."* I say, slouching back into my chair. *"But who is he?"* I ask, glancing at Luka. She doesn't respond. *"The vines...*

they appeared when I heard that song... Should I stay away from him?" My heart aches at the thought.

"You're safe, for now."

I let out a sigh of relief. Feeling eyes on me, I look around the table at the cambions watching. Clearing my throat, I squirm in the cushioned seat.

"Since I was... gone for a week," I say, skirting around the reason for my absence, "let's train this afternoon. The four of you have already been paired together, so"—I look to Lei Jing and Luka—"you two will be the last pair." Finished with my plate, I stand and place it on the wooden shelf for dirty dishes. "We meet in the garden at noon."

I leave the room, not waiting to see if they argue. But to my surprise, no one voices a complaint.

I'm making my way down the hall when a hand gently lands on my arm. I halt, spinning around. My eyes trail up from the ring-embellished hand to the face of the man currently consuming all my thoughts. He lets go, taking a step back.

"Are you... okay?" he asks.

My eyes trace each feature of his face. Though I still wonder if his powers are what entrance me, I can say definitively that he is the most beautiful person I've ever seen. From the sharp contours of his face to his somber eyes that hold more emotion than he lets on. Luka towers over me, a presence both intimidating and comforting—as if he could never actually cause me harm. *I'm here,* he had said... I remember that, at least.

"I'm okay. I didn't mean to worry you." And it's true. A deep part within me not wanting to disturb his peace. "It'll be a while until noon, do you want to take a walk?"

For a split second, doubt flits across his eyes as if we're back to day one. But he smiles, eyes crinkling as they turn into crescents. "I'd love to."

The garden—evidence of Azura and Oliver's brawl nowhere to be seen—twinkles with an airy lightness. As if the flowers, dew still resting on their petals, are alive once more and chattering away in the morning sunlight.

I smile as the sun warms my skin and a cool breeze blows through my hair, not yet tied for training. The wind grazes my cheek in a gentle touch, easing my worried mind.

Luka stands in the middle of it all, head turned to the sky like the night I saw him out here. His eyes are shut as he enjoys the warmth of the sun and breeze just as I am.

His body glows—even more ethereal in the day than he had been beneath the pale moonlight. A deadly beauty in this garden, yet I can't help but stare in amazement. Curiosity gnawing away at my resolve to keep my distance, even though Uriel says I'm safe. At least, for now.

"You're quieter than the others," I say.

His eyes open as he turns to me with that smile that tugs at my heart. "I have little to say."

I chuckle. "I doubt that. You seem—" I hesitate, my thoughts scrambling to describe what I see when I look at him. "Somehow, I think you've experienced the worst the world can offer."

My face falls as I recall what Meena told me—such nonchalance for a tragic story of abandonment and survival. But Luka is different. The truth of his experiences are hidden by a mask, one he doesn't dare take off. Something all too familiar to my own shielded heart.

"I'm here to help all of you, you know... Yet you're the one I know the least about. And after what happened...."

His eyes darken before he returns my chuckle. A low sound that heats my cheeks. "Maybe it's for the better." His smile doesn't fall, but there's pain laced in each word.

"I doubt that too."

We stare at each other for a moment that seems to last a lifetime. I search his eyes for the familiarity I felt when he played that song. For any answer his gaze can offer me. But what I see, what I *feel*, is not what I expect to find.

I always had a crush on Adrian—even if I never wanted to admit it to myself—butterflies flitting around my stomach whenever he was around. Best friends, but never more. Yet, here with Luka... This feeling is like a gentle wave holding me above the water's surface, rocking me in its calm grasp. Serene like the summer day around us, as sweet as the white rose he gave me, and as exhilarating as the cool breeze that seems to push me ever so closer to his side. And I'm not quite sure what to do with that.

Stepping away, I walk toward the grand fountain, playing with the flowing water as I follow its border. The phantom pain lingers over my lotus tattoo, a reminder, as Darkness had said to me.

"Tell me about yourself." I look up, meeting the gaze that follows me. "What are your powers? Who's your demonic parent?" Smiling, I think of the encounters I've had with the other cambions. "Or will you attack me to showcase your strength like the others have?"

He laughs that contagious laugh once more. "I won't attack you."

I smirk at him. "I didn't think so. But you didn't answer my other questions."

Walking around the fountain, I end up on the other side of him. Hands behind my back, I look at his face, tilting my head.

He smiles again, reaching forward to tuck a strand of hair behind my ear. My breath halts, frozen under the gentle touch.

Luka moves his hand back, raising it above us. I follow, watching as he releases shimmering light from his palm. My mouth parts as I watch the dancing lights intermix with the sunlight. Twinkling specks fall softly onto the flowers, and the petals vibrate as if struck with a wave of electricity. He lowers his hand, a shy smile resting on his face. Such contrast to the angular shape and sharp eyes that seemed so cold and distant, a facade to keep others—to keep me—from knowing the real him. And I can't decide if I hate it or want to know more.

"Beautiful."

23

LESSON ONE: WE'RE ALL MONSTERS

Looking at the group of cambions gathered in front of me, a smile falls on my lips. For once, I've got all six in the same space. We stand in the center of the garden, the disaster Azura and Oliver created a distant memory for us all. The afternoon is hot, even with the change in season—October already upon us.

The leaves are slowly changing color from vibrant green to yellows and reds. The skies are cloudier than during the summer, offering us a reprieve from the intense sun. But still, the heat remains.

"I'm glad you all came," I say, looking each of them in the eye. They don't wear the most conventional clothing to spar in... But I suppose I can only expect so much since I didn't give them specific instructions.

Tevari opts for his comfy oversized style while Azura beside him is in her crop top and black cargo pants. On the other hand, Meena wears a cute dress, and Oliver is dressed in his usual T-shirt and jeans. Lei Jing, as I've always seen her, is fully covered, wearing a long sleeve top that seems entirely too hot, and Luka... I almost blush as I look at him, remembering our private conversation earlier today. His style is elegant yet casual, wearing tailored black slacks with a flowy white button-up. Rings adorn his fingers. All are silver except for two on his right hand. Matching golden rings with an emerald gem set in each. One rests on his ring finger and the other on his pinky. I can't help but linger on them, on him. It suits him just like the beautiful lights he creates.

All are impractical compared to my athletic gear. I would argue with their choices if it wasn't for the fact that it took three weeks to get them all here.

"Today's exercise is all about teamwork. From what I've seen, you all have basic control over your powers, if not more than you let on. Now, I want you to think of not just using your powers for yourself, but using them in combination with your partner."

"It's not like we'll always be together. What's the point of learning to fight with them," Azura says, crossing her arms and throwing a side-eye at the others beside her.

I nod to her. "You're right, you won't always fight together. But if you want to survive, you better learn to. When you fight as a team, you need more control to complement each other's abilities. A dance, if you will. So think of this as a practice to see how well you can control your powers, so when push comes to shove, they won't get the best of you and hurt your partner."

They all nod, Azura backing down from the argument with a roll of her eyes. I try not to let it show, but if I'm being honest, I don't know what I'm doing. Teamwork wasn't the focus of Lance's teachings. Always keep moving; don't doubt your strength; fight to survive—these are the things he taught me during my fourteen years of training.

"And what about you?" Oliver asks, and I raise a brow at him. "There's only seven of us, and I'm not missing another opportunity to fight you. Especially with that delightful display you gave us before...." His eyes trail to the bracelet on my wrist, darkness swirling behind his gaze.

"What about Rishu? He's still here," Meena says, her pigtails swinging from side to side as she turns from Oliver to me.

"Well, he's a demon, not a cambion—"

Rishu appears in a puff of smoke. "Great idea, Meena. Other cambions won't be your enemy. Demons, *hunters*"—I meet his dark brown gaze with a harsh one—"will be."

I hate that he's not wrong. The cambions will need to know who their enemies are and how to defeat them. My hand reaches to the necklace Rishu gave me—hiding the angel wings on the back of my neck. *I'm their enemy too.*

"What kind of demon are you exactly?" I ask him, brushing my other thoughts away.

"Haven't you realized?" he says as his eyes glint red. I rack my mind but fall short on an answer. "My *human* name is Rishu Nagarajan. Think on that."

My mouth parts slightly as I stare at his bronzed face, black curls dangling dangerously in front of his eyes. The night when we first met comes to mind. Scales rolling across his skin beneath the street lights. I gulp, taking a small step back from him. *He's a naga.* Half-serpent, half-human demons from Southeast Asia. Some even worship them as deities. But they don't usually reside in North American territories, more typically in India, Malaysia, Laos, Thailand, and so on. Places far from Chicago, where Amon resides. How'd the two even meet?

His mouth forms into a grin as he watches the realization cross my face. "I suppose your past is useful after all...."

"Past?" Meena says, popping up in front of us. "What is your past, Nova? We don't know much about you."

I look into her bright gray eyes—innocent, even though she's killed humans to survive. My mouth dries as the rest of the cambions look at me expectantly. Guilt washes over me for hiding the truth. Demons and cambions alike, I was trained to hunt them. Every bit of skill I'm using to train them comes from the training of those that wish them dead. It feels cruel to keep lying, but the pain in my chest, the *fear*, tells me I can't say anything. If they knew, I'd be dead or worse.

We might be at least acquaintances now, but still... I never want them to know the truth. Not when it'd hurt us both.

Rishu places a hand on my shoulder and squeezes gently before turning to Meena. "You see, Meena, Amon also rescued Nova from a horrible past just like I did with you. But not everyone likes to share their history as you do." He pats her head, and she smiles adoringly at him.

"You're right. I won't ask anymore. You can tell us when you're ready," Meena says before bouncing back to Tevari's side on bare feet.

I nod, mustering up a smile. Glancing at Rishu, I offer a silent thanks. Only three weeks have passed, yet my life from before feels farther away than I ever thought possible. Being a hunter was the only thing I ever wanted—to prove to my father that I was capable.

Secrets, lies, half-truths... I wanted answers to it all. I still do.

I look at each of the cambions, so human despite their demonic heritage and yet also so much like me—kids looking for answers. I gulp, feeling a strange emotion climb its way up inside me.

"Since none of us have ever fought together, talk with your sparring partner on how you can utilize each of your abilities. Think offense and defense, who can play which part, and how can you switch between. Then we'll move to the clearing Oliver so kindly made for us."

Oliver grins as he walks away with Azura at his side. Hopefully, they don't tear each other's heads off. Luka's gaze meets mine as he wanders off with Lei Jing—as if something's on his mind, something left unsaid. Meena and Tevari head in the opposite direction of the two groups, and I turn to Rishu.

"You shouldn't have shown up. I can't... I shouldn't spar against them today," I say as I pull him aside so Luka and Lei Jing don't hear.

An annoying smirk appears on his face. "And why not? Afraid you'll lose as you did against those hellhounds?"

"I didn't lose! But no, that's not what I'm afraid of. Whatever you did to me to keep me alive... I feel weaker. Like my strength isn't quite there anymore." I look away from his gaze, the vulnerability eating away at me. The lotus burns almost constantly on my chest, the black vines threatening to cascade over my body if they ever break his seal. "How can I know it will last?"

He sighs, the smirk disappearing. "You told Amon to find a way to slow the lotus from killing you. This is his extension of your deal. And thankfully for you, I'm a master at sealing magick. We"—his eyes trail off in the distance—"I will be here if anything does happen. Nobody wants you dead when you're still needed."

"Needed? Will Amon ever tell me what he has planned for them? For me? He said he sees the past and future, so what is he so worried about? Are the hunters finally coming for him?"

Rishu smiles. "Ah, so you didn't miss that." I raise a brow, waiting. "All in good time, Nova. There's no rush. Not yet, at least."

"What is it with everyone holding back? I'm getting sick of hearing 'all in good time' every time I want to know something." He smirks, in no way inclined to answer my questions. "Fine, but until I'm fully recovered from what happened, you'll have to carry our team."

He salutes me, and I turn away as I roll my eyes at him. My gaze falls to Luka, staring right back at me from across the garden. Lei Jing stands in front of him, back turned to us. She speaks with her arms crossed; Luka's lips move every so often to respond.

His long black hair sways gently in front of his face as the breeze blows through the garden. My heart thrums in my chest, but I can't decide if it's the black vines pulling at Rishu's seal or something more.

This beautiful person in front of me—someone I strangely feel so calm around—I know he's dangerous. But I can't help myself. Even when being drawn to him is something I know as a hunter I can never allow. And somehow, I know it's not a hidden power of his doing this to me. So why do I feel this way?

I tear my gaze from his, breaking the connection. Maybe I don't want the answer to this question.

"Nova, we're ready," Tevari says, approaching from my side.

I nod. "Then let's get to the forest." I grin at him, mustering excitement for the sparring ahead of us. "We'll start with Tevari and Meena against Azura and Oliver."

"Don't you think... Meena is too young to fight?" Lei Jing says, glancing worriedly over at the cute pigtailed girl.

Rishu begins to speak, but I cut him off. "There's no need to worry about her." Meena's eyes meet mine, a devilish smile crossing her face, and I wonder how far she's come in the week I was gone. What new skills the girl has picked up since then.

My heart sinks, thinking of the time I've lost. A promised study session with Tevari, more illusion and puppeteering practice with Meena, not to mention the others I haven't even had a chance to work with. Lei Jing has her invisibility—her spying enough to clear that up for me—but what else can she do? Oliver has shown me the beast he can turn into, yet I can't help but wonder how much control he has of the thing that lives inside him. Azura has finally stopped threatening me every time I near her, but that doesn't mean she'd let me correct her stances or help her practice for more precise control of her flames. And Luka... Well, all I've seen is his light, nothing more of what he might be capable of.

I don't feel like I've lived up to my end of the contract.

"Give it time," I hear Uri whisper in my ear, and a wave of calm washes over me.

Arriving at the clearing in the middle of the woods, the two pairs meet in the center while the rest of us remain near the edge by the trees. It's messy—sticks and debris scattered in the dirt, fallen trees lingering in the center. Oliver sure made a mess of this place.

"There are only a few rules to follow while sparring," I say, calling out so everyone can hear me. "You can use any power you have, but please be mindful of injuring each other."

"You know we heal faster," Lei Jing says from my side. I turn to face her violet gaze and nod to her. Of course, I should have known that.

"Fine, then just don't hurt each other too badly and stay within the clearing. When I say begin, you may start, and when I say stop, you stop. Understood?" My commanding voice reminds me of Lance speaking to the first-year trainees, his clipboard in hand as he scribbled down notes. I never saw what he wrote, but this situation feels oddly similar. If only I had one too.

The two pairs in the clearing settle into fighting stances—ones that need a lot of work. Maybe I won't be so useless after all. "Begin."

Azura immediately summons fire to her hands as Oliver morphs his arms into long black talons—similar to the ones I first saw previously in this very clearing. Tevari raises thick tree roots from the ground to his side as Meena focuses her energy to make five illusions of herself. Each is tinted a faint pink, the only giveaway of her illusions. I nod in approval.

The clones of Meena race toward Oliver in a triangle formation as Tevari provides backup from behind, whipping the tree roots around as Azura fires off flames in Meena's direction. He flicks them into the air, where they explode, scattering embers around us. I wince, hoping we don't start a forest fire.

Azura boils with anger at the constant misses, and she starts pumping out fireballs faster than Tevari can deflect them. The tree roots fall to the ground once burned to their limit, and Tevari's face flickers with pain as if he feels the attacks himself. I make a note of it.

Meena's illusions are broken as Oliver's arms extend and retract, slicing into them with no remorse. His talons destroy them faster than she can resummon them, but Meena is quicker than he is, appearing between the shattered remains of her clones. Small and lethal, she zips under his arms to get close to him. Before he can react, she flips backward, kicking him square in the jaw with her grimy bare feet. I wince but can't help the grin that pulls at my lips.

"Who knew the girl could fight?" Lei Jing says at my side. I nod in agreement.

"I guess that happens when you have to survive," I meet her eyes and then Rishu's—a hard look on his face. I nudge him, but he shakes me off. "She'll be okay. I'll stop the fight before anything happens," I say to him.

Oliver's taloned arms retract as he shakes off Meena's blow. We all watch as she bounds over to Tevari, jumping to high-five him. A shy smile crosses his face. They make a pretty good team.

I step forward to end the session when a roar echoes throughout the clearing. Black feathers and scales ripple across Oliver's skin, the beast fully emerging from his once-human form. He's hunched over on his hands and knees, his body shifting into something between a wolf, a bird, and a snake. The skin of his jaw shrinks back as rows of razor-sharp fangs replace his teeth, and his lips curl back in a snarl. The whites of his eyes turn black, a red iris appearing at the center.

"Not good." I summon Kioren to my hand, the scythe antsy to intervene. This answers my question on how well Oliver can control the being inside him—barely at all. I step toward the clearing, but Rishu's arm stops me.

Oliver, now easily twice his previous size, races forward—faster than before—a flash of black across the clearing. He latches onto Meena's leg, lifting her into the air before slamming her into the ground.

"Why are you stopping me?" Rishu doesn't respond, his eyes trained on the cloud of dust rising around where Oliver threw her into the ground.

"What the hell is wrong with you?" Tevari screams at Oliver, the beast's jaws salivating as he paces in the clearing. Tevari raises his hand, using the tree roots to bring Meena closer to him. She looks dazed but otherwise uninjured. I cringe, knowing anyone else would probably be dead after a move like that.

Azura smirks, ignoring Tevari. Her flames grow around her, consuming her body. It's now two to one—Meena still unconscious. Azura and Oliver race to Tevari. He remains calm even as Oliver's rows of sharp teeth come crashing toward him. Meena jumps up at the last moment, kicking Azura so hard she crashes into Oliver. They tumble over each other in the dirt before rolling into a tree at the opposite edge of the clearing.

"Stop," I call out, brushing Rishu's arm out of the way.

My heart races in my chest as if I had been the one fighting. Even as an Undivided, I find them terrifying to watch. If I was just human—untrained with no angel or angelic weapon—I wouldn't know what to do if I came face-to-face with them. Fear traces my skin, an unwelcome feeling.

Meena runs to high-five Tevari again, dancing in a circle with a wide grin on her face. What a sneaky girl. Stepping into the clearing, I clap for the two winners as Kioren returns to the bracelet. "Congrats, you two won this round." Walking to where Azura and Oliver lay on the ground, I crouch down and extend a hand to each of them. "You two fought well."

Azura slaps my hand away, jumping to her feet. "We still lost."

Oliver, who's shifted back, remains on the ground, eyes diverted from the hand I offer. I stand. "There's always next time," I say to them. "You've just begun your training." Oliver keeps his gaze away from mine as I wait expectantly above him. "That's the first time I saw you lose control. Even when you and Azura destroyed the garden, you—"

"Say it how it is. I'm a monster." He stands, brushing the dust from his pants. When he meets my gaze, there's no trace of his usual arrogant self. Darkness lingers behind his eyes, the beast inside him prowling—waiting to be let out again.

I step back, my eyes widening. "You're not a monster...."

He chuckles humorlessly, a dark haze crossing his face. "You have no idea what I am."

I'm lost for words as he turns and leaves the clearing. We all watch him disappear into the woods, a heavy silence settling around us. The fallen logs around us burn with the last embers from Azura's fire, the dust still settling. Tree roots laying dead on the ground slither back into the earth with a wave of Tevari's hand. He still looks pained, guilty even, as they disappear beneath the dirt. Meena wipes sweat from her brow as she stares at the space in the forest Oliver disappeared into.

I glance back at the others. Lei Jing won't meet my eyes—her arms crossed, as usual. Luka, however, holds my gaze as if he wishes to step toward me even when he doesn't move a muscle. I turn away, staring at the dirt beneath my shoes.

Guilt rises in the pit of my stomach. He didn't believe me. Then again, I don't believe me. All I could see in his eyes was a reflection of myself. His monster just like the one that claws its way into my mind. Not the dark voice that haunts me, but my own inner being. A part of myself I never want anyone to see. It may not be a creature like the one inside of him, but it's a monster in its own right.

"We'll resume tomorrow." I turn and leave the clearing without another word, silence ringing behind me as I disappear into the woods.

24

Lesson Two: Never Underestimate Anyone

"Why aren't we sparring?" Lei Jing says, her arms crossed in her typical stance.

I walk the line of cambions standing before me in the garden. They've all joined me again for training—with the exception of Oliver. He's kept to himself since yesterday's events, and I'm not one to keep pushing. "Because I've realized we need to get your basics down before we move on to working with your partners again."

"Basics?" Azura scoffs, holding up a hand and summoning a raging flame. Closing her fist, she extinguishes it a moment later. "I have complete control of my fire. I'll be fine without your lame *basics*."

I stop in front of Azura, scanning her up and down. "Says the girl who lets rage get the best of her and has to revert to exhausting her powers since she can't handle herself in hand-to-hand combat." Tevari snorts, making all of us turn our heads to him. He looks sheepish as he regains his composure.

"Look, if you ever want control of your powers, you need to know at least the basics of throwing a punch."

"Then let's see you show us," Meena chips in, a broad smile on her face.

"Yeah, what are you skilled in exactly besides throwing that scythe around?" Lei Jing flips her long hair behind her shoulder, her eyes moving to the bracelet on my wrist.

A smile forms on my face. "I've trained in many forms of martial arts and close combat since I was young. But if my words don't convince you... who wants to spar? No powers, of course."

"I do."

My eyes dart to Luka standing at the end of the line. The lotus tattoo heats on my chest, the black vines squirming beneath Rishu's seal. I gulp, motioning for him to step forward. We've never seen each other fight, so this seems fair enough. The others move back to clear a space for us, taking a seat on the edge of the fountain.

"You seem confident."

Luka's eyes shimmer with mischief. "I am."

I smile, my heart racing with an excitement I haven't felt since I last sparred against Adrian. We never got a chance to spar once he returned from his mission abroad... I shake away the unhelpful thought. Lance's voice whispers through my mind as I take a deep breath, centering myself. *Don't doubt yourself. Be careful who you antagonize. Move your feet quicker.*

Getting into position, I watch Luka do the same—his stance far beyond that of a novice. "Ready when you are," I say, a smirk on my face.

"I want to call it out! Tevi, make me a platform," Meena says, and to my surprise, Tevari complies. Weaving plants together, he raises Meena a few feet above the others.

"Ready, begin!" she yells out, throwing her fist into the air.

I move in first, throwing quick punches that Luka easily blocks. He fights to be on offense, throwing a punch that I dodge. With ease, he transitions into an array of kicks and jabs that I swerve and duck beneath.

"So you're not a beginner," I say, getting close enough again to exchange punches with him—each one blocked, our skills evenly matched.

"I never said I was." He smirks, and I hold back a laugh.

I jump and kick, but he blocks again. We continue in a dance of skilled moves and dodges, neither of us able to land a hit. His arm slides past me as I dodge a hit, and I grab on to it, pulling my leg up to knee him in the stomach. Face-to-face, I see his smirk grow wider—his opposite hand blocking my attack. I try to pull back, but he grabs hold of my leg, keeping me in place.

Unbalancing us to break free, I tumble to the ground. Rolling over each other, we fight for the upper hand. Luka lands on top. He pins me to the ground, the smirk never leaving his lips.

"Had enough?" His silver eyes twinkle with playfulness.

"Not nearly." Grabbing his wrists, I pull him in and roll over on top of him, switching our positions. "What about you?"

Our eyes meet, and I'm suddenly all too aware of our proximity as I feel his breath mingle with mine. Warmth blossoms in my chest and spreads to my cheeks.

"Never," he whispers but makes no move to switch our positions.

The lotus thrums in my chest. Or is it my heart? I search his silver gaze for meaning, for answers, only to be gifted with another devilish smirk. A light pink tone graces his cheeks, and my face burns hotter.

"And Nova wins!" Meena shouts, breaking the spell holding me in place. She claps excitedly, urging the others to follow—albeit much less enthusiastically.

Quickly, I push off him, brushing the barely there dirt before offering an awkward hand. He takes it, his smirk morphing into a genuine smile that reaches his eyes. I turn away, taking a deep calming breath to cool my cheeks before facing him and the others again. What the hell is wrong with me lately?

"So, who's next?"

Rubbing my arm, I hit a deep purple bruise and wince. It's not something worth having my angels heal, but it's painful nonetheless. Training with the cambions is nothing like sparring with the first-years or Lance. They learn faster, hit harder, and are all the cockier for it. In a single week, they've learned skills that took me years to develop. A benefit of having unbelievable stamina, I suppose. Now a month has passed since I arrived, and I can only imagine how much stronger they'll get from here on out.

I gaze out a window as I walk down the hall, a sigh escaping my lips as I trail my eyes to the garden. Luka sits in his favorite spot at the edge of the fountain, ethereal even in this dreary weather—a hazy rain about to fall from the sky. Our eyes meet, and he smiles, but I turn away, quickening my steps.

He's... he's too much for me to handle.

Every time he's near, my heart, my mind... neither knows what to do when it comes to him. And Darkness is still there, lurking. And I don't want another one of his painful reminders.

"Nova." I hear my name called from behind. Turning around, I watch in surprise as Lei Jing hesitantly steps forward. "I—" She fidgets with her hands. "I want to apologize."

My eyes widen. "For what?"

She continues fidgeting, lips pursing together. "For not trusting you. I mean, I still don't. At least not completely... I have trust issues, okay?" She looks more annoyed with herself than at me, and I wonder what caused such issues, the tragedies in her life.

"You don't have to apologize. I hardly trusted you all either...." I say, but she just continues on.

"But like, I—Well, there's a lot you don't know about me like we don't know about you, which is fine because I also don't want to share... But my point is"—she lifts her head, violet eyes locking with mine. A long strand of her black hair falls over her shoulder, and she brushes it back—"I've always been scared to fight. So I should at least be thankful for you teaching us when you're human, and your kind usually hates us as much as we hate you."

I approach her, my gaze softening as I lift a hand toward her shoulder. She flinches, and my fingers retract before they touch her, hand falling to my side.

"You don't have to thank me either. I was still hired, in a sense, to train you. But I'm glad I can help," I say, and I mean it.

She bites her lip and looks off to the side. "If it was just because Amon brought you here with whatever contract you two signed, then we wouldn't be...." She pauses, her face scrunching up like the words are painful to say. "We wouldn't be"—she glances my way again—"friends?"

I can't help but chuckle. "Is that what we are now?"

She smiles, holding her arms close to her body. "At least something like that." We laugh together, something I imagine feels unfamiliar to us both.

"Look, I haven't asked because... it seems personal, but that tattoo... Are you really okay?"

My shoulders sag as I turn my gaze to the gray sky outside the windows. With a long sigh, I wonder if I'll ever have an answer to her question. "Honestly, I don't know...." I turn back with a forced smile. "But it's nothing for you to worry about. I'm fine, really."

She doesn't seem convinced. Thankfully, mind reading isn't one of her abilities. It's Meena I have to watch my thoughts around.

"I need to go find Rishu, but keep up the practice so one day you feel comfortable enough to show me all your powers, not just the invisibility," I say, and she nods with a soft smile.

I leave her where she stands, but her eyes burn into my back as I walk away. Things may be friendly between us, but we can never be *friends*. Crossing that line just isn't an option. Guilt claws at my stomach, but I know I can't allow myself any closer. Not with her, not with Luka. I'm safer when they don't know the truth.

"Are you?" Zera says, but I brush his voice aside. Nobody should have to deal with the things happening inside my mind but me. Even if the cambions knew and didn't try to kill me for my deception, there's nothing they could do.

Rounding the corner, I climb the stairs to the fourth floor of the château to find Rishu's room. When I reach his door, I knock until I hear his voice inviting me to enter. His room is laden with deep reds and dark browns. It's as plush and comfortable as my room, except smaller and without the balcony. He lounges on his bed, a dagger twirling in his hand.

I step into the room, closing the door behind me, and he arches an eyebrow as a slow, seductive grin slides across his face. "How may I be of service?"

I roll my eyes at how predictable he is. "I wanted to ask if you knew when Amon was going to tell me anything more. I know technically I was… out for a week, but it's been another two weeks, and"—I sigh, noticing the black claws extended from his fingers—"There's too much I don't know. I *need* answers."

"And what are your questions? Do you even know?" he says, sounding amused.

I scowl. "Of course, I know. It's all I can think about." My hand reaches for the lotus tattoo. One of many questions.

"Then ask me something." I watch as he sits up and sets the dagger aside, claws retracting. "You want answers? Ask the right questions, and you might get some."

A torrent of questions floods my mind. Who is Remembrance, the woman who showed me how to use Kioren? Who does she want me to remember? Who or what is Darkness? Why will the lotus tattoo kill me? Why do I have two angels? Why did my father keep me in his estate all that time? Who was my mother? What future does Amon see for all of us? So many options I can choose from to gain even an ounce of clarity in my life.

"Who is Luka?"

Rishu freezes, his eyes widening. He throws his head back with a burst of laughter, the low sound booming through the room. "Out of everything, *that's* what you're curious about?" Rishu stands, prowling over to me. "Luka is Luka. A being with the ability of light and darkness, even if he only wants you to see the good."

"But—"

"There are no buts, Nova. Luka is who he is. If you want to know more"—Rishu towers over me, his brown eyes flashing red—"instead of coming to my room to ask, go to his."

My scowl deepens as his smile turns sadistic. Truly a demon. Stepping away from him, I head toward the door. This was pointless. If he's not going to answer, then what's the point of asking him?

"You need to learn to ask the right questions if you want to get anywhere."

I turn back to him, pausing with my hand on the doorknob. "Is it the questions or the fact that you won't answer? I'm not some idiot human who can't read between the lines. You didn't lie, but there's no full truth in what you said either. Pretty tactless if you ask me."

I open the door and begin to leave when a hand latches around my wrist.

"All in due time, Nova. With some things, it's all about the timing."

I break my arm from his grasp. "Honestly, you're all beginning to sound the same. Between my father, my angels, Amon, and now even you—how are different sides when you all act exactly alike." I shake my head as I leave his room, shouting over my shoulder, "We made a deal, and I expect Amon to fulfill his side of it."

The door doesn't close behind me, and my steps falter as I hear Rishu mumble beneath his breath.

"He will. They both will."

25

DISCOVERY

Heading to the dining hall for dinner, I can't shake what I heard Rishu say. Did I hear wrong? It seems unlikely, but then who would *they* refer to in that context? There's only Amon and Rishu, and I can't imagine the latter referring to himself in the third person.

Outside the window, night has fallen. The stars are hidden behind dark gray clouds holding the promise of rain.

"Are you sure you two can't clarify anything?" I say quietly in the empty hall.

"We would if we could," Uriel says, her voice tinged with sadness. *"But you're treading in dangerous waters, Nova. You must be careful, or—"*

Her voice goes silent, and my steps halt. *"Miss me?"* My blood goes cold. Darkness is speaking as if all around me. His voice a nightmare I can't seem to escape, unknowable yet hauntingly familiar at the same time. *"You understand nothing, as always,"* he says, and I reach for the lotus tattoo burning on my chest.

"Was my warning not enough?"

"Stop," I plead, my voice trembling. The voice laughs at me—mocking and taunting as it soaks up the fear dripping off every inch of me. "Stop," I say again, but the laughter grows louder, consuming all other sounds around me. "Stop!"

"Nova?"

The hall grows silent, and I lift my head. Oliver stands in front of me, shock written across his face. He extends his hand to mine, but I recoil.

"Nova," Oliver says again, taking a step closer, "what happened?"

I shake my head, jaw clamping shut. *"Uri, Zera, what is happening?"* I ask in my mind, staring at my shaking hands. They're silent, but their presence bangs in the back of my mind, as if they want to speak but just can't.

Warm light spills into the hall as the door to the dining room opens, the others exiting upon hearing the commotion.

"Where have you been, loser?" Azura says to Oliver before her gaze travels to me. "And what's wrong with her?"

I lift my gaze and try to speak, but no sound comes out. My eyes meet Luka's, and my body trembles harder. What is going on? He pushes past the others, wrapping his hands around mine.

"Tell me what's wrong," he says. His eyes travel to where the lotus tattoo is hidden beneath my shirt, but I shake my head again. Panic flits through his silver eyes. *No.* I squeeze my eyes shut. I don't want any of them to see me like this. I can't let them know. I—

"Calm your breath, my child," Zera says, his voice rough, and I feel my breathing ease. *"I have created this space so that only we may enter. He cannot reach you here."* I open my eyes as my shaking stops and look at Luka, whose face is taut with worry. *"You're right that we are all alike—half-truths our only answers. All I can say is trust in the timing and keep moving forward through the pain. One day soon, it will make sense. I promise you that."*

Taking a deep breath, I pull my hands from Luka's. "I'm all right."

"You're not," he says, the others behind him nodding in silent agreement.

I swallow thickly. "I—" I don't know what to say. Can I really trust Zera's promise when promises seem to always elude me? A breeze passes through the hallway, brushing over my skin in the way it always has during difficult situations. It offers the reassurance that I can't find myself. "I'll be all right."

I meet Luka's silver eyes, and I jerk back as the realization hits me. How did I not see it before?

The figure I saw on the night of the blood moon... The one who stood on the church spire as the world was bathed in red... He was the one who caught me, and I remember those same silver eyes even when his face was blurred by pain as I fainted. Eyes that held me captive as they had when I first arrived at the château. Exactly who is Luka?

The ground trembles and I stumble forward into his chest. The others collide into each other while dodging the paintings falling from the walls. Rishu appears in a puff of smoke as Luka helps me regain my footing. The lights cut out, and an ear-piercing alarm begins to wail while the sky outside the windows—Amon's barrier—beats red in warning. With every tremor that shakes the château, the light fades in and out, briefly illuminating the frightened faces of the cambions.

"Everyone, downstairs," Rishu says, taking hold of Meena's hand. "Now."

"What's going on?" Lei Jing says as she and Azura hold on to each other as the floor quakes again.

A large ornate light comes loose from the ceiling, but before I can shout a warning, Tevari's vine shoots out and catches it before it lands on anyone. The vine tosses it aside as chunks of plaster rain down on us.

"Someone start explaining," Azura demands.

"I second that," Oliver says as he brushes dust from his hair.

Meena tugs at Rishu's sleeve. "Rishi, what's happening?"

A grimace crosses the demon's face. "We can't stay here. Now let's go, and then I can explain," Rishu says as he drags Meena down the hall.

Luka grabs my hand before I can say anything, dragging me with him. I tug my hand away and stop alongside the rest of the cambions.

"What the hell is going on?" I say as I look between Rishu and Luka, waiting for us at the top of the staircase.

"*Please*, we don't have time for this," Luka says, stalking back to take my hand once more.

He pulls me beside him, holding me tighter than I thought possible. I look over my shoulder to ensure the other four follow closely behind. Luka's hand clenches harder, and I scowl, unable to free myself. Skipping a step ahead of Luka, our hands still interlocked, I catch up to Rishu. His eyes blaze red as he charges ahead. This can't be good.

"Did someone find us?" I ask as we race down the stairs.

"I don't know. It shouldn't be possible," Rishu says, his voice strained.

Lei Jing comes up beside me with Azura, Oliver, and Tevari watching our backs. "Why would anyone be looking for us?" Lei Jing asks, her violet eyes glowing in the dark.

"I—" I look at Rishu. He said the barrier would be enough to prevent my father from finding us. If this is them... "Let's just get to wherever Rishu is taking us."

We reach the main staircase, descending to the first floor. Moving through the halls, we approach the front door, veering off to a side room. Decorations shake, some falling to the ground with the tremors. Oliver catches a vase, setting it right when the trembling subsides. I finally shake off Luka, my hand suddenly cold. Sliding a curtain open, I peer out the window. Another piercing bang and I cover my ears at the sound.

The tremors stop entirely after the bang, and an eerie silence falls over the château—the barrier fallen. Out the window, a city rises in the distance. My brows furrow together. Chicago?

"Rishi?" Meena says, her voice soft as it breaks the silence. "What's going on?"

Tevari pulls the girl close. "Seems we're about to find out."

Scanning left to right, I watch as fog rolls in from the edge of the property. The outside world invading the safe haven Amon created for us. Dark shadows stretch down the driveway as eight figures walk toward us.

My heart pounds in my ears, all other sounds fading around me. *Hunters*. It's only been a month, but they've already found me. But how? Calming myself, I assess the situation outside. This is a rescue mission; they won't know about the deal or the cambions.

Four warriors with angelic weapons approach the château—two with swords, one with a mace, and one with a large bow, arrow already nocked and ready to shoot. Two dragoons follow behind, dual pistols resting in each of their hands. Finally, a female tamer flanked by two hellhounds appears from the back. They all look young. I don't recognize a single face among them. Not until Adrian comes into sight.

I suck in a breath, stepping away from the window. This can't be happening... I told him not to come. That I had to do this but would one day return.

"Nova isn't that...." Meena says as she stares out the window.

"Stay here." I head toward the front door, not even sure of what I'll do.

An embellished hand grabs my wrist and spins me around. I stare hard into Luka's silver eyes, knowing at least one truth with certainty. Luka was there the night of the blood moon, lifting me from the ground when all my energy had been spent. He cradled me in his arms as if I was precious to him. But why? Why do that then and why act like a stranger now? I search his troubled eyes before gently removing his hand.

"You don't have to do this," he says, and I know he knows the truth of my past.

"They're here for us...." Tevari's panicked voice reaches my ears, and I look over at him as his vine tightens around his frame. "Hunters."

"They'll kill us. We're just... we're monsters," Oliver says. He pulls at his brown hair, eyes wild with fear.

Lei Jing curls into herself, and even Azura looks frozen in fear. Meena holds tightly onto Rishu's hand, and when I meet his eyes, it's clear what I need to do. They can't find the cambions.

"We fight together," Azura says as she stands from her chair, her tone not nearly as brave as her words. "Isn't that what we've been training to do?"

I close my eyes, turning toward the front door so I don't have to look them in the eye.

"We can't," I say, heart aching. I never thought my past would catch up to me so soon.

"Seriously? Why are you being such a hypocrite? You said we were better off fighting together," Lei Jing says, putting on a brave front as she comes between Luka and me.

"Nova, at least let me go with you," Luka pleads. He reaches toward me again, but I step out of his reach.

Looking around the room, I smile. I've only spent a month with them, but it's been by far the best one I've ever lived. Guilt and shame threaten to consume me, but I know there's only one option left for me to take. And there aren't enough sorrys to fix this mistake.

"Let me handle this alone. I'll be back soon."

26

BETRAYAL KNOWS MY NAME

Opening the front door, I slide through and gently close it behind me. I look to the gray sky, wishing for some sort of answer to all of this. *"Am I doing the right thing, Uri, Zera?"* They're quiet, but I can feel their silent support. There's no right or wrong when it comes to a situation like this. Only a decision to be made.

The hunters slow their approach as they see me standing in the doorway. I meet them in the driveway, hands at my sides to show I'm unarmed. Kioren heats on my wrist, itching to be let out, but I wait. The two hellhounds growl beside the tamer's side, waiting for their master to give them a command. It makes me sick to my stomach.

I study the seven standing off to Adrian's sides, wondering when he got his own team.

"Nova?"

Adrian stands only feet away, brow creased in confusion, eyes darting back and forth and up and down my body, making sure I'm unharmed. I'm sure he's thinking my rescue should have been far more challenging than this. The other hunters look at

256

one another as their weapons waver at their sides. Good. That means they really don't know anything.

"Adrian, you need to leave," I say, my voice surprisingly calm.

"What are you talking about?" He sheathes his greatsword behind his back and rushes to my side. His hands latch onto my shoulders, amber eyes searching my own. "I'm here to rescue you."

I move his hands off, stepping back. "You shouldn't have come here. Didn't you read my letter?"

"Nova..." He reaches for my cheek, but I slap his hand away. Hurt crosses his face, but I know it's necessary. Adrian can't help me now, not when he would kill the cambions.

He takes a step back as his eyes focus on something behind me. I turn and see the cambions exiting the château. My heart sinks. This can't be happening. Why doesn't anyone ever just listen to me?

I look sharply at Rishu and then Luka, who shakes his head gently; they couldn't stop them. Their powers hover at their fists, prepared for anything as they take in the hunters.

My voice shakes as I try to sound commanding. "Go back inside, *now*."

Meena steps forward. "He's the one..." she says as she stares at Adrian. "But he's a hunter."

"I said go back inside. I will handle this."

They don't move an inch. Shaking my head, I raise my wrist into the air and call Kioren to my side. The giant scythe eagerly shoots out from the black gem, the staff falling into my hands. I clutch onto it tightly, my knuckles turning white as I look back at Adrian. "Please leave. I don't want to fight you."

He scoffs, running his hands frantically through his hair. "You're siding with them?" He points to the cambions behind me. "This is ridiculous, Nova. Let's go *home*. I've been so worried about you." The last part comes out choked, and a pang stings my heart.

Adrian steps toward me, his hand outstretched. I swing Kioren in front of me to block his path. "I can't do that. I won't leave," I reaffirm myself. I taste blood as I bite down on my tongue in a futile attempt to hold back the tears that threaten to fall.

"I've barely slept since the day they took you. Come home, Nova," he says, a tear rolling down his cheek. "Come home to me."

I shake my head. Even if I were to return to that godforsaken estate, my father will never share the truth with me. There's nothing left for me there. Calming my voice, I say, "Adrian, I have to stay. I *want* to stay." He stares at me in disbelief, but I continue. "You saw what happened, what my father did. He's never going to tell me anything. Nothing will change."

"And here you'll find answers? You're abandoning your duty. Hell, Nova, you're an Undivided! How can you do this?" His eyes shine with tears.

"What is he talking about?" Lei Jing says from behind.

Adrian scoffs. "So they don't know?"

I tense, but I can't find the words to stop him. Adrian slips past Kioren, and my eyes go wide. He grabs the necklace I've not once taken off since arriving here, ripping it from my neck.

"Does this explain it?" he says, holding it before me.

The two sets of angel wings appear back on my neck, the wind swaying my ponytail out of the way for everyone to see. The truth of my identity on full display.

I rush forward to Adrian as tears roll down my cheeks. He steps back just in time as I swing Kioren at him, but the blade catches the necklace, slicing through the chain and shattering the gem. I scream, continuing to lunge for Adrian as fury and sorrow overwhelms me. My vision is blurry with tears, and my blade misses each time.

"Why, Adrian?" I yell through another wild swing. "I asked you to stay away!"

The other hunters rush forward to attack the cambions. Howls and gunshots ring out around me, and I catch glimpses of Rishu and the cambions fighting back, but I'm unable to keep track of them as I attack my best friend.

I scream and swing again, missing Adrian by a fraction. *Do I even want it to hit?* My best friend and only comfort at the Fandera Estate. Someone I loved. Someone I've betrayed.

Adrian finally removes his greatsword from its sheath, blocking my scythe with his blade. We clash back and forth as tears stain both of our cheeks. But the force behind each attack isn't there—for either of us.

I swipe Kioren at Adrian's blade, pulling the sword from his grasp and watching as it clatters to the ground next to him. He falls to his knees and stares up at me with amber eyes as red and puffy as my own. A worn, distraught boy is in front of me—not the courageous hunter I always competed against, always admired.

I freeze with my blade hovering above him. My entire body trembles with emotion as choked sobs leave my lips.

"Do it if you can," he says as the fight around us grinds to a halt. "I said do it!"

Yelling out, I slam the blade into the ground next to him. Falling to my knees, I let go of Kioren. The tears don't seem to stop, rushing down my face as all the hurt and guilt I've bottled up inside pours out of me. I look up as a soft touch grazes my cheek. Adrian's hands cup my face as he searches my eyes, matching tears streaming down his face.

"Please, Nova... We can forget any of this happened. I won't tell Solomon, I—" His voice cracks, and his teary eyes beg me to say yes, to follow him home. But the estate isn't my home anymore. I'm not even sure if it ever really was.

"Adrian... I have to do this."

His jaw ticks, and his eyes shutter—the hunter's resolve taking over. His hands fall from my face as my heart breaks into a million pieces.

"You're as bad as they are."

I exhale a shaky breath. "Going back to my father, to isolation and chains... You know that isn't an option." Calling Kioren back into the bracelet, I don't bother to stand. *I wish I could choose you, Adrian. But in choosing you, I'd have to choose my father, and I can't do that. Not when the scars are still raw on my skin.*

My lips tremble as I speak. "I'm sorry."

Looking up at him, his face mirrors the exact image of my father. Cold and stoic, barren of all emotion except disappointment and loathing.

"Your father should be ashamed of you." I close my eyes as I hold back more tears. "You're no hunter, Nova."

Rain starts to fall, the cold droplets washing away my tears and stealing the remaining warmth from my body, leaving me feeling numb and hollow.

"Leave them. They're not worth it," Adrian says to the group of hunters. "None of them are."

The hunters look skeptical, but still, they follow after him—leaving the cambions and me behind. I remain frozen in place as they fade from view, disappearing down the drive.

Standing, I wobble on unsteady feet. My head hangs low, hair damp with sweat and rain. I turn to the château, to the faces of the other friends I've betrayed.

"I'm sorry."

"You lied to us," Azura says, voice radiating anger.

Lei Jing scoffs. "So you're a hunter and an Undivided. I can't believe I called you a friend."

"How could you do this to us, Nova?" Tevari says, his voice deep with pain.

Lifting my head, I meet their eyes. Pain, hurt, anger, betrayal. The fire in Azura's eyes burns bright as she pulls Lei Jing closer. Tevari's vine wraps tighter around his body as Meena's eyes fill with tears. My gaze lands on Luka, and pain wells in my chest as I recognize a different emotion on his face. *Sympathy*. Maybe he always knew.

"I'm sorry," I whisper over and over again, knowing my words mean nothing.

Rishu takes a step toward me, Meena clinging to his hand. "Nova, you have to calm down. If you don't—"

My breath hitches in my chest, which feels like it's filled with flames, burning me from the inside out. I fall to the ground, grabbing at my shirt as I gasp for air. Rishu lets go of the girl and rushes to me, but Luka gets there first, catching me as I drop to the ground. He props me on against his legs, shielding me from the falling rain.

The black vines push against Rishu's seal, slithering over each other to try and break free.

"Nova, if this continues, the seal I put around the tattoo will break," Rishu says as he drops down beside us. Luka pushes my damp hair out of my face, his hand caressing my cheek.

I shake my head, unable to respond. His words only make me more anxious. The pain spreads faster as the vines pierce through the barrier. I sob, waiting for the moment they inch across my skin and kill me. The others rush to my side, standing overhead. *No, don't watch, don't look. Don't pity me.*

"I'm sorry," Rishu says, slamming his hand onto my chest.

The pain becomes tenfold as air returns to my lungs. The barrier around the lotus reinforced by Rishu's magick. It burns, and my vision goes black. I scream as tears stream down my face.

When he lets go, I jolt up, coughing violently. Luka rubs my back as my vision slowly returns. Glancing at the others standing around me, I can hardly meet their shocked and confused stares. Placing a hand on my chest, I try to regain control of my breathing, the lotus tattoo throbbing as the pain subsides. The vines curl around each other as they quiet inside the new seal. Looking at Rishu, I stare into his brown eyes filled with concern—waiting to know if I'm all right.

"Everyone, head inside. We can't stay here any longer," he says, but they don't move.

"What was that?" Lei Jing says.

"I said *go*." Rishu's eyes flare red, scales rolling across his skin as he exudes his power across the driveway. The cambions shudder but remain at our side.

Rishu and Luka help me stand, my legs shaky. I turn toward Rishu, unable to face the others. In all my life, I've never felt as much shame as I do now. Wanting nothing more than to curl up and disappear.

"Rishi..." I hear Meena whisper.

"Go now," Rishu says, softer this time. He eyes Luka over my head for a moment before I hear their steps fade into the château.

I don't move for a moment, unable to face my decisions and their consequences. I hold in a choked sob. Everything around me is crumbling. Adrian will never look at me the same, and the cambions will never trust a hunter.

"Nova, we need to leave. Are you okay?" Rishu asks, stepping back while still keeping a hold on my arm.

A low scoff escapes my lips. "I've betrayed everyone I know. Do you think I'm okay?" He sighs, silently keeping me upright on trembling legs. "Rishu," I say, needing someone to know what happened before the hunters came—know the voice that haunts my mind, "I—"

"This was bound to happen, Nova," Rishu says, letting my arm go, "but this isn't the end."

His words pierce like a knife as he lets go, walking past me as he enters the château—leaving me hanging before I can say anything. Rain splatters down harder as more clouds roll in. The wind wraps its cold breath around me, a comfort I can't accept. It rolls off me and fades into the night.

There's nothing I can do to pick up these fragmented pieces.

I'm so lost. I look up at the sky, raindrops gliding over my face. A clan I never want to return to—not that I even could anymore—and a place, this château with these people I've befriended... I put them in danger. There's no one else to blame but me.

They don't deserve any of this.

Closing my eyes, I wonder if the sun will ever come back or if this cold sorrow is all that will remain. I exhale a long slow breath as my mind reels. I can't leave, and I can't stay, but what choice do I have? All I know is that this is the end of something far more precious than those damn answers I've been after.

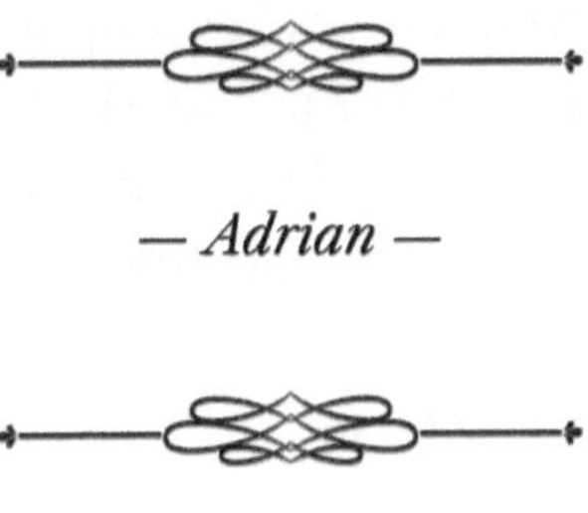

— Adrian —

I fall to my knees as my bedroom door shuts behind me. No tears fall. The well inside me drained and dry. She protected them as if they were *friends*. I shake my head, the image of her swinging that scythe down on me repeating over and over in a constant cycle of horror. A never-ending nightmare I can't escape. How am I supposed to report this to Solomon?

My hands dig into my hair as her words echo in my ears. *I have to do this.* But why, Nova? After all these years, after training to become the best hunter... How could you do this to me, to us?

"This is not the end," Michael whispers in my mind, the archangel's voice unwelcome in my distress.

"How is it not? She's drawn the line, chosen her side. I—"

Michael's words simply repeat. No clarification, just the promise of a different end yet to come. Standing, I pull off my sweat- and rain-laden clothes. I stare at myself in the mirror, rubbing the set of angel wings tattooed on the back of my neck, reminding myself of the mission I've devoted myself to.

An Undivided until death calls me into its tender embrace. And if... if this wasn't the end, then maybe salvation awaits Nova. Maybe in that future, I'll hold her face in my hands and see my best friend again. See the brave, strong, stubborn girl with those daring green eyes who egged me on with ever-witty comments while we sparred.

Maybe, just maybe, it could be something more than I ever imagined. A friend, a companion... A home.

Pulling her letter from my pocket, I rip it to shreds, throwing it into the waste bin. Maybe Michael shouldn't have led me to her... To see her like that, an ally to our enemy.

The bed feels like bricks as I plop onto it, my gaze fixating on the ceiling. "I'll fix this," I say out loud to no one in particular. "I'll fix this and bring you home. If not to Solomon, then at least to me." My resolve hardens, knowing that the path I've chosen will lead me back to Nova.

For better or for worse, the future of *us* is unraveling. The only one privy to our fate: our God above. Only *He* will know which way she and I will fall, and I'll be damned if she falls toward the silver-eyed devil Michael warned me about. The root of all this evil. The one who's changed everything.

A tear slides down my cheek—the well inside me giving up one final drip. It clears my head even as anger sizzles in my stomach.

"This is *not* the end."

27

Solar Eclipse

My arms are heavy as I scan my room for anything to bring with me. But there's nothing. Nothing that will change what I've done or the pain I've inflicted.

"Child, you must stay strong," Zerachiel says, his rough voice a needed comfort. *"Find power in these emotions that you push away."*

"How?" I whisper, but there's no response.

Closing my eyes, I hold back my tears—years of not crying, of staying strong and proving I'm not weak, shattered each time a salty tear falls. I shouldn't be the one crying. This pain is because of my own actions. Choices I made.

Still, I feel it all. Searching for the power they're supposed to have. Searching for any bit of truth in Zera's words.

Sliding to the floor, I lean against the bed frame, curling my arms around my legs. I sniffle as I drop my head to my knees, hiding in the cold comfort of my body. Kioren hums on my wrist, a gentle reminder of at least something on my side.

It doesn't ease me as much as it used to.

Lifting my head, I let it drop back against the bed. The light in the room looks dim, gloomy through my wet lashes. I hug my

266

knees tighter, pressing them into my chest. All this heartbreak, and yet I'm still far from any clarity.

A knock sounds at the door, which creaks as it opens. Luka appears, gently shutting the door behind him. His silver eyes shine with sympathy. It tugs at my shattered heart. *Our beloved,* my mind whispers.

"Are you okay?"

The tears fall.

His eyes soften, and he comes to my side. Sliding in next to me, he gently pulls my head to his shoulder, and I cry. Cry in a way I never have in all my life. Free, uninhibited, broken. Luka's hand strokes my hair, brushing away the pieces sticking to my face. He doesn't move, doesn't shift away.

"This isn't your fault. You aren't the guilty one," Luka finally says, tucking my hair behind my ear and holding my face in his hand. "I won't speak for the others, but your past... Being a hunter is only a part of who you are. It'll never make me leave."

"How can you say that? I've lied to everyone... I don't even know who I am anymore."

He wipes my tears with his thumb. "I know exactly who you are."

My heart thrums in my chest at the question prodding my mind.

"Luka..." The lotus tattoo heats on my chest, black vines held in place but stirring beneath Rishu's seal. Luka wipes another tear, patiently waiting for me to speak.

"Who are you?"

His hand freezes on my cheek, eyes widening as I search his face for an answer—those silver eyes I know I saw on the night of the blood moon. Something I've somehow waited my whole life for. *Remember. Our beloved.* The words Remembrance and my angels spoke to me... The threats Darkness gave looming overhead... It all swirls in my mind, threatening to drown me.

Conflict whirls in his silver eyes as he turns from me, and it's clear the answer I'm looking for isn't easy for either of us. I gently move his hand from my face, a somber smile on my lips. Right now isn't the time for this conversation. One day soon, I'll understand. Zerachiel made that promise to me. The only promise I truly trust. I start to stand, and he joins, helping me up.

"I need to explain to everyone."

Luka hesitates before he lifts his hand for me to take, those matching rings on his fingers glimmering in the darkness and mesmerizing me with some strange hold they have over me. *Remember.* Tentatively I take his hand. It's warm... I blush as I meet his gaze—soft and sad.

With a silent nod, we leave my room and head upstairs to the living space where I first met everyone. The hallways are dark, the red carpet black beneath my feet without the electricity that has yet to come back on. It's strange how I've become so familiar with this place in such a short time, the path upstairs ingrained in my mind that the darkness cannot hinder me.

When we reach the wooden doors, I let go of Luka's hand. He nods, encouraging me as he opens the doors. The room falls silent, five sets of eyes turning in our direction. The cambions are scattered across the furniture throughout the room, small bags filled with the only belongings they care about at their feet.

Their faces are cast in strange shadows from the few candles burning. A scene reminiscent of the day we all met—the broken window Azura sent me through long since fixed.

"I want to explain everything," I say, grateful the darkness hides my tear-stained cheeks.

Azura rises from a plush chair, crossing her arms as she says, "A little late for that."

"Give her a chance," Luka says, stepping closer to my side.

I glance at to him, thankful to have someone by my side—though guilt sits heavy alongside the reassurance. The other four don't comment, waiting to hear my excuses. I look up, meeting each of their eyes.

"My name is Nova Fandera, daughter of Solomon Fandera, leader of the hunters." The name hurts to speak out loud more than it ever did when other hunters spoke of me in ridicule, a curse on their tongue—this is somehow so much worse.

"You're *his* daughter?" Lei Jing says, her arms crossed tightly against her chest. She comes to stand next to Azura, the two girls sharing a similar look of disgust and anger.

I continue despite their glares, "I've spent eighteen years trying to prove myself to my father... But it was never enough for him, even when I became an Undivided with two angels—the first the clan's ever seen." I bite my lip, the memory still raw, the scars still around my wrists. "My whole life, I've never been allowed to leave our estate, but on the night of the blood moon, I snuck out and happened to meet Rishu. He came with an offer from Amon... I had no intention of taking it, but—"

"Boohoo, we all have a sob story, Nova. Hell, I was separated from my mother upon entry to this country and tossed around abusive foster homes my whole life." Azura's eyes flare as her past falls from her lips. "So you think you had it bad? What, because you became an even more powerful hunter? I knew something about you was off. I should have trusted my instincts."

"I never said my past was worse," I say, my voice harsher than intended. My irritation melts away as a new wave of guilt hits me. "I just thought you might want to know why I did all this."

"Continue," Tevari says from the plush couch. "I *hate* humans... But I want more than a shallow story. I want the whole truth." The green vine he wears travels across the floor, wrapping around my ankle. "So don't you dare lie."

I nod. The whole truth, then.

"My father was hiding secrets. Starting with this bracelet I wear. An angelic artifact he was intent on destroying. One I could never find a record of, and somehow only I can call it out—a name you wouldn't hear even when spoken." Lifting Kioren, I show them the silver bracelet that holds the scythe they've all seen. Remembrances words still ringing clear in my mind. "I stole it from him out of petty anger, and it changed everything... When he realized I had it after the blood moon, he put me in *chains*, threatened me with unknown consequences. And when I became an Undivided"—I stop myself, anger rising inside me—"Look, all my life I've trained to be a hunter, yet my father never let me. Even with everything that happened, he wouldn't let me leave his estate. I was basically a prisoner, or a princess, as everyone in the clan called me. But I still wanted answers, ones he promised. Why I had two angels, why the lotus tattoo appeared, why he kept me in his estate all these years, and what happened to the mother I never knew...

"But they never came. So I gave up everything with the hope that Amon could tell me what I wanted, what I *needed* to know."

"What is the lotus? It did that thing again...." Lei Jing says, eyes falling to the spot over my chest.

"What does she mean again?" Luka says, and I glance toward him. I never told anyone about what Lei Jing happened to see... One of Darkness's many reminders.

Pulling my shirt out of the way, I reveal the red-lined lotus surrounded by black vines tied in the white symbols of Rishu's seal. "I don't know what it means, but during my angelic trials, this was tattooed along with the angel wings. And..." I'm scared to say the rest out loud. As if telling them makes it more real.

"And it'll kill her." Rishu appears in the center of the room in a cloud of smoke.

I nod, swallowing the knot in my throat. Reaching to the tattoo, my fingers graze the circle of black. "I saw it during my trials. These consumed me...."

Luka takes my hand from my chest. "I won't let that happen."

A low laugh sounds in the room, and we all turn to Oliver, hidden away in the shadows. "You're a monster like we are"—his gaze lifts to meet mine, and his lip curls as he snarls—"just the *human* kind. Should we pity your daddy issues and the pain you suffer from? Who's been pitying ours?"

"Watch your words," Luka's voice is dark. A side of him I haven't seen. Hidden beneath the mask of light. His hand squeezes mine tighter.

"He's not wrong," I say quietly. I didn't come here for them to pity me. "This is my truth. I honestly don't expect anything from any of you. Not forgiveness or understanding."

Darkness seems to chuckle in my mind, relishing the despair in my heart. He doesn't speak, sitting in the back corner of my subconscious to watch the show. I don't dare mention him to them without understanding who or what he wants.

"What about the contract?" Azura says, her flaming eyes dying back down to hazel. "Has Amon told you anything? You don't seem to"—she hesitates—"to know more."

I shake my head. "Only that the black vines which Rishu has been able to hold back will one day kill me, though it was more of a confirmation than anything new." I glance at Luka. There's much Amon hasn't shared with me.

"Nova, I don't care about any of that," Meena says, stepping around the couch where Tevari sits to stand before me. "But you lied to us. Made us trust you when your kind hunts us for sport."

My heart sinks. No apology can fix this. "I'm sorry."

There's nothing I can say to justify my actions. My past, my lies, and the reality of who I was trained to be. A killer. I'm the real monster among us.

It's strange, though, how in this short time with them, I've grown comfortable with not being a hunter anymore. A life that seems distant now, unfamiliar. Eighteen years washed away after only a month with these people—these friends. *They're not your friends anymore.* The painful reminder stings my heart. When did I stop wanting to kill demons?

"As much as it'd be lovely to keep chatting, we must go," Rishu says, looking over my head to Luka. A silent conversation passes between them. Dread gathers in my stomach. "*Now.*"

Kioren hums on my wrist, the metal heating against my skin. Not in the comforting *I'm on your side type* of way, but with an urgency warning of impending danger. I lift the bracelet to my face. The black gem bubbles though I haven't called the scythe forth. Streaks of vibrant color—like rainbow veins—pulse as if coming to life. My heart thunders in my chest as ice-cold nails brush down my spine. I can feel Darkness creeping over my shoulder to whisper in my ear. *"You've come of use."* I almost gag as he slithers back, his words racing through my mind.

"What's happening now?" Lei Jing asks, her arms dropping to her sides. Weariness clouds her violet eyes that dance between Rishu and me, then to Luka. So I'm not the only one who's noticed Luka's difference. From simply watching from the shadows to equaling—if not surpassing—Rishu's command...

Rishu's lips move as if to say something, but he decides against it. My nerves don't quell. Even Uriel and Zerachiel seem to pace inside me, their anxiety adding to my own.

"What is it?" I say within my mind but gain no response from the two angels. I gulp, the feeling not sitting well in my stomach. It's almost as if a blockade is stopping them from speaking to me.

"Only take what's utterly important," Rishu says, grabbing Meena's single bag before taking her hand. "Teleporting all of us at once isn't possible on such short notice, but there's a van out front to take us to Amon's building."

Nothing inside or outside the château signals danger. No sound, no presence, *nothing*. Still, Kioren buzzing on my wrist and whatever Rishu and Luka sensed is more terrifying than when the barrier around the land shattered and the hunters found us.

Luka slides his hand into mine and leads us out of the room. His palm is warm against my own, and it feels natural as he hurries me down the stairway. My mind is too scattered to question why it feels so calming, and why I continue to allow the simple touch. Glancing over my shoulder, I make sure everyone is following behind. Panic is written across their faces as our steps quicken down the carpeted halls.

Squeezing Luka's hand tighter, I try to rein in my fear. Rishu and Meena are just ahead, and I pull us closer—matching their pace. This feels like déjà vu. I can only imagine what Darkness meant and who is coming this time.

"Rishu, what's going on?" I say, holding my voice steady.

"No time." His eyes don't even move to mine, focused entirely on our destination.

"Rishu," I say, grabbing his arm with my free hand, "you're scaring us. What did you sense?"

Rishu glances out the window at the morning light peeking over the horizon; rain drizzles down the windows in the brightening hall. Red eyes meet mine as he says, "Listen, we don't have time for questions. If we don't leave now...." He purses his lips, shutting his eyes in frustration. "We just need to leave."

"Okay." I don't argue more, but my heart races with what he won't share.

Luka laces his fingers through mine and squeezes gently. "It'll be okay," he says, but I'm not sure even he believes it.

Reaching into my mind, I call again to Uriel and Zerachiel as we hurry to the main level. Only Zera responds, bringing us into our private space within my mind. His words do nothing to calm the raging fear churning in my stomach.

"My child, I am sorry I couldn't warn you. A promise I had long ago made to you. Just remember, within the darkest of days, the truth comes to light."

"What does that mean? Zera, what's happening?"

"I have always been with you, finally awoken by Uriel in this lifetime." My stomach turns. The images I saw during the trials—the lifetimes I thought I had mistaken for something else. *"I can only do so much to ensure you awaken in this life. But the enemy, the one you hear, the one that reeks of darkness... it's closer than I expected. He sends unforeseen enemies I had not been privy to."* Zera's voice is clearer than it's ever been. A sound that should be reassuring instead instilling newfound terror. *"Trust that no matter what, I will keep you alive. This time... this time, you will not meet an end. You will reclaim."*

My hand covers my mouth as nausea overwhelms me. *"Zera, what enemy?"* He doesn't respond, leaving me in silence as our private space dissolves around me.

"What is it?" Luka's voice draws me back to the present moment. His hand holds mine tighter as if to pull me closer. Does he know who's here? The enemy Zera speaks of? I cringe, not sure if I want to answer his question.

The front door comes into sight, and I almost breathe a sigh of relief.

Instead, I gasp as the door suddenly blows open with a tangible wave of darkness and bloodlust. We all freeze midstep, and my heart hammers in my chest as the intense power settles around us. *Darkness.*

We're not prepared; we barely escaped the hunters. Whoever or whatever has come, we are not ready. I place one foot in front of the other, pushing myself toward the swaying front door.

The driveway is empty, but I don't let that calm the terror racing through my veins. A large black van waits for us at the bottom of the stairs—the one Rishu mentioned. I hesitate at the door, my hands shaking as I look around but don't find anything out of place.

"This isn't good. Amon should've warned us," Luka says, his eyes trained on the sky as if he can see something I can't.

Rishu turns to Luka as he says, "You could—" He cuts himself off as a wave of darkness shoots from Luka's free hand to wrap threateningly around his throat. Rishu's eyes flare red, anger tracing the sharp lines of his face, but he says nothing more.

My eyes go wide. How is it that Luka holds so much power over the demon? Daring a glance behind, I see that the other cambions have also noticed the interaction. Reeling in my fear as best as I can, I pull Luka toward the van. We need to get out of here.

Cool raindrops slick my skin as we descend the steps to the driveway. The murky gray sky rumbles as the storm rolls in, blotting out the rising sun. I hurry my steps, eager to get in the van and away from this place.

A bolt of lightning shoots across the sky, staining the clouds a sickly green color. I skid to a halt, staring at the clouds, mouth gaping. My breaths quicken against my will as pure untethered terror crawls across my skin.

Meena screams as the van in front of us is suddenly crushed beneath a monstrous shadowy creature. Humanoid in shape but easily twice the size of an average person, its sinewy gray limbs drip with that all-too-familiar inky substance. Glossy black eyes turn to face us as leathery wings unfurl from its back. I step back, pulling Luka with me.

The creature lets out an ear-shattering scream, and Luka tucks me into his side as if to protect me. I gently push off, releasing his hand as I study the creature. It's too similar to the hellhounds, to the child I saw on the night of the blood moon. But where the child was just a vessel, this creature has been *combined* with the shadowy essence that the light I called forth destroyed. Kioren vibrates aggressively on my wrist.

"Back inside, *now*," Rishu says, dropping the bag and dragging Meena toward the front door.

We scurry toward the château when a loud creak stops me in my tracks. I turn back, my gaze moving to the gray-green clouds.

"Rishu..."

A large grand stone doorway appears out of nowhere, hovering over the drive about thirty feet in the air. The doors crack open, the sound like a war drum in my ears. My feet freeze in place as Luka grabs my arm to pull me inside. But I can't look away. Terror immobilizes me as Darkness roars with laughter in my mind.

"Nova, we have to go," Luka yells, and I finally turn to him, only daring to look away from the doors for a moment.

"Please, Nova." His eyes search my face with panic and fear. Not of the impending enemy but for something else entirely. "We can't stay here."

I turn back to the sky as the doors open fully. Kioren's scythe bursts from the gem, the black tendrils connecting us laced with vibrantly colored veins as it wraps around me protectively. The scythe stands at the ready—just out of my reach as if someone else is holding it, ready to fight.

Through the doorway, I can see a black void cast with the same putrid green light. Bile rises in my throat, fear and disgust threatening to bring me to my knees as the darkness leaks out like a toxic fog. It's *vile*. I can taste it on the wind and feel it in the raindrops pelting my skin. Loud steps echo from the doorway, slow and calculated. The hair on the back of my neck stands on end as a malevolent power, greater than anything I've ever felt, crawls across my skin. When two figures enter into sight, I stumble back.

"Father?"

My eyes widen as I try to make sense of what I'm seeing: My father, blond hair plastered to his face with the thickening rain. His face seems younger, a light glowing from within as he grins down at us. The second figure steps around to stand at his side, and my eyes widen more.

"Theo?" My voice quakes, unable to hide my surprise and terror.

*"Nova, whatever happens—do not believe everything he says. He will not give you the full trut*h*,"* Zera's rough voice yells in my head, but I can hardly hear as if Darkness is determined to quash the warning.

Theo laughs, squatting down on the stone platform jutting out from the doorway. His eyes are black pits; shadows slither around his lean figure. I can feel the hatred and anger oozing from his soul. "Surprised to see me? You know, I'm much stronger than I was before. I'd love for you to get a taste of me now," he yells, moving to jump, but my father stops him with a wave of his hand.

"Don't forget our purpose."

Theo's face pulls into a frown, but he doesn't move from Father's side. I inhale a deep, shaky breath, taking a step forward, Kioren's tendrils moving with me.

"Wasn't Adrian enough?" I yell through the rain. A shiver runs over my skin, and I can't tell if it's because of the cool rain or my father standing in the sky in front of this horrid doorway.

Theo laughs as my father ignores me, his eyes narrowing on Luka. "If it isn't the False King himself. No wonder it took so long to find this place," he says, his voice colder than ever.

I don't dare glance back at Luka. The False King? Dark energy swirls alongside me as Luka steps to my side. Rain drips from his black hair, the strands falling in front of his eyes. White light curls at his knuckles, the power rolling off him as strong as the wave of bloodlust we first felt from inside the château.

"But I'm not here for you." Father's gaze moves from Luka to me. "Not this time."

Father jumps from the platform, landing directly in front of me. He grabs onto the black tendrils surrounding me, yanking them from around my body. Kioren slashes forward, but he catches the blade between the palms of his hands. The scythe attempts to push through Father's grip but remains steady in his grasp. Father turns his cold eyes to me. *Green eyes.*

"Who are you?" My voice is barely a whisper.

The man smirks. Reaching through the tendrils, he grabs me by the throat. He pulls me through to him faster than should be possible, jumping us away from the others, back toward the crushed van and shadowy creature. He dangles me above the ground, a crazed look on the face identical to my father's. But how? My father has no siblings. I hear Luka snarl, running toward us.

Choked sounds leave my lips as I struggle for air, clawing at his hands and kicking wildly. Kioren stills, rendered immobile by the green darkness seeping from the man's fingertips and down to the bracelet. His hand tightens, and tears form in my eyes, lungs burning for air.

"Would you put this thing away already?" He throws the tendrils aside. Panic builds in my chest at seeing Kioren so easily overtaken by this man's power. "It's useless, my dear." I shudder at the pet name, the one Darkness likes to call me. Is this him?

I watch helplessly as Kioren, weaker than I've ever seen, is forced back into the bracelet.

Darkness curls around our feet, almost circling up the man's leg, but the man just grins. He spins me around by the throat to face the one charging at us. His nails elongate, the tips cutting into the flesh of my neck as he leans in and whispers softly. "This is the monster beside you."

There's no sign of the light Luka once showed me, only darkness, bloodlust, and rage. "Let her go," he snarls as he comes to a halt, the man's claws digging into my skin.

Behind Luka, the cambions summon their powers to their hands as Rishu shifts to his demonic form. Iridescent purple scales cover his bronze skin. Two horns curl out from his brown curls as his eyes turn red and ears elongate into pointed tips. As terrifying as he looks in his Naga form, it's nothing to the man chuckling in my ear.

"You heard him. Let her go." Rishu growls, snake-like tongue slipping through sharpened fangs.

Black dots flit across my vision as the man squeezes harder—my strength failing me. "Now, why don't we go, my dear, before things get out of hand."

Green tinted darkness seeps from the man's clawed fingertips, spreading up the stairs to entwine around the feet of the cambions. It renders them immobile, all-consuming fear seeping into them. Shadows burst from Luka as he charges forward again, Rishu at his side with dueling blades.

The man lets me go, and I suck in a breath as I drop to the ground. Before I can move, he hits a pressure point in my neck, and I go limp. Lifting me into his arms, I fight the darkness at the corners of my vision. My stomach lurches as we leap into the sky, the ground zooming out of sight along with Luka and Rishu. Faintly, I see more black shadow creatures beginning to surround the others, and a pit forms in my stomach.

Cradled in the man's arms, my head lolls back, fading in and out of consciousness as we land on the stone platform protruding from the grand doorway. Luka's blurry face follows us through the horde of black creatures; his sweet voice transforms into a raging howl as he screams my name. A black mass of energy forms in his hands, and from it, the jaws of a beast.

Before I can get a clear view, the man laughs and turns us away. He casually walks us through the stone doors, which close behind us, before Luka's attack can hit. Black collapses in on me as I succumb to the unnatural power that seems to delight in eating away my strength and energy. Without Kioren or my angels, there's nothing to ease the terror of this nightmare.

28

GONE

Cold.

An all-consuming chill that penetrates deep into my bones. Every part of me aches as I regain consciousness. I shiver as I lie on the cold, hard ground. Warmth feels like a distant memory. My eyes flicker open; everything is hazy in the dim green light. I lift my numb hands in front of my face. The skin is pale and gaunt, my fingertips purple. Pressing my palms onto the gray stone floor, I push myself up on weak arms. I feel as if I might black out again, but I force myself to scoot across the floor to lean against the wall for support.

It feels like days have passed, though I'm unsure how long I've been here. Time itself seems distorted. Maybe it's only been hours since I first opened my eyes. Maybe it's been days.

I lick my dry, cracked lips. My mouth is parched, my stomach growling as I rot in this godforsaken cell. I know I must have a fever. Chills and sweats rack my body, my hair and clothes plastered to my skin.

It's dark here, always. And with only four walls and a locked metal door, it's terrifying. A single barred window above lets in the sickly green glow from the unknown world outside, which smells both sweet and rotten. Only the haunting sounds of screams and growls give me any clue of what lies beyond. Maybe more creatures like that horrible beast that crushed the van as if it were nothing but tin foil.

There's not even a bed to lie on in this cell, or anything remotely soft, for that matter. Zero comfort for the prisoner—only a bucket in the far corner to relieve myself. The man who looks like my father dropped me here, and I haven't seen him since. He got what he needed, and now he'll force me to wait. At least Darkness hasn't spoken to me since getting here—the only good thing that's happened in this place that reeks of death.

A key twists in the door, and I scurry to the far corner with the last remains of my energy. I wobble as I stand, my feet numb and aching from the cold. Kioren is silent on my wrist, as are the angels in my mind. Darkness may be gone, but unfortunately, so are they.

The door opens to reveal a burly man, easily twice my size. Large, gruesome scars trail over his gray skin, but his face is covered with a black leather mask resembling a muzzle for a mutt. Black energy coils around him, just as it did with the child I saved the night of the blood moon. This man—if he can even be called a man—is wrapped in even more of the repulsive darkness, more similar to the creature that crushed the van than the child. Dread washes over my drained and exhausted body.

As he walks into the room, he doesn't say anything, black eyes peeking through his mask, massive body blocking the only exit. If he moves far enough into the room, I could get past him—escape this cell. With his size, he might be on the slow side... I wouldn't have to fight. He steps in, and I make my move. A large hand grabs my hair, wrenching me back and slamming my face into the ground. I scream as my head cracks against the stone.

The world spins. The blood trickling down my face provides the only warmth I've felt since arriving here. My stunned head is lifted from the floor as the man drags me by my hair.

I whimper as I'm pulled from the room, scalp stinging and throbbing. Blood oozes its way into my crusty eyes, and I blink it away as my senses come back to me. The taste of copper on my tongue urges me to fight back, and I claw against his grip, fingernails ripping into his leathery skin. The black energy burns me just as it had with the hellhound. But I don't care.

I *need* to call for Kioren. I can't fight on my own in this state. I try to force words to come out, but no sound escapes my dry throat. Only the sound of my torn clothes and skin dragging on the stone tiles breaks the silence of the dim hallway.

Bright light surrounds me as a door opens, my vision blinded by the sudden exposure. The brute lets go of my hair, dropping me in the center of the room. I force my upper body up as my eyes adjust but I have no strength to wipe away the blood now dripping to the floor.

My gaze turns upward, and I see the man who brought me here. He sits on a black throne, skulls—both human and demon—built into its frame. The room is as empty, gray, and cold as the prison cell he keeps me in; only the throne, this man, and his brute inhabit the space. The man—his face so like my father's—wears an expensive-looking modern suit, and his face is clean-shaven. His nostrils flare in disgust as he studies my frail form.

"Do you know who I am?" he asks, his legs crossed, a glass of dark red wine in his hand. At least, I hope it's wine. "I suppose you wouldn't, though I must say I am *thoroughly* hurt by that."

I attempt to spit at his feet, but my mouth is dry from having been denied water for so long, and only a scant amount of blood sprays from my lips.

Clicking his tongue, he stands from his throne. "Now, now, we can't be having this kind of behavior." He towers over me, his green eyes piercing into my own. They're somehow even colder and more terrifying than my father's stern blue gaze. "I do expect respect from you, my dear."

His leather boot slams into the side of my head faster than I can make a sound. The kick sends me sprawling out onto the cold stone. The world spins again, and my vision grays around the edges. At this point, I'm probably concussed. More blood runs down my face, and I reach up to touch my head. Warm liquid sticks to my hand.

Gritting my teeth, I push my body up again, mustering a grin despite the new throbbing pain. It's met with a kick to my ribcage. I bite my tongue on impact, and more blood flows into my mouth. This time I don't rise.

"So this is how you want to play?" The man crouches to the ground, grabbing the front of my shirt and lifting me to him with ease. "Then let's play."

He uses his thumb to wipe away the blood dripping into my eye before smacking me hard across the face. Blood flies from my mouth and spatters across the floor. I glare daggers at him through the damp hair dangling in front of my face. The man smiles, and my blood runs cold.

"What do you want with me?" I croak out.

He drops me, and I land hard. My arms shake as I prop myself up.

"So she can speak."

The smug grin doesn't leave his face. His eyes sparkle as he pushes his pale blond hair back with a stroke of his hand—my blood leaving red streaks in the strands.

"But, it only works if you show me respect."

I spit again, the taste of copper lingering on my tongue. "I don't care who you are; you don't deserve my respect."

He lets out a maniacal laugh. The sound reverberates through the throne room, bouncing off the walls and echoing eerily around the room. "Oh, my dear, you should care. For I hold a secret far darker than any you seek." He spins around and heads back to his ghastly throne.

I tense. How does he know I've been searching for answers? Theo comes to mind, but he wouldn't have known about my whereabouts. And anyway, even knowing my whereabouts wouldn't tell him I'm searching for answers. My breath hitches. Darkness...

"Now are you curious?"

I remain tight-lipped. There has to be a way to get out of here before he can do more damage to me. Pulling my body up higher, I bite back a whimper as my ribcage protests the movement. Did he break a rib? I brush aside the thought and the pain.

"*A door has opened,*" Zerachiel says faintly in my mind as if he's struggling to get the words to me.

A door... Zera isn't wrong, and he did warn me before that it might be more half-truths than anything, but still. A door is a door.

I hesitate before agreeing. "I'll listen if that's what you want."

"Good." The man's grin widens. "My name is Camus Fandera, my dear *niece*. But you may call me Uncle."

My heart drops to my stomach, and my arms give out from under me. Father doesn't have any siblings. Even with their nearly identical faces, it has to be a lie... I scour my memories for anything, a clue I might not have picked up on at the time. Father never brought up the Fandera family tree, let alone a twin brother. Hell, he wouldn't even tell me who my mother was.

The image of my father and grandfather from my angelic trials flashes through my mind. There was someone else there. Someone with the same blond hair. The only feature of the blurred figure that I was able to make out. My stomach churns. My angels tried to warn me, and Darkness kept them from saying anything again.

"Surprising, isn't it?" Camus says with amusement.

"You're lying," I choke out.

"Ah, but alas, I am not." Camus taps his fingers repetitively on the armrest of his throne; his other hand clutches the skull protruding beside him. "Your father is my twin, older by a few minutes."

The quiet sound of blood droplets hitting the tile fills the silence as my mind reels. How could Father have a twin nobody knew about? Or did they know and not tell me? The latter seems more likely.

"Oh, Nova, he hasn't told you anything, *has he?* Not who you are or why he so desperately tried to keep you in that estate of his. Is having an uncle really that farfetched?"

I struggle to my knees, my eyes burning with rage. "So you're his brother, who cares? If that's true, then you were a hunter. What happened to the hunter's code?" I spit my words at him even as the irony of them hits me. I've practically done the same, but this place reeks of death and despair. He's either the one who created those shadowy creatures or the one who leads them—or both. Either way, there's no hunter's code left in his actions. No humanity in his gaze. At least, I still have that despite all I've done and everyone I've betrayed.

He stands once more, the tapping of his shoes sending waves of terror through me as he approaches. "The hunter's code?" He breaks out in a fit of laughter. "What would you know of such a thing? You sided with *demons*. I'm not nearly as disloyal as you are."

Crouching to the ground, I wait for another blow—expecting the crushing pain. His hand reaches forward and caresses my cheek instead.

"Aren't we the same? The hunters turned their backs on us, so we turned on them."

I pull away, disgusted by his touch. "We're nothing alike."

Retracting his hand, he stands, walking over to a window in the room. "Do you know why you know nothing about me?" I don't answer, so he continues. "Because the hunters chose to believe I was dead. And Solomon is to blame." He speaks with a resentment that runs deeper than his words let on.

"What did my father ever do to you?"

"He was born first," he says, not turning away from the window. "But look where I am now. I have joined the side of the True King to bring about a new world. Your father could never stomach what it would take to do just that."

The laughter begins again, my skin crawling at the sound. This man isn't sane. A door to answers or not, I need to get out of here.

"Is he why you kidnapped me?" I say, scanning the room for an exit.

"Kidnapped?" He turns to look at me, hanging his head over his shoulder. "I *saved* you. You, of all people, cannot be with those demons. Especially not with the False King, my dear. Don't you know those black vines will kill you if he's around?" He clicks his tongue, his green eyes glimmering with the same sickly glow as the world beyond the window. "I must say, I thought you were smarter than this. Maybe this lifetime has rendered you *dull*." He turns back to the window with a sinister smile.

I freeze. Lifetimes. What does he know about the images, the *memories*, I saw during my angelic trials? I hold in my questions. Who cares what he knows. I need to get out of this place before he decides he's had enough of me. The blood running down my face is proof enough that he has no intention of keeping me alive.

"Uri? Zera? What do I do?" I desperately call for them despite whatever is blocking their voices.

"Help is coming," Zerachiel says, the only one able to respond. Uriel is silent, not even a hint of her presence in my mind.

Closing my eyes, I wish with all my heart that Zera's response implies the cambions made it out alive. I saw those... those unnatural shadow creatures attack them. But if they survived and are coming here... I don't want to put everyone in danger. Not in this wretched place.

"What about my scythe?" I ask Zera, silently watching Camus admire whatever's out that window. I shudder. If the growls and roars are any indication, I don't think I want to find out.

"Frozen in place, it will be of no help in this dimension." Dimension?

"Come, my dear. Let me show you how I plan to create the new world in the name of the True King."

The brute comes over and lifts me off the ground by my arm. As I struggle against him, he pulls it out of its socket. I scream in pain, but no one pays me any mind. Dangling my body at his side, he throws me toward the wall, and I barely catch myself. Bracing my body against the cold stone wall, I scrunch my eyes in pain. Camus gestures for me to come forward, and I oblige, much to my displeasure.

I slide slowly along the wall until I reach his side. I grasp onto the iron bars, breathing heavily as I hold myself up. My stomach turns to an empty pit at what I see before me.

A barren wasteland is occupied with thousands of shadow-like monsters. Blank black eyes and sinewy gray limbs. Creatures that don't look human or demon—but some horrible cross between the two. Shadows have taken control of their bodies, the inky substance dripping off them. They're all shapes and sizes. From those flying overhead on leathery wings to ones that appear similar to the hellhounds I fought, except so much worse. Larger with longer fangs hanging from their gaping jaws as if they were remade after the blood moon to be more effective killers. Others are smaller, and I gag.

Children. Like the child I saved, yet these beings hardly resemble that little girl. Consumed completely by the deathly black energy that pollutes the landscape. Deformed shapes pile on each other as they stare up at the window. They wait for a command, puppets to their master beside me. Beings with their sentience stripped from them.

Tears well in my eyes as I sink away from the window. "What have you done?"

"Isn't it beautiful? My king's creations—the *Krav*. Human-demon hybrids of the finest quality, unlike the cambions you associate with." Camus turns to me, his eyes crazed. "They'll bring about the new world my king envisions."

I pull myself back to the window and stare at the mass of creatures. Humans and demons corrupted by this shadow of darkness. *Darkness.* This has to be his doing, whoever he is. This "king" Camus worships... He'll be the death of us all. The lotus on my chest throbs, yet this time not with pain but with urgency. A desire to free them from his control as a fleeting memory passes through my mind. A piece of news I hardly paid attention to.

"It was you...." My words are soft. "The refugee children going missing... Why"—I reach out to the collar of his shirt, latching onto it—"why would you do this to them? What the hell is wrong with you?"

Camus doesn't even flinch; a sly grin curls over his lips. Reaching up, he grabs my wrists, removing my hands from his collar. "Why?" He leans in close to my face. "Because this world is corrupt. I will bring it to its destruction to help my king begin anew. But don't worry, I didn't take anyone who would be missed."

"Screw you." With all the strength I can muster, I punch him across his face. His cheek reddens, but all he does is laugh, pushing me away from him.

I topple to the floor, air hitching in my lungs as I hit the cold ground. My head reels, and I close my eyes, trying to block out his cruel laughter and the nauseating glow of the poisonous sky looming outside the window. With this army behind him, he's capable of so much destruction. Forcing myself to rise again, I watch Camus walk to his throne.

"Sir."

A voice comes from the door, pulling Camus's attention from me. Turning my head, I see Theo, the white of his eyes strained with black veins. The dark shadows cling to him, leeching away his humanity. Slowly but surely, it will corrupt his soul. What happened to him?

"Did you bring it?" Camus says, casually crossing his legs and taking a sip from his wine glass.

"Yes, sir."

Theo approaches the throne and extends his hand, a golden lotus flower in his palm. The lotus tattoo burns on my chest, calling to the one Theo holds. I drag myself toward them, reaching for those golden petals.

"You see, Nova," Camus says as he takes the flower, his gaze flitting to me with a sadistic grin, "you will be of use to me." Chills run down my spine. Darkness had said the same thing...

"Take it," Remembrance whispers in my mind.

I try to rise to my feet, to fight the agonizing pain in my body. Camus laughs, handing the lotus back to Theo.

"Begin preparations," Camus says. "She'll be needing this if our plans are to work."

My heart stops at his words. What else is this man planning? Theo nods, leaving the room with the golden lotus. His eyes meet mine one last time before he disappears into the hallway. Camus's attention falls back to me, and I can't help but cower beneath his stare.

"Now, I think it's time for you to return to your room. But, Nova, I will make you see why this is the right thing to do."

The brute approaches me once more, and I struggle to not let him take me. If they lock me up again, I don't know when I'll be let out again—how I'll get that lotus. Camus grins as the burly hand of the brute latches onto my hair and drags me out of the room. I wrestle against his grip, but all my energy is spent, my body too battered.

No, I can't leave yet... I need to fight. I need to stop him. *"Uri, Zera, please, I beg you! Lend me your powers to fight."* They don't respond, and my head slams into the stone floor.

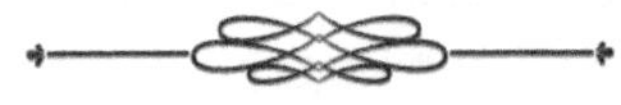

— Luka —

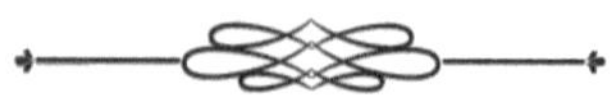

I slice through the last of the godforsaken creatures that man damned us with. The others are burned out, exhausted after fighting the horde, but the fire of rage is still lit inside me. He *took* her. Just like Solomon once had... and he will pay for it.

Quelling the shadows at my feet, the sword in my hand disappears back to the shadow realm—Gehenna. I shouldn't have summoned Zin for aid. He'll keep his mouth shut, but I saw the questioning look before he slithered back out of this dimension.

"What now?" Rishu says as he comes to my side.

I consider for a moment. There's a trace of that vile dimension lingering in the air. If I use my powers... If I use them, I can summon a portal that could take me there.

"I know that look," Rishu says, and I glare at the demon. "I'm going with you. Amon is still responsible for the girl despite—"

I silence him with a glare, noticing the cambions approaching us.

"Luka, what's going on?" Lei Jing says, fronting the group as the eldest among the five.

"We're going after Nova, right?" Meena says from behind Tevari.

I look between them. Consequences of this deal. "I'm going, Rishu too. The rest of you will head to Amon's building."

"Since when do you give the orders?" Azura says, her flames somehow still flaring in her eyes despite her obvious exhaustion.

I frown. I don't have time to argue with them. The trace of that dimension is already diminishing. I have to—

"If you go, we go," Tevari says.

The others nod in agreement, so I turn to Rishu. Can I really risk their lives when none of this had anything to do with them before Amon brought them here? To help me nonetheless... Rishu shrugs. The naga is much easier to deal with when he's not bowing at his waist for me.

"Fine," I say as I turn toward the crushed van.

My portal will lead us to Nova, but it'll come at a cost that I know I'll have to pay someday soon. Just hopefully not before I can save her from the Lotus Pond, the misery my mistakes have inflicted on her...

I close my eyes but have no one to pray to for Nova's safety. No god I trust, no hope in a destiny beyond that of my own making. Extending my hand, I summon the portal. A swirling gray energy, a mixture of shadows and light.

"Don't say I didn't warn you," I say, not bothering to see if they follow behind.

I won't lose her again.

29

The False King

Blood oozes from my scalp, but the pain is fuzzy. My vision drifts in and out of darkness as I regain my bearings. The brute dumped me back into the cell, leaving me to bleed out onto the stone tile. My lips twitch. I guess Camus really wants me dead...

My angels are the ones who have kept me alive until now, even if they can't fully communicate with me—Zerachiel's voice is fainter than ever. If not for them, this blood loss would have easily killed me already.

Hours pass. Then days. Or at least that's how it feels, lying on the cold floor, unable to lift my limbs.

The door squeaks open; footsteps approach my side. The figure is blurry as it kneels beside me, lifting my body from the cold floor.

"Look at you now. I could laugh," Theo says, but no sound of laughter follows. A wet cloth presses against my forehead. The wound stings as he disinfects it, but I don't move from his hold.

"Why are you here?" I mumble to him, my eyes fluttering shut.

"Sadly, I was the one ordered to keep you alive."

"No. Why are you *here*, with him."

He's silent as he continues to wipe away the blood on my forehead. What made him choose to come to Camus's side? Was it me? The thought grips my heart. When we sparred, did I push him so far over the edge to abandon his sense of justice? Has he given up on being a hunter? All to join this lunatic in destroying the world?

"Theo, just tell me." My voice is hoarse, and my throat feels like I've swallowed nails, but I push the words out.

He glares at me. "Are you really one to ask? You abandoned your duty and sided with demons."

"Better than Camus." I struggle to sit up, wanting to look him in the eye. "You saw the monsters he leads, the Krav. He kidnapped *children*—and who knows who else—to make them."

"And?" He drops the bloody cloth in a small bucket of water beside him. "This world is corrupt. Camus wants to make things right again. To end demons once and for all. I'm *better* than all of you in that aspect. I will actually do what needs to be done."

My jaw drops. "*Children*, Theo. They're not demons. What have they ever done to warrant this cruelty?"

He shrugs. "A means to an end, Camus needs an army to end all demons. Those kids won't be missed anyway."

I'm stunned. Barely able to comprehend what he's saying.

"And you think demons are the evil ones...."

He scoffs. "Seems they've corrupted you too. If you weren't his niece, you might've been turned into one of the Krav." I cringe at the thought.

"No, they haven't corrupted me. I've just realized the hunters have been wrong all along. The demons I know, the cambions I've befriended, they aren't all evil. They were born with demonic powers, but they don't deserve to die because of it. They're just fighting to live like we are. We're alike, even if no one wants to see it."

Theo sticks the wet cloth back to my head, soaking up more blood. I hiss but let him continue cleaning the wound. Not that I could stop him anyway.

"Your cambions wouldn't have been born with those powers if demons didn't exist in the first place."

I grab his wrist, somehow forcing my arm up. "But they do exist, and their lives are proof we can't keep killing just because we don't understand."

"Fine, think that way and see how far it gets you." He stands, towering above me. "As for me, I'll stay here where I can make a difference. For once in my life, I won't be second to anyone, not to you and not to Adrian."

He turns swiftly and heads for the door.

"Theo, think about what I said. It's not too late, you can leave with me. You want to make a difference? Then don't let this man take everything from you, including your humanity."

He turns his head ever so slightly, only glancing over his shoulder. "This is where I need to be."

The door slams behind him, and I close my eyes. I knew he was always compared to Adrian... But I was only tough on him because Lance needed me to taunt them, pick at their weaknesses to assess them for the angelic trials. I let out a soft sigh. His parents must be so worried.

Turning to the medical supplies he left, I consider my options. The only choice I have now is to regain my strength. If Kioren can't function in this dimension and my angels are barely keeping me alive, then all I can rely on is my own ability. Even if that means sneaking out of this godforsaken hellhole without the lotus.

Closing my eyes, I take a deep breath before pushing my arm back into place. I hold in a scream before the pain lessens, and I let out a long breath. Feeling my side, I check for broken ribs but determine they're only severely bruised. My head feels heavy, but the bleeding has stopped, thanks to Theo. Hopefully, it stays that way.

Leaning back against the stone wall, I let out a sigh. Between the brute, Camus, and this dimension itself—I don't think I've ever taken such a beating.

Standing slowly, I wince as I prop myself against the wall and begin to make my way to the door. I fiddle with the handle for a moment before freezing in shock. Theo left it unlocked? Pushing the door open carefully, I peer out into the hallway, looking for the brute. At my current strength, he'll be able to whip me around again without breaking a sweat.

I step timidly out of the room, holding my breath. Candles light the hallway, giving me enough visibility to find my way. All I can do is search for the door that brought me here and hope it leads to an exit that isn't hovering high off the ground like how it first appeared when Camus came. I continue on, but the hall is never-ending. Doors line the walls in a repeating sequence. I don't dare peek into any of them, not having any desire to come face-to-face with whatever is making the unnatural sounds coming from inside, but my heart longs for the lotus he *stole*. To take it before he can act on whatever he has planned.

One of the doors cracks open as I pass. I freeze. Heart racing, I slowly turn around and flatten myself against the wall. My palms are clammy as they curl into fists.

"My dear, ready so soon?" Camus's voice rings out from inside the room. "Come join me."

My eyes shut tight. Do I have a choice? Slow steps carry me to the door, and I stop at the entrance before peeking inside. It's different from his throne room. Though it boasts the same ugly gray stone walls and floors, there are blessedly no windows looking out at the ghastly Krav horde. Yet, somehow, it feels even more like a prison than the one he put me in.

A long table in the center is covered with serving platters piled high with various foods. It stands alone, opulent despite the barrenness of the room. Camus sits at the head of the table, an empty place set to his left. Candles have been lit in empty corners with large candelabras flickering amidst the food. The light casts a dim glow, causing shadows to dance eerily on the walls.

"Please, take a seat," Camus says.

Hesitantly, I do as he says, my eyes following his every move as he swirls another glass of red wine.

"You must be hungry. Eat." He motions to the food, but I don't pick up the silverware. "I promise there's no poison in it. Even I wouldn't do that to my niece."

I meet his eyes, unwavering from mine, as he waits for me to eat. I lift the fork, poking at the food. It looks delicious, and my stomach aches, begging me to eat. Gulping, I spear a piece of meat and place it in my mouth. The moment the food touches my tongue, I don't hesitate to shove more in, the hunger taking over.

"So tell me, Nova, what do you know? Has Solomon told you anything?" he says, and I pause my chewing.

"Why do you want to know?"

He chuckles, taking a sip of his wine. "Because there is much I want to tell you, but no need to rehash old news."

I sit up, placing the silverware back on the table. "I know the tattoo on my chest will kill me if that's what you're wondering about."

He hums to himself as he takes another sip, mulling over my words. "And? Anything else?"

I stay silent.

"Then let me tell you a story about the Fanderas," he says as he sets his glass down, leaning forward on his elbows, eyes gleaming ominously in the candlelight. "A thousand years ago, demons went on a rampage when Lucifer broke into the moon and bled its power for them to feed from. Hunters already existed to fight demons, but Lucifer's actions caused an outbreak unlike anything before. Solomon the First is the one who led humanity to victory."

"Everyone knows this," I say, returning to my food. Anything to regain my strength.

"But do you know why a Solomon has always led the clan to this day?"

I pause, considering his question before barely shaking my head.

"I thought so. You see, when God gave us the angelic trials to bond our soul with an angel, he promised Solomon something more. A fraction of his own soul to be passed down from Solomon to Solomon."

"Impossible," I say as a sadistic grin grows on Camus's face.

"Oh, but it is possible, my dear. There's even a book, *The Eternal Keeper*, that guides the sons of Solomon in their journey to... well, that part isn't important right now. But this is how your father became the leader of the Fandera clan." And why Camus hates him, he didn't need to add.

My heart beats faster. The angels showed me the book in my trials. Grandfather giving it to my father when he was much younger. So I wasn't mistaken in seeing Camus's blurred face in that strange memory. But this can't be true, right?

"However, your father wasn't an only child but a twin. Meaning half of the power Solomon the First was gifted is now within me."

"There's no way *God* would do that. He'd never give one human such immense power," I say, scoffing at him, turning back to my meal. Zerachiel mentioned that half-truths would be at play with Camus.

He smiles. "Your father fights against his gift, but I won't do the same. With this power I can recreate this world in *His* image, our True King of Creation."

I drop my silverware, and it clatters against my plate. He really believes this. No evidence of a lie in his tone or features. Whether it's true or not, he believes it as the truth. I gulp, suddenly thinking of Darkness. If Camus's "True King" and the dark voice inside my head are one and the same, it can't be God.

"You expect me to believe you?" I say, looking him dead in the eye. Maybe I can pull more information about what powerful force could convince generations into believing he's a god.

"Believe it, or don't, it's the truth. And He speaks to me of all the secrets left unsaid"—he sighs as he seems to reminisce in the feeling—"and they are vast and glorious."

"And what secrets would those be?" I say, trying not to sound too eager.

He lifts his wine glass to his lips. "My dear, some things are best left unsaid for those who aren't worthy to hear," he says before standing from the table, leaving his food barely touched. "Now, some uninvited guests seem to be making their way here. Oh, how I hate those who intrude on quality family time."

The brute enters the dining room, Theo at his side. I shake my head, standing from the table, my eyes pleading. If the others have come... With his horde of Krav, we don't stand a chance.

"Please let me leave," I say, almost begging.

"I'm sorry, my dear, but there is one more thing you need to know."

He motions to the brute, who then approaches my seat. I back away from the table, not wanting him to grab my hair again—to drag me back to the cold prison cell. I trip backward, falling as I stare at the masked brute, and scoot back on the floor to avoid his burly gray hands. But he just stands above me, black eyes shining behind his mask. A puppet without emotion.

Theo snickers, catching my eye. Looking past the brute with a frown, I stare at him—he quickly looks away, unable to hold my gaze. I claw my way to my feet, holding myself up as much as possible. This won't be how things end. If my friends have come to rescue me, then I will protect them with everything I've got. We'll all leave here together.

"And so they've come," Camus says.

A large gust of wind blows into the room as a portal opens in the wall. Shadowy figures step through, entering the dimly lit dining room. Luka leads the group, Rishu following close to his side in his naga form with iridescent scaly skin and curling black horns. The others are behind them, powers at the ready to fight against the people who took me. Luka's eyes immediately find mine. The face that has always looked at me with such softness is now hard, cold, and extremely pissed.

"If it isn't the False King. To have you in my dimension, what an honor," Camus says, bowing in a mock welcome.

I tense at hearing the name. Luka ignores Camus, trailing his eyes up and down my body, examining all the injuries inflicted on me. My eyes remain on him, trying to look strong, to convince him it's not as bad as it looks. His face hardens further, and I know, despite my bravado, I didn't pass his inspection. His eyes seethe with anger as he strides to Camus, grabbing hold of his collar.

"I don't care who you are, but taking her was your death wish," Luka says.

Camus lets out a breathy laugh. "Be careful what you say, False King. Or do you want her to know your secret?"

Luka's jaw clenches as he tightens his grip, but ultimately he lets go, shoving Camus away from him as he does so. His head turns to me, and I furrow my brows. *Our beloved.* The words resonate in my mind as if Remembrance is whispering it into my ear.

"Camus, please," I say, stepping around the brute as far as I can. "*Please* let us go."

Camus's head rolls toward me, his eyes completely black like the abominations of the Krav horde he leads. "Leave?" Cackling erupts from his lips, and he suddenly appears before me in a blur of movement, shoving his brute aside and into the stone wall. I flinch as the stone wall crumbles on impact. The brute lies unmoving as pieces of stone fall around him. "Why, when we're having so much fun?"

His hand shoots forward and wraps around my throat, squeezing tightly and cutting off my breath. I claw at his wrist as my feet leave the floor, my eyes unable to look away from his vacant black gaze. My knuckles turn white as I try to pry his fingers from my throat.

Luka appears behind him and pulls him off me, and I fall to the ground, coughing. Camus whips around to face Luka, shoving a punch into his stomach that sends him flying back into the others. I have to do something, *anything.*

Dark rage flares in Luka's silver eyes. Standing, I reach deep inside for the energy I need to fight back—to safely get everyone out of this wretched place.

"*Please, Uri, Zera, lend me your strength.*" Their voices are faint. Too quiet to decipher.

Camus strides to Luka, the others too stunned to respond to his attacks. Lifting him by the collar, he presses Luka against the wall, whispering into his ear. He turns his head back to me, speaking louder.

"A serpent has been hiding in your midst." Luka pushes Camus off, dense shadows forming in his hands. Camus laughs. "Care to know who this man really is?"

I look between Luka and Camus, my mind racing. I have to stop this madness and get us out of—

"Meet the False King, Lucifer Morningstar."

30

SHADOWS ON THE WALL

"You're lying," I say, looking past Camus into Luka's eyes. *He's not lying.*

Luka's shadows die in his hand.

"You can't even trust the people around you, my dear. Why would you want to leave? I'm the only one who's given you any semblance of truth."

"Luka, is that true?" Azura asks, the bravest to speak up. We look to Rishu for confirmation. He turns away, red eyes downcast.

"Rishi, did you know?" Meena says, grabbing onto his scaly hand. He glances at her but remains silent. She lets go of his hand, hurt shining in her stormy doe eyes, and moves back to stand by Tevari, who wraps his vine around her protectively. Lei Jing and Azura move to flank them, faces hard and eyes alight with anger.

"So we're all monsters with secrets." Oliver sneers, black talons shrinking back into his fingers.

I turn to Luka, searching his face for answers. Silver eyes waver between guilt and anger. "I'm sorry." His voice is but a whisper as the pieces start to come together.

Our beloved. It clicks in my mind. He knew me. In whatever these past lives were, he *knew* me. Long before we met here as Luka and Nova.

My eyes move to Camus. His black eyes trained on me with that cruel smile. I'm done with this game he's playing, toying with us like we're his puppets. Uncle or not, this is the end. No matter what the truth is or the reason Luka lied to us—I will get us out of here.

"We're leaving, whether you let us or not."

My body is weak, drained from my time in this frigid dimension of death and despair. But a spark alights inside me, screaming for retribution. A will to get the cambions out of this wretched place. A will to put an end to Camus's plans.

"I don't think so." A knife comes to my throat from behind, softly pressing into my skin.

"Theo, don't repeat past mistakes," I say, not daring to move, the knife drawing a thin line of blood along my neck.

"Mistake? You mean when we sparred?" He scoffs. "I was weak, following a worthless leader. A lot has changed since then."

The knife digs deeper into my skin, and I hold my breath, trying not to move. Theo won't be baited into defeat like he was when we sparred. There's newfound strength in his grasp, the tall, lanky boy I remember no longer standing behind me.

Reaching up to his wrist, I pull the knife from my throat, quickly spinning his arm around to his back. Theo twists the knife in his grip, the blade pointed directly at me.

It shoves into my gut, and my grip on his arm loosens. I stare down at the handle protruding from my side. A rough cough rips from me as blood floods my mouth, drizzling down my chin to the stone floor.

"Nova!" Luka races over to my side, the others right behind him.

The room around me blurs as I put pressure around the knife, my fingers drenched in my blood. I fall backward, Luka catching me in his arms.

Theo stares wide-eyed, mouth gaping. He moves out of the way, returning to Camus's side. Camus raises a hand, shattering a hole in the ceiling. Krav immediately begin to break through, crawling in from the horrid land beyond these walls, waiting for a command from their master. They hiss unnaturally, black eyes fixed on us. The inky shadows swirl around them as they crawl in and out of the darkness as if they have become one with it.

"We need to leave, now," Rishu says, two twin blades forming in his hands with a puff of black smoke. Turning his attention to the Krav, he stands in front of us, ready to fight.

"Can we hold them back?" Tevari says, his vine changing shape into a sharp briar.

"Hell yeah, we can," Azura says, fire blazing at her fingers.

Meena summons a few of her decoy illusions, and purple energy crackles at the tips of Lei Jing's fingers. Oliver's arms shapeshift into long black talons, feathery scales spreading across his skin. Even with his fear of the creature inside him, he looks set on fighting.

"Please go," I say, clenching onto my side. If they leave now, they'll be safe; they don't have to fight. I bite my lip, whimpering as the knife shifts.

"I won't ever leave you," Luka says, caressing a hand over my cheek, wiping away the blood streaking my face. "Not again."

The others nod in agreement, turning to the approaching Krav. Camus watches in amusement as he flicks his hand forward with a final smile. The Krav rush toward us, and he and Theo disappear behind the oncoming mass.

As the Krav reach us, my heart breaks as I see the faces of those who were once human and demon, now completely distorted by madness and chaos. Rishu and Oliver rush forward into the fray, slashing left and right at the crazed creatures. Tevari and Azura protect their sides, blocking the monsters with thorns and fire. Lei Jing summons an energetic barrier to protect us while Meena attacks with her illusions.

But it's not enough.

A horned Krav rips a gash in Oliver's side—his cry rings out among the many others as the black substance burns his skin. Rishu cuts down the shadows, but where one dies, another takes its place. He seethes as claws cut his skin, his demonic power healing them only for them to be reopened by another attack. More Krav latch onto Tevari's briars, pulling him closer to the battle, and Azura's fire is dwindling. Meena breathes deeply as she lifts her hands, raising the fallen Krav to do her bidding as she opts for the skill we worked on together. But it doesn't matter as more and more Krav crawl through the ceiling.

"You can save them." Remembrance's voice whispers in my head, her words stronger than when the shadow brought me to her. Stronger than it's been since she showed me how to use Kioren.

"But how?" I cough, blood splattering out on the floor.

"You have unimaginable strength to help others, to make things right."

"I don't understand. Without Kioren or my angels...."

Her voice is a twinkle of laughter—one filled with more sadness than delight. *"The only thing you have ever needed is yourself. It will be an arduous and painful journey, but when you reach the Lotus Pond, all will be clear. Embrace the anger, the call for retribution."*

A swirl of pink petals floats in front of my eyes, a soft smile hidden behind the flurries. The floral scent wafts to my nose, overtaking the scent of death and decay that permeates this dimension. Her silver hair floats behind her; a hand reaches out to my eyes once again. A warm light flows through me, enveloping me. It hurts, and my body stiffens as the lotus on my chest heats and the black vines threaten to break loose. Memories of the blood moon flash through my mind—ones I could hardly believe were real. Using a strange light—this light—to heal the child, freeing her from the shadows.

"These beings are beyond recognition; free their souls."

Her image fades, and I look at Luka. He caresses his hand against my face, not moving from my side. Reaching out, I gently grab onto his hand with a smile and pull it away. He furrows his brows, but I only shake my head.

I push myself up from the ground, Luka and Meena coming to my aid. They hold on to my arms, so I remain steady, but I shake them off, knowing I can stand on my own now. Wrapping my fingers around the blade wedged deep into my side, I yank it out. Blood gushes to the floor, but I feel nothing.

"What are you doing?" Luka says, panic lacing his voice. I smile as the blade clatters onto the stone tiles.

"Nova, you're bleeding even more now," Meena says, rushing to press her hands to the open wound.

I take her hands off me, shaking my head softly.

"Whatever you plan on doing, don't even think about it," Luka says, blocking my path.

"What's she doing?" Lei Jing says, her hands held up to maintain her energy barrier against the Krav—a power I've never seen her use. The energy field is holding, but her arms tremble, and sweat trickles down her forehead.

"Saving us," I say as I turn to Luka, running my bloody fingers over his cheek.

He lied to me, to everyone, but I can't find fault in this moment.

"You have one chance. After this, the power won't be accessible. Not until you find the Lotus Pond." I wonder what she speaks of but turn my attention to the chaos we're fighting. Stepping forward, I pass through Lei Jing's barrier.

"I'll fight, Nova, just please—" Luka says, grabbing my arm. His eyes search mine, begging me to stay.

I shrug his hand off, pushing him back into Lei Jing's barrier. "Stay here."

The pain is gone, the torture Camus put me through becoming a distant memory as the warm light leaks from my body into the world around us. A power deep within me awakening to free us from this nightmare.

The horde of Krav hovers over us, caving in on my weakening friends. Running forward, I jump in, kicking one off Oliver. The being bursts into a ball of light, disintegrating on the spot. Moving faster than I ever have, I zip around the four cambions in combat. My light travels from my fists, punching holes in the Krav horde—returning them to peace. But more fill the empty space—a never-ending army. How many lives did Camus take?

Digging through the Krav, I search for Camus and Theo. The cowards who ran from this battle. Believers of the actual False King—no, a false god.

Claws rake down my side, and I scream as blood flows from my wounds, soaking the ground around me. Turning on the creature, I shove my fist through it, watching it disintegrate in my light.

Out of the corner of my eye, I see Luka, Lei Jing, and Meena join the battle—no longer behind the energy barrier.

Five cambions, a naga, and the long-lost fallen angel Lucifer all fight side by side. Raining chaos down on chaos. They're merely a blur at the edge of my vision—my focus solely on the shadowy Krav before me.

The light expands from my chest, filling the room. The creatures screech as they're bathed in the warm glow, unable to run away, commanded by their master to fight. Closing my eyes, I summon more of the power, digging deep even as I can feel the black vines pushing against Rishu's seal.

Through the horde, Camus and Theo reappear, grinning slyly at me. I push my light toward them, but they disappear before it reaches them. I yell out, throwing my arms wide, and the light erupts from my core.

It expands out in a brilliant shockwave, disintegrating all the Krav within a wide radius. Restoring order to the world—even if only by a mere fraction. The lotus on my chest burns, and I scream as Rishu's barrier around the black vines shatters. Black vines burst forward, racing over my body.

I collapse to my knees, clawing at my chest. My fingernails leave long red marks, but I can't stop. The vines extend down my left arm and ribcage before coming to a halt. Air rushes into my lungs, the pain and light fading around me.

My hair falls in front of my face; black dots dance across my vision.

"Until we meet at the Lotus Pond."

Luka rushes to my side, taking me into his arms. I stare into his silver eyes as the world fades to black.

31

UNBOUND MEMORIES

My eyes open to a dark room, a blank white ceiling above. As I sit up, a thin blanket falls from my shoulders. Curtains are drawn closed, blocking out the daylight. Only a small crack lets in the faintest amount of sunlight.

The room is familiar. Similar, if not the same, as the one Amon let me rest in before setting off to the château. Standing from the bed, I turn to the doorway, my bare feet cold against the tile flooring. My mind is a blur, steps uneven with dizziness as I walk out of the room. Every muscle and bone in my body aches. A part of my brain wants to say none of what I remember is real.

I rub my bare arms, the heat too low to keep the shivers away.

I step out of the doorway to find myself at the end of a long hallway. Multiple doors line the way to an elevator at the other end. The lights have been turned off—apparently a common occurrence in Amon's building. I slowly make my way toward the elevator, my feet moving on their own.

A door opens, and panic floods my body. I try to run as my breaths come faster and faster. The brute's heavy steps follow behind me, his hand reaching to grab onto my hair and drag me to Camus. I can't let that happen. I need to escape, I—

A hand lands on my shoulder and spins me around. I scream, pushing myself away and stumbling back. Strong arms catch my fall, and I fight against them, tears falling as I struggle against the hold. A familiar scent reaches my nostrils, and my heart rate begins to calm. My eyes trail up the black silk shirt to the face of my captor.

"I got you. You're safe. No one can hurt you here. I promise." His dark brows draw together in concern as he gently wipes the tears from my face and helps me regain my footing. He waits for me to calm down, though the memories of my time in Camus's dimension still haunt me. Letting me go, he steps back and gazes at me with sad silver eyes.

"Luka?"

"I'm here if you need me."

He begins walking past me, but I grab onto his sleeve. We need to talk. One of my questions was finally answered. The truth came out... Luka is Lucifer.

"Why did you lie?" I ask softly.

"Nova..."

His face is drawn in a frown, cheeks gaunt as if he hasn't been eating or sleeping. Dark circles line his silver eyes, which appear dull, somehow devoid of the radiance they always seemed to shine with before. Still, a faint light seems to shine around him, and I stare in awe. Even in his current state, he's more beautiful than anyone I've ever seen. God's favorite fallen angel.

"Why did you pretend to be someone else? Who is Luka?"

"Nova, I never—"

"I have no right to judge your choices. We both lied to everyone," I say, not letting go of his sleeve. "Just answer one thing... Who are you to me?"

Lips part to speak, but no words come out. He stays silent for a long moment, his face contorting as he grapples with whatever is going on in his head.

"Nova, it's much more complicated than—"

"Uncomplicate it."

He licks his lips nervously. His eyes meet mine, and we look at each other for another long moment. My heart aches as I await his truth. Even without Remembrance's voice in my head, the two words she kept whispering are stuck in my mind. *Our beloved.*

"Okay." He takes my hand into his own, my fingers brushing against his rings. "Then instead of explaining, how about I show you... everything." I tilt my head, and he smiles, soft and sweet. "Only if you want me to."

He doesn't make a move, waiting. Staring into his silver eyes, I search for answers. My heart flutters, and a blush rises to my cheeks despite everything that's happened. I hesitate, nodding softly after making my decision.

"I want you... to show me."

With a magick I don't quite understand, Luka—no, *Lucifer*—has transported us into one of his memories.

We stand atop a hill with a small stone house, smoke billowing out its chimney. I spin in a slow circle, gazing out at the open field beyond the house. An ancient-looking city rests on the other side of the hill. Nothing in the architecture resembles anything I've ever seen.

I absentmindedly reach for my chest, fingertips grazing the fabric of my shirt that rests over the lotus tattoo. Black lines catch my eye, and I pause. The sinuous pattern covers down to the middle of my forearm. I drop my hand, shaking my head as I focus on the memory Luka brought us to. I'll worry about those vines later.

A woman speaks from behind, and I turn to face her. Her face is wrinkled, the corners of her eyes creased deeply—it is the face of a woman who's led a happy life. Gray strands fall around her tanned face as she smiles at me. The woman is robed in a muted orange and white dress, with loose sleeves laced in an ornate design. A piece of fabric covers her hair, hanging low behind her. Beside her, a tall, burly man stands with dark hair speckled with gray and a thick beard at his chin. He wears clothes of dark brown, simple and airy for the apparent summer weather. The couple laughs together, but their gazes look straight through me.

Turning around, my breath hitches as I watch a girl my age, if not a little older, climb the hill. My mouth drops open as she comes into view. Her face... While the features aren't quite the same, I recognize them. But it's her green eyes that tell me all I need to know. She is me, *was* me.

Dark hair falls in long waves over her shoulders. She wears a similar dress to the older woman, her mother, I'd assume, but in a brilliant green to match her eyes. The girl smiles fondly at the couple behind us as she passes through me as if I'm not there. I turn and watch as she greets them, speaking in a language I don't recognize. She turns back to us with a broader smile, and I follow her gaze.

My mouth parts as I see Luka climb the hill. He looks the same except for the ancient clothing he wears, and his hair... it's braided loosely to one side, reaching down past his chest. Much longer than the modern cut he has today. *He's beautiful.* Shaking my head, I stumble back. I've seen this place before. This stone house, these two people, even this girl. My head throbs as if the memory isn't meant for me to see, to remember.

"They were your adopted parents," Luka says from beside me as his past self walks through us to the girl and her parents. "They found you abandoned when they moved here to Nicaea."

"Nicaea..." The name doesn't ring a bell. Just how long ago was this?

The scene changes, and we're standing out in the field beyond the stone house. A boom sounds, and I look to see Lucifer falling from the sky. He lands hard, lying lifeless in the tall grass. His white robes are covered in blood, black feathered wings slowly shrinking into his back. I go to reach out to him, but a hand stops me. I turn to Luka, but he just shakes his head.

Feet pound in the distance, and soon the girl is by his side. She calls out for her father, who was chopping wood, and they carry Lucifer's battered form to the stone house. The girl's mother prepares water and herbs, beginning to treat his wounds.

"This is when we first met," Luka says as we watch the scene unfold before us.

"Is this when you became a fallen angel?"

He shakes his head. "For years, I was in disagreement with the reigning God and the angels beside him."

"Reigning God?"

He sighs. "You see, the Heaven's work differently from what humans know. About every two thousand years, a new God is chosen. We angels support the new God, but...." Luka's eyes turn dark. "This God, he's a tyrant. Despite having served as an archangel for over a millennium, he demoted me because I couldn't—wouldn't—support his ideals and was constantly arguing with my siblings. On this day"—he motions to the scene in front of us, pain etched in each word—"I fought with Michael, and I just let myself fall to Earth. Injured or not, I didn't care. I just wanted to escape for a while."

I process the information in disbelief. Has everything we've been taught been false?

The scene morphs again. This time, we're standing in the city center surrounded by beautiful ancient stone buildings.

The girl and Lucifer smile together as they walk through the marketplace, joking and laughing as they look at the different stalls. Lucifer reaches out as they stop in front of a table of jewelry, landing on a pair of gold rings. I look down at Luka's right hand, recognizing them. The girl giggles as he places it on her ring finger, but she quickly takes it off and hands it back to the vendor. An emotion I can't identify stabs my chest, and I close my eyes as I take a deep breath.

"You loved her—me, I guess. You didn't want to go back to Heaven, did you?"

Luka—his other name foreign to me—doesn't say anything, and I can't bring myself to face him. If he was in love with her, then what now? Did he lie to be close to the reincarnation of the girl he once loved? Was the whole deal with Amon just a scam to meet me? My heart breaks at the thought, desperately hoping it's not true.

The scene changes again, and we're standing back of the hill. The setting sun casts red rays across the city; everything is eerily quiet. The stone house behind us is silent, and dread washes over me.

"This is what changed everything," Luka says quietly, his voice pained.

Lucifer and the girl arrive back at the stone house. Smoke no longer billows out of the chimney, no light comes from within, and the door is slightly ajar. They both pause before entering, but when they do, the girl screams.

Swallowing, I take a few steps closer. Her parents lay motionless on the ground, their throats slit, blood still oozing from the wounds as it stains the floor. The girl falls to her knees, cradling her parents' bodies in her arms as she weeps. I stumble back as my mind begins to race. The black vines threaten to inch across my skin, but I can't turn away.

Lucifer reaches for the girl, holding her face in his hands. He speaks quickly, and the girl argues with him. But he lets go and disappears from her side.

"What did you say to her? Where did you go?" I ask, turning back to Luka.

"To Heaven. They were the ones who did this."

"What?" I take a step away from him. "Why? It doesn't make sense."

His eyes are sad as he watches. "Because God wouldn't let me love a human."

The scene changes yet again, and we watch from above as a siege rains down upon the city. Luka climbs the hill in front of us, longsword in hand. His face is grim, and dark energy swirls around him. The girl rushes to his side, grasping the black cloak he wears. She yells at him through tears, and the words are suddenly clear in my mind.

"Please, don't go. My parents are gone... I can't lose you too."

"I have no choice. Run from this place, and I will find you again at the lake."

The girl reaches out to Lucifer, but he disappears before she can stop him—his wings pushing him toward the sky. She crumbles to her knees, tears streaming down her face. I press my palm into my chest; this pain is unbearable.

"Stop." My voice is a whisper as I bend over, the black vines inching further down my forearm. Luka doesn't move from my side. "Make it stop!"

I squeeze my eyes shut as I curl in on myself.

"You wanted to know the whole truth. You died because of my love for you, and I fell from Heaven fighting to keep you."

I feel the air change, and I open my eyes. We're back in the hallway, Luka standing in front of me. He lets go of my hand, and I suddenly feel cold without his fingers wrapped around mine. I stare at him, conflicted. A replacement, a stand-in. That's all I am.

"You left her, and what? Broke open the moon to raise Hell? Then came here a thousand years late to apologize?"

He looks away, eyes hard. "No, I would never do that. I admit it worked in my favor, but I don't know who broke into the moon for its power." His eyes meet mine, and I know he's not lying. "The reigning God threatened me with your life after having your parents killed, so I rebelled. Then the hunters kidnapped you and sided with God and the other angels. I raised Hell, became their *king*, to find you. To fight for you."

"But what did us humans do to deserve that chaos?"

"He killed you!" I freeze, my heart thundering in my chest. "Solomon killed you... Burned your body so I could never find you."

I step back from Luka, and his eyes dart away from mine. I bite my lip, processing everything. Tears prick my eyes.

"That's not me... I'm not the same girl you loved. Why bring me into it a thousand years later? Hell, why have I even been reincarnated all this time? What, did this reigning God decide to torture you with my existence by reincarnating me—"

"Nova..." Luka's voice is pained.

"No... No, no, no...."

I let out a shaky breath, stepping out of his reach. My hand reaches for my chest, gripping the fabric of my shirt. The black vines don't grow, but the dark voice in my head laughs at my distress. *Darkness.*

"I didn't know until Amon told me and showed me proof. But when I saw you the night of the blood moon, I knew."

My fist tightens, knuckles turning white. Damn Luka, damn the girl from my past life, damn everyone. Hell, I'll even damn the Heavens for all they've done. But a nagging pain in my chest renders me immobile—the picture still isn't complete. *Until we meet at the Lotus Pond.* The words Remembrance spoke—a final message.

"And now what? Why will these black vines kill me? What about the lotus tattoo? Please explain to me how any of this makes sense." He's silent, and I let out a heavy breath as I walk past him toward the elevator.

"Did you do all this so that—" I shake my head. "You know what. Forget it. I don't want to know. I think it's time I talk with Amon and the others."

"I didn't do this so you'd love me." His words stop me in my tracks; I close my eyes. "I just wished to see your face, to apologize for the mistakes I made and free you from His curse. That's all."

My throat tightens. I'm slowly drowning in a wave of thoughts and emotions I hardly understand. What do I do with these feelings? Everything I've ever known has turned out to be false. My sense of self crumbling more with each piece of the puzzle that falls into place... I wanted, *needed*, these answers, but all I've found is confusion. Pain.

"It's enough to love you from here."

I spin around to him. "You don't get to say that. Not now, and maybe not ever." His eyes shine with sadness as a tear slides down my cheek. "Luka, or Lucifer, whatever this is, whatever you want... I don't care anymore. Put yourself in my shoes. What would you do after someone you trusted tells you everything you just did? Especially knowing this isn't the end of it."

"Nova—"

I hold up my hand, stopping him from continuing. "Just stop. I've had enough."

Walking away, I don't dare turn back—even as my heart wrenches in my chest. Damn these feelings that aren't even mine. Damn Remembrance for ever mentioning a *beloved.*

In all the time I've wondered why things are the way they are, nothing like this ever crossed my mind. When I first saw glimpses of those lifetimes in my angelic trials, I never would have imagined they—and everything else—only happened because Lucifer had loved me, and God wouldn't allow it.

And there are no words either of us can say to fix the destruction that love has caused.

32

AFFLICTIONS

Entering the elevator, I push the button for the top floor. The doors shut, and I let out a long sigh, leaning against the metal wall. My head and chest ache. *This is too much for me.*

"What am I supposed to do?"

Uriel eases into my mind. *"My child... You have learned so much in such little time... There is fear in your heart, as there should be. But we—"* She stops herself, quieting in my mind. *"I am here to protect you in the only way I can."*

"We all are...." The elevator doors open to the top floor, and Uri goes quiet.

Sunlight pours into the hallway from the large windows as I step out. I don't stop to admire the city in the daylight, marching straight toward Amon's office. Reaching his door, I take a deep breath before knocking. His voice rumbles from the other side, and I enter.

Amon sits at his desk, facing the window. I look around for Rishu, but he's nowhere in sight. To my surprise, the cambions are all here, sitting in various office chairs spread around the room. They look up, and my breath lodges in my chest. After everything I hid from them, they came to save me without knowing what they might face... How do I ever repay them?

"Nova! You're awake! You were so cool back in that other dimension; I mean kinda scary but totally amazing," Meena says, jumping from her chair and running to me.

"Thanks?"

"You were pretty cool," Lei Jing says as she approaches behind Meena. Her lip twitches as if she's holding back a smile.

"You went wild," Azura says with a crooked grin as she leans back in her chair. "Obliterated those things and healed yourself at the same time. It was seriously badass. When were you gonna show us how to do that?"

I stare at them at a loss for words.

"You didn't change?" Lei Jing asks, looking me up and down.

I look down at the torn, bloody clothes I still wear—my feet bare. Too distracted by Luk—*Lucifer* to even think about them when I left my room. Reaching down to my side, I feel the skin beneath the hole in my shirt left by Theo's knife. Only a faint scar remains. My mind runs miles, adding more items to the list of things I don't understand.

That power... where did it come from? It most definitely wasn't my angels. Does it have to do with my father? Camus mentioned a part of God's power being passed down to the firstborn son, but could it apply to me as well? I close my eyes and pinch the bridge of my nose as I feel another headache coming on. What if the power isn't God's at all but some third party... The voice of Darkness inside my head would make sense then if my father passed this curse onto me.

"I forgot to...." I say, meeting Lei Jing's gaze. She tilts her head as if silently asking if I'm okay. I shake my head. Another time, another day for that conversation.

Amon spins around in his chair to face us. "My dear Nova, it's so good to see you awake again." A wide grin rests on his porcelain face, and his long platinum hair swept over his shoulders. "We have much to discuss. Beginning with what Lucifer has shared with you."

The cambions look to me. I doubt Amon has shared with them what Lucifer is doing here, what my role in all of this is. Even their role is just to fill a gap between the two of us. A frown pulls at my lips. Whatever Amon has planned, I'm sick of it. The deceptions, the secrets, the lies. When does it all end?

"You mean the fact I've been reincarnated for a thousand years because Lucifer fell in love with a past version of me, and now I'm being punished for it? Is that where you want to start? Or maybe we should start with why you offered me a contract in the first place. Some sick deal to get me beside, him all while knowing about a war my uncle's starting. Yet you felt no need to warn me about it while I trained the cambions who got caught in the crossfire."

Amon smirks, his blue eyes twinkling as murmurs from the cambions rumble around us. "Smart girl. You weren't brought here just because I needed you to train my cambions." He stands from his chair and makes his way around the desk. "In fact, I wasn't the one who brought you here at all. Though we'll get to that later...." His steps are slow and calculated as he makes his way to me. He stops close enough for me to smell his cologne, the scent mingling with the smell of the blood staining my clothes. "Lucifer is under my control. I at least have to thank you for that," he says as he takes a loose strand of my hair, twirling it between his fingers.

I remove his hand, stepping out of his reach. "What are you talking about?"

His smile widens, and I almost shudder. A predator sizing up its prey, waiting to pounce and kill. The cambions are nothing like this demon before me. I have to remember exactly who I'm dealing with.

"After disappearing a thousand years ago because his human lover died, he let Gehenna fall to ruin after taking control of it as its king. The hunters thought him dead, but I knew he was not. You see, my visions of what's to come were still filled with him. But he's stubborn, and the only way he'd ever listen to me was to get you out of the hunter's hands and into his."

I groan as my headache intensifies. "This just keeps getting worse."

"And it'll continue to get worse. Thousands of possible outcomes that all end with the world burning—humans and demons alike. The only hope I've seen for this war is you in Lucifer's hands. I've made plenty of deals to get you and him to this moment."

Amon comes closer, taking my chin in his hands. He lifts my gaze to his, searching my face. "But everything's changed now. My visions of you... I see death closing in but nothing more. And no one is strong enough to block me from seeing their past and future." He seethes as he leans in closer. "Yet you, a human girl... I cannot read you. Even the great fallen angel Lucifer is as open to me as a child. It makes you... far more interesting."

"Take your hands off me." Amon grins, the look enough to turn my stomach rotten, but he steps away. "If it wasn't for Camus and the cambions, I'd leave and never help you again. I should have listened to the hunters' number one rule—never make a deal with the devil," I say, grumbling and crossing my arms.

"Perhaps, or maybe the truth scares you. You and my cambions were meant to be connected to Lucifer, yet the only way I can see any piece of your future is through them. As unclear as it continues to be, I have to believe you are more than what my king has let on." My jaw clenches as unease swirls in my stomach. We were all part of Amon's game. "Now the dice has been cast, but I'm unsure which side it'll land on."

"Excuse me, what exactly is going on?" Lei Jing says from beside me. Meena's doe eyes dart back and forth between us, the tension in the room tangible.

"I am also very confused," Oliver chips in from the other end of the room, and Tevari lifts his book in agreement.

"I hate to say it, but I'm with Oliver," Azura says.

I sigh, turning to them. "Amon got me to sign a contract with him, one I'm assuming was the last part of whatever contract he signed with Lucifer. Training you all was just an excuse."

"Not entirely," Amon cuts in. "While there are thousands of possibilities of us failing, I never said I didn't see us win. All five of them here must play a role in this war. Yet, somehow, their precise roles are obscured, and all I can think is that they must be closely connected to you, Nova."

I consider his words. If he can see everyone's futures, why are only ours obscured to him? Is it because of Darkness or Remembrance? They're the only beings I can imagine who might be able to hide such things from Amon.

"And this war? It has to do with those shadow beings?" Lei Jing asks.

Azura sits forward in her chair. "Don't forget about the psycho we saw. Who is he again?"

I sigh. "My uncle, who's my father's twin, apparently. He believes the world needs to be destroyed and remade, so he created the Krav, or his *king* did. Oh, and he believes God has given him the power to do so, something about it being passed down since Solomon the First—the one who led the hunters during the Great Demonic Fall. But the only conclusion I can come to is there's a third party involved that we're not yet aware of."

Amon hums thoughtfully. "The Krav... Like the god of military and combat from the Ellim Mythos. The champion of Eden. Obviously, he's delusional, but there must be some kernel of truth in what he told you."

Azura stands and steps forward, looking between us. "Well, this is hella disturbing and super unclear." I nod in agreement. "Also, maybe dumb it down a little bit. I personally don't know much of demonic or hunter history. I hardly even know anything about Avnas, my demonic deadbeat dad."

She's right. The cambions don't have the same knowledge as Amon and I do—it's wrong of us to expect them to keep up. And Avnas... I might not technically be training them anymore, but I can't help but consider Azura and her demonic parentage. Her powers make so much sense now. A demon of pure flame. No wonder she has anger issues.

"Wait!" Meena shouts, and we all turn to her. "Your father." She rolls her eyes when none of us catch on. "Your psycho uncle's twin? If anyone knows anything about all of this, it would be him, right?"

My heart sinks. She's not wrong, but... I never expected I'd have to return so soon.

"Excellent thought, little one." Amon lights up, causing Meena to flash her wide grin. "Nova, what do you say? Is it time for the disgraced daughter to return? I, personally, am dying to know the truth."

Everyone looks at me expectantly, waiting for my response. "He has a book...." I watch Tevari perk up, finally looking up from his own book. "I saw it before, *The Eternal Keeper*. Well, technically, I didn't see the actual book, but I know where we might find it."

"A book? How would that help?" Oliver says from his seat.

"Books are knowledge," Tevari says as he fiddles with a leaf of his vine.

I nod in agreement. "My angels showed me a vision of my grandfather giving it to my father. Camus said it explains the fraction of God's soul that has been passed down from Solomon to Solomon. If anything, we might get an idea of what we're up against."

"If it's even really God or not," Lei Jing chimes in, and I nod.

"Okay, then let's go get it." Flames flare from Azura's palm. Already ready for another fight. I almost chuckle. Almost.

Seeing my father again after so long, after everything he's done... I could go a thousand years without meeting again.

"It's not that easy," I say. "You're all demons, so you won't be able to enter the compound, and I'm a deserter who's sided with said demons." The room grows silent. "But, I think I should be able to at least speak to my father before they try to lock me up."

"Well, now that that's settled," Amon says, clapping his hands. Rishu appears in a puff of black smoke, making a quick bow to Amon. He's returned to his human appearance with no sign of horns or scales. "Rishu, make the preparations. We have a book to retrieve."

33

HOMEBOUND

"**I**s this really a good idea?" I ask Rishu, looking behind him at everyone. Luka raises his gaze to mine, and I quickly turn away. Now's not the time to deal with him. Not with what's ahead.

We stand outside a blue boathouse just beyond the Fandera Estate. It rests on the lake I always dreamed about crossing, to escape to the freedom I was denied.

So much has changed since then.

I scan the group, the cambions ready to charge into the Fandera Estate with powers blazing. I sigh. Maybe I shouldn't have let them convince me to take them with me.

It's cold and cloudy today, the mid-October sky as unwelcoming as this town. The leaves are already turning brown with the coming of winter, frost sticking to the ground in the early hours of the day. It was only a blip in time that I was in Camus's dimension, although it felt like days, weeks. But a full day hasn't even passed for everyone else. Apparently, time works differently in his dimension.

The cool wind brushes over my cheeks, the all too familiar scent of *home* carried with it. The path back to the estate is

328

easy to follow, a single paved sidewalk leading the way. I rub at the scars that line my wrists, reminders of the angelic chains my father put me in only a few weeks ago. Chains I now know can be cut by Kioren. I brush a finger over the black gem of the bracelet, grateful for the responding quiet hum against my wrist.

"We wouldn't want to miss out on the family drama," Rishu says, glancing over his shoulder at the others. Meena, nose, and cheeks pink from the cold, gives us a thumbs up.

I sigh again, stuffing my hands into the pockets of my jacket. "Okay, then the plan is simple. We won't fight if it's not necessary. The guards at the estate should recognize me, and then I will enter alone to speak with my father...."

"You're not going in alone," Luka says.

"We don't have a choice. No demons can enter clan property. You should know." His silver eyes are sharp as I look at him. Dark energy hovers around his frame, but I continue, ignoring the stubborn look of disagreement on his face. "I'll talk with my father, find the book, and you all will wait in the woods next to the estate for me to either escape or throw the book out to you."

"How do you know this will work?" Lei Jing says, her violet eyes uncertain.

She hugs herself tighter as she shivers. A wave of guilt passes through me. I betrayed them, yet they're still here with me to figure out the missing pieces and stop an impending war. My debt to them, it seems, keeps stacking up.

"If it's not there, we'll figure something else out. My father only keeps things in his office at the estate or at his campus manor. If we don't find it, we'll go to plan B and look in the manor."

"What about the other hunters and Undivided?" Oliver asks.

"Just try avoiding contact with anyone. Hopefully, they'll only notice me and not any of you," I say with a not-so-reassuring smile.

"This isn't a solid plan...." Tevari says, his vine peeking out from inside his coat.

"And the hunter"—Luka says derisively, crossing his arms—"what happens if you meet him again?"

I suck in a breath. Adrian has been the furthest thing from my mind if I'm being honest. Looking at Luka, I raise my chin. Nothing and no one will deter me on this mission. Not even Adrian.

"I'll be fine. Let's just go and get this over with."

We head out onto the curved sidewalk, laying low to not draw attention to ourselves. Thankfully, we're passed by only a few cars and a single morning jogger with their dog. The dog barks, catching the scent of demons. I panic briefly, but the owner apologizes, and we continue on our way without causing more of a scene.

When we reach the halfway point, the estate almost in view, the cambions and Rishu fall into the shadows of the woods. Luka hesitates at the edge, eyes pleading.

"Go," I say. "You can't come with me."

He steps toward me and presses his hand to my shoulder. Looking down, a black butterfly the size of my palm rests on my jacket. It gently flaps its wings, which shimmer faintly with an almost-silver sheen. My mouth parts. Of course. All the black butterflies I've seen have been from him. He disappears into the woods before I can comment.

Standing on the open sidewalk, I take a deep breath before continuing down the path to the estate—a path back to the cage I grew up in. I tighten my ponytail. After everything that's happened, after abandoning my old beliefs, I never imagined I'd return here like this.

The gates to the estate come into sight, memories washing over me. I always wanted to get outside those brick walls to hunt demons. Now look at me.

Four hunters I don't recognize stand on guard, the weapons I know they carry concealed. I approach without hesitation, stopping before them.

"I think you know who I am," I say, looking between the hunters whose eyes have gone wide, disbelief written across their faces. "Is my father home?"

The hunters look between each other before one radios into the house. Finally deciding it's safe for me to enter, one of the hunters leads me to the front door. Stopping at the entrance, he speaks quietly. "He's in his office."

I nod, releasing him to his duty. Entering the main foyer, a shiver runs up my arms. It's no longer in pieces from when I left, though it holds the same coldness. I guess my remodeling didn't help any. A laugh escapes my lips at the thought as Kioren warms on my wrist—a silent offer to repeat the chaos.

I take my time as I climb the grand staircase, running my fingers up the wooden railing. Pausing at the top, I look to the opposite end of the hall where my old room is. A subtle ache weighs in my chest. The room I left everything behind in. The hunter's code, Adrian, Lance... Even if I was a prisoner here, at least everything was so much simpler then.

I turn away from the past, heading to my father's office. The same path I took before making my decision to go to Amon. And for a moment, I hesitate at his door. There's no way to know if this plan will succeed. My father is unpredictable. I can pretend to be confident in front of the others, but the truth is I don't know anything.

Knocking on the door, I wait for his voice on the other side. No sound comes, and I push my way into the empty room. Closing the door behind me, I race to his desk. Sifting through papers, opening his drawers, and skimming the large bookshelf—I search the office as fast as I can. I feel beneath the desk, hoping to find a hidden drawer, but come up short.

The door handle jostles, and I freeze. I haven't found the book yet. I spin around as my father opens the door, and his cold blue eyes meet mine. Somehow, in the last few weeks, his face has aged. His hair looks flat and lifeless, and his clothes are wrinkled and unkempt. In his hands, he carries a large leatherbound book. Neither of us says anything for a long moment as he enters.

"Nova." His voice sounds pained, hoarse.

I clench my jaw so hard it pops as I fight to keep my emotions under control.

"Father," I respond in the cold tone he always used.

He walks around the desk to stand in front of me. His eyes are tired, the skin beneath a dark purple. I've never seen him like this before.

"I'm sorry," he says.

I inhale sharply as he reaches a calloused hand to my cheek, holding it softly.

"I promised myself I would protect you after what he did to her...." Tears fall from his eyes. The sight unfamiliar, warm. "I've put you through so much, and yet I still couldn't protect you."

A tear unwillingly streams down my cheek, and he wipes it away with his thumb. "Nova, I know why you're here, and I—" He closes his eyes, grunting in pain. I hesitate as I reach for him, my mouth moving but no words coming out. When he looks back at me, the coldness I remember isn't there. "Listen to me, I can only help you so much now." Shoving the book he had been holding into my hands, he wraps my fingers tightly around the edges. "Take this and run."

"Father... you're scaring me," I say, unable to pull my hands from his.

"I know you know part of the truth, otherwise—" Grunting in pain again, he steps back, his hands falling from mine. He recovers and looks at me with wide, pleading eyes, urgency written across his face. "The book can help you find the answers I wasn't able to share with you. Find the Lotus Pond and make things right."

"Father, what's going on?" I step toward him as more tears fall from my eyes.

Placing a hand back on my cheek again, his cold blue eyes somehow turn warm. "I may not have ever truly been your father, but everything I did... Everything was to stop this cycle of pain. The curse we've punished you with for far too long. I'm so sorry, Nova."

His gaze drops to the butterfly resting on my chest and a sad smile across his aged features. "I'm glad he found you."

My heart blossoms at his words, but it vanishes in an instant as Father's hand falls from my cheek in a scream of agony. He claws at his face, pulling at his blond strands. Paper and books fall from the desk as he thrashes around the room in pain. I back up, watching in horror.

"Go!" he screams as he falls to his knees, clawing at his eyes. Tears glisten down his cheeks. I take a step forward, reaching my hand to his shoulder.

"Father—"

"Go!"

Another agony-filled scream leaves his lips before it just stops—the room growing too silent. A low chuckle sounds under his breath as I scoot around the desk to the door. His hands fall from his now bloody and tear-stained face.

"Oh, Nova, you should have left when he told you to."

I freeze as he stands from the ground, fixing the sleeves of his dress shirt. That voice... It can't be. Father looks to me, the blue of his eyes and even the whites have gone—becoming the thing I have come to fear. *Darkness.*

"Solomon always had too soft a heart, *weak* in more ways than one," Darkness says, eyeing the butterfly, "Too think he's grateful for the False King...."

I back away as he prowls around the desk, each step deliberate, a predator stalking its prey. My skin prickles as he nears, breath quickening in my chest.

"Nova, leave now!" Uri and Zera scream in my head, shaking me out of my terror-induced stupor. Looking out the window, I see the wall to the forest beyond.

"Kioren, come forth!"

The scythe emerges, black tendril shattering the glass pane. I race toward the window, but Father moves faster, cutting off my exit. Grabbing Kioren's handle, I swipe down but hesitate at the last moment. The blade shrinks back in the confined space.

A roaring laugh bursts from my father's lips. "Have you become so human?" Father grabs one of Kioren's tendrils, pulling me close. "You made a mistake coming here. Haven't I warned you enough, my dear?"

Staring into his black eyes, I scream as the black vines inch across my skin. Gritting my teeth against the pain, I plant Kioren's staff and swing around to kick the man in the chest. He lets go with a laugh, and I race out of the office, holding the book close.

"Run, run, run. But you won't ever outrun me," he taunts in a sing-song voice.

I clutch the book harder as I pick up speed, sprinting down the hall, the black vines slowing their assault on my body the more distance I put between myself and the evil being who has possessed my father.

Two guards enter through the front door upon hearing the commotion, drawing out a sword and gun as soon as they see Kioren coming down the stairs.

"Don't let her leave," Father's voice rings out from behind me, shouting to the waiting hunters.

Jumping down the rest of the stairs, Kioren's black tail twirls around me protectively. Bullets fly in my direction, ricocheting off the tendril as it expands to block the assault. They pierce the hunter's soft flesh, and I wince as he howls, falling to the floor. Slashing Kioren down on the next hunter, the scythe's blade cuts easily through the metal of his sword.

The hunter steps back with wide eyes. Glancing up one last time at the smirking figure of my father, I stare into his—no, *Darkness's*—pitch-black eyes one last time. Turning back, I race toward the open doors.

The two other hunters waiting at the gate approach with their weapons drawn as soon as they see me. Feeling a tug from Kioren, I let go of the handle and watch as it swerves around, cutting their weapons down and knocking them out with its whip-like black tendril. I don't stop running, needing to get as far away from the estate as possible and back with the others. Kioren slides back into the bracelet once the estate is out of sight, no one following me down the sidewalk. The silver bracelet pulses against my wrist in sync with my desperate heartbeat.

The black butterfly on my chest shatters, and I slow, eyeing the forest. Wind nips at my exposed skin as more clouds form in the sky above. Snow starts to fall, and my cheeks, wet with tears, begin to freeze. How did it come to this? I look at the leatherbound book Father gave me, *The Eternal Keeper*. How did he know I'd come for it?

Seven forms emerge from the trees, but there's only one face I focus on. More tears well in my eyes as I meet Luka's concerned gaze. Rushing to my side, he envelops me in a warm hug. I hold tightly onto his coat, digging my head into his shoulder as I sob.

"Nova..." I hear Azura say, but I'm too overwhelmed to respond.

Voices yell down the street, and I let go, coming back to my senses. I take a deep breath and wipe the tears from my face. "I have the book; let's go."

Glances are shared between the group, but no questions are asked. We race back to the boathouse to the parked van that brought us here. A gunshot echoes around us, followed by a scream. Rishu falls to his knees, a dark circle of purple blood spreading slowly across the front of his jacket. Meena and Oliver help him up as the hunters gain on us. The chapel bell starts ringing, and my stomach sinks. They've alerted all the hunters.

I turn to face the hunter, recognizing him as one of Adrian's team. Tall, dark-haired, with piercing blue eyes. We make eye contact, and I remind myself never to forget his face. He aims another bullet at the cambions, and I call Kioren forth once more. I have the scythe spread out the black tendril as a shield as we make our way to the van. I reach into Rishu's pocket and grab the keys, unlocking the car as Tevari and Oliver lay him across the seat. A groan escapes Rishu, and I know the bullet wound hurts more than he's letting on.

"Who can drive?" I say, looking around as Kioren deflects more bullets.

"I can," Luka says, and I toss him the keys.

The rest of us climb into the car, and Kioren shrinks back into the bracelet. We slam the doors shut quickly as more bullets hit.

"Lei Jing, can you hide us until we're out of Falgens?" Luka says from the driver's seat.

"I can try." Lei Jing presses her hands against the back window. Her face scrunches up in concentration as her purple energy begins to spread out from her hands and encompass the vehicle.

"Meena, can you make an illusion of us to send in the opposite direction?" Luka asks, looking at her in the back seat from the rearview mirror as he peels out of the parking lot.

She looks between him and Rishu, then over to me. I nod to her.

"I can," she says, sitting up straighter with a look of determination on her face.

Climbing over Oliver and Azura, she moves to Tevari's lap and presses a hand to the window. She closes her eyes, and a moment later, an exact duplicate of our van appears beside us. Meena sends it down the opposite street, bullets flying in its wake. Luka speeds away as hunters swarm the parking lot behind us—thankfully focusing on the illusion and not us.

Out of immediate danger, I lean over Rishu and unzip his jacket, peeling back the blood-soaked shirt beneath.

"You just had to get shot," I say, and he chuckles.

"I must say, your angelic bullets hurt a lot more than expected," he says with another laugh while also wincing in pain. "At least I was only hit once."

I shake my head. Angelic bullets are deadly to demons. They lodge themselves into their flesh and release angelic essence that will eventually poison them. So even if the shot itself doesn't kill them, it will still end with their death. Rishu's a high-tier, but if we don't get this out sooner rather than later... I look up and see Meena's worried gray eyes. I'll get it out.

Wiping the area as best as I can, I study the wound—the veins around it are already turning black as the poison sets in. I summon Kioren again, this time asking for something more like the butter knife it first showed itself as. A small, wickedly sharp blade lands in my hand.

"This is going to hurt," I say, looking at Rishu before slicing the skin wider even as it tries to heal itself. He lets out a muffled scream, writhing on the car seat.

"How can I help?" Tevari asks, his vine lifting out of his coat to examine Rishu.

I take a deep breath to steady myself as I call forth Kioren's tendrils to aid me in my search of the bullet lodged in Rishu, only daring a quick glance at Tevari. "When I get this bullet out, we'll need to clean the wound and cauterize it. His healing will probably be much slower because it's an angelic bullet, but he should be fine, I think."

"Not helping," Rishu says through clenched teeth as I use the pointed tendril like tweezers, digging inside the wound.

"Tevari, summon water to wash it out once it's out, and Azura"—I meet her fiery eyes—"I hope you've gained some precision because you're gonna have to cauterize it."

Azura nods, hopping over from the backseat to my side. A steady flame sparks at her fingertip.

"I'm impressed," I say as my makeshift tweezers find the bullet. Kioren wraps around it, transforming inside Rishu to ensure we get every piece of shrapnel. The tendril carefully lifts out of Rishu, dropping the bullet into my hand. "Now your turn," I say to Tevari.

It takes a moment, but he summons a small amount of water to run over Rishu's open wound. Ripping my shirt, I wipe the wound before handing him over to Azura. She presses the flame to his skin, and Rishu screams as she helps close the wound, his healing abilities doing the rest. Sweat beads on his forehead as his eyes roll back.

"Here," Tevari says, pulling out an herbaceous-smelling poultice from his bag. "Pack the wound with this."

I raise a brow but don't question him, trusting his photographic memory and knowledge. Packing the wound, I examine Rishu, satisfied that he'll at least survive. Letting out a long exhale, I slouch back into the seat.

"Everything okay?" Luka says, glancing back through the rearview mirror.

I nod, meeting his silver gaze. I can't believe I got so caught up in my emotions that I let him hug me. Cried into his shoulder... After everything... And yet I still want more, and I can't decide if I hate myself for it or not.

"Man, I wish teleporting was easier," Meena says, voicing what we all think.

No one says anything, the hum of the car lulling us to silence as we leave Falgens and begin our three-hour drive to Chicago.

34

DIVINE INTERVENTION

— Adrian —

She had been here. At the side of those *demons* again, according to Aril. I could hardly believe my second's report of seeing her and then the van she had supposedly been in shattering into an almost pink-tinted glitter.

I hate myself for not getting there fast enough to stop her. Another failure on my part. Michael chuckles in my mind but offers no advice.

My cadre stands around me outside the Fandera Estate, the sounds of the chapel warning bell still blaring across the city. A hunter had come racing in from the campus, storming into the estate after Solomon. "I have to alert Solomon!" had been all he said, pushing past us with such urgency that no one stopped him.

"What now?" Ewan, my red-headed warrior, asks from my side.

A scoff from Roman garners my attention. "The princess is a demon lover. What is there to do but put her down."

I shoot him a glare. "You will do no such thing," I say, and the hunter rolls his eyes. Michael urges me to put him in his place, to wipe the grin from his face. I don't comply.

My cell rings, Lance calling. I answer, putting the phone to my ear.

"Get here fast," Lance says, the sound of growls reverberating through the phone.

The call ends, and I turn to my team. Before I can say anything, a sinewy gray creature flies down from the sky, latching onto the wrought iron of the estate's gate. We shrink back, assessing the unfamiliar creature.

"I'm guessing this is what the call was about," Aril says as we pull our weapons into our hands.

My greatsword, Severance, is a welcomed weight to distract from the cacophony of emotions raging inside me as I nod to my second. Cain approaches my side like a shadow, his katana poised for battle. The others of my team retrieve their weapons while Eva moves to the back to summon her creatures.

"I've never seen anything like it... What is it?" Callan says, drawing his bow.

His twin shrugs. "Who cares as long as we can kill it," Cain says, no remorse in his voice. Not that remorse is necessary for whatever this *thing* is.

"We shoot on your command," Anders says, hooking his mace back onto his belt to retrieve his gun—not his preference, but the long-range weapon is a better choice against a winged beast like this.

The door behind us bursts open, and Solomon strides down the drive to our side. A cocky radiance shines around him, abnormal to the usual stoicism. I don't look long at him, my attention on the creature, waiting for it to strike. With its wings, we'll be at a disadvantage.

"Kill it," Solomon says, and I'm happy to oblige. "Then I have a mission for you."

— Lance —

A blizzard crashes down on Falgens. Snow flurries cloud the campus as smoke rises into the hazy sky. Screams resound in the street, gunshots and the clinking of angelic weapons accompanying them. The chapel warning bell rings loudly, the sound reverberating through the campus grounds.

I watch as people run for their lives as dark, sinewy creatures pounce on them, tearing them to pieces. Hunters fight back, unprepared for such an attack—the campus meant to be the one place demons can't enter. Are these even demons?

"Get all non-hunters back inside the buildings," I yell out into the storm, commanding the other hunters. "This is an unknown entity, so don't lose sight of your team."

"Any capable hunter should be fighting; this isn't the time for weakness," Darius yells out over the small group. His tone is strong, but a wave of uncertainty flicks through his deep-brown eyes.

We stand at the top steps of the academic building as the other hunters break off into their teams. Pulling out the gun I have holstered, I quickly aim and take out five of the approaching creatures before they get too near. They fall limp to the ground, but where one dies, two more take its place. Darius heaves his heavy mace over his shoulder, a scowl drawn across his scarred face.

"It's time," I say, rolling up my sleeve.

"You're one sneaky bastard, Lance. I never would have guessed you had an angel let alone one in the faction," Darius says, chuckling as he tucks his other hand into his jacket pocket.

I smile softly. "Archangel Azrael knew I would need this." I motion to the autumn-colored gem hanging from my ear. "And this," I mumble an incantation under my breath, and the symbol of my angel appears across my forearm, soft light emanating from the black lines. It grows brighter until I'm able to reach inside my arm and pull out the golden necklace lined with seven rubies—one ruby missing from its setting. Archangel Azrael knew I'd be lost without these two things. One to hide our identity, the other to aid us in our mission.

"Azrael's angelic artifact, how did you get your hands on that?"

A guttural sound echoes around us. "We have company. I'll explain everything you need to know when we get to Nova."

"Always an excuse," Darius says, heaving the mace into both hands. "Now, let's kill these bastards."

I quickly place the ruby necklace around my neck, a thin golden blade forming in my hands the moment the gems settle on my chest. I smirk and bolt forward into the horde, slashing them down with the incredible speed and agility gifted to me by my angel. A grayish form lunges for my side, but I swivel my body, slashing down on its neck. Its head rolls across the ground, black blood leaving a trail in the gathering snow. My eyes narrow as I examine the creature, its mouth open in horror despite the rows of teeth and protruding horns.

"Damn show off," Darius mumbles under his breath.

He rushes forward to join me in the fight, slamming his mace down on the ungodly horde with a force that shakes the ground.

I don't linger behind, Azrael's blade bringing sweet death to the enemy as we clear a path, making our way to the main street outside the campus grounds. My hand tightens around my weapon as a car pulls up to the curb, a dark-tinted window rolling down.

"Ready?" The driver says, a clicking sound reverberating as they unlock the doors.

"It feels wrong leaving," Darius says as he spins around and smashes a final creature that followed us.

"We don't have a choice anymore. At least Adrian's on his way here... But it's beginning; I know you feel it too," I say, directing the statement to both the hunter at my side and our driver. "This is why I had no choice but to make the deal."

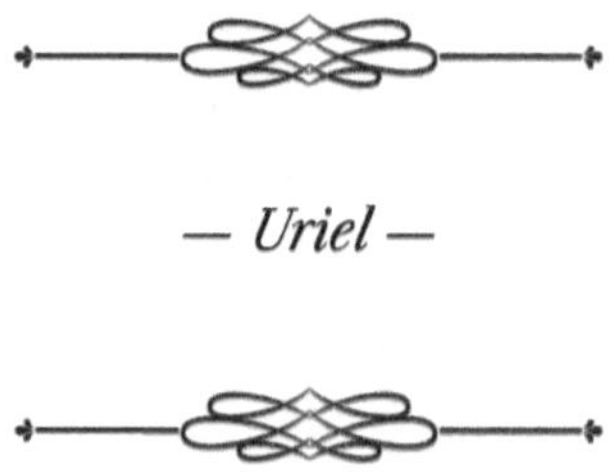

— Uriel —

"The time is nearing."

The room is dark, only the faint light of the moon shining through the ceiling. White hoods are drawn over the heads of everyone in the room, veils covering their angelic faces.

"Azrael, Zerachiel is alive," I say softly. We speak in hushed voices, knowing our words could mean our destruction.

"Impossible, his heavenly body is gone, Uriel," another says, his voice a harsh whisper.

"Because the only part of him left remains within Nova. It was unexpected to feel his presence awaken when I bonded with her soul... He must have known the truth four thousand years ago when we had been too blind to see it." I glance at the moon above, lost in the bright white held together by our angelic power. "*Asari* must have said something to Zerachiel as he's been guiding her all along. A promise, he said, one he wouldn't clarify...."

Murmurs echo in the cavern. Our lost brother, alive... and helping *her*. I was just as surprised as they are. "Falren doesn't seem to know, at least for now. And he's still convinced I'm on his side, misleading the girl. I don't know how long it'll last, but I can finally feel change coming."

"It is, and soon," Azrael says, and I hope it's true. "Uriel, continue to guide her until we can join you." I nod. "Barachiel, make sure your partner trusts mine. We both must do our part, no matter the cost."

"Azrael, what of our fallen brother, Lucifer? He is also by her side," Barachiel says.

"Do not fret over his presence for now," Azrael says to the angel.

"His presence isn't what worries me."

"She won't choose him," I say confidently, breaking the growing tension between the two angels. "Not when she learns the truth and what's at stake if she were to fail."

The room grows quiet, the other angels not daring to speak on the matter. We're all here for the same reason. A faction with one goal in mind.

To fix all that is broken.

"The moon is fading. Leave now to your places." Azrael turns away from the group, his gaze moving toward the white moon peeking through the ceiling. "There is much to be done before the sun rises."

35

THE ETERNAL KEEPER

I trace the engraved letters on the leatherbound book. *The Eternal Keeper.* My father... He wasn't acting like himself even before that dark being possessed him. *Darkness.* I'm sure of it. But my father mentioned the Lotus Pond—something I've only heard Remembrance speak of.

And I'm scared.

I know this book holds the answers I've longed for, yet I can't bear to open it. After what I learned from Lucifer, the convoluted history between us, I'm terrified of what my father has been trying to protect me from. *End the cycle.* I don't know if I can handle this cycle of pain he's referring to.

Luka approaches, reaching out as if to touch me but drawing away at the last moment. "We don't have to do this now. Tomorrow or the next day. Just tell me what you need."

We lock eyes, the longing in his silver gaze painfully obvious. He said he wants to protect me—save me—that he's not here to love me again. My eyes fall on that ring on his pinky. He kept it with him all this time... Is it a reminder to protect me? To atone for my death in that lifetime? Or is it a reminder of a love that I will never amount to? I stare down at the book.

My whole life, everyone has tried to protect me. It's never been what I've wanted or asked for; I've only ever wanted to be free, to understand who I am. Lucifer and my father are both guilty of sheltering me, hiding the truth from me. Yet I can't bring myself to blame either of them.

I sigh deeply. "No, I—" I look around the room. The cambions who've supported me even after everything, and Amon who's trying to save us all—even with his wicked heart. There's no time to wait with this war coming. "I'll read it aloud."

"Nova, you don't have to. We can read it once you finish," Lei Jing says, but I shake my head.

"My father wasn't himself, his body was being taken over like how we saw Camus, but before the possession took hold, he was desperate for me to take this and run. I've never seen him like that before...." I take a deep breath as I remember the look on Father's face, the urgency with which he put this in my hands. "So I don't want to do this alone. Whatever secrets are in this book, I want to face them with all of you."

Lei Jing nods along with the others, giving me time to open the leatherbound book. The smell of ancient paper wafts up to my nose as I crack the stiff binding and open to the first page. The words are inked in an aggressive but delicate looping script. I begin to read the first passage.

From the hands which gave us strength, we struck a deal. To stop the plight of demons upon our land, we must now comply with the request of our Lord. His godly power in return for finding the cursed child born of the Lotus Pond. A place that exists yet does not. The tether of His power guides us to the location that is never fixed.

As the firstborn son, you have become the next Solomon to take on this responsibility. He will guide you to the Lotus Pond to retrieve the child. Raise them as your own, taking on a wife to match the child born. Teach this child to fight against its dark nature, to hate the demons as a human does. It is imperative that you also bear a son to ensure the passage of this sacred lineage.

When the time comes, our Lord and Savior will command you to complete your final duty as a Solomon: kill the child of the Lotus Pond and teach your son of his lineage and responsibility to find the child once again.

A tear slides down my face, a ball forming in my throat. "This has to be a lie...." I manage to choke out, but I can feel the truth in my soul.

"Nova..." Meena tugs at my shirt, her stormy eyes shining with tears.

"So wait, you were born in a pond?" Azura says as she kicks her feet up. "Wow, that's messed up. How does that even work?" Oliver hits her arm, and I almost chuckle at the irony of it all.

Luka wipes the tear from my cheek, no longer able to keep his distance. "I brought this on you." He steps back, hands balled into fists, eyes hard. "The Heavens will pay for their tyranny."

Calming myself, I go over everything I know. My father was protecting me from this cursed truth—that he'd have to kill me one day, that he's not even my father. I recall the vision of my grandfather passing the book down to him. No wonder he was so upset after reading this. I am too. But what about Kioren? The silver metal hums on my wrist. My father spoke of consequences because I summoned it—but what is Kioren? And this power... It must have unintentionally been split between him and Camus. But why is everything different in this lifetime? Father never had a son... Not one I know of at least. And what is the Lotus Pond, aside from the place I'm apparently born in? Remembrance is too *real* to be nothing.

Summoning Zera to our private place in my mind, I ask, *"Is what this book says true?"*

"True to a point, but you are no cursed child. This I promise you."

Taking a deep breath, I look at everyone's expectant faces. "Apparently it's somewhat true, Zerachiel just told me."

"Did you say Zerachiel?" Luka asks, and I nod. He stares as if he's seen a ghost. "That's impossible... He died before I ever fell from the Heavens."

"What do you mean he died? It's definitely him."

He shakes his head. "He was one of the seven archangels along with me, but one day he disappeared, never to be seen again. The reigning God had him replaced by Selaphiel once he was declared dead."

"Wait, if you can talk with your angels, can't they tell you everything?" Azura asks, short brown-black hair swaying as she cocks her head.

"Azura's right. Wouldn't they know about this deal between Solomon and God—also, did you say *reigning* God?" Lei Jing says, directing the question to Luka.

"It's a secret system within the Heavens... Divine beings called godlings are trained to become the next God. A new God is to be chosen every two thousand years, but the current one has refused to step down and has been in power for over four thousand years now."

"So it seems this reigning God is potentially our enemy." Tevari looks thoughtful as he considers the new information.

"There's a reason I had disagreements with him long before I ever fell from the Heavens," Luka says, and the room falls quiet.

Without thinking, my hand reaches for him, and his eyes soften. I pull back, irritated with myself but not letting it show on my face. This is so frustrating. All of it.

"Whatever happened with Solomon the First and this reigning God, my angels can't tell me anything right now. I haven't told you all this yet, but"—I shiver, remembering the voice of Darkness speaking through my father and Camus—"there's someone listening in to my conversations with them. He... he's warned me before to stop looking for answers. When I didn't listen, he caused these to spread," I say, lifting the sleeve on my left arm where the black vines almost reach my wrist. I haven't dared examine how far they've spread beneath my clothes.

"Nova, why didn't you tell me?" Luka takes my hand in his, looking over the markings covering my skin.

I meet his eyes. *Because I was scared...* He seems to understand, not pressing me more on the matter.

"But the thing is, this being is dark. Truly evil. I can't imagine him being a god of any kind. There's nothing holy about him."

"So you're saying it's possible we're dealing with a trickster," Oliver says, speaking up from his seat at the far corner. He looks overwhelmed, as we all do. His eyes darken as he looks to me for confirmation. All I can do is nod.

"So now?" Tevari chimes in. "We find this pond, and what? How does it help any of this?"

"Or give us answers about our enemy," Lei Jing adds.

I nod again. None of us have an answer. My father—though I suppose he really isn't; I have yet to wrap my head around that—told me that finding the Lotus Pond would end the cycle of pain I'm stuck in. But how can we decipher anything when it seems like we're still missing so many pieces of the puzzle?

"Rest for now," Amon says, finally speaking up from his desk chair. "We'll talk more tomorrow."

Everyone nods in agreement, tired looks plastered on their faces. The city lights shine through the office windows as the sun dips behind the buildings, the deep blues, and purples of dusk beginning to creep across the sky. They've all powered through so much recently. We all need a break, even if it's a short one.

"I'll check on Rishi first," Meena says and quickly leaves the office. The others trickle out behind her.

I remain, moving to stare out the window at the glimmering city below me. Luka casts a longing look in my direction, but I nod for him to leave as well. He listens for once, exiting the room along with the others.

"You should rest," Amon says, a long sigh leaving his lips.

"I wish I could," I say, not moving from the window, "but there's something I need to ask you first."

"Let me guess, you don't think God inflicted this fate on you to force you apart from Lucifer?" he says as he comes to stand with me at the window. I look at him, waiting for his answer. "It took Lucifer a thousand years before he found you in the hands of the hunters, where you'd been all along. The girl he had loved out of reach and hating who he had become. But I think being reborn and taken by the hunters means more than just punishment for Lucifer. I think you know that too."

"But why?"

He sighs with annoyance. "There's only one place you can go to find answers now," he says, turning his blue gaze to me. "The Lotus Pond."

I nod, turning back to the twilight sky. My eyes are heavy, shoulders drooping. "I'll read more of the book tonight. Hopefully, something will clue us in on where this Lotus Pond is, maybe even about this deal Solomon the First made." I spin around, heading toward the door.

Amon's words stop me as my hand touches the handle.

"Don't burn yourself out, Nova. We need both you and Lucifer to have a chance at winning this war."

I open the door, leaving his words hanging in the air.

Jolting up in bed, I breathe heavily, pressing my fingers into my eyes as images flash through my mind. The same ones I saw during my trials, repeating in my dreams. I thought they had faded, becoming a distant memory, yet they stain my mind like nightmares. Maybe because of what Luka, as I still prefer to call him, showed me. My mind has lingered on those memories... And what it all means for the both of us.

A knock sounds at my door, and I stand from the bed. The leatherbound book falls from my lap to the floor with a loud thud. I reach to pick it up, placing it back on the sheets. I walk to the door and hesitate before opening it, knowing in my gut who's on the other side.

"Can we talk?" Luka says.

His long hair is disheveled, but he still looks as annoyingly handsome as always. I cross my arms, rubbing away the goosebumps his stare invokes.

"I don't think that's a good idea."

"Nova."

My name on his lips almost sends me falling into his embrace. A single word begging me to listen. A small part of my mind revels in the power I hold over him, the emotions *I* invoke in him. It makes me want to reach out and brush the hair from his face, to feel the electric shocks every time we touch.

"Please, Luka... just go," I say, my voice small, unconvincing. Another part of me, weaker than my desire, wishes to see him suffer for all he's done.

"I won't," Luka whispers under his breath, his voice as soft as mine.

Closing my eyes, I take a deep breath before finding the courage to meet his eyes. My mouth opens to speak, but he steps forward, his body just grazing mine as I'm pushed back against the wall of the room. He raises a hand to the wall, leaning in close enough that our breaths mix together. His eyes stare into mine, not releasing me from their grasp.

"I know what you're thinking... and you're not her."

His other hand traces up my arm, fingers lightly brushing against my skin before reaching my face. He cups my cheek softly, tucking a strand of hair behind my ear, his eyes never leaving mine. I suck in a breath, my heart beating rapidly. My lips move, wanting to say something but unable to find the right words.

"Now, we talk," he says, a smirk playing on his lips.

I nod, dazed. He steps back, smiling in victory as he enters farther into the room. Shaking myself out of my stupor, I shut the door and follow him in. He stands by the bedside, his hand gently resting on the book. I lean against the wall on the other side of the room, trying to keep my distance, to not succumb to the yearning of my heart. He flips the book open, skimming the pages.

"I fell asleep reading it," I say to him, and he hums in response. "The Lotus Pond is never in the same place. They kept records of where they found it each time, but it's always scattered across the world."

His face darkens. "Even for my punishment, this is too much." I don't respond to his statement. "And I don't quite understand the light I've seen you use not once, but twice now. How does that fit into all of this?"

"I don't know," I say, walking over to the opposite side of the bed, my heart thundering in my chest. The mattress sinks as I take a seat, looking up at him. "The other pages seem to be in a code of some sort; notes from past Solomons would be my guess. Only my father's notes are legible, but there's nothing about this light, and they're—" I can't finish my sentence. My father's notes are difficult to read. An indescribable pain conveyed in each sentence. *I promised myself I would protect you after what he did to her...* Father had said that to me before Darkness took him too. His notes speaking of a sister—a woman I used to be. I swallow hard, willing myself to brush the harsh reality of that away.

"You still call him father," he says, and I nod. "What did he write?"

My eyes cloud as tears well up, but I hold them back. "When he learned what he had to do, he fought against his father. He wrote of how he would have to kill me... Of how when he found me as a baby, he knew he never could."

I never thought I could feel anything but contempt for my father. Yet all along he wanted me to live, to disregard the rules written in this book. Maybe locking me away was his way of trying to give me a normal life—at least as normal as possible, considering the circumstances.

"Do you want to talk about what happened?" Luka says, putting the book aside. I turn away from his gaze and shake my head. He sighs, the bed dipping as he takes a seat. "I'm scared, Nova. I've seen what wars can do—I've been responsible for a number of them. There's a reason I disappeared...." He places his hand under my chin, turning my face to him. "We can't run away, can we?"

Those beautiful silver eyes search mine, but the answer is already clear.

"We can't." Because even if we did, our time would always be limited.

"I know." His eyes well with tears. Tentatively, I reach up, brushing them away as they roll down his cheeks. Despite everything, it breaks my heart to see this man shed tears for the cruel fate we cannot escape.

"We will make things right... But I need you to promise me something." His brows furrow together as his hand finds the one I have pressed into the bed. I hesitate, my breath catching in my throat, but I force myself to continue, "I know you're scared to lose me—we don't even have the answer to the black vines yet." His hand tightens around mine, and I can feel the markings slithering down my arm ever so slowly. "But promise me, whatever happens, you have to keep fighting. Camus, his God. They can't get away with what they've planned."

He sighs, shoulders drooping. Earlier I told everyone every detail I could remember from my time in Camus's dimension. From the Krav brute to the golden lotus to his plans to refashion the world with his horde. Everyone is aware of what's at stake if we don't stop this war.

"I'll fight, no matter what. I'll make it my promise to you." He lets go of my hand, holding his pinky up as he waits for me to hook mine with his. I admire the gold ring that rests on it, the emerald gem that matches the one on his ring finger.

"Really?" I ask with a soft chuckle. "A pinky promise?"

"I take my promises seriously," he says, a watery smile forming on his lips.

"Then I have one more thing for you to promise me." His head cocks to one side as his smile falters. "Don't leave me this time."

My heart pangs in my chest as he takes my hand, hooking my pinky with his. His silver eyes, like the glittering moon, lift to mine, holding me with such intensity I almost forget to breathe. "I promise. I'll never leave even if you command it so." He stamps our thumbs together, sealing the vow. Light laughter falls from my lips, and soon he follows as we savor the simple moment together. Taking pleasure in what little joy we can.

"Can I ask you something?" Luka nods, our pinkies still laced together. "You said Zerachiel died before you fell from Heaven. So how is it possible for him to have bonded with me?"

He shakes his head, lowering our hands to the bed and unhooking our fingers. "I wish I knew."

I brush the question aside as a look of sadness crosses his face. "So, I'm curious. You look like, well... you"—I smile, waving my hand toward him—"but what does Zerachiel look like? And Uriel too, she's my other angel."

"You've never seen them?"

"No... With the Undivided, at least in my experience, they're just voices. Which was alarming the first few times they spoke to me." He smiles softly as I continue. "Do they all look like you? How are the features of angels decided? It's not something we're taught as hunters... I don't think they really know or care."

A happier smile rises to his lips, a light blush dabbing his cheeks. "We represent humanity, so we all look different even though we're brothers and sisters—just like humanity. My features resemble those of East Asian descent." His fingers find mine again, rubbing circles on the back of my hand, and my heart jumps at the electricity through the touch. "Zerachiel, I'm not sure how he'd look anymore. He always had pale skin, dark hair, and wide, ocean blue eyes. His face was kind, though always serious."

"Maybe a little too serious?" I say, and we laugh.

"But he was beautiful, strong. An angel well respected until... until he suddenly vanished." He looks off at the wall as if lost in thought—or in memories.

"I can ask him what happened...." I offer, but it's met with a shake of his head.

"No. I may have inadvertently been the cause of the creation of Undivided, and I don't understand what bonding is like, but I still respect my brothers and sisters. Zerachiel had his reasons, whatever they may be, and he'll share them when he's ready." Luka traces up my arm. A thrill races through me under the gentle touch, and my blush deepens. "Not to mention I don't want these marks to spread any further."

I nod, distracted, willing myself to change the topic. "And Uriel? What's she like?"

He smiles wider as his fingers end their pursuit. "The most beautiful of the angels. She glimmers with light as if she were light herself. It's been a thousand years, but I still remember her luminous dark skin and bright silver eyes, much like mine—and the face of someone who recognizes her worth," he says, and I wonder if he recognizes his own worth. His beauty—even with the darkness he hides away inside. I don't dare voice my disagreement, but I honestly don't know how anyone but him could be considered the most beautiful of the angels.

"My sister and I were always close since we both use the power of light, but I doubt she'd wish to see me now. She always greatly respected the divine Source of all life, the only thing we truly needed to honor...." He didn't need to add that it's this Source—a separate entity I don't press him on explaining—that he disrespected with his actions against the Heavens. The regret too obvious in his silver gaze lost in memories.

I try to picture my angels as he's described them to me, but I still have only an incomplete idea of what they may look like. His silver eyes turn back to mine, and I smile, reaching a hand to brush his silky black hair from his face. He grabs my wrist, stopping the movement.

"Nova, I need you to know I wasn't lying before. I'll never force anything on you. Not my feelings or questions about yours." My breath hitches, a blush rising to my cheeks. "While you may share her soul, you are uniquely you. I'm just grateful I found you again, to have the opportunity to apologize for leaving you in that past life and to vow to protect you in this one."

I look away, unsure of what to say. It still hurts. This feeling of being replaceable. If I were to die today, would I just reincarnate at the Lotus Pond? Could everything end so quickly to just begin once again? I sigh. How can I not feel replaceable?

He lets go of my hands, standing from the bedside. I watch his movement as he stalks around the bed, stopping in front of me. I look up once more into those beautiful silver eyes, his lashes long and dark as he hovers over me. Tangible desire whips between us, and all I want to do is feel his lips on mine.

Luka smiles softly and cups my face. "Get some rest." Leaning down, he kisses my forehead before heading toward the door.

I bite my lip. "Luka," I call out, and he stops. "Your siblings may be beautiful, but so are you." His eyes widen—hand falling from the door handle. "And one day, I'm sure your brothers and sisters will want to see you again."

His lips part, a soft smile rising. "Thank you, Nova. You should know you're beautiful too. You always will be." He slips out of the room, leaving me breathless where I sit.

Flopping back on the bed, I pat my chest, desperately trying to calm my raging heart. His scent lingers in the room, and a deeper blush rises to my cheeks. What the hell is wrong with me? I roll over, burying my head in the sheets. *You're beautiful too. You always will be.* His words repeat in my head, a never-ending cycle of his sweet, low voice.

The lotus tattoo pricks my chest, the black vines inching across my ribcage. I muffle a scream in the bedsheets, wrapping my arms around my torso.

When the pain subsides, I roll onto my back, staring at the white ceiling above. My mind still lingers on his lips despite the black vines urging me to rethink.

These feelings... How can they feel so good yet hurt so bad? Maybe it makes me a masochist to never want this to end despite the pain. Something new blossoming between us, regardless of the history only one of us remembers. I splay my fingers over the lotus tattoo on my chest.

He should've just kissed me.

36

CAN WE TRUST AGAIN?

I stand at the head of a long glass table in a conference room near Amon's office. The cambions and Luka sit around it in black seats. Afternoon light trickles in through the large window—thin shades drawn to keep the sunlight from blinding us.

The room holds that new office smell as if the space is hardly used despite the vastness of the company. Amon's corporation—as I've learned from my research now that I finally have access to a computer—goes beyond what I originally thought. From imports and exports to real estate and construction to philanthropy. Though I suspect his regular employees aren't privy to this top floor and the things that happen here. I look around the table as I hold my father's book, tapping my fingers on the leather binding.

"I can't make you fight." I meet each of their faces. "After everything I've done, everything we've learned... I'm terrified knowing I can't run away from it." My gaze pulls to Luka, our promise an unspoken thread between us. "There's a war coming, and I'd never force this on you, but... will you fight with me?" My heart thrums in my chest; I hate asking this of them. Even though

Amon said they have a role to play in this war, I won't make decisions on their behalf. Not even with this gnawing feeling that tells me he's right. "It's your choice to make. If you want to leave, I'll have arrangements made—"

"You think we'd say no?" Lei Jing says. "As much as I hate to admit it, I kind of understand why you did what you did and what will happen if we don't do anything."

"I have to agree," Oliver says. He props his elbows on the table and rests his head in his hands, looking out at the city view. I never got a chance to talk with him after what happened at the sparring pit. But he's here, even if he's still hiding from himself.

"But what's going to happen now?" Meena asks. "When we find this pond, will you be okay? Will it stop Camus?"

I'm drawn back to Luka's hard stare. Maybe I should have talked with him first. "I don't know exactly, but hopefully, it'll stop these from spreading." I lift my arm, the black vines close to reaching my palm. "Maybe it can even help us fight Camus in some way. I don't have all the answers yet."

"How?" Tevari says, his vine wrapping around his head like a crown. "Do you know where this pond is?"

"Or how to find it?" Azura adds.

I bite my lip, shaking my head. "I don't."

This book my father gave me only has handwritten accounts of the past Solomons. Of their voyages and travels—but only for the last three hundred years or so. Only some of the locations are mentioned, and those that are seem to be scattered across the world in no apparent pattern. Not even my father wrote where he found me. If my father thought this book could help us—to find this Lotus Pond, to be the solution to our problems—I think he overestimated its worth.

"We'll figure it out," Luka says, and I force a small smile.

The door bursts open, and Amon strides in, grinning from ear to ear. "Or you don't have to." His gaze turns to me as his long pale hair swishes behind him. "Nova dear, do come with me for a moment."

"Amon," Luka says, a dark look crossing his face.

"My king, do hold your temper. This will help your precious beloved."

I cringe at the name. *Beloved.* A word I've grown uncomfortable with. Even if... I internally shake the thought away. "Luka, it's fine," I say, stepping over to meet Amon. "Where are we going?" His smile turns venomous, but he remains silent as he turns and leaves the room. "I'll be back soon," I say to everyone before following him out.

We head down the hall toward his office. Uriel's silvery hum resonates in my mind, and I raise a brow in question. Amon opens the wooden office door for me, light from the large window trickling into the hallway.

"After you," he says, waiting with the door held open.

"You know, you could tell me why you brought me—" As I enter the office, two men rise from the chairs in front of his desk. My mouth drops to the floor when they turn to face me. "Lance? Darius?"

"Miss this pig-headed brute?" Lance says, a smile on his deceptively young face. A piercing pain stabs my heart as I realize how much I've missed him.

"Nice to see you, princess," Darius says, looking as intimidating as ever.

I step farther into the room, running my eyes up and down their forms, barely able to believe my eyes. "What are you doing here?" Spinning around, I point at Amon. "You know he's a demon, right?"

The two hunters chuckle. Outfitted in tactical gear and angelic weapons, they look like they've come from a battle. Up close, I notice a small cut—the blood now dried—on Lance's cheek.

"Who do you think made the original deal that brought you here?" Lance says, and my jaw drops farther. "What? Did you think a *demonic* necklace got you out of your father's estate with those angelic chains?"

Darius gives Lance a light shove, and he almost falls over. "Leave the girl alone. How would she know you're an Undivided with Azrael's angelic artifact."

"Undivided? Azrael?!"

He smirks. "We have a lot to talk about."

The door slams open, Luka pushing his way in with the cambions in tow behind him. Their faces are dark, bodies tense, ready to fight. Dark energy curls around Luka, no trace of the light he once showed me.

"*Hunters,*" Tevari says, his vine curling protectively around him as sharp briars grow out of Amon's carpet.

Oliver growls and steps forward. Meena and Lei Jing stay back but drop into the fighting stances I taught them.

Raising my hands, I step toward them. "Okay, let's all take a moment."

"Hell no," Azura says, the air around her wavering with heat as fire sparks at her fingertips.

Lance scoffs, raising a pistol in their direction. "I'd recommend you back down, little girl. You may be part of Nova's deal, but honestly, I couldn't care less. We didn't come here for you, any of you."

Azura yells, sending a fireball at the two hunters. Summoning Kioren with barely a thought, I slice through the fire, the black tendrils spreading out to protect me from the blast. The fire parts around me sputtering out when it hits the walls, leaving them singed and blackened.

"That's enough!" I shout, déjà vu washing over me. Hopefully, this time I don't go flying out a window. Even my angels wouldn't be able to save me from a fall this high. "Before we go killing each other, can't we at least find out why they're here and what deal they made? Hunters don't make deals with demons... often."

Tevari huffs, gold flaring in his eyes and cracking through his skin. He turns, leaving the room. Azura still burns from within but crosses her arms as if to mimic Lei Jing.

"Nova, I know you know them, but after everything...." Luka says, his dark energy spreading around the room like a shadow. "I don't think this is a good idea."

"We can decide what to do after we hear them out. If they can help... We need it."

"I don't like them."

I look at Meena standing behind him, gray eyes thunderous. Her usual soft, innocent look has worn off, revealing the hurt, angry child within. Oliver stands beside her, a pained look crossing his face as his hands shift back to normal. He doesn't meet our gazes, eyes downcast.

"I can't imagine how this must be for all of you, but please, let me talk to them, and then we can all decide together. I'm not forcing any of you into working with more hunters."

"You're barely a hunter, Nova," Lei Jing says, and I wince. She's not wrong, though. "But you're right. Let's hear them out."

Lance puts his pistol back in its holster as the demonic power in the room fades. I breathe a sigh of relief, mentally summoning Kioren back into the bracelet. Amon claps, a dangerous smile written across his pale face. His eyes blaze red with anger.

"Dear me, what a *splendid* reunion." No one responds. "But I must say, raise your weapon at them again, and you won't be walking out of here alive." He glares at the two hunters. Darius takes a small, hesitant step back, but Lance holds his ground as Amon steps toward him. I inhale sharply as the wave of Amon's energy washes over the room. True demonic power.

"It won't happen again," I force out, giving Lance a pointed look.

"It better not." Amon twirls around and saunters back to his desk. He takes a seat, crossing his legs as his eyes return to their usual piercing blue. "Now, I have other business to attend to. The conference room will be *much* preferred for your little reunion."

He laces his fingers together, nodding to the open door where the cambions stand frozen. They shuffle out of the room, Luka and the hunters following closely behind. I linger for a moment longer, but Amon dismisses me with a wave of his hand, not even looking up from his computer as he begins tapping away at the keyboard. I comply, the door slamming behind me. A long, uneasy sigh leaves my lips. Just one thing after another...

Loud arguing can be heard from the open door down the hall. Pushing my way into the conference room, I throw harsh glares around the room. When it goes quiet, I turn to Lance.

"You have one chance. Explain yourselves," I say as I take a seat beside Luka.

Lance nods, standing in the far corner with Darius at his side. "Listen up," Lance says, stepping up to the head of the glass table. The cambions sit in the same seats as before—though Tevari remains absent. "I'll keep this simple for all of you. Both of our angels are part of a faction determined to help Nova—"

"Help with what exactly?" Azura says.

Lance shoots her a look, and she seals her lips with a huff. "As I was saying, we're here to help Nova find the Lotus Pond. We don't know the specific details, the angels are keeping it a close secret as it somehow affects them... My angel, Azrael, directed me to make a deal with Amon so that I could support Nova on this mission. Unfortunately, none of this could be started until you were separated from Solomon." Lance examines the black vines crawling down my arm. "And it looks like we don't have a lot of time."

"How can you help?" I ask, moving my arm out of his sight. "I have my father's book, but there's no record of where the last Lotus Pond was found. How can you help if even this can't." I push the book toward them.

Darius arches an eyebrow. "Princess, I don't think you're getting the picture. The only one who can find the pond is you."

"What? That's not true, though. The book states that each Solomon has been led to the pond to retrieve me." Saying the words out loud is painful, but I repress the sudden burst of emotion, refusing to let the others see how much it hurts me.

Lance sighs, picking up the leather book. "I don't know much about this, but what I do know is that whatever energy is within you connects you to the pond and the lotuses."

"Lotuses?" Luka asks from my side.

"Seven, to be exact. Each will have to be found before you can enter the Lotus Pond."

I feel my angels stirring as a scene from my angelic trials passes through my mind. Seven lotuses of different colors resting on my body as it floats in the center of a pond. My stomach twists at the thought of the golden lotus in Camus's hands. That must be one of them.

"Lance, what does this all mean, though? If you know about the pond, then you know I've been reincarnated and...."

His face grows soft, solemn. "I know. And I know you will be freed of those vines—you must be freed to stop the coming war." My eyes widen. "Amon told us what happened... And our angels knew some of it too." I take a quivering breath, turning my gaze from the pity in his eyes.

While I told everyone what happened in Camus's dimension, I left out some of the darker details. The inescapable cold that bit into my bones, the devastating pain that somehow managed to grow worse with every injury Camus and his brute inflicted. Closing my eyes, I try to ease my breathing. A hand covers mine, and I look to see silver-and-gold-embellished fingers, warm to the touch. I glance at Luka, unsure how to feel with this new information.

From wanting freedom and answers to this... Something I never wanted, but something impossible to walk away from nonetheless. Luka smiles, reassuring me with the simple gesture. My heart aches yet flourishes. Reveling in his touch while resisting the urge to pull away.

"How?" I meet Lance's face, his eyes trained on the hand over mine. "How can you help me find this pond?"

— Adrian —

Blood and ash line the streets of the campus grounds. The horde of shadowy creatures had seemed unending until Solomon was able to fix the angelic wards. Apparently, they can be disarmed—something even I wasn't aware of. Then the creatures all but disappeared. No reports of any more attacks from other hunters around the city.

I punch a metal post, my knuckles beginning to bleed.

"Weak," Michael says, his voice cold in my mind. *"Do you know why those creatures attacked?"* I don't answer, so the angel continues. *"They did because of the girl you wish to protect. As I said, this isn't the end, but the end is not something you will get to decide."*

"What the hell are you talking about?" I say out loud when no one is in range of hearing my one-sided conversation, everyone too busy cleaning up the bodies and wreckage left behind.

"She will bring death and carnage."

I step back, a shiver racing down my spine—unsure if it's because of my angel's declaration or the snow still falling to the ground. He has to be lying...

Solomon comes into view, and Michael retreats within my mind. I wait for my leader at the edge of the sidewalk, the skin on my knuckles already healing.

"Adrian," Solomon says, his face contorted with more emotion than I've ever seen. Pain, guilt, sadness. Nova's letter traces in my mind, *do not trust my father.* I wait for him to speak again. "You must find Nova."

My brows scrunch together, and my words sharp. "So now you're actually interested in where she's at?"

Solomon looks away, scanning the pile of dead bodies being loaded away. "It's different this time." He turns back to me, determination set in his gaze. "She will soon start her search for the Lotus Pond, and I want you to help her."

I blink. "Lotus Pond? What the hell is that?" I say, fed up with the cryptic words and half-truths. No wonder Nova said not to trust him...

A sigh leaves the hunter's lips as his gaze turns to the falling snow.

"It's the only chance she has... to save us all."

— Nova —

Lance and Darius leave the room to give us a chance to discuss their offer. They say they can help me connect to the pond and lotuses through a ritual of sorts, something Azrael apparently can help with, being the angel of death and whatnot. They keep mentioning how this is more than just saving my life but won't clarify beyond that.

"So?" I ask everyone. "What do you all think?"

The room goes silent, looks passing between the cambions present. At the far end of the room, the door opens, and Tevari slinks in. His face is hard, anger still simmering in those dark eyes. But his vine is relaxed around his body, which I hope is a good sign.

"I heard everything," he says, taking a seat in an empty chair, "and I trust you enough to do what's right. Even if that means working with *hunters*."

Trust. The word seems painful for him to say. What if I break it again? After everything... I close my eyes, my head hanging low. No, not again. We *can* do this, together.

Lifting my eyes, I look around the room. The others give a soft, quiet nod, Tevari's conviction enough for them to agree. And it hurts to see. Guilt washes over me as I pull them farther into this confusing and dangerous world I now live in. My eyes land on Luka, a sigh escaping his lips as he notices my hesitation.

"You know I'm not going anywhere," he says, and I can't help but smile.

"Then we shouldn't wait much longer. I'll tell Lance I'll go through with this ritual—as soon as possible."

No one speaks as a wave of unease settles over the room. There's no way for us to predict the outcome. Not if Amon can't see my future or even the role I have to play to stop this war. And now, with the new information about the lotuses and the pond... everyone's just as lost as I am.

"Everything's changing," Lei Jing says quietly, the others nodding along with her.

"Hopefully for the better," I agree, and somehow, those words make it feel like everything has been set in motion. A ticking clock counting down.

Night is falling, the glow of sunset illuminating my room through the open curtains. I sit in a plush chair, staring out as the city lights turn on for the evening. Shadows cast along the walls seem to cave in on me, threatening me in the early hours of the night. As if waiting for me to let down my guard and fall asleep—to attack while I'm exhausted.

Closing my eyes, I pull my arms close to my chest, comforted by the slight hum and heat of the bracelet on my wrist.

"Uriel, Zerachiel, did you know Lance and Darius were coming?"

"Uriel was aware, I was not," Zera says, his voice fuming.

"Are you saying you two haven't been in on this the entire time? What aren't you telling me now?"

A barrier not of my own making forms in my mind, Zerachiel pulling him and Uriel into the only safe space where Darkness can't reach us.

"I cannot hold it for long, but the one you call Darkness will not hear our conversation," Zera says.

A twinkle chimes, Uri's voice moving to the front of my mind. *"I am part of a faction set on helping you, Nova. But I cannot speak of why just yet, as knowing would kill you."* I gulp, glancing at the black vines encasing my entire left hand, the rest trailing down my ribcage. *"Zerachiel was thought dead, but he has been with you since—"*

"Silence! We all have our promises to keep," Zerachiel's voice booms, cutting Uriel off.

"What promise?"

"A promise to help, just as Uriel has made. However, the promise I made forbids me from speaking of it. I am only a guide."

The barrier shatters, the private space within my mind gone. I frown, hugging myself tighter. Another secret, another uncertainty. A faction and a guide, so many promises I don't quite understand.

I lean back in the soft chair. Do I even want to know the truth anymore? There's such sadness in the way Zerachiel and Uriel speak... The only hint I have is that the truth goes far beyond what any of us can imagine. Beyond what Luka has shown of our history together and beyond the truth my father has revealed to me with that godforsaken book.

Looking at the purple sky out the window—to the stars and heavens hidden above the clouds—I curse the one who started all of this.

He who condemned Lucifer's love for me. *Darkness.* Low laughter echoes in my head. "*You'll never win,*" he whispers to me, a promise and a threat.

"Like hell I won't."

37

THE MIND MAZE

Sitting on a metal table in a private lab on the top floor of Amon's building, I watch Lance carefully mix different substances into a long vial. I wrinkle my nose at the smell—bitter and tangy—dreading having to drink whatever it is. I turn my attention to the others in the room. With everyone here, the space is far too crowded.

"How's Rishu doing?" I ask Meena to distract myself from what lies ahead.

She's been caring for him since we got back. The angelic bullet clearly did more damage than he let on, considering he's hidden away from the rest of us. *Weakness isn't tolerated in this world.* Those words I once spoke. Seems like it isn't just me who's been taught to think that way.

"He'll be healed soon," she says with a soft smile. Her eyes flit to the vial, her nose scrunching as mine had.

Luka comes over, taking a seat beside me on the metal table, closely watching Lance. "You're sure this won't hurt her?"

"She'll be fine. This concoction will allow her to go deep into her subconscious without interference from outside sources," Lance says as he pours another foul-smelling liquid into the vial.

My fingers press into the cold tabletop. I'll take anything if it prevents Darkness from lingering in my mind. Luka doesn't seem convinced. He catches my gaze, and my heart stutters, pounding in my chest at our proximity.

"You haven't asked yet," Lance says.

"About what?" I ask as I tear my eyes away from Luka's alluring gaze.

"Adrian."

My whole body tenses as Lance fiddles with more ingredients. I haven't thought about Adrian since I saw one of his hunters shoot Rishu. Not the best memory to associate with my best friend... If I can even call him that anymore.

"Or what happened at the campus."

My brows furrow. "What happened at the campus?"

Darius steps forward from the back wall, his thick arms crossed and bulging. "Those *things* attacked. Broke through the wards like they were never there to begin with."

I jerk back in shock. "The Krav? How's that possible?"

"Princess, I'm surprised you're still asking that. How is any of this possible?"

I look at the ground, feeling the stares of the cambions on the other side of the room. I know they can't understand. Even though I left my previous life behind, I would never wish harm on the hunters or the regular students at the campus.

"And Adrian? Is he okay?" My nails dig into my palm, unable to look at the man beside me. His hard stare burns into the side of my face.

A pit forms in my stomach as Lance says, "I called him to help fight at the campus, but we left before he showed up."

I shut my eyes tight. Please, *please* be okay. Luka's hand covers mine again, but it's not as comforting as it might have been before.

"I think we should leave," Lei Jing says, ushering the other cambions out of the room. I mumble a thank you under my breath, unsure if she heard me or not.

As soon as the door shuts, it opens again as Rishu enters with a lotus flower in hand.

"Rishu?" He looks refreshed, his bronzed skin glowing even in the dim lights. He gives me a lazy smile, handing the flower to Lance.

"What? You look like you've seen a ghost," Rishu says, his gaze turning to Luka beside me. He offers a slight bow before rising and meeting my eyes. "Something so little wouldn't kill me."

I shake my head, laughing softly. An angelic bullet definitely isn't what I'd consider little. "No, I can't imagine it would."

Lance moves quickly as he tears a petal, dropping it into the vial. A cloud of purple smoke puffs up, and a satisfied smile blossoms on his face.

"That's not one of the lotuses, right?" I ask as my nose wrinkles again.

Lance shakes his head. "No, just a substitute to emulate the ones you'll need to find." I nod as if I understand. "Drink. Then we'll tie you up."

"Excuse me?" I ask as he hands me the vial, the brown-green liquid swirling ominously.

"For your safety," Lance says.

"Of course." I roll my eyes and force a smile before taking a deep breath and downing the liquid in one shot. It slides down my throat like ice and fire. Burning and freezing my insides. The lotus burns on my chest, the vines inching farther across my skin. I raise my hand to my chest, but the pain eases.

"That wasn't so bad."

Lance gives me a sheepish look. "I must mention"—He gently pushes me back onto the metal table, wrapping the straps around my wrists and ankles. I try not to dwell on the horrible memories that come with them, fighting the urge to flee. Luka meets my gaze, nodding reassuringly—"it'll be worse from here on. When you're in your head, remember it's like a nightmare. I can always pull you out, though."

Lance's eyes flicker with hesitation as he looks at me, his gemstone earring twirling above. I chuckle to myself, recognizing the gem. The same one Rishu gave to me to hide my angel wing tattoos from the cambions. No wonder none of us knew.

"But that doesn't mean you can't get hurt, so you must be careful and move quickly. Those black vines don't want you to find the lotuses," Darius says over Lance's shoulder.

"Go figure," I say, biting my lip as the lotus tattoo heats on my chest. "So tell me, Lance, how did you become an Undivided? After all these years I've known you... I don't think I know you at all." I force the words out to distract from the pain beginning to bubble beneath my skin. Luka picks up on my distress and peers down at me with worried eyes.

The corner of Lance's mouth pulls up into a half smile as he tests the strength of the bindings. "I was almost eighteen and snuck into the chapel. I was eager to prove myself to your father, much like you always wanted to. I found the hidden entrance, somehow ignited the angelic statue, and Azrael called to me. He bonded with me without much of a trial. I was going to tell your father despite the possible consequences, but when I returned to my room, this earring was there, and Azrael said to hide that I was now an Undivided. And so, when I was chosen to go through the trials the following year, I rejected the offer. But Solomon still placed me as your trainer that same year."

I can't find the words to respond. "Not what I was expecting," I mumble through gritted teeth.

"You never told me either, bastard," Darius grumbles, going to lean against the far wall.

A volcano erupts inside me, bursting through my lips in a scream. The hold on the black vines loosens; pins and needles dance across my skin. Copper fills my mouth, the heady scent of lotuses rising to my nose. Luka's hand grabs onto mine, his face contorted as if enduring the same pain.

A red glow emanates from my chest, growing brighter by the second. I yell out as the pain increases, pulling at the straps to be free. Tears fall from my eyes as I writhe around on the table. The light grows stronger, the black vines freeing themselves and growing across my skin. I feel them inch up my neck and farther down my side, consuming me.

Damn, Lance... He could've warned me about the pain.

From the corner of my teary eyes, I see Luka struggling to try to unlatch my straps, Lance and Darius pulling him away. He flings them against the wall, but the sound of their cries never reaches my ears. A dark void creeps around the edges of my vision before slipping into the deepest parts of my mind. My head lolls back, silence enveloping me.

Soft grass brushes my skin, gently waking me. The sun shines brightly, warming my skin with its rays. I sit up and breathe deeply as a gentle breeze drifts lazily around me. The moist scent of dirt and fresh flowers eases my mind.

A crack of thunder echoes above, and I jump to my feet, looking at the blue sky, which has begun to bleed red. A full moon appears overhead, a crack almost severing it in half. Blood oozes from it, dripping to the earth below. The smell of bitter decay overshadows the earthy notes from before.

My heartbeat quickens as the screams of tortured creatures resonate around me. I scan the area. I take a deep breath, desperate to hold back the fear threatening to overwhelm me. *I have to be strong.* Closing my eyes tight, I pray the horrible sky and screams will fade. *This is just a nightmare.*

"Be calm," a woman's voice says. *Remembrance.*

The world turns quiet, and I open my eyes to the peaceful paradise it once was. My lips part as I take her in—clear for the first time. But it's not her eyes of pure gold or silver hair so pale it's almost white that takes me by surprise. No, it's the face that matches my own like a reflection.

"You have a task to do," Remembrance says.

Raising her arm, she points behind me. I spin around, the surroundings slowly blurring and changing into the same pond I saw during my angelic trials—the one everyone keeps mentioning. Lotus leaves rise out of the blackened water.

"But what am I supposed to do?" I ask, turning back around, but Remembrance is gone.

With hesitant steps, I approach the pond. The scent of lotus flowers wafts to my nose even though no flowers rest on the pond.

The green jungle closes in behind me, entrapping me in this circular pond with no way to go but in. Stepping forward, I dip one boot into the black waters and then the other. It pulls me into its depths, dragging me deeper until I'm beneath the surface. I don't resist, letting the pond take me under. The inky water swirls around me, clinging to my limbs and holding me in place without room to struggle.

My lungs burn as I wait for the slideshow of images to appear once more. Instead, my feet hit the bottom. The water in front of me clears—a pathway leading me to a plain wooden doorway slightly ajar. I wade my way to it—the water thick, slowing me down. But I trudge forward, desperately urging my feet to keep moving.

I reach the frame of the doorway and push my way through. Air fills my lungs in a rush, and I gasp, resting my hands on my legs as I look around. Rolling hills covered in an endless field of golden stalks—much like corn but towering higher than any I've seen—surround me, extending far past the horizon. There are pathways meandering through the stalks—a maze of shimmering gold. Sunlight shines down from the cloudless blue sky, reflecting off the golden stalks and blinding me with every sway.

The stalks in front of me part, revealing an opening into the maze. Remembrance materializes at my side, her white dress swaying in the breeze.

"Find the seven pieces," she says, looking toward the entrance.

I stare ahead into the endless rows of gold. "The lotuses?" I ask, but when I look over at the woman, she's gone once again.

Steeling myself, I walk toward the entrance. The ground is littered with golden flecks, and up close, I realize the stalks are quite thin and lined with tiny flowers, rising even higher than they seemed from afar—almost triple my height. The rich, intoxicating scent of lotus blossoms reaches my nose. The lotus tattoo on my chest tugs like a burning string pulling me in the right direction. My steps falter as the flowers curl in behind me, closing off my only exit.

The maze is quiet. Silent and predatory, it watches me with eyes I can't see. A breeze ruffles the golden stalks, the lotus scent growing distant.

"I feel like a dog," I say to myself, somehow knowing if I lose its trace, I won't find it again.

But there's only one path. It doesn't veer or curve; it's straight and unending with the slight rises and falls of hills. I walk and walk, my pace quickening as I pass rows and rows of golden flowers. My eyes dart back and forth, and my ears remain alert. This may be my mind, but I don't trust it.

A dead end comes into sight, but as I reach it, I realize that the path is off, splitting in two opposite directions—identical in every way. I pause to listen, smelling the air once more. The lotus scent is faint in both directions, but my heart pulls me to the left. A gentle tug from the burning tattoo guiding my way.

As I move down the path, the golden stalks curl in and close behind me. I wince as I watch the flittering plants overlap, sealing me in. Not sure if this means I chose correctly or if I'll never get out of here.

"I'll never find anything at this rate." It feels like a clock is ticking above me—winding down the time I have to find all seven lotuses.

I set off at a jog to cover the ground faster. It's quiet as I continue to pass the never-ending rows of gold, nothing remotely different no matter how far I run. Just the sway of the thin stalks bristling together in the breeze as the tiny flowers reflect the sun above. A curve comes into sight, veering to the right. I break into a run, panting as the air becomes heavy in my lungs. When I reach the bend, I skid to a halt.

Ahead, a black jaguar stalks down the path. Night flows from around its feet, stars dancing in its tracks. It moves with precision, one step after another, unaware of my presence behind it—or undisturbed by it.

My gaze moves to what it's stalking, and my heart jumps. A ball of black energy flits around, stopping momentarily to unravel into a black lotus flower. The lotus tattoo sings on my chest, urging me forward with a dancing joy. I take a step, and the jaguar stops. Its head swivels around, golden feline eyes locking with mine. The jaguar snarls, an almost human grin forming on its face. My breath stutters in my chest, and I take a small step back.

Run.

I turn and run faster than I ever have. Enormous clawed paws pound the dirt behind me; I can hear teeth snapping at my feet. The jaguar is toying with me—its prey. I call out to Kioren, but the bracelet is silent on my wrist.

Not good, not good, not good.

A new opening appears to my right, and I leap toward it, rolling to the ground. I jump to my feet, watching the golden stalks lock together. They intertwine as the jaguar paces on the other side—the smirk still on its feline face. Dread washes over me even as the opening closes and the creature fades from sight. *One.* Remembrance's voice chimes in my head.

Taking a deep breath, I turn to face the new path ahead. My brows knit as the scenery changes before me. Continuing to follow the path, I step out from the golden stalks and onto a sandy shore. Waves lap at my feet as I look out over the vast ocean before me, turquoise blue extending as far as my eyes can see. The air is salty, masking the lotus scent.

I've never seen an ocean before, at least not in person. A rumble shakes the ground at my feet, and I watch as an island rises from the blue depths. It's hazy and unclear in the distance, but the tug of the lotus pulls once again.

I walk into the waves, the water rising higher and higher until all I can do is swim. I glance behind me as another rumble echoes, the golden flowers falling into the path as it caves in on itself, turning into a pit of darkness. I don't stare long, pushing my arms and legs to swim faster as the growing abyss races toward me.

The water turns violent, dragging me into its cool depths. Beneath the waves, I see the black void nearing, and the water tugs me backward as it cascades into the pit. My muscles ache, but I kick harder, rising above the waves. *It's just in my head.* I remind myself, yet it provides no comfort.

I swim harder. Waves crash into my mouth, and I taste the salty water, gagging and gasping for air as I force myself onward. The island appears closer, but so does the chasm behind me.

Another wave crashes against my head, and I'm pulled under, the current dragging me back. Panic grips my heart, but I fight back to the surface once more, lungs aching. I'm relieved to find the island just a few breaths away.

My feet scrape the sandy floor, and I push harder to reach the shore before the black void takes me. A blue orb floats out from the tropical forest atop the island. It lands on the white sand beach, a lotus of the same color unfolding. *Two.*

I'm pulled back with a scream, the dark abyss sucking me in with a roaring laugh. My fall is endless, the breath leaving me as if no end is in sight. Minutes feel like hours. I flail in desperation, hands grasping for anything to stop my descent.

Serpentine flesh coils around me—vague in the dark abyss. A roar thunders in my ears, blasting my eardrums. From the darkness, a purple orb floats above me, unraveling to show the lotus within. Another laugh—female and unfamiliar—and I land hard on a rough floor. *Three.*

With a groan, I prop myself up, thankful the landing hadn't been harder, considering how long I'd fallen. I look around the room, but it's too dark to make anything out. *Darkness.* How can I not think about him in a situation like this...

Endless black, slithering like the vines tracing my skin. The lotus tattoo on my chest throbs. My lips pull back with a hiss of pain. These *are* the black vines. Encasing me within this room, shrouding me in pain and darkness. I stand, turning in a circle.

I look up and watch in horror as the speck of blue sky high above—the only light in this pit—disappears as the darkness caves in. My heart pounds in my chest, and I struggle to stay calm. This is a prison. Another way for the real Darkness to mock my efforts—to threaten and taunt me.

I reach to my angels, calling their names. No response. I call to Remembrance, the woman whose face is my own, but there's nothing.

A red glow rises from my feet, an orb growing from the ground. It illuminates the dark space, and the vines on the walls recoil from the warm light. Tentatively, my fingers reach for it, and I suck in a breath as strength fills me as if a missing piece of my soul has been returned. The light suddenly unfurls to reveal a red lotus. Then hundreds more form around it until red flowers completely fill the bottom of the pit.

I spin in a circle, no longer able to find the first red lotus. *Four.* They shrink into the ground, and I fall to my knees, reaching after them. The red light wraps around me, and I can't even manage a scream as I'm pulled into the ground, the world tilting as I land back in the maze.

The lotus tattoo aches and pounds along with my racing heart. I tug at the fabric of my T-shirt, dragging the heavy air into my lungs as the power of the red lotus fades. Somehow it saved me from Darkness... My connection with it felt so natural, so complete.

I *need* them. And I'm not entirely sure why. Rage swirls inside of me, that dark, unfamiliar feeling that is of my own making. *Embrace the anger, the call for retribution.* Words Remembrance spoke. I pound my fist into the dirt as I let out a roar. All the wrongdoings left in the wake of Darkness... He won't get away with it.

With a sigh, I sit up and let the anger seep out of me. Three lotuses have yet to be found, and I don't know how much time I have left here. I pull myself to my feet and begin navigating the maze once more. The path ahead is as straight as an arrow as it had been before, but this time a closed door waits for me in the center. Its wooden frame appears simple from a distance, standing in the middle of the path, attached to nothing on either side.

As I approach the doorway, I feel a slight breeze drifting through the slightly open crack, carrying with it the faint scent of lotus flowers. I run my fingers over the wood. Up close, I realize the door is carved with delicate illustrations that seem to tell a story. There's a girl and a... baboon? The door creaks wider as I trace the lines lightly with my fingertips. Hesitantly pushing it open the rest of the way, I peer inside but don't step through.

In the distance, a rocky cliff juts from the ground, surrounded by rolling hills covered in tall yellow grasses and sparsely dotted with trees. Lush green trees grow from the top of the cliff. Barks and grunts carry on the temperate breeze. Turning my head to the sound, I notice cattle circling in a pasture that spreads out to the side of a simple small hut. The baboon from the doors engraving trails behind the herd as if guiding them. I rub my chest. Why does this feel so familiar?

A white orb flies toward the hut and cattle, the lotus scent intoxicatingly sweet as it stops its flight as if peering in my direction. *Five.* It zooms over the cliff, disappearing from sight.

The door slams shut in my face as it slips out of existence. A sigh of longing leaves my lips. I can't take these lotuses back with me from within my mind, no matter how I wish to.

Continuing through the maze, I follow the tug of my tattoo—the golden flowers intertwining and closing off the path behind me with each turn I take. Only two lotuses are left to find, and we will have a plan, a way to potentially stop Camus. How though? The question circles in my mind, an answer nagging at my brain.

Looking down the path before me, I find myself at another dead end. Three pink lotuses sit on stone altars, a selection for me to choose from. A test. On one altar, a swan is engraved in the stone. On the next, an elephant. The last stone pillar depicts a tiger.

I close my eyes, giving myself over to the tug of the lotus tattoo. Letting the pain, the urgency, consume me. To pull me toward the one that is real, the one that is mine. A tear slides down my cheek. I *need* these lotuses to live, to survive, to save everyone and everything I care about. They are a part of me, and they've been missing for a very long time.

Taking a step forward, eyes closed, I reach out my hand, allowing the power from the lotus tattoo guide me. Black vines prick my skin, threatening me with every inch they spread, but I breathe through the pain. My fingers graze soft, delicate petals, and relief washes over me. As I open my eyes, I catch a glimpse of the two other lotuses disappearing along with the altars. Power emanates from the pink lotus in my hand, and another tear falls as I watch it vanish. *Six*.

A flash of lightning followed closely by a booming crack of thunder startles me from my melancholy. I tremble as the sky above turns green, and a putrid smell reaches my nose. One I haven't been able to forget. *No...*

The ground sinks beneath me, and I scream as I fall into another dark abyss. I land hard and scramble to my feet, pushing through the putrid essence clinging to my skin and weighing me down. I hold back the urge to vomit as an unearthly cold seeps into my body.

"This can't be...."

I stumble forward, searching for a way out, but when I reach the edge of the darkness, I freeze. Fear rises in my stomach as I see my father's twin, Camus, with Theo. I made it out—I *saved* us—he can't hurt me here. *This is just a nightmare. None of this is real.* The thoughts don't comfort me as the black abyss pushes me closer to the scene as if begging me to watch.

Camus and Theo stand before an enormous glass container filled with green liquid at the center of a stone room. A dangerous smile rises on Camus's face as he rests his hand on the glass. Gulping down the fear even while my feet beg me to run, I move in closer, sticking to the shadows even as his Krav phase in and out of them.

From his suit jacket, Camus pulls out the golden lotus. *Seven.* My muscles burn with the need to lunge forward and snatch the lotus from his filthy hand, but I restrain myself. *It's not real.*

Daring another step closer, I peer into the container he stares at so vilely. Bile rises in my throat, and my hand rushes to cover my lips before I can empty my stomach on the stone tile. Inside, a naked body is curled up, suspended within the liquid. Long black hair floats behind her. I choke back a sob as my heart wrenches in pain.

Cold black eyes turn in my direction. Dark energy radiates from Camus, and fear builds inside me, freezing me where I stand. A smirk rises to his lips as he reaches for a knife in his pocket. He sends it flying in my direction, but the abyss sucks me back in before the knife lands. I flail as I tumble through the darkness, fear, and panic taking control of my limbs. I couldn't have been there. He *couldn't* have seen me.

The darkness turns to liquid, and I fight my way up through the inky water to the surface of the pond. Breaching the top, I suck in the clean air—the reek of Camus's dimension still lingering in my lungs. Wading out of the black liquid, I crawl onto the grassy shore and collapse as tears fall from my eyes. It's impossible. I couldn't have been there.

"Seven have been connected, seven still left to be claimed."

I look from the ground to Remembrance's face—to my face. Though her hair is almost white and her eyes are golden to my green, it's like I'm staring at a reflection of myself. Before I can say anything to her, the ground shakes beneath me as the pond and jungle crumble, breaking away to reveal a nightmarish scene. Towering buildings collapsing, screams echoing in the distance. Hunters, angels, demons, and the Krav all fighting against each other. The sky above beats red as the full moon bleeds.

The cambions and Luka materialize behind me, rushing forward into the battle while I remain frozen, unmoving as I behold the destruction in horror.

"Make it stop," I plead, begging the images to end but unable to tear my gaze away.

"This future will come."

I spin around to face Remembrance once again. "No," I hiss, "I won't let it." Striding toward her, I grip the white collar of her dress. "Why show me these things if you can't explain any of it? My friends will die? The world will crumble? And all you can say is this future will come? Tell me something useful! Why have me find these lotuses and this godforsaken pond if I can't do anything to save the people who matter the most?"

Tears stream down my face. Her hand reaches for my cheek, brushing the tears away. "You search for the Lotus Pond without remembering the blossom is you. I can't free you of the vines until you reach it, but I can give you time. Trust yourself, Kioren, your friends, your beloved. The answer, the key, has always been within you, *is you*." I look at her face, glistening tears falling down her cheeks—her pain mirroring my own. And I finally see how translucent she is. A mere shadow, only the essence of whoever she really is, or was.

"Who *are* you?" I ask, letting go of her collar.

She smiles softly, sadly. "I'm sorry you have to bear this burden."

My hands fall to my sides, and I take a step back. "*Please*," I beg again, holding her golden gaze. Something so inhuman, so foreign, yet entirely familiar. "Please help me. I can't do this alone."

Leaning forward, she places a kiss on my brow. "You're never alone."

She bursts into a cloud of lotus petals, drifting off on the breeze as the scene around me returns to the misty warmth of the Lotus Pond. Two figures cloaked in white stand in front of the pond before me.

Beautiful wings spread wide, feathers gently fluttering in the wind. The white hoods fall to reveal their faces veiled in a thin, nearly translucent fabric. My mouth parts as I realize I'm about to see my angels for the first time.

"You have been given time," Uriel says, her voice silvery and clear. She lifts ebony hands to her veil, gently lifting it from her face.

She's beautiful.

Silver braids laced with glittering pearls are partly tied up in a top knot, the rest of the long braids falling around her cloak. Thick full lips smile at me, her eyes large and bright. Wisdom shines in her silver eyes—the color so similar to Luka's. Her rich dark skin seems to glow from within. The one known as God's light, she shines even brighter than I ever imagined.

"But time it will take," Zerachiel's gravelly voice says as he pulls back his own veil. His face is pale and almost as translucent as Remembrance's. But it appears as if the lack of color comes from having been locked away, hidden from sunlight for an exceedingly long time. *Hidden within me.* I remember what he had said. Zera has been with me since long before Uriel and I bonded. Zerachiel's hair is a deep black, falling in waves to his shoulders. His eyes—like Luka said—are as blue as the ocean waves.

"We cannot give you more time," Uriel says, stepping forward and taking my hand in hers, "but we can offer you the help you will need to reach your final destination."

Power radiates through her fingers, and I gasp. Never have I felt so close to her powers. Her energy fills me to the brim, reminding me of the light Remembrance gifted me. But while Remembrance's power felt warm, Uri's is like the cold touch of starlight.

Zerachiel steps forward, wrapping my other hand between his long pale fingers, "Seven pieces you must find, seven tasks ahead of you."

More power radiates through me, currents of it running over my skin. His power is more intense than Uriel's. Like a gush of wind. And right then and there, I know that all those times I felt the wind beckoning or comforting me, it was him. Guiding me as he had once promised to do long ago. What that promise was and to whom it was made, I can only guess, but the power awakens memories of my childhood. Of the gentle nudge to keep training despite the brutality of my teachings. Of the caress that would graze my scrapes and bruises. Of the wind beneath my feet as I took the leap from my bedroom window.

A tear slides down my cheek.

Uri's silver eyes burn bright with her light as she says, "So we give only what you as an Undivided can take."

My eyes slip closed as I feel the connection with these two angels deepen, strengthening our unbreakable bond.

"With each lotus you find, the black vines will spread. Time will not be in your favor against the one you call Darkness, but with our powers, we will keep you alive," Zera's voice is less strained, as if fully awakened.

"I don't understand," I whisper, their power overwhelming me. I feel dizzy with a mix of bliss and terror at what I suddenly possess.

"Here it is quiet, undisturbed, but time is short," Uri says, her hand squeezing tighter, "Use our powers, find the Lotus Pond, restore order."

A scream leaves my lips, pins and needles digging into my back. I clutch their hands for support, barely standing as they hold me upright. Beneath my skin, I feel my bones shift and alter, my muscles rearranging. A pop sounds, and relief washes over me as feathery wings unfurl from my back. I stumble under the weight as my angels release me, allowing me to stand on my own. I glance over my shoulder—two sets of wings just like the tattoo on the back of my neck. They extend wide and powerful, more beautiful than any depictions I've ever seen. The bottom set, Uriel's wings, glitter with ancient starlight, while the top, Zerachiel's, are pure white and seem to radiate sunlight.

"Doesn't this go against everything the angels stand for? Working with a hunter turned ally of the demons. Of Lucifer." Luka's real name feels strange on my tongue. And I wonder, though dare not ask, if they miss him as much as he does them.

They smile. Soft and sad, as Remembrance had. As many people around me seem to. Uriel reaches for my cheek, gently brushing the hair behind my ear. "There is no other who should wield our power. No hunter, no human."

I search her face, trying to read whatever thoughts are crossing behind her silver eyes. I look from Uri to Zera, who wears a somber expression on his face. "Thank you." Another tear slides down my cheek, and I quickly wipe it away. "Thank you for guiding me, for keeping me alive."

The pond beyond them gurgles, black liquid bubbling at the surface. Folding their wings tight, they spin to face it—guarding me from it. Black vines rise from the surface, the abyssal prison emerging from the pond. Overwhelming fear threatens to drown me. Clenching my fists, I hold on to the power they shared.

"You must leave, now," Zerachiel's voice booms. A warning and a command.

"Can't we fight it together?" I ask as they block my view of the pond.

"The vines are fighting against this place Zerachiel has created. He will see you here if you stay longer. You *must* go. And do not fear if you do not hear us—we are always with you," Uriel says, her wings extending to push me back.

Dread permeates the air around their forms, a fear maybe even stronger than my own. Just who is Darkness? The vines burst through the pond, shooting in my direction.

"Remember all that you saw and heard. Now *go*." Zera grabs me and throws me into the sky.

My wings catch me and pump upward, aching with the strain of the new movement. Peering down, I watch as light engulfs the scene below—the world in my mind disappearing beneath me. My heart races as I push harder, higher, trying to outrun my fear.

Dark spots cloud my vision, blurring the sky as it changes to that sickly green glow. The air around me wavers, and I stumble mid-flight. Shaking out my wings, I look down once more. Black vines burst toward the sky, aiming right for me.

My eyes grow wide as they rush toward me, like hundreds of hands grasping toward me to drag me back down. With a final push of my wings, I burst out of the world within my mind, pieces of it shattering around me.

38

UNRAVELING

"**N**ova, wake up," a loud voice yells from above. Hands grip my shoulders, shaking me hard.

"She has to wake up, we're out of time," another says.

My eyes slowly blink open, bright light temporarily blinding me. I jolt up, the straps no longer attached to my wrists. Power surges through me, and I grab at the lotus tattoo, curling over in pain and ecstasy. Everything blurs, fading in and out of sight. Arms wrap around me; a hand lifts my chin.

"Luka..."

I feel Uriel and Zerachiel fighting the black vines within me. Remembrance gave me time, my angels gave me more time and power, but it won't last. There really is a ticking clock over my head. I look to my hand, the black marks frozen in place for now.

The building trembles and I stumble from the metal table, steadied by Luka's hand. I look between the two hunters and the shattered glass scattering the floor. "What's going on?"

The door bursts open as Amon strides into the room. "Camus has found us."

My stomach heaves, the stench of his dimension lingering beneath my nose. Did I... Did I lead him here? Leaning over, I

393

empty the contents of my stomach onto the floor. Luka holds my hair back, rubbing my back as my body shakes.

"Did you accomplish everything?" Lance asks, grabbing my shoulders when I finish retching. I can only offer a nod in response. He lets out a thankful sigh, nodding to Darius behind him.

Luka shoves Lance's hands off me, pushing him back. "You should ask if she's okay first, which she obviously isn't." He looks me over, silver eyes examining the halted vine tattoo. "Are you okay? What happened?"

I open my mouth to speak, but no words come out. How do I even begin to explain everything I saw? Everything that happened within my mind... But my angels' powers reassure me. We finally have direction, even if I don't know exactly where it'll lead us.

"I don't know. I don't think I have enough time to explain," I say to Luka.

"You don't," Amon says, his eyes burning red. "Now the question is, fight or flee?"

Rishu appears at the doorway, the cambions trailing behind him. "We have a problem. He's brought his horde."

I close my eyes and take a deep breath, feeling the tingling power of starlight and wind at my fingertips.

"We fight," I say as I reopen my eyes. "He can't get away with this. But... but you have to know that he found me in my mind. I think... I think I led him here." I almost puke again, remembering the girl he had in that container, not daring to consider what he plans to do with her and the golden lotus. "I'm sorry."

Mumbled curses fill the room. My shoulders slump, and I look at the floor, unable to meet their eyes. We have to fight. Otherwise, he'll just trail after us no matter where we run... But we're so unprepared.

"It's not your fault," Luka says at my side. "None of us could've predicted what might happen."

"Luka's right. We should've been preparing while you went through that," Lei Jing says, coming to stand beside Rishu.

Amon tsks. "This Camus is more troublesome than I thought. Not even my sight predicted this."

"If you saw him, then it means he has a lotus," Lance says, Darius uttering profanities under his breath. I nod, and more curses follow.

Meena screams as a black form snatches her from the doorway. We hear a sickening *snap* as we run to the door, exiting into the hallway. Meena stands there looking unfazed, holding the dead form of a Krav.

"That felt good." We stare at her in silence. She cracks her neck, twin pigtails swaying behind her.

I look around Meena out the large window before us, and my heart sinks. Black forms amass in the sky. Leathery wings encased in inky shadows beat furiously, growing closer; growls and shrieks reverberate through the window. The horde parts to reveal a stone doorway appearing from within the shadows. *Camus.* The door is wide open, the dark abyss of his dimension leaking into our world—green light bleeding into the sky.

I suck in a breath. Can we even fight against this?

Glass suddenly shatters as a Krav flies through the window next to us. Azura is the fastest, blasting it back out with her flames. Glass cracks with a loud thump, and I swivel to face the opposite end of the hall where another is ramming itself into a window.

"Nova, what do we do?" Oliver says at my side, the beast prowling behind his eyes, antsy. But the boy... the boy next to me is fidgeting anxiously, fear present in his swirling gray and yellow gaze. I look around to find the others staring at me with similar looks in their eyes, depending on me to guide them. My stomach twists. What have I led them into?

"We need a plan," I say, scanning over Amon, Luka, and the two hunters, "and fast."

Lei Jing approaches the glass, peering down at the long drop to the cement roads. "They're breaking into the lower levels."

Various curses resound around the room. Tevari blazes gold as he extends his arms to the sides, briars shooting from his hands down the hallway. He seals both ends shut. "Seems like we don't have a choice other than to fight," he says, turning to face the window.

"Kids, you better prepare yourself," Darius says, heaving a large angelic mace over his broad shoulder. "I hope Nova trained you well."

"She did learn from the best," Lance says, lifting his sleeve. A glowing angelic symbol forms on his forearm, and he pulls out a ruby necklace. He places it around his neck, a thin blade of gold and ruby forming in his hands. The angelic artifact of Archangel Azrael. Black curls fall in front of his face as he pulls his fedora from his curly hair, tossing it aside.

"I—"

"You trained us as well as you could with the time we had," Azura says, fire flaring in her eyes. There's reassurance in her stern gaze. The other cambions nod behind her.

Amon clicks his tongue. "Then I suppose it's our turn." He motions to Rishu, who bows his head, transforming into his naga form. Iridescent scales climb over his bronze skin, red eyes replacing deep brown. Two horns curl out from his skull, brown curls brushed aside to reveal pointed ears.

"As you command, my lord," he says with a hiss as his forked tongue darts out to taste the air like a snake.

Amon's lips curl into a wicked grin as he takes on his demonic form. We all step back as bones crack and bend. His pale skin turns to a bluish color, black wolf claws replacing the nails of his fingers and toes. Limbs grow longer, leaner with each snap of his bones. Black feathers replace his long blond hair, and a snake tail whips out from behind him.

I find myself smiling with appreciation at his demonic form. Now this, *this* is what I expected when I first met him.

Amon turns to me, a twinkle in his blood-red eyes, clearly savoring the fear and curiosity written across my face. He sniffs his nose as if gaining a new sense and his eyes trace over me, lingering on my back. "Let us see if your wings can keep up with mine, Undivided." Fire burns in his mouth as he speaks, the sound low, dangerous.

"Wings?" Luka says, and I turn to him with a smirk. Maybe we do stand a chance.

Amon runs forward and crashes through the glass window, feathery black wings bursting out of his back and catching the wind. I raise my hand, Zerachiel's power bubbling at my fingers as I cast a gust of air at Amon to help him lift higher into the sky. I shudder a breath as the unfamiliar power ebbs away.

The shrieks of the Krav horde intensify as the demon charges. Rishu follows quickly after, jumping out and catching Amon's hand as he swoops past the window. He throws Rishu up, twin blades forming in the naga's hands with a puff of smoke. The two demons raining Hell on the horde.

"This isn't a plan!" I yell out over the howl of wind.

Neither demon pays me any attention. Amon attacks with a fierceness unlike anything I've ever seen, fire shooting from his mouth, turning the creatures to dust. Rishu jumps from one Krav to the next—his bloodlust palpable. And when he begins to fall, Amon is there to catch his hand and throw him back into the melee. Despite being heavily outnumbered, they carve through their enemies with ease.

While Amon and Rishu are holding back the horde, I spin back around to the others. The rest of us still need a plan. "Luka and I will join Amon and Rishu," I say, holding a hand up before Luka can argue with me. "If we can take out Camus here and now, we'll be that much closer to ending this madness. And to do that, we need everyone who can fly out there fighting through the horde." He frowns but concedes my point, pulling a broadsword from a shadow with a growl. "I know we weren't able to finish our training, but I believe in you all. Fight together, watch each other's backs, and hit them hard."

The cambions nod, calling their powers forth.

"We have nowhere to escape to if things go wrong," Tevari says, his hand reaching to the side as he reinforces one of his barriers as the Krav slash at his briars. More and more Krav are rising from the lower levels. I wince, knowing he's not wrong.

"We don't have much choice," Lance says, sounding resigned. If he doesn't have a better plan, then this is all we can do.

Darius swings his mace from his shoulder, taking it into both hands. "Damn these bastards. Princess, we got one end if your little cambions can watch the other and the windows. We'll regroup if anything goes wrong."

I nod, and the two hunters set off. Lance casts a final look back, offering a quick nod to me. *Approval.* My heart warms as I turn to face the others.

"Don't worry about us," Meena says, grinning confidently. "We got this."

Kioren hums on my wrist. "Okay, then good luck."

"I can't," Oliver says, panic in his eyes as he sinks to the floor, head in his hands. "I *can't* do this."

Oliver's voice is filled with pain. My heart breaks at his slumped shoulders, at the tips of his fingers shapeshifting into black talons against his will.

"Luka, go," I say, shouting over the deafening roar of the battle outside. I don't watch him leave as I turn to Oliver. Even as I hear his wings unfurl, a battle cry erupting from his lips.

I look to the others as I crouch down next to him. "Azura, stay here. The rest of you take your position at the other end." They nod, racing off as Azura protects our backs from any Krav that might near the broken window.

"I can't fight, Nova... I"—Oliver's voice cracks, tears falling down his pale cheeks—"I'm a monster. I fought in that dimension, but it almost took me over... I just—" He closes his eyes.

I spare a glance at the battle raging outside. I have to get out there and help. They're all fighting—swords and claws and fire clashing into the Krav horde. But more and more come through that doorway. A never-ending nightmare of Camus's creation. Thousands of lives taken for his army. Both human and demon.

I focus back on Oliver, taking his face into my hands. "You're not a monster, Oliver, you never have been." I brush away a tear that rolls down his cheek. "It's okay to be scared to lose yourself to the power inside you. I know I'm scared, but we have to fight if we want to survive... Or at least to escape long enough to find a way to survive."

"I shouldn't survive."

"Don't say that." My hands tighten around his face, heart breaking for him. What has this boy been through? "Don't ever say that again."

He gulps, meeting my eyes. Letting go, I step back. Oliver seems smaller, shoulders hunched, hair messy on top of his head. Not the cocky, teasing boy I first met. A facade, I realize. Something I recognize all too well.

"Embrace your entire self, Oliver, even the side you fear. No matter what, you're still you, and you control the power. But I'll never force you to fight. Just... just stay safe, okay?" I stand and look to Azura, who nods, her fire flaring. If he won't fight, then we will protect him as best as we can.

"Good luck," I say and race toward the window. Taking a deep breath, I jump without hesitation, summoning Zerachiel's wind to catch the two sets of wings unfurling from my back. My wings pump, the movement harder and more painful than it had been within my mind. Untrained muscles threatening to give out and drop me to the cement far below.

"Kioren, I call you forth," I yell out over the howling wind as a Krav beast flies toward me. I use Uri's starlight to blind the Krav as the scythe appears in my hands, slashing down on the beast. It shatters into dust as it had that night of the blood moon so long ago.

With Kioren in hand, I slice one Krav after another, desperate to make my way to that unholy doorway—to end Camus. Luka flies by on black wings, his gaze falling to the two sets of wings holding me midair. He doesn't watch long as a Krav crashes into him—cut in half by the swipe of his blade. I watch in both terror and admiration. This side of him much like the Lucifer I read about. A soldier, a destroyer, but also a protector.

A Krav slams into me, sharp claws raking my side. I yell as it knocks me from the sky. My wings struggle to stop my descent. Kioren's handle is locked in the creature's jaws, but it curls around and slashes the Krav off me.

Spinning my body around, I try to catch the wind. I reach a hand forward to summon Zerachiel's power, but it only lifts me for a moment. Razor-sharp teeth latch onto a wing, and I scream, looking over my shoulder as two giant Krav tear into my wings. We tumble in the air as I fight them—Kioren's tendrils ripping holes in their inky bodies. Blood oozes into the white of my wings feathers as we race closer to the ground.

A roar reverberates in my ears, and the two creatures are torn off my wings. The power and energy of my angels fade, exhausting the last of their reservoir. My wings burst into pieces of light and feathers, and I fall—weightless in the cold sky. The wind surrounds and caresses me but is unable to stop my descent to the street below.

Luka dives toward me, hand outstretched. My eyes flutter, tears falling from my eyes with the bite of cold licking at my bloody wounds. Kioren moves its black tendrils out of the way, and Luka catches me, wrapping his arms around me. My stomach flips as we come to a sudden halt, his black wings pumping with ease.

"Nice wings," he says as his scent envelops me, his arms tightening around me. Reaching around his neck, I hold on to him with the last of my strength. The wounds I endured on the wings a phantom pain that lingers on my back.

"I couldn't keep them summoned," I mumble in his ear, my gaze moving to the amassed horde above us. The wounds on my sides ache in the bitter cold. Uriel's power ebbs through me, slowly healing the injuries.

Luka pulls me back, his silver eyes staring into mine. Blood oozes down from a cut across his brow.

"You did good, love," he says sadly, "but we can't win this fight."

I don't want to agree... But how can I not? The horde grows thicker while we grow weaker. We're not enough to take on an army. Above, Rishu is flung into a window, the glass shattering around him. Amon holds his own, but the creatures keep coming—ripping and tearing at his wings and skin. He howls in pain, slashing them down. But for each Krav he kills, twenty more take its place, with hundreds exiting the doorway.

Fire sputters out the window I jumped from, and I know Azura must be pushing for flames she doesn't have. It doesn't seem the others are faring any better than us.

"What do we do?"

His face hardens, arm tightening around my waist. "We run."

I freeze. How can we run? I look away from him. The thought of letting Camus get away with this makes me sick. We can't let him win.

But how can we not run?

"I—" I start, searching Luka's eyes—begging for another answer, another option.

"We don't have another choice," he says as if reading my unspoken words. "We're not enough to stop his army. He caught us off guard... Even if I were to summon all my power, we would not win." Luka pulls me in closer. "I won't lose you again. Not when we can live to fight another day. To assemble an army of our own."

A tear falls down my cheek. "I hate this."

Luka presses his forehead to mine. "I know."

Approaching screeches startle us out of the moment, Luka zipping out of the way of a dozen Krav. Kioren wraps a tendril around us to keep me secure as I take its handle into my hands. Luka holds me tight as he switches his sword to his other hand. We fly back toward the broken window, cutting down any creatures in our path. The feel of his arm around me is comforting as we fight as if this is what we've always done.

Breaking through the horde, Luka lands us gracefully back inside the building—Azura halting her flames to let us enter. Kioren unravels from around us as Luka's wings fold in and disappear to accommodate the space.

Calling Kioren back into the bracelet, I see just how exhausted Azura is. The other cambions race from down the hall upon hearing our return. Beads of sweat drip from their foreheads, their chests heaving with heavy breaths. Their powers are at their limits. Cuts and bruises line their skin, and I wince. We have no choice but to run.

Rishu bellows from the other side of Tevari's briar wall. He fights through a swarm of Krav as Tevari opens a doorway, letting him pass before quickly twining the wall back together. He slumps when he finishes, the vine around his body a paler green than I've ever seen before.

"You have to go," Rishu says, out of breath, blood oozing from his iridescent skin.

Azura spins on him as Meena rushes to his side. "We can still fight."

She throws a fireball out the broken window, the flames latching onto the leathery gray skin of a passing Krav. It licks at the creature's wings before dissipating in the wind. The creature seems to laugh, diving toward us. Black talons shoot forward and tear the monstrous beast apart. The arms retract as the Krav falls from the sky. We all turn to Oliver huddled on the ground. He meets my gaze—that beast of his still prowling behind his eyes but contained for now. I nod to him, and he looks away, his head dropping to his knees.

"Can't you use your light again?" Meena asks, her gray eyes dull.

I shake my head. "Not until I reach the Lotus Pond... or it'll kill me if I do." Maybe I should call it forth, extinguish all these creatures once and for all. Save my friends, save Luka...

"Don't even think about it," Luka says, his words harsh—scared.

"But... I..." I stammer, desperate for a solution. There has to be something we can do. "I—"

Amon crashes into the room, falling to the floor littered with shattered glass. Lance and Darius run back from down the hall, blood oozing from various cuts along their skin. I look around the enclosed space; we're all beaten and battered by the Krav. My eyes heat with tears. I never should have encouraged us to fight; we never stood a chance.

"Nova," Lance says, sweat and blood making his black curls stick to his face. "You have to go. Find the Lotus Pond and end this. It's the only way."

Darius nods from beside him. "We'll stay behind and distract them while you run."

"No. If I run, you're coming with me."

"Run, Nova." Amon rises from the ground with the help of Rishu, and I turn to him, my heart racing. Amon's wings are torn, blue blood trickling from the slashes. His eyes return to pale blue, the black feathers around his head falling to the ground as the long pale strands return. "Take the others and *go*."

My ears ring as a burst of violent purple energy erupts from Lei Jing's hands, her power exploding as it hits three Krav passing the broken window. The horde rises in the sky, circling the building and stone doorway. She stumbles to her knees, sweat beading on her forehead as Tevari helps her up.

"I was right that my king led us to you," Amon says, and I turn back to his battered face. "Your hunters are right when they say to find the Lotus Pond. The visions of you are starting to clear, more than they have ever before...." He coughs, blue blood dripping from his lips. Rishu holds him upright as his blood stains the carpet purple around his feet.

"He'll destroy the city," I say, "and anyone who stays behind."

My eyes move to the two hunters. I can't let them stay behind to die. I wouldn't be able to live with myself.

A laugh echoes from the doorway in the sky. The shadowy creatures shriek and growl, spiraling in chaos. Their master is coming. My body tenses, the rage inside of me calling on me to fly back out there and tear into Camus, to end this now. I clench my fists, nails digging into my palms as I withhold the urge knowing I wouldn't make it past the horde.

"There's no time, Nova. Even Azrael says this is for the best," Lance says, that soft and sad smile I've seen too often resting on his face. My trainer of fourteen years... How can he expect me to leave him here?

Amon turns his slowly shifting body to Luka. His demonic form fading back to his human appearance. "My king, form a portal. Take Nova, take the cambions, and find the lotuses." Amon's voice is firm—commanding even through his exhaustion. His eyes are glassed over as if a vision is passing through. A truth only he can see.

"No," Meena's voice is quiet as she looks between Rishu and Amon. "Rishu has to come too."

Rishu doesn't move, standing over the girl with a coldness I've never seen him show her. "Amon and I will stay behind with the hunters."

I shake my head. I can't let them do this. *I won't.* A hand touches my shoulders, and I look at Luka. His eyes are filled with pain. This isn't any easier for him.

"We should all just go," Lei Jing says with a shaky breath. Her long hair sticks to her face and neck. I catch sight of tattoos through the rips in her long sleeves, but when I blink, it's gone. She reaches to push her hair back. "There's no reason for any of us to stay behind."

"I agree," Tevari says.

Azura gently pulls Oliver from the ground, a limp in her leg as she wobbles over with him at her side.

"No," Amon says. "We must stay behind. I was right that the colored strings of fate connect my cambions, connect Lucifer, to you, Nova. If we go with you, you will undoubtedly die. But without us, there's hope. This is the way it must be."

I meet his eyes before looking back to the sky behind him. Shadowy forms cloud the sky, the screams and cries of the Krav piercing not just my ears, but my heart. Blond hair appears through the dark mass, and my body freezes, throat tightening. We're out of time.

A spinning gray portal forms and slowly begins to widen beside me, Luka tense, conflicted, as he works to create one strong enough to send the seven of us through. I look between the two demons and two hunters standing off to the side and then back to Luka—his face scrunched in concentration. The lotus tattoo tugs on my chest as it had within the maze, and I place a hand on his shoulder. Closing my eyes, I send my energy—the energy of the lotuses—to him. Guiding and strengthening our only exit.

When I open my eyes, the others are staring at me with wide eyes. The portal swirls before us, solid and unmoving. *To the first lotus*, I hear Remembrance in my mind.

A command is called out from the sky, and the Krav horde races toward the building as one solid form. With no time left, I make a choice. Grabbing Lei Jing's arm, I pull her close. "Sorry."

She screams as I shove her into the portal before anyone else can object. Stepping forward, I grab Azura and Oliver firmly, using my last strength as an Undivided to push them into the portal.

Tevari holds up his hands as I turn to him. "I'll go myself, thanks," he says, jumping in after them.

Meena latches onto Rishu's arm, tears streaming down her cheeks. "Please, Rishi... *Please*, don't do this."

Rishu takes her wrist, dragging the fighting girl to the portal. He cups her face in his hand. "You'll be okay. I promise we'll meet again," he says, staring into her stormy eyes. Her cries are cut short as he pushes her into the portal.

The horde closes in, and Luka steps in front of me. He blazes with an energy darker than I've ever seen. I look over his shoulder and stare out the window—black symbols form in a circle in the sky above the doorway. A roar shakes the building as a giant black serpent emerges; it looks at us with silver eyes before racing toward the horde and diving into the black mass. The sound is horrible as it bites its way to the stone doorway, the shadowy creatures writhing in its jaw before their limp forms fall to the ground below.

Luka falls to one knee, his breaths heavy. I reach down to help him up as the portal begins to fade.

"Go now," Lance says. I turn to him, shaking my head even though I know we must leave. A conflicted feeling of guilt and knowing that Amon is right.

Behind him, Amon, Rishu, and Darius all nod in agreement. Tears fall down my face as I shake my head. How can I do this?

"I'm sorry," Luka says.

His hand latches onto mine, pulling me into his arms as we tumble into the portal as the Krav horde descends on the room. I reach toward the disappearing figures with a scream as the portal swirls shut.

We spin through the vortex, my stomach twisting and turning with it. Luka's arms tighten around my back, holding me to his chest. I cling onto his shirt as I cry, overwhelmed by the guilt. We left them behind. *We left them behind.*

My heart squeezes tight, knowing leaving them behind is a death sentence.

I led him right to us. *This is all my fault.*

We tumble through the other side of the portal, my body falling on top of Luka's. I groan, every muscle in my body protesting. Tevari offers his hand, gently helping me up as I stare at the world around us. Humidity latches onto my skin, but I shiver at the sound of unknown animals chattering around us.

Turning back, I help Luka to his feet. His side is soaked red with blood. Ignoring everything around us, I lift his shirt. The wound is gruesome. How did I not see it before? His hands grasp mine, pulling them away.

"I'll be okay," he says with a soft smile.

A misty rain splatters my skin from the towering trees above, and I finally take in the lush green jungle around us.

"Where the hell are we?"

Epilogue: Hostage

Pieces of the wall skitter to the ground as the Krav horde climbs Amon's building. Their claws dig into the exterior as their roars fill the hazy night sky. Their souls ache for the light, the warmth of a peaceful end—something their brethren killed this night were not gifted.

These howls pierce the air, but no one hears; no one responds to their pain. An interdimensional barrier separates them from the human lives below. An act of kindness on Amon's part. Or maybe just a convenient way to keep the truth hidden. Neither he nor the blond devil before him can claim to care what happens to the humans. But it's critical to keep them from getting involved. Humans cause more problems than they're worth when it comes to war.

Camus sits in the leather chair behind Amon's desk, his gaze pointed toward the city. The office is dark, only the blurred lights of the city bleeding into the room. He laces his fingers together with a long sigh. The chair swivels to face the four hostages kneeling on the carpeted floor. Krav shadows—creations that didn't survive the entire process, physical bodies no longer entirely tangible—hold the hostages immobile with the same darkness lacing the dimension they were created in.

"A shame she escaped," Camus says, a smirk tugging at his face as if holding back a laugh. "All my hard work wasted."

"You let her escape once. At least this time, we ended up with them," Theo says, and Camus shoots a deadly look in his direction, silencing the boy.

The hostages are quiet as Camus rises and prowls around the desk. Each step is calculated, deliberate, his eyes scanning the four kneeling before him. Crazed with power that isn't his, lost in the madness of his goal.

"Hunters and demons working side by side," he says, his nose crinkling. "*Disgusting*."

"You know I never had a problem shitting on Solomon," Darius says, his bulging arms tugging against the Krav shadows' hold to no avail, "I'm thinking it'll be more fun with you, you fucking coward."

A boot lands across the hunter's mouth, sending him to the floor.

"Quiet," Theo shouts.

Blackness eats away at the whites of Theo's eyes, the inky substance beginning to drip like tears. The darkness spreads through his veins, pale skin turning gray.

"Boy, did you kick me?" Darius growls, shooting back to his knees. His eyes burn with anger as he looks at his former student.

Theo wavers, but only for a moment.

"What do you want with us?" Lance says, his voice calm despite the injuries he's sustained—ones still dripping red onto the floor.

"Isn't it obvious, hunter," Amon says, rolling his eyes. "He wants to stop Nova. But he won't. Her future has started to clear itself to me. A journey he cannot deny."

A laugh bursts from Camus. It fills the room with its sickly sound even as Rishu says, "You'll never find her."

Rishu's eyes are honed on the ground in front of him. His iridescent skin is dull; purple blood drips from a slash across his chest. Slowly he lifts his gaze to Camus, determination set in his red irises.

Camus's laughter fades as he leans back against the desk. "If only that's what I was after." Rishu grimaces as all eyes turn to their captor. "What? Did you really think I brought her to that realm to have her join my side?" Theo goes rigid in the corner of the room, his pacing halted. No one speaks, so Camus continues. "Pathetic that you would even think I'd stoop to her level. She may be my niece, but not by blood."

"To her level?" Lance says, and the attention is pulled to him. "I know the truth, and she's finding the one place you never wanted her to."

"And where's that?" Camus rises, prowling over to the hunter.

Lance looks up with hate. "She'll find the Lotus Pond and end you. End all of this. The truth will shine through the darkness you've created, and she will be free to reclaim what was never yours."

Camus's eyes turn black, a laugh bubbling from his mouth once again. "Pity you think you know it all." Crouching down, Camus caresses the hunter's face. "I know Azrael has betrayed me, Barachiel, and Uriel too," he says as another voice, Darkness, speaks through him, deep and menacing. "You chose the wrong side, my sweet angels."

"We chose the only side," Lance says, his gaze holding firm despite the threat lingering in Camus's words.

"Word of warning, hunter, you don't know anything." Pushing Lance's head back, Camus prowls back to his desk. "The one you worship is a fake. She will only bring death and despair to us all. But think of all the good I can bring to the world. Yes, there are casualties involved, but the humans owe me their feeble lives if we are to end evil once and for all. If you think about it, we should be on the same side."

"Screw you," Darius says, but this time Theo doesn't intervene.

"You're delusional," Lance says with disgust. "You won't win."

Camus smiles. "I already have."

A vision passes over Amon's pale blue eyes, clouding them with each word Camus speaks. "He wanted this..." he finally says once the images pass. The three hostages turn to him as Amon locks his gaze with the blond devil.

Camus's smile becomes predatory. "You have no idea what a favor you've done for me. You think in sending her to find the lotuses, the pond, you're helping Nova." He lets his words linger as dread settles around the four hostages. "Remember, it is I who controls the fate of her life. She won't die by my hand on this journey. She will find the remaining six lotuses, and when she reaches the pond which I cannot enter, I will take what was never hers to steal from me." A laugh seems to bubble at Camus's lips as he prowls toward the hostages. "Solomon may have chosen to disregard his duty to give our Lord an heir, to pass down the lineage that should have been mine entirely... but the child he raised is far more than I could've hoped for."

Realization crosses Lance's face, the hunter frozen with fear. "No..."

"Oh yes, hunter. You've gifted me with the knowledge of the angels I can no longer trust, and you've sent Nova on the journey to her end, granting me my victory. Really I should thank you," Camus says as he heads back to his seat behind the desk.

Lance hangs his head, sagging closer to the floor. "What have I done?"

Amon's eyes cloud over, another flash of the future passing through his mind. A future he often sees where they're all dead—the world crumbled and broken. Nova's failed. It's as Camus predicts, whatever power lies within the Lotus Pond now swimming through his veins. The sky bleeds red like the broken moon. Humans, demons, gods, and angels alike are gone from existence. Only one true power reigns overhead, basking in triumph.

Amon's head swims as he takes in the vast number of outcomes leading to this end. An end Amon has been fighting against all along—the result of a war he's failing to prevent.

A golden image pushes to the surface—of Nova, the future that had been hidden from him. She floats atop the blackened waters of the Lotus Pond, seven lotus blossoms, each softly glowing with a different color—black, white, pink, blue, purple, red, gold—emerging from her chest and circling above her body. Seven blurred figures stand evenly spaced around the edge of the circular pond, colored strings matching the seven lotus flowers connecting to the young girl. The lotuses align with the seven before spreading out into their outstretched hands, and Nova rises from the blackened waters that fade to a clear pool, reborn.

The golden light she emanates is more potent than anything he's ever felt before, piercing from the vision behind his eyes to his current reality. An essence of something beautiful and free and powerful. A truth unspoken—lost to time.

Amon blinks, and his vision shifts. The red string of fate that ties Lucifer and Nova together is stretched even tighter than Amon realized. When the truth is revealed, it might rip them apart, break the soul of the very girl Lucifer loves.

He had seen a piece of this foresight before he sent Nova, his king, and his precious cambions away. Only now, it had become clearer, a vision filled with hope and heartbreak. A singular outcome that could change everything despite the dark manipulations at play.

Like a master artisan crafting a stained-glass window, Amon pulls fragments from the images he's shown, piecing together the story he wishes to see unfold. He holds tight to the final image, mending the cracks that threaten to shatter the beautiful scene. Somehow he brought six of the seven together for Nova. While he initially believed the cambions were meant for his king, the story is finally making sense to him.

Amon's eyes clear, and he hangs his head so that his long pale hair falls around him, hiding his face as his lips turn up in a small smile.

Eyes now returned to their natural green color, Camus leans forward, pressing his hands into the wooden desk. "As much as I like to chat, we have work to do."

He gestures to the corner of the room, and a young woman steps out from the shadows and into the dim light. The hostages tense at her appearance—one all too familiar yet completely unrecognizable. She ignores their questioning looks as she twirls a dagger casually in one hand. Her eyes are vacant, detached, as she stares ahead, waiting for an order. No better than the Krav army he commands, yet entirely too human to be one of his shadowy creations.

Camus smirks as he leans back in his seat, lacing his fingers together as two more shadows appear at the girl's side. "Find our lotus, Asa. We wouldn't want to miss the fun."

GLOSSARY

- **Amon:** A Grand Marquis of Hell said to have a wolf's head and serpents tail, and vomiting flames. He can see the past and what's to come. S-class ranking.

- **Angel Faction:** A group of angels set on fixing what's broken.

- **Angelic Artifact:** An ancient artifact created by the angels for the Undivided. It is usually in the form of wearable jewelry—always with some sort of gem—that is connected to an angel and grants the bearer a weapon or power. When the artifact is in use the color fades from the gem only to return once the power has been returned.

- **Angelic Metal:** The only metal capable of killing a demon. It was created by the first artificers who mimicked the angelic artifacts. The metal can be fashioned into any kind of weapon including, but not limited to, swords, arrowheads, and bullets, to make angelic weapons.

- **Angelic Trials:** A test within the mind where a selected hunter must pass through seven moral gates in order to become an Undivided. While the rules and process are known by hunters, whether selected by an angel or not, it is forbidden to speak of the experience.

- **Archangels:** Seven are chosen by the godling who is to become the next reigning God to assist them in leading humanity into the next age.

- **Artificer:** A hunter classification that creates angelic weapons.

- **Ansiel:** He is the angel known as The Constrainer. His angelic artifact is a silver pocket watch with a blue gem.

- **Avnas:** A President of Hell that appears in flames before taking human form. He rules over thirty six legions. S-class ranking.

- **Azrael:** One of the seven archangels. He is the angel of Death, presiding over dead souls. His angelic artifact is a gold necklace with seven ruby pendents.

- **Barachiel:** An angel whose name means Gods Blessing. He presides over lightning.

- **Bishop:** A renowned hunter family that has maintained their status as the Fanderas seconds.

- **Blood Moon – *Night of Helel*:** A rare occurrence where the full moon turns red, dripping its essence to Earth and granting demons even greater strength. The Night of Helel refers to one of Lucifer's many names, meaning the son of dawn or the son of the morning.

- **Buer:** A Great President of Hell that rules over fifty legions. He teaches natural and moral philosophy, logic, and the qualities and uses of herbs and plants, and is also capable of healing all infirmities. High-tier ranking.

- **Chlorokinesis:** The ability to grow, manipulate, summon, and control plant life.

- **Dragoon:** A hunter classification that specializes in firearms.

- **Exorcist:** A hunter classification that specializes in banishing demons.

- **Fandera:** The founding demon hunter family.

- **Falgens:** A fictional town three hours north of Chicago in Michigan.

- **First-years:** Trainees in their first year of becoming a hunter. They are usually new recruits and not hunter-born.

- **Full Moon Patrol:** One of two nights—the other being the new moon—where demons become more active and hunters send out patrols to monitor areas that might have more activity.

- **Gabriel:** One of the seven archangels. His name means God is my Strength, and he presides over messengers.

- **Gehenna:** Another term for Hell, most commonly used by demons and fallen angels.

- **Ghoul:** A humanoid demon that feasts on flesh. Mid-tier ranking.

- **Godling:** Beings that are trained for thousands of years in order to become the next God.

- **Healer:** A hunter classification that specializes in healing demonic wounds.

- **Hellhound:** A wolf-like demon that normally sticks to graveyards to hunt lost spirits. Low-tier ranking.

- **High-tier:** The third highest ranking in demonology. These demons can take human form but aren't as much of a threat as the two highest rankings.

- **Hunter-born:** A hunter born into a demon hunter family.

- **Hydrokinesis:** The ability to manipulate, summon, and control water.

- **Kioren:** An ancient sentient artifact of immense power. Only Nova is able to call it forth and hear its name.

- **Krav:** Monstrous creatures created from human and demon in another dimension.

- **Lamia:** A night-haunting, child-eating demon. Mid-tier ranking.

- **Lotus:** A water lily flower that only blooms during the day, sinking beneath the blackened waters only to rise again the next day unblemished.

- **Low-tier:** The lowest ranking in demonology. These demons cannot take human or humanoid shape, instead they are usually some form of creature or beast.

- **Mara:** A demonic celestial king associated with death, rebirth, and desire. He is the personification of the antagonistic forces against enlightenment. S-class ranking.

- **Magick:** A separate type of power a demon can wield that isn't usually one of their inherent abilities.

- **Mid-tier:** The second ranking in demonology. These demons can take on a humanoid shape but are unable to maintain it for long periods.

- **Mind-weaver:** A demon with the ability to take images from someones mind and create tangible illusions. They may also be able to replicate the images of objects and people.

- **Moonlit Château:** A château with French aesthetics that is protected and owned by Amon. It is hidden from the world beneath a powerful barrier.

- **Naga:** A semi divine half-human, half-serpent being that can take form of either or a combination of the two. High-tier rating.

- **Pyrokinesis:** The ability to manipulate, summon, and control fire.

- **Raguel:** One of the seven archangels, his name means Friend of God, and he presides over justice.

- **Raphael:** One of the seven archangels, his name means God Heals, and he presides over illnesses and healing.

- **Reigning God:** Every 2,000 years or so a godling is selected to be the next God, or reigning God, to bring humanity into the next age.

- **Selaphiel:** One of the seven archangels, her name means Prayer of God, and she presides over worship.

- **Shapeshifter:** The ability to transform your natural shape.

- **S-class:** The second highest ranking in demonology. These demons can take on impressive human shape and are very powerful. These demons are the high-ranking royals of Hell.

- **SS-class:** The highest ranking in demonology. These demons are not only the most powerful within Hell, but the ones who pose the greatest threat to humanity.

- **Tamer:** A hunter classification that specializes in taming spirits and low-tier demons.

- **The Eternal Keeper:** A book detailing the agreement made between Solomon the First and the current reigning God.

- **The Great Demonic Fall:** The war that led to the creation of the hunters and the Undivided when Lucifer rebelled against the Heavens.

- **The Heavens:** A glass kingdom in the sky where the godlings, reigning God, and angels reside.

- **Undivided:** An elite group of hunters with souls bonded to angels.

- **Warrior:** A hunter classification that specializes in melee weapons.

- **Zerachiel:** A angel long thought to be dead. His name means Gods Command and he presides over the sun, wind, and children who's parents have sinned.

- **Zin:** A giant black serpent that resides in Gehenna and can be called forth by Lucifer. S-class ranking.

Acknowledgments

Wow. Just wow. To finally be here: my book published and people reading this story that I've spent ten years creating. It's truly a dream come true that has nourished my inner child, the kid who always wanted to write and share stories. This wouldn't have been possible without my incredible mom who's supported my passion since day one. From bouncing ideas off each other to listening to me ramble on and on about characters, even joking by saying, "I know them better than some people in my life." Her support means the world to me, and I'll always be thankful for her and everything's she done.

To my grandma who's read every single draft of this book and even helped me with the final proofread by reading it aloud together. I appreciate you immensely, and I'm excited for you to read the rest in this series.

To my editor, Samantha Holtgrewe, who really dove inside my brain, asked the right questions, and helped me give this story the final pizzazz to tell it exactly how it was within my mind. I'm so glad I went with my intuition to work with you, and I'm incredibly excited to work on the rest of this series with you.

To Anders Grapes, the best group of writers to work with! Our weekly Friday meetings for the last year and a half have been the best part of my week. To Camilla, Charity, Natalya, and Jennifer, the four of you have helped make this book a reality with all your insightful and helpful critique. I look forward to seeing your stories published and for you to continue with me on this journey of writing the rest of the Undivided series!

To my illustrator, Elaine Cheng, who created the perfect cover to convey this story. Your art is amazing, and I'm excited to design the rest of this series with your help.

To my new readers who are just entering into the world of Undivided. I look forward to hearing your thoughts on *Blood of the Lotus,* and I hope you continue with the Undivided series as the story progresses into the next book and more and more of the twisted things happening behind the scenes are revealed!

To BTS and my extensive writing playlist that helped me get through some of the hardest times of my life, inspiring me with the lyrics of your songs and boosting me up when I was low. It's amazing how much you've impacted me in such an amazing way, and I sincerely appreciate all the work you put into your artistic craft.

To booksellers, librarians, reviewers, and bloggers on all platforms, my fellow authors and bookworms in general. I'm so proud to be a part of this community that is so kind, welcoming, and supportive, especially to a newbie indie author.

Undivided contests, incorporates, re-imagines and/or was influenced by a number of myths, legends, and historical contexts. I owe a significant amount of debt of inspiration to real life stories and events of the past.

But most importantly, I'm acknowledging myself for all the work I've put into this book, and I'm proud of myself for how far I've come since first coming up with the idea for Undivided in 2013 while on a trip in Costa Rica. Unfortunately, it was at the same time that my grandpa passed away, but I can't help but believe that this idea was the last thing he sent me. So this story I'll forever hold close to my chest, and I'm excited to share the rest of this series with all of you amazing new readers.

And for all of you dreamers out there, remember that there are always ups and downs when it comes to pursuing passions that others might not deem worthy, but striving past those difficulties will make your victories even sweeter. So here's to never giving up on your dreams, to believing in yourself, and to many more stories to come.

ABOUT THE AUTHOR

Sade Louise—otherwise known as Sadie Peterson—is an author, model, actor, and digital content creator. She grew up in Grand Rapids, MI before moving abroad to Paraguay at the age of fifteen where she lived for four years. She's applied her unusual life experiences into the characters, settings, and stories she writes. Beyond writing, she loves traveling, learning languages, creating art, and spending time with her friends and family—including her two adorable cats Suki and Yeon.

You can connect with her on:
www.sadelouise.com
Instagram: @author.sadelouise
TikTok: @thesadelouise
Twitter: @thesadelouise
Subscribe to her newsletter:
https://www.sadelouise.com/newsletter